Kept in the Dark

Lindsey Acosta

To my grandfather

Garfield "Papaw" Dingess

For my first fiction novel, I found it only fitting to dedicate this book to the man who introduced me to stories. His storytelling was truly a gift and I believe my love for words was sparked by him. Thank you for teaching us that you're never too old to use your imagination.

I love you so much, Papaw.

Acknowledgements

This part of the writing process is the hardest. So many people have played a vital role in the writing and publication of this book. I first want to thank my husband, Tony. Thank you for believing in me and my stories. You're the reason I'm able to make my dream a reality, and words will never be able to express how thankful I am for you.

My sister, Brianna, and my mother, Ellie: your support is so appreciated. I can always count on you both to encourage me and be my biggest fans.

Chief Andy Ray of the Bartow Police Department (formerly Chief of the Auburndale Police Department): Thank you so much for being willing to answer all of my questions concerning police procedure. You were so helpful and kind!

Lynda Hill: I so appreciate you taking the time answer all of my crime scene questions. I know the plot has changed quite a bit since we spoke, but your expertise helped tremendously!

Dr. Erin Hanson: Dr. Erin Hanson: You were such an immense help to me while I was drafting this book. Your expertise in the field of DNA brought so much clarity to the story. Though much of what was in the original plot was later changed, I appreciate you so much for taking the time to answer all my questions!

My ARC/Publishing team managers | Kyrsten Burley and Kristin Turcio: You both have gone above and beyond and have been nearly as dedicated to this book as I have been. If I become a million-copy-bestselling-author, I'll have you two to thank for that.

My Beta readers | Karissa Blankney, Susannah Pearce, Josie Pattishal, Leah Fowler, Lauren Schugg, and Kaci High: You were the first people I allowed to read my nearly-unedited third draft and I felt so vulnerable giving it to you; especially after keeping it a secret for almost fifteen years. But each of you were so encouraging and you all helped shape this story into something even more beautiful than I could imagine.

My ARC readers and street team members: Y'all helped set the foundation of marketing for this book and you were so willing and ready to get Kept in the Dark in front of the world. I truly have the best teams! *Names listed at the end of the acknowledgements section.

Honestly, there are so many more people who played an intricate role in the publication process of this book and I'm forever grateful for those who were by my side through this journey. So many of you have encouraged me and inspired me and I hope this book makes you proud.

And of course, thank you to all of my readers. This wouldn't be possible without you.

<u>ARC & STREET Team Members:</u>

Alanna Wiediger, Alexandria Linde Andersson, Amanda Masek-Black, Amanda Price, Amanda Shook, Andrea Schilaci, Annie Pruitt, Ashley Ashley Jacobs, Tucker, Ashley Walby, Astrid Pizarro, Autumn Ganes, Bethany Blanton, Bianca Norfleat, Brad Deiter, Brianna Henry, Brittany Whitman, Candice Sawchuk, Carina Powers, Carissa Herrera, Cat Ramirez, Celeste Velocci, Chelsea Bailey, Christina Faris, Cierra Allen, Cynthia Pinto, Danielle Folk, Denita Holman, Destiny Harvey, Devon Conaway, Diana Cooper, Dwaya Harrison, Emily Ambrose, Emily Booth, Emily Stellmar, Erika Murphy, Erin Hanson, Evangeline Herter, Heather Flaherty, Holly Gates, J L Hyde, Jamele Medina, Jaquline Lutes, Jasmine Maddy-Taylor, Jasmine Malzahn, Jeannine Neale, Jen Jensen, Jen Slagel, Jenna Seward-Hatfield, Jennifer Horton, Jess Adolfo, Jess McCallops, Jessica Heatherly, Jessica Lamboo, Jessica Lasinskas, Jessica Thornton, Jessie Swisher, Jessika Atland, Julia Force, Julie Maleski, Kailey Laiza, Kaitlyn Skiscim, Kaley Gillis, Kate Forsman, Katie Foster, Katie Materni, Kaylen Ostendorf, Kayleigh McManus, Kaylene McPhee, Kelly Falcone, Kelsey, Kelsey Kleinheider, Kerri Grace, Kiley Compson, Kirstin Wood, Kristie Woodard, Kyla Grant, LaToya Wells, Lauren Lynch, Leilani Laurencio, Livia Hertel, Lorayne Gohl, Logan Munkeby, Lorraine Carpenter, Luaren Fritz, Lyndie Dison, Madelin Tucker, Mallory Sorrells, Marcy Sorenson, Marie Cashel, Marisha Lunde, Mary Baumgarten, Mary Debord, Mary Kuhlmann, Megan Blazer, Megan Dick, Meghan Ginelli, Melanie Gordon, Melissa Duchaine, Melissa Ingram, Michaela Baker, Michelle Madrid, Nicole Garcia, Nicole Hine, Nicole Roha, Nikki, Nikki Lee, Paige Fortner, Reagan Hopper, Renee Arieno, Samantha Cooper, Sara Carver, Sarah Richardson, Shannon Demaio, Simone Machado, Simone Praylow, Stacey Grubich, Stacy Burkhart, Stefani Rae Lange, Stephanie Bulcamino, Tabitha Morton, Tasha Spaniel, Terah Hansen, Teresa Brock, Tiana Hardy, Tiffany Case, Tiffany Clayton, Tiffany Ewald, Tonya Hoselton, Victoria Atweh, Yinka Boudreaux, Zachary Holmer.

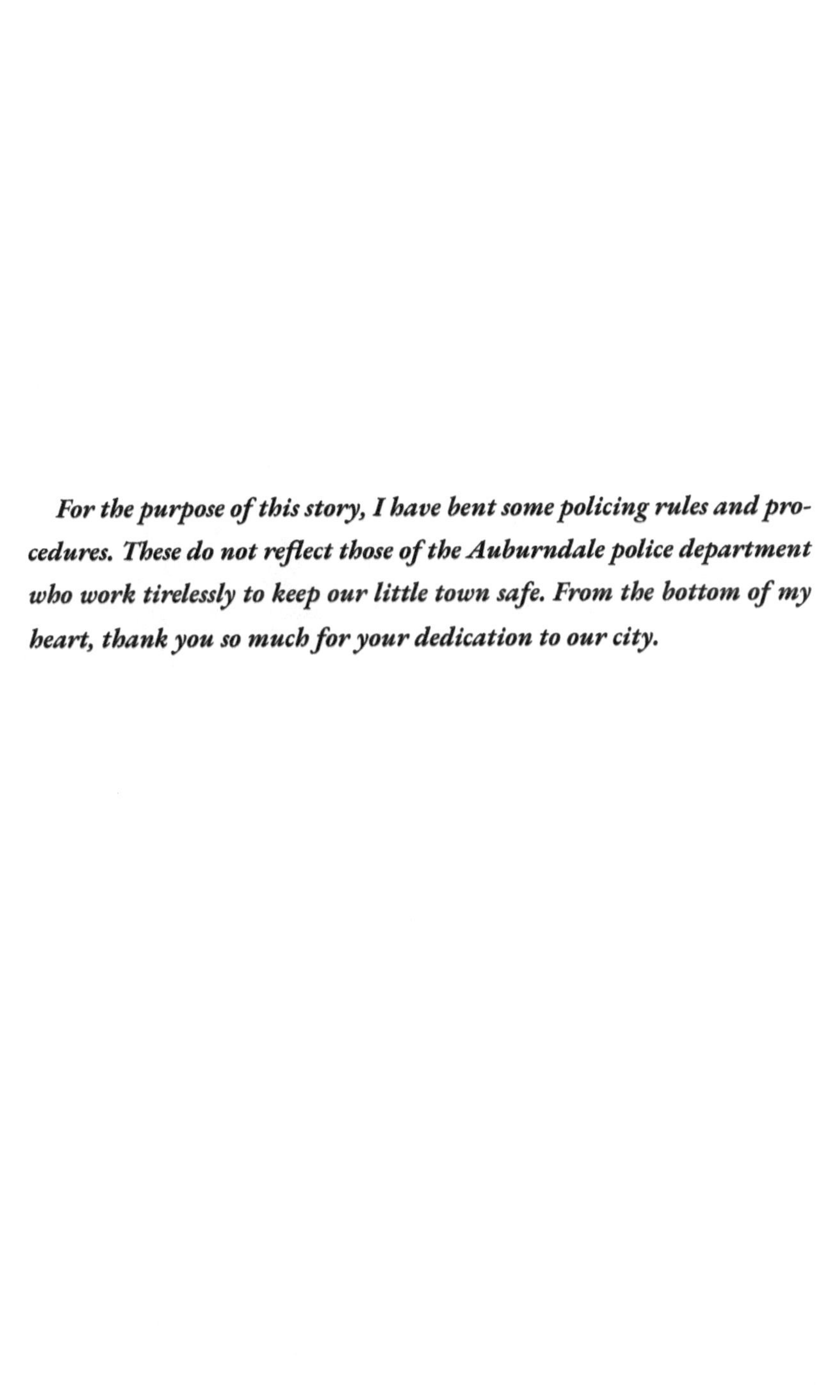

For the purpose of this story, I have bent some policing rules and procedures. These do not reflect those of the Auburndale police department who work tirelessly to keep our little town safe. From the bottom of my heart, thank you so much for your dedication to our city.

Chapter 1

June 10, 2011
11:26 am

A flock of birds flew across the open sky. There were few clouds to block the rays of the Florida heat as the sun beamed down on Sara Gallagher's face. Though she had only been outside a mere thirty seconds, she was sweating profusely and a part of her wished to go back into the prison if only for the air conditioning. Instead, she closed her eyes and took a deep breath.

Freedom.

Though tan lines, beaches, and vacations came to mind when people thought about summers in Florida, Sara had a different sentiment. She spent the last thirteen years hating the season, though not for reasons most other Floridians dislike it.

It's no secret the natives hate the one-hundred-degree weather that accompanies the summer as well as the tourists that flock to the sunshine state to vacation and sight-see as if it were some glorious place. Politicians will claim it keeps the state thriving, but all it really does is hike up living costs and crowd the roads with both lost and bad drivers.

And the humidity all but makes living here miserable. It's not enough to be hot, you have to be damp, too. It feels like the heat has wrapped you up in a wet blanket. And then, rolling in with the heat and humidity, are the daily afternoon showers.

Misery loves company.

Sara, though, hated summer because it was a reminder of all she lost. Summer was supposed to be a time of freedom and happiness. A time to cast your cares aside and live in the moment, making memories that last a lifetime. But for Sara, it only ever reminded her that she was a prisoner; that she lost everything. It only ever reminded her that one fateful summer night had changed the trajectory of her life.

Until today. Today she was free.

The outer gate to the prison buzzed loudly as it closed, jolting Sara from her thoughts. After serving thirteen years for a crime she didn't commit, she was being given a chance to become a "functioning member of society." Whatever that meant.

She had spent more than a decade being treated in the most inhumane ways. She had to fight for basic human needs, had absolutely no rights, and even fewer options or opportunities. Though the government would have everyone believe that prisoners were given life's necessities, that was far from the truth.

Sure, you had a bed and food, but even those were fair game along with anything else you could get your hands on. If you wanted a bed, you had to fight for it. If you wanted food, you had to be more violent than the woman trying to take it from you. And, when it came to commissary items like snacks and feminine products...well, you had to learn to think smart, hit hard, and pray the other prisoners believed you were tougher than you truly were. Violence is the language of the prisoners and it's a language Sara knew well- a gift her father gave her long before she was ever thrown behind bars.

Sara spent most of her life being looked down upon, forgotten about, and tossed away like trash, which worsened once she was thrown into a cage. How anyone thought she could go from being a ward of the state for over a decade to a functioning member of society was beyond her.

Her freedom didn't matter, anyway. Her family turned against her, her friends abandoned her, and her hopes and dreams disintegrated the moment a guilty verdict was read.

She had been eighteen then and was sentenced to thirteen years for second-degree murder. It hadn't been a fair trial, and the judge wanted to make an example out of Sara, despite the fact the entire case was circumstantial at best.

Although, it didn't help that Sara pled guilty.

She found it quite ironic she was getting out the same week she had been put away, only years apart. She chuckled cynically. She was free, but what good was freedom when you've lost everything? She didn't have a place to live, a family to help her get back on her feet, or a job waiting for her. Even her twin sister, Hailey, turned her back on Sara.

Sara may be physically free, but she was still bound to her past, a ball and chain she would drag behind her for the rest of her pathetic life.

Sara turned to take one last look at the place she begrudgingly called home for the last thirteen years.

Good riddance.

She fanned her face with her hand, trying to cool off. The fleece sweatpants she wore trapped the heat and, despite wearing a light t-shirt, she was still soaked with sweat. She should be grateful the prison gave her the standard-issued clothing to wear, but she wasn't. She was angry she had to wear them at all.

It was yet another painful reminder of all she'd been through.

The smell of freshly cut grass assaulted her as she made her way to the busy road and began walking, sticking her thumb in the air as she did. It didn't take long for an older gentleman to pull over and roll down his window. "Where ya headed, Darlin'?"

He was missing some teeth, his head nearly bald except for a few patches of gray toward the back of his scalp. His old pickup truck sputtered as it sat idly, waiting for Sara to pick her next destination. She wanted to name a random town where she could start over, but truth be told, she longed to go back to where it all started.

Sara was out for blood.

She walked up to the truck and yanked on the rusted handle of the passenger door. The vehicle smelled like hay and horse feed and the floorboards were a mosaic of mud, oil, sand, and grass. "Can you take me to Auburndale?"

"That's a long drive. I can take you about thirty minutes up the road, but that's it," he said.

Sara shrugged. What choice did she have?

She paused before climbing in.

As a little girl, she had grown up hearing horror stories of people who were never seen again because they climbed into a stranger's vehicle. She could see it now: "Hitchhiking Gone Wrong: convicted murderer released after serving thirteen years, killed by serial killer."

Would she be his next victim?

Sara laughed to herself. How ironic it would be for her to serve her sentence for murder only to be murdered on the day she was released.

But her need for retribution was far greater than the fear she felt.

Hell, she had nothing more to lose, anyway. And there's a special word for when you have nothing left to lose:

Freedom.

And unfortunately for everyone else, Sara was now free.

With that, she climbed into the truck.

Chapter 2

June 23, 2011
7:32 pm

Trey Harbor hated being on call, but unfortunately it came with the territory. Being the Chief of Police of a small town like Auburndale, Florida wasn't difficult or overwhelming. It was simply mundane. There was hardly any crime and, if there was, it was small-town issues being blown into big-city proportions.

His days consisted of speeding tickets, expired tags, and connecting with the community. However, a more exciting day included getting a call about kids playing ding-dong-ditch or some new form of tag in an old cow pasture that hasn't had a cow inhabit it since the early 90's.

To say his job was rather uneventful was an understatement, something he never thought he'd say. His younger self would be both impressed and shocked by Trey's career choice. He had always expected to end up in jail by the time he was twenty, but life was full of surprises.

Trey smiled when he thought about his teenage years. He had made a name for himself as the town prankster, the local rebel, Auburndale's very own bad-boy. Something he still found rather amusing.

He spent many days doing exactly what he was now paid to stop others from doing. He had been known to graffiti old bridges, play pranks on unsuspecting neighbors, and run wildly around the city. And one couldn't forget the many fights he'd been in or the time he almost caught a felony charge for running through the orange groves.

Needless to say, he found trouble and trouble found him; a match made in hell for his poor mother.

Now he was the Chief of Police. How he pulled that off he didn't know.

Yes, most days were filled with mundane tasks of keeping the city in order. Today, however, had been anything but quiet.

Trey walked toward the crime scene tape that warned passersby not to enter the residence. He lifted it above his head and crouched underneath, making his way toward the other officers that were inside.

It was an old mobile home that had seen better days. The missing shingles and the overgrown grass were the least of the owner's worries. He swatted at a bee that had ventured from the hive that hung from the corner of the roof.

What initially started as a wellness check quickly turned into a missing persons report and possible homicide.

From what Trey gathered about the alleged victim, Nicole House had been working at the local pizza joint since it opened, first as a waitress and now as a manager. From all accounts, she was great at her job. Miss House was known to make her customers and staff feel welcomed, heard, and cared for. She was never late to her shifts and had only called in sick a handful of days over the years. So, when she didn't show up for work and no one could get a hold of her, the assistant manager requested a wellness check.

Trey had expected the woman to be playing hooky, maybe nursing a hangover, or pushing a one night stand out the front door. Instead, he was shocked to find her home in complete disarray. Pictures had fallen from the walls, an end table had been knocked over, and knick-knacks had become shards of glass that glistened in the now-setting sun.

Then there was the blood pooling on the kitchen floor along with the spatter that covered the cabinets and ceiling.

There had definitely been a struggle, but there was no sign of Nicole.

Though Trey heard good things about the woman, he didn't know her personally. He was, however, familiar with her son. Ryan House and Trey Harbor had a unique history, one plagued with fist fights and death threats.

The last time Trey threatened to kill Ryan was thirteen years ago.

Trey had been at the Strawberry Festival with Hailey Gallagher, unaware they had been split up in the crowd. As one of the top fairs in the country, the festival brought thousands of people to the small town of Plant City. And, unfortunately for Trey, they had gone on one of the busiest nights.

After a few minutes of mindlessly wandering, Trey had finally found Hailey standing near the Ferris Wheel. His heart had plummeted as he saw Ryan gripping Hailey's forearm as he whispered something to her. Her entire body had tensed, and her eyes rounded as she tried to pull away.

Ryan's grip had only tightened. He had attempted to drag Hailey away, her shouts of protest falling on deaf ears as the crowd either didn't notice or purposefully ignored her, not wanting to get involved. Trey had heard her soft cries across the sea of people, and he took off after them, a guttural instinct pushing him to protect her. Rage overtook him and a brawl had ensued as he pummeled Ryan to the ground.

Though Trey was strong, Ryan hadn't given up easily. Blows were shared back-and-forth and after the drawing of a crowd, Trey had managed to get the upper hand as his fist connected with Ryan's nose, breaking it. By the end, they had both dripped with blood.

Trey had shoved his forearm into Ryan's throat, cutting off his airway. *"If you ever lay a hand on her again, I swear I'll kill you."*

And he had meant it.

Ryan had simply smiled as crimson smeared his face and leaked into the dirt.

Trey had taken Hailey to get ice cream after that, hoping to ease her anxiety with something he knew she loved. Thankfully it worked, and they had laughed together the remainder of the evening.

Hailey never told him what Ryan had said to her that night, and Trey had respected her too much to push her into revealing what she wanted to keep secret. Even after all these years, Trey still felt uneasy just thinking about it.

The crime scene techs were hard at work collecting any evidence, working in sync like the hive of bees just outside the door. Though there weren't many techs present, the house was still full of life.

Trey stepped around one man who was dusting for fingerprints on the knife block. Three of the five knives were accounted for in the block, and one had been found in the dishwasher, leaving one lonely knife they needed to find.

Trey didn't think they would locate it. Nicole had likely been murdered, the killer using Nicole's own knife to do it. The amount of blood alone was enough for him to believe she was dead.

But, without a body, the case would remain a missing persons case.

He shivered as he thought about her last moments. Did she see it coming? Did she call out for help only to be met with violence? Did she survive an attack just to be taken to an isolated area to suffer even more?

There hadn't been any signs of forced entry; no broken windows or splintered door jambs. Someone who knew Nicole had likely harmed her, in the safety of her own home, no less. She opened the door for a friend only to find they were actually an enemy.

"Harbor."

Trey looked to his right to see Jason Shuarts near the back door just off the kitchen. He made his way over to his friend. "Hey, Jay. What can you tell me?"

Jason was crouching down to study the floor, his brown skin glimmering in the sunlight that was slowly fading into the night sky. Once Trey got close, Jason stood up. "I can tell you need some sleep. You look like shit."

Trey laughed. "I don't think you've got much room to talk. It's a wonder you managed to lock down someone like Angie looking the way you do. She's clearly out of your league."

Jason returned the laughter then slowly became somber as he pointed toward the backyard. It could be seen through the sliding glass door which remained open as officers and CSI techs came and went, collecting evidence as they did. Trey followed Jason's motion and eyed the small droplets of blood that stained the concrete steps descending into the yard. He noted the weeds that were sprouting through the cracks, eager to feed on the sun's fading rays.

"She went out the back door or someone carried her. Could be the perp's blood, too. Either way, the blood stops in the grass." Jason walked outside, carefully following the trail of violence to its stopping point. Trey went behind Jason, studying each drop.

"Footprints?" Trey asked.

"Not that we found. But if there were any, the rain washed them away. Thankfully the porch protected the blood, so we'll run DNA testing to see if it's Nicole's or the perp's."

Trey nodded. Florida was known for its sunshine by the tourists, but for the locals, it was the afternoon showers that everyone begrudgingly anticipated. Trey looked up at the sky. There wasn't a cloud in sight, the wrath of the thunderstorm hardly evident in the aftermath.

"Do we have any leads?" Trey asked.

Jason shook his head. "Not yet, but it's still early. As soon as I find anything, I'll call ya."

Wanting to talk about something less gruesome, Trey said, "So are you ready for your big day?"

The man beamed. "You know, it sounds lame, but I'm ready to settle down."

Jason was finally marrying his high school sweetheart, Angela Moretti. Trey and Jason had been friends since grade school, and now Trey had the privilege to stand next to him as Jason's best man. He was happy to celebrate his friend's special day. It was the least he could do after everything Jason had done for him over the years.

Jason had seen Trey through some of his worst and best moments in life. He was there when Trey's mom was diagnosed with cancer and when she beat it; and when it came back with a vengeance that eventually took her life. He was there when Trey got his first arrest at thirteen years old and when he had to do community service as his punishment. He was there when Trey passed eighth grade after thinking he would fail. And Jason was there to pick up the pieces when Hailey left and never looked back.

Trey wasn't proud of the fact that a woman nearly broke him beyond repair. Trey thought Hailey was *the one* and when she left without so much as a goodbye, he was devastated. He poured his pain into one bottle of bourbon after another until Jason dragged him out of the hole he was in.

"Trey?" Jason said.

He snapped out of his thoughts. "Sorry, I just can't believe you two are tying the knot after all these years. Took you long enough."

Jason chuckled. "Yeah, well, I would have done it sooner, but you know she wanted to finish school."

Trey winked. "Better late than never."

Jason smiled and shook his head. Then, he became silent, looking around as he shifted slightly.

"Don't tell me you're getting cold feet," Trey teased.

Jason hesitated for a split second before saying, "No, not cold feet." He ran a hand through his hair and let out a breath, a tell he'd had since they were kids. He did it every time he had an internal battle of wills. You could almost see the little angel and devil on Jason's shoulders as he contemplated whatever it was he wanted to say.

"You're doing it," Trey said.

"Doing what?"

"You want to tell me something but aren't sure if you should. Just say it. I've got shit to do today." Trey shouldn't be annoyed but he was. Though a man's man, Jason was still relatively empathetic in a way that few men were. He'd rather ignore a situation altogether than potentially hurt someone's feelings by talking about it.

Not Trey. He went looking for trouble, sometimes even created it out of boredom. If there was something going on, he wanted to know about it. He'd deal with the repercussions later.

Jason sighed. "Hailey is coming to the wedding. We didn't find out until today and I figured you'd want to hear it from me instead of running into her."

Trey's heart slammed against his chest at the sound of her name. Memories of her flooded his mind, ones he'd buried long ago.

Thirteen years ago, Hailey left town and never looked back. To his knowledge, not so much as a phone call made its way to or from Auburndale.

Trey chuckled, wondering if this was Jason's sorry attempt at a joke. "Why would she be coming back for the wedding? She and Angie haven't talked since Hailey left."

Jason looked away and said, "No, they've been talking on and off for years."

Trey froze and he lifted a brow. He tried to hide his surprise but failed miserably.

He shouldn't be shocked by the news, though. Like Trey and Jason, Hailey and Angie had been best friends and Angie had been devastated when Hailey left. And poor Jason had been left to deal with the wreckage of both Trey and Angie in the aftermath of Hailey's departure.

"What are you talking about? You never told me they kept in touch," Trey said.

"I know." Jason continued to avoid Trey's glare. "Angie didn't talk to Hailey until almost two years after she left. By then, you seemed to have moved on and weren't a total mess anymore." He added quickly, "I didn't want you to get hurt again."

Trey crossed his arms over his chest. "So, they've been talking this whole time and now she's coming back for the wedding?"

Jason simply nodded.

A pang of jealousy creeped into Trey's heart. He wished he still held a place in her heart the way Angie did. He spent countless nights wondering when Hailey would come back to him, but she never did.

Now he was sure she wasn't even thinking of him anymore. She was probably playing house with a man whom she loved deeply with three kids running around. Trey bet she even had a dog and a white picket fence.

And as angry as he wanted to be at the life, he pictured for her, he loved her too much to wish anything else. If she didn't choose him, he hoped she found someone who gave her butterflies every time she saw him.

Trey tried to hide his conflicting emotions about the woman he still loved. He shook his head. "I doubt she'll even show up. She's never come back before, why start now?"

"Look, I just know things were messy at the end and I didn't want you to be blindsided." Jason paused for a minute. "What happened between you two, anyhow? One minute y'all was talking about getting married and the next she just up and disappeared."

Trey could never bring himself to tell Jason the whole story of why Hailey left. Truth was, he was embarrassed he broke things off with her and didn't want to be called to the carpet. He had tried to reconcile with her a few weeks after her mother's death, but she refused to see him. And, according to her father, she wanted nothing to do with Trey.

So, Trey never admitted his stupidity and Jason never pushed too hard. Thankfully, Jason didn't let Trey drown himself in bourbon like Trey wanted, despite Trey's secrecy.

Looking back, Trey was mortified at how desperate he was when Hailey left. But, then again, he was a kid at the time... twenty, full of life, and naive as hell. He thought he found the love of his life and she had taken his heart the moment she left.

Now, though, he could clearly see it was only a whirlwind romance that had been exhilarating and filled with lust. She had been his first love. And like most first loves, they weren't meant to last.

As time went on, he found himself thinking less and less of the brunette who lit up his life all those years ago. The sparkle in her hazel eyes was defiant yet soft, daring yet cautious. She was always the balance between his rebellious side and the caution that came with being responsible. She somehow managed to keep him on his toes while simultaneously keeping him in line.

"Not much happened, honestly. She got mad and left. I'm sure her mother's death didn't help any and then her sister gets hauled off to jail for the murder." Trey shook his head. Hailey had been through so much in a short summer's time.

Jason pointed at Trey. "People don't just 'get mad' and completely uproot themselves, Trey. Y'all were going to get *married*. You're telling me she wouldn't stick around for *you*?" Jason crossed his arms. "Like I said: more to the story."

Jason was now hardly able to keep his anger at bay, a rare sight for Trey. A vein throbbed on his forehead as he said, "And how could she do that to Angie? She was devastated when Hailey left. I just want to know what you did to make her leave like she did."

Jason's words cut Trey to the core, and he tried not to shrink at his friend's accusation.

So that's what this was really about.

Jason was worried Hailey would hurt Angie again.

What Jason didn't realize was that Trey didn't like to talk about that summer because it still hurt him. Though the wounds Hailey left had healed, the scars still burned. And as much as he would deny it, that was the truth.

Trey spent a great deal of time being angry he wasn't enough to keep her here. She'd never given him a chance to explain why he broke things off with her. He often wondered if he'd tried hard enough.

Feeling old wounds split open, his own anger gripping him, Trey said, "Well, she did. So, mind your damn business. If I wanted you to know, I'd tell you. I didn't want to talk about it then, and I don't want to talk about it now."

"Why, Trey?" Jason flung his arms out, matching Trey's anger. The two received glances from the other officers who took notice of the heated conversation. Jason lowered his voice and said, "If you're over her like you claim, why won't you talk to me about it?"

"Why do you care? It's done and over so let it be."

Jason shook his head. "Who are you trying to convince: me or you?"

Trey let the silence answer for him.

Not wanting to talk about Hailey any longer, he changed the subject. "Look, tomorrow is your wedding day. Don't let Hailey Gallagher ruin it."

Jason sighed and nodded. "Yeah, you're right."

"And Angie is a grown woman who can take care of herself. Give her some credit."

Jason smiled. "She definitely can. I shouldn't worry so much, but I love her. Plus, that whole 'protect' thing kinda comes with the vows."

"I know." Trey smiled back.

Trey turned to walk away but Jason stopped him. "Watch out for Hailey. We don't need a repeat of thirteen years ago. I don't want to spend my days peeling you off the bathroom floor after your dates with Jim Beam night after night."

"Don't worry, she's been a memory since the day she left."

The two finished the conversation by promising to keep one another in the loop about Nicole's case. Trey made his rounds and spoke to a few other officers and CSI techs, none of whom had anything helpful at the moment; something Trey wasn't surprised by given how fresh the case was.

Trey left the old mobile home and headed toward his truck where his thoughts turned back to Hailey, much to his dismay. Even after claiming he'd long since forgotten about the woman, he couldn't get rid of the conflicting emotions that were now surfacing.

He was angry at her for leaving without so much as a goodbye or an explanation. Then his anger toward her turned to resentment toward himself for not stopping her or going after her. Then it all turned into sadness as he mourned what could have been.

Yet, as infuriated as he was with her, he couldn't blame her for leaving the way she did. Her mother had been murdered and her sister was to blame for the violent act. So, instead of losing just one person she loved, she lost two that night.

To make matters worse, her father had never been kind to her and Sara, which had worsened a few months before her mother passed, so there was no more familial connection keeping her here. Trey suspected David had much to do with Hailey's departure, despite his claims of not being involved.

It didn't help that Trey broke things off with her that night out of his own insecurities. He'll never forget the way her face contorted in pain, the tears that streamed down her face as she ran off. He had spent the last thirteen years hating himself for it, though Hailey had never given him the chance to make things right, to tell her he loved her so much he thought his heart might explode.

He climbed inside his truck and quickly blasted the air, welcoming the coolness. Despite the sun having been replaced by the moon, the Florida heat never seemed to retreat along with it.

Before pulling out of the driveway, he took out his wallet and retrieved a necklace he kept within its fold. It was a small, gold locket with a single rhinestone embedded in the center. It was Hailey's and she had given it to him the night he first told her he loved her. He never could find the nerve to toss it. It was the last piece of her he had left.

He ran his thumb over it, letting the memories rush through his mind.

As much as he hated himself for it, he still loved her. She was the one that got away and no woman had ever come close to outshining Hailey Gallagher.

Life was about to get interesting if she returned.

Jason was right: Trey should stay away from her if he knew what was best. But that was the problem. Trey always went looking for trouble. And Hailey had been a whole new kind of trouble, which was why he had wanted her so badly.

Their relationship had been a whirlwind of emotions that he never wanted to repeat. Trey pushed her out of his mind long ago and he planned to keep it that way.

However, he found himself painfully aware of the fact that once Hailey left after the wedding, she'd never have another reason to come back to Auburndale again. This would be the last time he would see her, and he wasn't ready for such a permanent goodbye, even if he saw this one coming.

But no matter what happened, he had to stay away from her, for both their sakes. Being with her once had ended horribly. Trying it for a second time might just kill them.

Chapter 3

June 25, 2011
5:38 pm

Jason cried as soon as Angie walked through the doors of the church. He eagerly took his bride's hand, smiling so hard even Trey's cheeks hurt. Trey had never seen a couple so in love with each other.

Angie glowed radiantly, her tanned skin complimenting the white gown she wore. Or was it ivory? Was that even a color? Women had specific names for colors that all looked the same. Trey couldn't keep up.

He caught a quick glimpse of Hailey sitting in the back row. She looked slightly older, and her brown hair now had blonde streaks that highlighted her features well. She smiled as the couple read their vows.

Trey couldn't help but notice the young girl sitting next to her.

Did she have a daughter?

She looked just like Hailey. Aside from having jet-black hair, her bone structure and olive skin were that of her mother's. Trey wasn't ready for that punch in the gut, and he hated that he still felt something for the woman who broke his heart.

Yet, he felt a stab of betrayal as he envisioned her having a family with another man. There was a time when he had been the one whom she wanted to start a family with. However, he quickly noticed she wasn't wearing a ring and was embarrassed by the sliver of hope he felt.

Trey now stood at the dessert table, filling his plate with random delicacies: a slice of pie, a few cookies, and some good ole' apple dumplings. His stomach growled in anticipation of the sugar rush. He probably shouldn't eat so many sweets, but it was better to stuff his face with calories than drown himself in liquor again.

He turned to walk away when he nearly crashed into a woman. She was petite, about a head shorter than he. "I'm sorry, ma'am," he drawled.

"That's okay, I-" Her smile quickly faded, and her body became rigid as a ruby shade slowly dusted her cheeks. Her lips were pursed tight in a frown, not even attempting to hide her distaste.

Some things never change.

Trey's breath caught in his throat, and he pulled at his collar, attempting to cool himself. "Hailey," he stammered.

Trey chastised himself. *Really? You haven't seen her in thirteen years and all you can say is her name?*

"Trey," she spat.

"How are you?"

"Fine." She quickly left and sat back down at her table, not bothering with dessert or a second glance his way.

The lady could seriously hold a grudge.

He knew things might be awkward with her coming back to town, but to still be so angry after all this time was a bit dramatic. But leave it to Hailey to be dramatic. She always had a flair for the theatrical, something he found both irritating and endearing.

Right now it was irritating.

Yet, he couldn't help but notice the way her dress hugged her hips as she walked away. Or the way her calf muscles contoured with every step of a heel. He pushed those thoughts from his mind. He didn't dare think about anything else or he may need to leave early for a cold shower.

Sitting at the table with Hailey, the teenager glanced at Trey and raised a brow, eyeing him suspiciously. Trey guessed she was about twelve. After seeing her more closely, there was no doubt she was Hailey's daughter. The girl even pouted like her mother: lips pushed down, and eyes narrowed. A look that could kill and had often made Trey wonder if Hailey was, in fact, plotting his death from time to time.

He thought about approaching them but knew it would only make things worse. Trey wished he and Hailey didn't have to be at odds. Even though things ended badly, they shared many special moments together and he desperately wished they could have remained friends after she left.

Instead, Trey began walking back to his table to finish his plate of desserts, though now he seemed to have lost his appetite. He shoved the plate back and watched the crowd dance in excitement. Angie and Jason were making their rounds, thanking everyone for coming.

Though he was enjoying the wedded bliss of his friend, he couldn't help but sneak glances at Hailey. She was still just as beautiful as she had always been. She threw her head back and laughed as an older woman chatted with her, probably about memories from her childhood.

He missed hearing her laugh. He also missed her sense of humor and her playfulness. Hell, he even missed her stubborn-ass attitude.

Sensing his gaze, Hailey met his eyes. But instead of looking away from him, she held his stare. He nodded to her and smiled. It was only then that she quickly looked away.

He cursed at himself for allowing her to still have some sort of hold on his heart. He hadn't thought about her since the day she left. He didn't want to start now.

Well, that wasn't entirely true but he would pretend it was.

He dreaded going back to his quaint little bungalow later, where he knew he would spend the entire night wondering how to get rid of the image of the beautiful face that still haunted him.

———————

Being back in Auburndale had unwanted memories flooding Hailey. Gosh, she hated it here and she hated that she had to bring Trinity with her. When Hailey moved away, she planned to never come back at all. And had it been for any reason other than Angie's wedding, she wouldn't have.

Of course, running into Trey had been the icing on a very bitter cake even though Hailey had prepared herself for it. What good that did.

She didn't realize all of her anger and animosity would come rushing to the surface once she saw him. She knew they wouldn't be friends, but she didn't want there to be such dread either. Quite honestly, she had hoped to avoid him at all costs but obviously that plan had been thwarted.

Luckily, she'd be leaving town in a few days so stewing over her teenage love interest was pointless. If she hadn't promised her stepmother they'd come for family dinner, she'd head back to Alabama tonight. But after that, she really wouldn't have any ties left to this awful town.

However, someone she hadn't been prepared to see at the wedding was Ryan House. She'd nearly vomited at the sight of him, talking herself down from a panic attack as he smiled and waved to her. A chill raced down her spine as she recalled the violence that seeped from him, the evil that lurked behind his gray eyes.

"Momma, are you okay?"

Hailey snapped back to reality, meeting her daughter's worried gaze. Though Trinity resembled her father more than she did Hailey, she had inherited Hailey's piercing green eyes, along with her stubbornness, attitude, and piqued curiosity that seemed to bring about trouble just as it had for Hailey.

Her thirteen-year-old daughter was growing up quickly and Hailey found herself missing baby snuggles and toddler giggles. But those days had long disappeared and now stood a teenager, though she would always be Hailey's little girl, her little ray of sunshine.

Hailey had given Trinity the same nickname Hailey had been given as a child, though Trinity brought new meaning to the name Hailey loathed.

She remembered the day Trinity was born. It had been a rainy day, a great boom of thunder announcing the arrival of the storm and her daughter. She had been in labor for nearly thirty hours when the nurse laid Trinity on her chest. When Hailey held her six-pound, four-ounce baby in her arms, she cried. She was holding a miracle in her arms.

After having just lost her mother, her sister, the love of her life, and the life she once knew, Hailey was no longer alone in this world. She had Trinity, and Trinity was the only thing Hailey would ever need. She had been Hailey's ray of sunshine after her darkest days.

Not to mention she was a literal miracle.

Trinity shouldn't even be alive after the attack Hailey had suffered. But here she was.

Hailey smiled and sighed. "I'm fine. There's a lot of memories here that I don't want to think about."

Trinity lifted a brow and Hailey immediately regretted her answer.

"It's nothing. Don't worry about it."

Trinity rolled her eyes and crossed her arms over her chest. "That's a lie, but whatever."

Hailey ignored the comment and watched as everyone danced, talked, and laughed. She knew most everyone here, small town living. Many people asked where she had disappeared to and why she hadn't come back all these years. Others just stared at her, afraid to ask their nosy questions.

Every now and then, she would catch Trey staring at her. She hated that she still got butterflies despite the fact she didn't want to have anything to do with him. They had planned a life together, claiming their undying love for one another, only for him to leave her.

She looked around the room and spied Ryan House walking toward her. Her stomach dropped and she hoped he would walk past her. For reasons unknown to her, he had hated her and Sara, but more specifically Hailey.

He would go out of his way to pick on her and, oftentimes, even torment her. When she was fifteen, he put a dead frog in her locker, its intestines hanging out. She had nearly vomited from the smell of decay.

The first time he had physically hurt her was at the Strawberry Festival where he had threatened her and attempted to drag her away, everyone turning a blind eye as he did, despite her cries for help. She had been terrified until Trey tackled Ryan and a fight broke out. Unfortunately, that wasn't the worst of Hailey's run-ins with him. A few months later, he tried to kill her...and almost succeeded.

To her dismay, he walked up to the table, drink in hand. He always smelled of whiskey and cigarettes. And he was always drunk.

His beard was thicker now and his hair a little longer. He wore a scar near his hairline, compliments of Hailey. She inwardly smiled to herself, satisfied to have left her own mark on him as he'd done to her. He was disheveled with his dress shirt halfway untucked and his gray eyes nearly turned black when he spied her; hatred always present when he looked at her.

"Hailey Gallagher. Didn't think I'd see you again." A dark smile tugged at his lips.

"Go away, Ryan." She glanced at Trinity who perked up, noticing a shift in Hailey's energy. She furrowed her brows as her eyes darted between Hailey and the stranger.

"What are you gonna do? Tell your daddy?" he mocked.

She stood, wanting to send a clear message that she was no longer afraid of him. "Go. Away," she said through gritted teeth.

He stepped closer, getting in her face. A few guests glanced in their direction, both worried and curious about the exchange. She stepped back and he grabbed her upper arm, bringing her close, much like he had years ago.

She pushed against his chest, and as hard as she tried to fight it, her lungs tightened, and she felt a panic attack surfacing. He had done the same thing right before he had tried to kill her. She glanced at Trinity who was now standing, unsure of what to do.

Before Hailey could say anything, she heard a deep voice behind her. "Let her go."

She turned to see Trey standing behind her, his jaw tight as he glared at Ryan. Duty or protection? She wasn't sure, but she was glad he was there. Even after all this time, Trey still made her feel safe. She wasn't exactly sure what that meant, so she refused to acknowledge it for fear of what feelings might reemerge if she spent too much time lingering on such thoughts.

Ryan exchanged a glance between Trey and Hailey. Trinity was fidgeting and her voice had gone up an octave. "Mom?" Her daughter's eyes darted between Hailey and the two men, and then to the crowd that was now staring at them.

Angie quickly walked up to them, gathering her dress as she did, and gripped Ryan's arm. Her southern accent was as thick and as sweet as honey as she whispered, "If you don't disappear from my reception, I'll have Chief Harbor here throw you in a jail cell." She smiled, though they all knew she was anything but happy.

Ryan released Hailey's arm and said to her, "If you stick around long enough, eventually Trey won't be around to protect you. Just like he wasn't the night your Ma died."

"Ryan!" Angie snapped.

Trey stepped between Ryan and Hailey, daring Ryan to throw the first punch. But Ryan threw his hands in the air and laughed as he sauntered off, amused by Trey's reaction. He disappeared out the back door and Hailey prayed she would never see him again.

Her body involuntarily shivered. He would make good on his threat if given the chance. That much was clear, given that he promised the same thing the night of the festival and a few weeks later he came to collect. Trey hadn't been with Hailey when her car broke down after their fight and she had almost died at Ryan's hand because of it.

Trey turned to her. "Are you okay?"

"Yes, I'm fine. Thanks." She tried to steady her breathing as Trinity raced around the table and clung to her. Trey smiled at the girl but she didn't return the gesture, suspicion still present in her hazel eyes.

"What was his problem?" Trinity demanded, her voice cracking. Hailey rubbed Trinity's arms trying to calm her.

"He's not a nice guy. That's all you need to know."

"Clearly," Trinity said. Her daughter was not pleased with her response, but Hailey didn't care. Despite her teen's constant protests, Hailey wasn't obligated to share everything with her daughter.

Thankfully, Angie interrupted. "God bless it, I hate that man. Always stirring up trouble. I told Jason I didn't want him here, but since he's Jason's cousin, his momma about had a conniption when I declined inviting him." She rolled her eyes. "They're not even blood-relatives. They're related by some far-off uncle that's been forty times removed, or some such bologna."

Trey looked at Hailey, and Hailey smiled briefly before carrying on the conversation with Angie. She was thankful he intervened, but she still had no interest in talking to him.

After an awkward, lingering moment, he got the hint and quietly walked away. Her gaze followed him for a moment before she turned and responded to Angie. "It's okay. I'm just glad I got to come back and see you on your big day."

"I've been trying to break away from these guests to come see you!"

"Don't worry about it, Ange. I know being a bride is the hardest job." Hailey winked as they embraced each other. Hailey held her friend tight, not realizing how much she had missed her. Angie was the only person Hailey kept in contact with after she moved, but even those phone calls were seldom and sporadic.

"I've missed you so much!" Angie said as she sat down. She turned toward Trinity. "And this must be Trinity."

Trinity smiled and went back to reading her book.

"Yup, that's my girl." Hailey beamed.

"I can't believe how much she looks like you."

Hailey was used to the comment, but she also knew how much Trinity looked like her father, something she was glad Angie didn't disclose. All Trinity knew of her father was that he was from Auburndale and that he had broken Hailey's heart. And Hailey planned to keep it that way.

She always told herself she'd tell Trinity about her father when she turned eighteen. Right now, she was too young to understand all that had happened between Hailey and Trey. Trinity simply wasn't ready to hear the truth.

But maybe it was time. After all, they were back where it all began. A torrid love story, a princess and a knight in shining armor, a fairytale that many girls dream about...but it all ended in heartache.

Except Trinity. She was the only good thing to come out of that devastating summer.

But Hailey wasn't ready to face her demons. So, Trinity's father would remain in the shadows.

Angie leaned in, more serious than before. "Have you talked to your sister?"

Hailey was taken aback by the question, though she shouldn't be since her sister had gotten out of prison two weeks ago.

"No, there's not much to say," she said curtly.

"I mean, I get there's a lot to clear up between you two, but I'm surprised you feel that way."

Angie was interrupted by a couple coming to say their goodbyes. Hailey waited patiently for them to walk away, hoping the interruption would cause a change in subject. Angie had always been known to talk about things at the worst time, a trait she clearly still possessed, unfortunately for Hailey.

"Anyway," Angie continued, "I just can't believe she ended up serving time. That video was proof she didn't do it. She literally had her alibi recorded and was still convicted?" Angie simply shook her head in disappointment.

Hailey furrowed her brows. "What video? The reason she was even a suspect is because she was found next to my mother's dead body."

Hailey couldn't believe the audacity her friend had to bring up her mother's death. Angie knew firsthand how distraught Hailey had been over her sister's conviction, and even more so, her mother's murder. Hailey had refused to discuss any of it during their few phone calls over the years. That Angie would bring it up the first time they saw each other in over a decade struck a chord with Hailey.

Aware of Hailey's anger, Angie put her hands up. "I didn't mean to start a fuss. Really. I thought you knew all about it. I mean, I gave the video to *you*."

"What video?" Hailey said, irritated by the turn of the conversation. This was the last thing she wanted to talk about.

Angie frowned and let out a sigh and Hailey immediately felt bad. "I'm sorry. This is still really hard for me to talk about." Hailey calmed herself before saying, "What video are you talking about?"

"Remember the package I brought you a few days after your mother died? It was actually from Donna Sheldon. It was a video of her, Sara, and a few others at the time of the murder. It was time-stamped and everything. Donna thought it proved Sara didn't do it." Angie paused for a moment and shook her head. "When Sara was convicted, I just thought the judge tossed it."

Hailey was bewildered.

Angie asked, "Do you really not know what I'm talking about? It was in a large box because Donna didn't want anyone to know what it was. She labeled it with your name, and it had a bunch of packing peanuts in it..."

Hailey's heart sank and a knot formed in the pit of her stomach. A week after Morgan died, Angie dropped off a package to Hailey. She didn't want visitors at the time so Genevieve, the family's housekeeper, brought the box to Hailey. Except she never opened it. She didn't care about the box or about Angie or people's empty condolences. All she cared about was trying to figure out how to put back the pieces of her now-shattered life.

So she had shoved the box into her closet and forgot all about it.

She truly hadn't cared about anything in the weeks and months after her mother died. She hardly ate or slept. She didn't get out of bed unless it was necessary. She would simply stare at a spot on the wall for hours, wishing she were dead along with her mother.

Her whole life had changed that summer's night. Trey broke up with her after swearing to love her forever. Her mother was killed and Sara was arrested for the crime. Then Hailey herself danced with death. On top of that, she found out she was pregnant that morning.

After everything was said and done, Hailey wanted to run away and never come back. And she had done a pretty good job thus far.

Hailey took in a deep breath to try to steady her racing heart. Heat pricked her skin and she felt the desire to run away again. She tried to focus on what Angie was saying, but everything was muffled and the room slowly started to spin. She reached out and grasped the table to steady herself.

If what Angie said was true, Sara was wrongly convicted for their mother's murder.

And for the last thirteen years, Hailey had the evidence that could have exonerated her.

Chapter 4

Hailey tried to fight the dizziness that came and went in waves as she attempted to keep herself from panicking over Angie's revelation about the video. After catching up with Angie for another thirty minutes, Hailey said her goodbyes and made her way to her childhood home to find the tape.

When they spoke on the phone yesterday morning, Genevieve mentioned that all of Hailey's things were still in her old room. Hailey had been surprised to hear the housekeeper was still taking care of the Gallagher home after all these years.

Apparently, David Gallagher had no desire to change anything about the old estate, despite his new wife's claims they needed to update the space. Hailey found it slightly eerie that her father hadn't changed the house since Hailey left and Sara was arrested. Especially given the fact it was where his first wife had been murdered.

Hailey wondered if the tyrant had a heart after all. Though, if he did, it was miniscule. Maybe after all the terror he'd rained down on his family, David felt a sliver of guilt and somehow didn't want to give up old memories that undoubtedly haunted the home.

It was even more surprising, though, that her stepmother willingly lived there. If Hailey were in Lauren's shoes, she would have convinced her husband to sell the home that harbored so much pain and cruelty. Who would want to live in a house where someone was murdered, even if it was grand and beautiful?

It gave Hailey the creeps.

Hailey's heartbeat quickened as the two-story home came into view. She rolled down the window in hopes that the evening breeze would ease her anxiety. Those walls contained so many memories- more bad than good, unfortunately. Hailey drove the long, palm tree-lined drive, the lake peeking from behind the house as the driveway wound its way to the place she spent the first eighteen years of her life.

She circled around the massive fountain that had been built in the middle of the yard and parked the car. Her mother loathed that fountain, claiming it was a drowning hazard. But her father always loved the extravagant things in life and waved off Morgan's concerns. He quickly revoked his judgments of his wife when Sara nearly drowned a year or two after it was built.

Though Hailey never recalled the fountain spouting water after the incident, a soft melody of splashes now joined the dusk's lullaby as it beat against the pebbles at its foundation.

Hailey hated the site of it.

She didn't immediately get out of her car. She sat motionless for a few minutes as dreadful memories surfaced. Her mind was replaying that night, the one where she had become motherless and found her own flesh and blood was the cause of her pain. Even after all these years, she could still vividly recall the sounds of the police as they swarmed her home, drowning out the familiar summer night song of croaks and chirps.

After suffering her own trauma hours earlier, she had come home to what became her worst nightmare.

She had been walking up the driveway toward the house when the flashing red and blue lights demanded her attention. As she had gotten closer, the crime scene tape and police officers had blurred together as her body fought off exhaustion and shock.

The hairs on her nape stood at attention and she had innately known something awful had happened. She had wanted to sprint toward her home and find answers, but after what she'd been through, she didn't have the energy or the strength. Yet, despite her body's protests, she had been instinctively drawn to the scene of the crime, every step becoming harder than the last.

Hailey had stopped for a moment, realizing she wasn't presentable.

Should she change? Her mother would have a heart attack if she came home like this.

Her clothes had been torn and she was missing a shoe. She had brushed off the grass that clung to her jeans, the green streaks irking her. She had pulled a stray leaf from her hair.

Assessing herself, she had grasped at the locket she always wore and nearly cried out when she had realized it was missing. She had quickly remembered she'd given it to Trey weeks before.

However, it was the blood that had startled her. She had still been covered in the crimson stains that mixed with dirt, though at that point it caked her skin. She had aggressively scraped at her arms and hands, trying to erase the terror her body had just endured. When it wouldn't come off, she had ordered her legs to walk forward toward whatever violence occurred on such a warm summer's night.

Every step had been heavy, as if her body was trying to protect her from the monsters that lurked in the shadows. Tears had flowed down her cheeks, as if they were attempting to wash away the dirt and horror that stained her face.

"Mom," Trinity said from the passenger seat, "snap out of it. You're being weird."

Hailey was startled back to reality. "Sorry, there's just a lot of stuff you don't understand about this place and it's really hard for me to be here."

"Well, that doesn't mean you have to be all spooky about it and zone out."

Hailey smiled and shook her head. "Alright, alright. I'll stop being spooky."

The two of them climbed out of the car and Hailey took in the magnificent structure. As much as Hailey wanted to stay elsewhere, there were no other options in town. Since tourists very rarely came to Auburndale, there were no bed-and-breakfasts, inns, or hotels. At least none that were kept clean and weren't used to run small criminal enterprises.

After getting their suitcase out of the trunk, she and Trinity mounted the large steps and knocked on the front door. A woman answered, streaks of gray visible throughout her blonde hair. Her brown eyes gleamed as a wide smile crept on her face.

"Gen!" Hailey exclaimed.

"Hailey, my sweet girl!" The woman wrapped Hailey in an embrace and Hailey smiled at the housekeeper who had also helped raise Hailey and Sara.

"How are you? I can't believe you're still working for the slave driver." Hailey pointed toward the house, indicating David. It had been an ongoing joke between Hailey, Sara, and Genevieve.

Genevieve's mother started working for Henry and Camila Gallagher when Genevieve was six years old. She and David grew up together, though Genevieve was a few years older than David. The two had spent many days playing together but as time passed, socio-economic status, different schools, and opposing social circles caused them to drift apart, though they still shared many secrets and confided in one another.

When Genevieve turned seventeen, she began working for the family as a housekeeper alongside her mother. Even when her mother passed away, Genevieve continued to dedicate herself to the Gallaghers. Especially to Hailey and Sara.

Hailey thought Genevieve may be a saint for entertaining David's malicious and controlling demeanor for so long, though he never seemed to show the woman that side of him. Genevieve had never hesitated to put him in his place, and he respected her because of it.

Genevieve let out a rambunctious laugh. "The slave driver still needs my help."

Hailey introduced Trinity as she awkwardly twirled her hair, waiting to be acknowledged. "Oh, Gen, this is-"

"Trinity. I know! She looks just like you." Genevieve embraced the teen as if she had known her for years. Trinity stiffened as she hugged the woman back.

The three of them made their way into the foyer and Hailey's gaze drifted to the end of the staircase where her mother's body had laid. From what she understood, Sara had pushed their mother down the stairs where Morgan Gallagher met her demise. Hailey wondered if her face flashed through her mother's mind in Morgan's last moments. Did she cry out for help or for her husband or maybe even for her own mother?

She visibly shook as chills ran up her spine. Hailey clenched her teeth and willed herself to look away from the spot that once held her mother's dying body.

Genevieve said, "Your father is working right now, but Lauren is watching TV in her room. I'm sure she'll want to see you."

Movement caught Hailey's eye, and she looked up to see Lauren standing on the landing.

"He hasn't changed much since you were young," Lauren said with a smile as she descended the stairs. "He's at a shooting fundraiser with a few City Commissioners. You know how much he loves his guns. Every now and again I'll tag along, but he claims I'm not nearly as good a shot as he is."

Hailey's arrival had interrupted her stepmother's night as she was clearly getting ready for bed. She donned a pink shorts-and-button-down pajama set and her face was void of makeup.

A curvaceous blonde with eyes as blue as ice, she was a sweet woman and drop dead gorgeous. Though she'd never admit to it, she had a nose job and breast implants that enhanced her already natural beauty. Hailey didn't have to wonder why her father chose to marry her. Lauren looked good on camera, and she stroked his ego.

Maybe that wasn't fair to the pretty blonde, but it was the truth. Sure, the woman was kind and engaging, but David only cared about one thing: his reputation.

Trying her best to push her way into the inner circle of the local politicians and businessmen, Lauren became her father's secretary when Hailey and Sara were sixteen. She wasn't overly ambitious, but she was driven enough to get her foot in the door at the mere age of twenty. That clearly paid off because she played a significant role in David building his political career.

Hailey suspected Lauren fancied her father for some time and took her chance with David when Morgan died. Surprisingly, it worked, because David married Lauren only a year after Morgan's death.

Truthfully, Hailey didn't dislike Lauren, but she didn't love her either; something that was largely due to Lauren only being four years Hailey's senior.

Granted, Hailey didn't know much about her. Only that she'd been raised by a simple country couple who adopted her when she was three and that she'd moved to Auburndale shortly before she started working for David.

"Hi, Lauren. Thanks for letting us stay here," Hailey said. She motioned her hand toward Trinity. "This is my daughter, Trinity."

"Hi," Trinity said softly as she raised a hand to wave.

Thankfully, Lauren didn't try to hug Hailey or Trinity, and Hailey appreciated that Lauren didn't force a relationship. Hailey had moved away by the time Lauren and David started dating, so she never had to wade through the awkwardness of living with a stepmother.

"Of course. Y'all can stay anytime." Her thick Kentucky accent oddly soothed Hailey. "Help yourself to anything you'd like. Nothing has changed since you left, even though I keep trying to convince David to update it a little." Lauren winked at Hailey, and she immediately felt at ease being back in the grand estate.

The four stood silently until Lauren took in a deep breath and smiled. "Well, I'm going to hit the hay, but y'all are more than welcome to stay up and get settled or just relax. I figured you'd want your old room, Hailey, and Trinity can stay in Sara's since they're adjoining."

Hailey smiled. "That's fine with us."

Lauren walked back up the stairs and disappeared down the hall.

"Well, I'm heading out, girls," Genevieve said. "I told Lauren I would wait around for you because I just couldn't wait to see you." She kissed Hailey on the cheek, then Trinity.

Once Genevieve was gone, Hailey carried their small suitcase up the stairs and showed Trinity where they would be staying. The teen stopped abruptly in the hallway to look at the photos that sat on a decorative table. She picked up a small gold frame that had been shoved to the back of the table, all but hidden behind another framed photo. Hailey assumed it was Genevieve who made sure it didn't get put into a box or thrown into the trash.

Trinity studied the faces that stared back at her. "Is this your mother?" Trinity asked.

Hailey gently took the frame from her daughter and smiled. It was a candid shot of Morgan holding Sara and Hailey on each hip. The twins were four years old, both in corresponding outfits. All three girls smiled brightly, Morgan's sparkle in her eye still present. It would be years later, but that sparkle would eventually diminish. Hailey could hardly remember it all.

"Yes, that's my mother," Hailey said proudly.

"She was really beautiful. You have her eyes."

A lump formed in Hailey's throat, and she quickly blinked back tears. "Then so do you."

Trinity smiled and Hailey placed the photo back on the table as Trinity walked into the bedroom, leaving Hailey alone.

Her heart ached all over again, remembering that Trinity would never meet the woman Hailey called mother. Trinity was right; Morgan Gallagher was beautiful. But more than that, she was funny, kind, and smart. All things Trinity inherited from her.

Wanting to push her thoughts aside, Hailey went to her room.

Hailey's mouth fell open as she took in the sight. Her room really hadn't changed in the last thirteen years. The bedsheets were still the same pink floral pattern, and the drapes, though faded, still cloaked the balcony that sat right outside the French doors. Even her old set of drawers and vanity sat untouched. It was as if she had died, and David wanted to freeze her in time.

Maybe the old man really had changed. After all the years of abuse, had the patriarch of the Gallagher family finally found himself wishing he could go back in time before their lives had been shattered? Or was he still the same heartless father who always gripped control so tightly he'd draw blood from those he claimed to love if they didn't allow him to have it? Was this yet another way to seek that control, to keep everything the way it was before it all spiraled out of control and their family disintegrated?

Walking to the French doors, she opened them and stood on the balcony, taking in the moon that was beginning to move the sun out of sight. She looked over the sunset that painted the sky beautiful shades of red, orange and yellow. She had seen it a million times, but tonight it somehow seemed sadder.

She had watched the sunset with her sister and her mother before bed as a little girl. Then it was just her and Sara when they were teenagers, always talking about boys and the latest school gossip. And she had watched it with Trey on more than one occasion when he snuck in through the window to say goodnight, slow dancing as dusk turned to darkness.

As much as she wanted to hate him, she couldn't. Hailey smiled to herself, remembering the many times she and Sara climbed down this very balcony to meet up with Trey and Chase or when she and Trey spray painted their initials together on an old bridge just over one of the lake canals. Memories flooded her and this time, she let them, basking in the surge of bittersweet happiness she felt.

Breathing in deeply, she walked back inside and closed the French doors behind her. She stopped just short of the bed. She wondered if anyone had found the hidden compartment in the floor she had used as a hiding spot for her diary and other treasured items.

Curious, she knelt down and lifted the bed skirt and began pressing on the wooden planks. As one gave way and popped up, a sly smile pulled at her lips. She carefully slid her hand into the hole and felt for the old photos she had left behind. She was happy to find they were still there.

Pulling them out, Hailey studied the stack of polaroids. There were some of her and Sara at a party they had snuck out to. Others were of the twins sitting together on the lanai and then a candid shot Trey had taken of the two girls. Sara smiled wildly in all of them; always feeling like the world was hers for the taking.

For a long time, Hailey believed Sara would conquer the world and all its glory. Sara wanted to be a fashion model, and her future had been bright in that regard. Hailey knew in her heart of hearts her sister would walk the runways in Milan and Paris one day.

Unfortunately, drugs and alcohol consumed Sara. She had been on various narcotics cocktails in most of those photos and throughout most of their teen years. And she had paid dearly for her addiction.

So did the rest of the family.

Something Hailey could never come to terms with was the roller coaster of emotions brought on by her sister. She loved Sara to death, but with that love came pain. It was painful to love Sara; she was so destructive and chaotic.

Instead of focusing on who Sara had become and where she ended up, Hailey focused on the good memories. Then she moved on to the other photos.

The ones of her and Trey.

The ones she left behind hoping she could forget about the man who shattered her heart.

There was one in particular that stood out to her, though. She and Trey were sitting on a picnic blanket in a random field, their favorite place to go. There was a twinkle in their eyes as Trey pulled her close to his chest. Hailey had melted into him as if she had been doing it forever. It felt so natural to her. His hat blocked the sun, and her hair was pulled into a ponytail, allowing her locket to be shown off.

Hailey clutched at her chest where the locket would have hung if she had kept it. She had given it to Trey that day, after he told her he loved her. That was the moment they had made a promise to love each other for all eternity.

And she had meant it.

But he hadn't.

She shouldn't still be stuck in the past. After all, they were kids then. Neither one of them knew what love was, let alone what it meant to love someone forever. But his betrayal still stung.

Before Hailey could stop herself, she wondered about all the what-ifs and what-could-have-beens, all of the hopes and dreams that shattered along with her heart.

Hailey sighed.

She missed Trey and the life she thought they'd share. She missed the dreams she so desperately desired. She missed her mother so much it hurt. She missed who her sister had been before Sara had become an addict and murderer.

What she wouldn't give to go back to that night and stop it all from happening.

She hated how emotional this trip was making her. She felt like a teenage drama queen.

Hailey pushed her feelings aside, no longer wanting to relive the hurricane of choices that destroyed her life in one fell swoop. She tucked the photos back in their hiding spot and closed the hatch, locking them away. Much like she wished she could do with her memories.

It wasn't until she sat on the bed that she realized how much her feet ached from the heels she'd been wearing all evening. She took them off and tossed them on the bed next to her.

Her eyes fell on the closet doors that were now closed, the wooden panels unaware of the potential truth that was concealed behind them.

Pulling on the doors, she found it was now empty aside from a few boxes. She hadn't taken much with her when she moved, just her clothes and makeup. She had wanted to leave behind all that she could and start over. It looked like Genevieve had boxed up old keepsakes and used the closet as storage. To the far left sat a lonely box, her name scrawled in bubbly letters across the side panel.

Hailey anxiously fetched the cardboard and walked to her bed where she began opening it. Her heart thudded loudly as she tugged at the flaps. Part of her wanted to throw it back into the closet and leave. How could she live with herself if what Angie said was true?

It wasn't too late. She could ignore what Angie told her and finally move on with her life. Once she left town, her past would be left here, no longer able to dig its claws into her and drag her down.

Then she thought of Sara and how much she had loved her sister once upon a time. She remembered who she was before the drugs and alcohol, before their father began beating them into obedience, before she was named a murderer.

Pushing past her selfishness, Hailey folded down the tops of the box and peeked inside.

Sure enough, just as Angie claimed, there was a single video tape inside hidden under green packing peanuts. Her heart sank as she realized the magnitude this video could have. How it could turn everything upside down if it did in fact prove Sara's innocence.

She popped the tape into the VHS player that still sat on the opposite side of the bed. She turned the volume down low, not knowing what to expect. Hailey hit play and held her breath as she watched the screen come to life.

Donna was drunkenly talking to the camcorder about the group's plans. Hailey could make out Sara, Jake Nelson, and Thomas Smith in the background. They all sang loudly to the music that played on the radio in the car. Donna laughed at her friends and turned the lens toward them. Sara sang to the camera, always the life of the party, slurring her speech as she did.

It then panned to Thomas who was at the wheel, also intoxicated. He shoved the camera out of his face, causing Donna to curse at him. Hailey felt sick knowing all of them had been driving drunk that night, though during the video they seemed to be in a parking lot.

Sara grabbed the face of the camera so that Donna was focused on her. Sara started crying, her words hardly intelligible. "I love Chase *soooo* much, but I can't give up my dream of modeling. Doesn't he love me enough to wait until I get my big break?"

"Forget about him! You can have any guy you want. Just wait 'til you get to New York," Donna said, sending Sara into hysterics. Donna set the camcorder down on the dashboard revealing that they had been parked at a local corner store. The camera went black after that, and Hailey sat motionless for a moment before rewinding the tape.

As Angie claimed, the camcorder had the date and time stamp of the murder: *June 03, 1998, 10:42 pm.*

Angie was right: Sara hadn't killed Morgan Gallagher.

And Hailey unknowingly had proof for the last thirteen years.

Chapter 5

June 25, 2011
9:47 pm

A knock at the door startled Sara. No one knew she was staying at Angie's, and since today was Angie's wedding, Sara knew the woman wouldn't be expecting company. Assuming it was a neighbor, Sara didn't get off the couch and instead ignored the knocks.

She planned to stay with Angie until she could get back on her feet. Thankfully, with Angie's recommendation, she had been able to score a part-time job restocking a small shop a few evenings a week. It wasn't much money, but it was enough for now.

All she wanted to do was lay low until she was able to get her life in order...and until she could plot her revenge. The last thing she needed was for word to spread that she was back in town. And since Angie would be on her honeymoon for the next four weeks, Sara had ample time to set things in motion. The happy couple was celebrating wedded bliss and Angie's recent doctoral degree graduation with a month-long vacation.

The thudding continued and she grew more and more irritated. Whoever it was knew she was inside. Sighing, she got off the couch and opened the door.

She hadn't expected to see the pretty face that stood on the other side. It was like staring into a mirror, except the other woman didn't look like she'd been to hell and back. Hate flamed within her as she stared into her sister's eyes. Anger, her oldest friend, came right after.

The two stared at each other for what felt like an eternity. *How did Hailey know she was here?* They hadn't spoken to each other since Hailey left town, making it very clear her womb mate deemed her guilty like everyone else.

Sara was surprised to see Hailey had added blonde to the lifeless brown hair she wore as a teen. She always vowed she'd never go blonde, a knock at Sara since Sara had taken pride in the platinum color she loved so much. Hailey looked older and more mature, but she didn't look like life had beaten her down or that she spent the last decade fighting for her life.

Jealousy roared right below the surface, just as it always did when it came to her sister. Hailey was loved by everyone, and Sara was second best.

"Wow, the perfect little princess returns," Sara mocked. "What do you want, Hailey?"

Sara didn't want anything to do with her sister, but before she could slam the door closed, Hailey nervously said, "I know a lot has happened, but I need to show you something...it's about *that* night."

Immediately on edge, Sara said, "What about it?"

That night was the beginning of Sara's nightmare. What could Hailey possibly need to talk about that required her to all but hunt Sara down this late at night? Whatever it was, it wasn't good. Hailey wanted nothing to do with Sara so if her twin was standing on her doorstep, no doubt a hurricane of trouble wasn't far behind.

Bothered by Sara's hostility, Hailey began picking at her nail polish. "There's something you need to see." Hailey looked around, shifting as she did.

Sara was nervous now. She didn't like that Hailey was jumpy. It was unlike her and it put Sara on edge more than she already was.

Sara hesitated at first but then simply opened the door and gave Hailey the space to come in, not saying a word. Hailey walked inside, slowly taking in the cozy bungalow. Angie decorated her home with a lilac, white, and pale-yellow color scheme. Not something Sara would have chosen, but it suited the bubbly redhead.

Hailey walked to the couch and sat where Sara had been sitting previously. Sara wanted to protest but reminded herself she wasn't in prison anymore. She didn't have to be territorial. She was clearly having a harder time adjusting to freedom than she thought she would.

Sara then considered throwing Hailey out of the house out of spite but, again, decided against it. Sara was anxious to know why Hailey was so flustered and had gone out of her way to talk to her after all these years.

Sara sat on the other side of the couch, keeping her distance as suspicion filled her. "How did you know I was here?"

"Angie told me while I was at the wedding."

Sara rolled her eyes. She wasn't surprised, Angie couldn't keep a secret to save her life. Sara nodded, wanting to get Hailey out of her hair. "So, what do you need to show me?"

Hailey retrieved a VHS tape out of her purse, irritating Sara even further. "If you're wanting to watch a movie together, you can leave."

Hailey furrowed her brows. "What?" She looked down at the tape. "Oh, no. It's not a movie." Hailey sighed. "A few days after Mom died, Angie dropped off a tape, but I never watched it. It sat in a box in my room until I found it tonight. And you need to see it. Just...just trust me."

Sara bristled at the remark. Her sister had lost a grip on reality if she thought Sara would ever trust her again. She walked out on Sara when Sara's world crumbled around her and never looked back.

Hailey wasn't the only one to lose something that night. Sara mourned their mother's death just as much as Hailey. If anything, the last thirteen years proved that Hailey wasn't worthy of Sara's trust.

Unprompted, Hailey turned on the TV, popped the video tape into the player, and hit play.

Sara wasn't expecting to see a video of herself and her friends. It felt like a lifetime ago, as if she was watching a complete stranger. And she was. Sara no longer knew the girl in the video. That girl had died along with Morgan Gallagher.

Studying the screen, she cringed at how irresponsible they were. They had no business drinking and doing drugs, let alone driving under the influence.

When Sara heard her remarks about Chase, she immediately became rigid, embarrassment heating her body. A few moments later, the screen went black.

"Is this some kind of joke?" Sara stood up and crossed her arms. "You abandoned me all this time and now you come here to show me some stupid video. For what, Hailey? To remind me of how messed up I was?"

Hailey thrust her finger at Sara. "That's not fair. You're not the only one who went through something and you're not the only one who lost Mom. I was traumatized, too."

"So, abandoning me was your best option?"

Hailey matched Sara's anger and stood up. "I didn't abandon you! I ran away from my own problems."

Sara shook her head and laughed. "That's rich, Hailey. What problems did you have?"

Stunned, Hailey said, "Are you serious? You don't know anything about what happened to me. I went through something too and it almost cost me my baby! I was in shock and didn't know what to do so I left. The world doesn't revolve around you, Sara."

"Baby? What are you talking about?"

Hailey closed her eyes and sighed. "I found out I was pregnant that morning. I have a daughter."

Sara didn't speak at first. Once again, she felt betrayed by the person she once trusted the most in this life. How could Hailey not confide in her? How could she have missed out on thirteen years of her niece's life?

Hailey was so selfish!

"You have a kid, and you didn't think I'd want to know? Just a courtesy call: 'Hey, I know you're locked up, but you have a niece,'" Sara mocked.

Hailey rubbed her temples. "I see you haven't stopped being dramatic."

"Oh, get over yourself! Goody-freaking-two shoes."

Hailey's mouth hung open. She had always been called goody-two-shoes growing up and Sara knew she hated it.

"Selfish drunk," Hailey responded.

"Judas."

"Murderer."

Sara narrowed her eyes at Hailey.

Hailey's eyes rounded. "I'm sorry, I didn't mean it. I just-" she sighed, pausing to gather herself. "I was a kid and didn't know what to do, so I left. I didn't really know what to think in the beginning, but when you pled guilty, why would I have believed differently?"

"Because you're my sister. No, you were more than that. You were my other half. You knew me better than anyone. You left and never looked back while I was left to rot in a cage for someone else's crime."

Hailey looked away, knowing Sara was right.

Sara shouldn't be surprised that the first time they've seen each other in thirteen years would result in a fight. Growing up they had been both best friends and mortal enemies, a special bond only understood by sisterhood. And the last few years leading up to their mother's death had been plagued by heated arguments, silent treatments, and purposeful distance. They had hardly talked before all hell broke loose that summer.

Sara had been chaotic and impulsive while Hailey was controlled and wound too tight. The two were at odds as Sara's destruction seeped out around her and into Hailey's life. Hailey desperately tried to wade through it, only to nearly be drowned by it.

It made Hailey's appearance all the more peculiar. Sara still wasn't sure what Hailey's end game was. What was her sister trying to do?

Calming down, Sara asked, "Why did you bring me the video?"

"Did you notice the time stamp? It's the same date and time as Mom's death. This is your alibi."

"What do you mean 'my alibi?' I'm literally free after serving thirteen years in prison, no thanks to you."

Hailey ignored the slight and pointed toward the TV. "This could clear your name. You didn't do it, and the video proves it."

Sara threw her arm up. "It's a little late for that. I don't need your pity or your help. I know you're used to cleaning up my messes, but I don't need you anymore."

Sara was fuming. She began pacing, a habit she picked up while behind bars. *What the hell was going on?*

She had come back to town to seek revenge, though that plan proved to be much harder than she anticipated. And now Hailey had the audacity to show up unannounced after ghosting her for the last thirteen years? To add insult to injury, Hailey believed she was guilty this whole time but all of a sudden wanted to prove her innocence?

It infuriated Sara.

Hailey wasn't around when Sara's entire life was being turned upside down; when she was being railroaded, manipulated, and made to be the patsy. But *now* she was all in? *Screw that.*

Screw her.

Sara didn't care about the guilt her sister clearly felt about abandoning her. Hailey deserved for the guilt to eat away at her, to create a darkness that would slowly devour her from the inside out. It was just like Hailey to come swooping in, claiming to save the day when all she did was make Sara's life more miserable.

Just like when they were kids.

Any time Sara was in trouble, Hailey tried to bail her out. Only it didn't help Sara. No, Hailey got a little gold star of approval from their father while Sara was gifted bruises and scars.

There was no way in hell Sara would let Hailey ruin what lousy life she now had.

She had served her time and wasn't about to open up that can of worms. Whoever killed her mother had gotten away with it so why bother?

It's not like Morgan was around to appreciate the hard work of her golden child and the impossible redemption of her wayward daughter. She nearly laughed at the thought of herself making her mother proud. What a foreign concept that was. Why should she start now?

Everyone already thought she was guilty, there was no use trying to prove them wrong. She could easily move away and start over where no one knew about her past.

But that would have to wait. Sweet revenge was beckoning, and she had a busy schedule ahead of her. One that included dining with the Devil and his demons. A dinner in which she may just poison the very people responsible for her nightmare of a life.

And the guest list was long, her father being at the very top. He wouldn't even know it was her doing until she was long gone. Hell, she may even add Hailey to that list if Hailey continued to piss her off any more than she already had.

And after Sara was done leaving a trail of destruction, she would get a new identity and disappear. She definitely had criminal connections now.

She rubbed her face. All she ever wanted to do was proclaim her innocence, but she had been silenced and manipulated into taking a plea deal. So, at eighteen years old, she signed her life away and entered a guilty plea knowing full well she was innocent.

And no one came to her rescue. Not Hailey, not Chase, not Genevieve. Certainly not her father. He had been the one leading the mob who demanded she be shackled and chained.

Hailey's gentle voice pulled Sara out of her trance. "What happened that night?"

Sara didn't want to talk about it. She didn't want to relive the pain that came with the memories. Though, maybe she should. Maybe she should submerge herself in the revenge that flamed within her, sharpen the hate that intensified with each passing day.

She hadn't always wanted revenge. But what could she say? People changed.

Initially, Sara had been surprised her father was trying to bury her, though she shouldn't have been. He was a tyrant, a liar, and a manipulator. If he thought Sara was guilty, he was going to make the verdict stick.

Ever since she and Hailey were kids, David Gallagher made it his life's mission to make Sara miserable. And now she would return the favor.

Hailey's voice was nearly a whisper, "I know I can't undo what happened to you, but if you let me, I'll try to help clear your name."

Sara wanted to scream. Hailey spent a lot of time standing up for Sara, taking on their father's rage. But Hailey wasn't there to defend her when the whole world called for her to be jailed.

Funny how she only wanted to help Sara on her own terms and in her own time.

Sara smiled and clapped. "Bravo, Hailey. Another halo to add to your collection. What a saint for finally apologizing even though you should have done it years ago. Not to mention you're so ready to help me 'clear my name' when it's convenient for *you*. What a joke."

Hailey stiffened.

Sara continued, "And who are you fooling? The only reason you came here is because you feel guilty about having that video all these years. So big of you, Sis."

Hailey's mouth gaped open. "I'm trying to clean up *your* mess, per usual!"

Sara stepped closer to Hailey and crossed her arms. She silently threatened her sister, just as she had when they were growing up. But Hailey didn't step back or cower. She stepped closer, surprising Sara. It was clear she wasn't going to be intimidated.

If it weren't such a heated argument, Sara might have been proud of Hailey.

But right now, she hated her.

There was a time when Sara would have lost her temper and lashed out. Not now. She had spent a decade learning how to manipulate and play the enemy in a way they would never see coming.

Just like her father.

The irony of it wasn't lost on Sara. She just didn't care.

Instead of yelling, Sara calmly said, "News flash: I never asked you to. See, that's your problem, Hailey. You think you're everyone's saving grace but you're really just everyone's pain-in-the ass. So do me a favor and walk out on me like you did thirteen years ago."

"Screw you, Sara!"

Sara walked to the door and opened it wide for Hailey. "Oh look, you already have."

Hailey stomped out the door, leaving Sara to dwell on all of her sister's betrayals.

Chapter 6

Hailey had nearly cried at the sight of her sister the night before and was taken aback when Sara first opened the door. She hadn't been prepared to see that Sara was no longer a teenager, but a woman.

She had taken in Sara's petite frame and wild dark hair. Natural brown locks now took the place of what was once dyed icy blonde. Her once bright, hazel eyes were etched with anger and suspicion. She had a scar on her neck that hadn't been there before her arrest; Hailey heard rumors about a prison fight.

Hailey hardly knew the woman who had stood in front of her. Though, maybe she had never really known the real Sara. Her sister had been toxic, only revealing what she wanted you to see.

Growing up with Sara had been painful for Hailey. She had loved Sara with every fiber of her being, while, simultaneously, hating her with those same cells and molecules.

Strange how those two conflicting emotions could coexist.

And Hailey had been content hating Sara because Sara had made Hailey's life difficult. Her twin always came flying in like a gust of wind from a hurricane, demolishing anything she touched. For Hailey, hating Sara was easier than trying to make sense of the destruction and chaos. It was safer that way. Keeping Sara at arm's length ensured Hailey wouldn't be collateral damage. She just didn't know Sara would become a casualty of her own chaos.

After driving around to calm herself, it had been nearly eleven o'clock by the time Hailey had gotten back to the Gallagher Estate. Thankfully, Trinity hadn't cared that Hailey had disappeared for a short time. It gave her a chance to relax without Hailey breathing down her neck. Apparently, Hailey suffocated her daughter. She nearly laughed when Trinity had said it (typical teenage antics).

Unfortunately, she hadn't slept well, her fight with Sara plaguing her throughout the night. She had anticipated Sara's anger, she had every right to be upset, but Hailey hadn't expected the hostility that seemed to seep from her twin.

But today was a new day and Hailey decided she would clear her sister's name with or without her help. She owed it to Sara and their mother.

Hailey threw on jeans and a pink blouse and applied her makeup. Trying to find her hairbrush, she dug around in her suitcase until she clutched the bristles. She quickly ran it through her hair and assessed her reflection.

She planned to talk to Sara again, after they both had some time to calm down. It's what Hailey had always done while they were growing up, anyway. They would have a huge fight and the two would go their separate ways. And, like clockwork, Hailey would inevitably apologize to Sara and the two would go on with life like nothing happened.

Hailey hoped it still worked after all these years.

Until Sara agreed to help, Hailey would have her work cut out for her as she pieced together the facts of that night. Of course, she needed to figure out what to do with Trinity. She didn't need Trinity finding out about Hailey's past.

To make matters more complicated, she still had family dinner with her father and Lauren later, something she desperately needed to mentally prepare for.

Hailey sighed and made her way downstairs.

She was nowhere near ready to have a family get-together for the first time since she left. If Hailey had it her way, she wouldn't have to speak a word to the man who was neither kind nor loving to her growing up.

He claimed to always have his family's best interest at heart, but both Hailey and Sara saw right through his facade. David Gallagher was a selfish man who would do anything to stay ahead and look good in the public eye, even if it meant misery behind closed doors.

And misery it was.

She thought about inviting Sara just to stick it to her father. She'd pay good money to see the look on his face if Sara were to walk through the door. If they weren't fighting, Sara would do it just to piss off the old man.

Once downstairs, Hailey beelined for the back patio where Trinity was swimming. Lauren was sunbathing on the far side of the pool, her tan skin glistening in the sunlight. She smiled and waved, and Hailey returned the gesture. Trinity was swimming laps with another young girl in what looked like a race.

Coming up for air, Trinity spied Hailey. "Hey, Mom!"

"Morning. How'd you sleep?"

"Good!"

With that, she was back to racing her friend.

Genevieve came out of the door after Hailey, carrying a tray of orange juice and toast. "That's my granddaughter, Cecilia. I figured Trinity would like to have someone to hang out with."

Hailey was glad Trinity had made a friend, especially because it looked like they would be staying a little longer. "I was actually wondering if you'd be willing to watch her on and off over the next few days. I need to meet with some people, and I don't want Trinity to go with me and be bored."

Genevieve's face beamed. "Does that mean you're staying longer?"

Hailey smiled. "It does. So, I may need some help with Trinity if you're willing."

"You know she's always welcome to stay with me. I'll make sure I bring Cecilia along." Hailey gave the woman a hug. She had missed Genevieve when she moved away, but her stubbornness was stronger than the empty void she had felt. And she hadn't kept in touch, something she now regretted.

Hailey walked over to Lauren and sat in a chair next to her.

Lauren said, "Hey, Sugar. Did you sleep okay? I know it must be weird being back in your old room."

Hailey shrugged. "It wasn't too bad. I was pretty tired from the drive here and the wedding, so I slept like a rock."

That was a lie. Once she actually fell asleep, she had nightmare after nightmare. Triggered by her fight with Sara, no doubt. Some about her mother, others about Sara or Ryan or Trey. All of them had her waking up, heart racing and panicked. Lauren looked at Hailey, lifting her hand to her forehead to protect her eyes from the sun. "Well, I'm glad. Are y'all still joining us for dinner?"

Hailey wanted to decline but held her tongue. "We'll be here. Six-thirty, right?"

"Mhm. Your father is very excited to see you. He's happy you're home."

Hailey wanted to roll her eyes but didn't. Lauren meant well, but she also didn't understand what it was like living under the tyranny of David.

"Actually, I was wondering if Trinity and I could stay a few more days. There're some people I'd like to catch up with, but I don't want to outstay our welcome."

Lauren's face lit up. "Of course you can. Stay as long as you'd like."

"Thanks, Lauren. I really appreciate it."

"No problem, Sugar. We're family, remember?"

Again, Lauren was being kind, but Hailey still thought it was weird that David had married her, given the nearly thirty-year age gap.

Hailey went back inside to get a drink before leaving again. She wanted to talk to her Uncle Eli and get his thoughts on the video. Since he was the Chief at the time, and first on the scene, he would have a lot more insight into the situation than anyone else.

Genevieve walked into the kitchen and said, "I need to give you something." She motioned for Hailey to follow her. When they got to the mudroom in the back of the house, Genevieve retrieved her purse and pulled out two books.

"You're giving me books?" Hailey asked.

"Diaries. They were your mother's and it's the only ones I could sneak out of here before your father threw the rest away." She paused for a moment. "I think Sara would like them too, but I don't know where she is now or how to get them to her."

Hailey didn't know what to say. She hadn't even known her mother had kept diaries.

"Have you read them?" Hailey asked.

"I wanted to. I miss her so much, but it always felt wrong. So, I saved them, hoping you'd come back. It might be nice for Trinity to read too, to get to know her grandmother."

Hailey's eyes misted. It was odd to think that Morgan was a grandmother, just one who would never know her grandchild. Hailey spent a great deal of time being angry that Morgan would never meet Trinity, or that she missed out on her first steps and first words. Morgan wasn't able to come to any soccer games or dance recitals. And Hailey was still grieved she had to be in the delivery room alone when she should have had her mother there to hold her hand.

"You don't have to read them now, but Trinity is occupied if you want to." Genevieve kissed her forehead and left the room.

Hailey stood motionless, staring at the books. She wanted to read them. To see her mother's words, to feel close to her again, but she was afraid of the rush of emotions it would surely bring. Thirteen years later and she was still grieving.

Yet, she was drawn in.

So she went back to her room, opened the French doors to the balcony and sat in one of the rocking chairs that was still in the corner.

Before opening the first diary, she traced its cover with her finger, reminiscing about a time long before their world was turned upside down. Then she took a deep breath and flipped to the first entry dated *1977*.

The journal started with everyday routines and a few personal thoughts of Morgan's. Her handwriting was girly and bubbly, much like Morgan herself. Hailey smiled as she could recall many times when her father claimed that if Barbie could write, her handwriting would be that of Morgan Gallagher's.

As Hailey read, she could almost hear her mother speaking through the pages as she told the story of meeting David for the first time. Eventually, the story changed and the two were engaged and then getting married.

The entries got shorter toward the end of the diary and were few and far between. Hailey didn't read anything alarming until the third to last entry.

Morgan's tone changed from a woman who was madly in love to that of a suspicious wife:

> *David has been acting strange. He's staying late for meetings, isn't speaking much during family dinner, and seems distracted. I continually ask him if something is upsetting him only to be met with excuses of new laws and political problems. I'm not sure I believe him.*
>
> *What kind of a wife does that make me? A wife who doesn't trust her husband isn't a good wife at all. My heart is heavy with guilt for feeling this way, but my instincts tell me something is wrong.*
>
> *I can only hope that in time he will be honest with me. I can only hope that I am wrong and foolish for thinking the worst of the man whom I've vowed to spend my life with.*
>
> *I can only hope he is not having an affair.*

Hailey re-read the entry, making sure she wasn't misreading the words that had been written decades before, even before she and Sara had come into the world.

Morgan's words didn't change, and Hailey's heart broke for her mother.

Though she was shocked to see that Morgan suspected David of having an affair, Hailey somehow wasn't surprised by the accusation. He was, after all, the most selfish person she had ever met, and he cared very little about anyone but himself. Including his beloved wife, and especially his daughters.

David hated that he had daughters.

He had made that apparent since the twins were in diapers. It was no secret her father wanted sons to carry on the Gallagher name and family legacy. And much to his dismay, Morgan refused to have any more kids after almost dying while in childbirth with the twins.

Hailey checked her phone for the time and realized an hour had passed. She had been so immersed in her mother's thoughts and life that time seemed to stand still as she read the secrets that were being revealed in the pages.

Moving to the next diary, things appeared to have settled between Morgan and David. Morgan's entries had simply become that of daily updates along with any accolades David received as Mayor. The entries were still few and far between, but nothing was alarming.

Every so often, Morgan would make known her regret of dropping out of nursing school. She wholeheartedly wanted to be a nurse but was convinced David deserved a doting wife. So, she gave up her dreams for him. She wrote that she sometimes felt lost, as if she had given up a piece of herself and didn't know how to get it back.

As time went on, the once bubbly woman now seemed to be losing her love for life. Hailey hated that Morgan's light was being diminished by the man who was supposed to ignite it.

Wanting to confirm her suspicions, Hailey began skimming the entries for anything that may lend itself to the truth of an affair. Much to her dismay, she found what she was looking for.

Dated two years before Hailey and Sara made their appearance into the world, Morgan wrote:

The love of my life has betrayed me. I've known for some time, but he admitted his infidelity and I can no longer live in denial. I can no longer make excuses and now have to face the truth.

The affair started shortly after we were married.

Part of me doesn't want to live anymore.

And to make matters more humiliating, his mistress is pregnant. My heart has shattered into a million pieces. I have been trying to conceive for a year now and I still have yet to feel the kicks of a sweet babe. But how easy it was for this woman to conceive my husband's child. I feel awful for feeling such hatred toward the unborn child; they have done nothing wrong. But I can't help but feel that something special has been taken from me and my future children. My children will not be his first born.

I have promised not to divorce him under the condition that he remains faithful and leaves his mistress and his child. It is a selfish condition, but I feel no remorse in asking. David has agreed and we will move forward in our marriage.

Hailey's jaw dropped and her hand flew to her mouth. She found herself heartbroken for her mother.

Looking back, she had seen her mother be the doting wife who made sure the family was taken care of. She was always by her husband's side for all his events and campaigns and photo-ops; her arm linked in his, placing a sweet kiss on the cheek every so often.

That was who Hailey remembered Morgan to be. The loving and dedicated wife and mother.

However, the more she thought about it, the less she could recall any moments in which her parents kissed, or touched, or even laughed together. Sure, they were loving while in the public eye. But behind closed doors, the two were cold toward one another.

Now she understood why.

She then realized she had a half sibling. One she spent thirty-one years knowing nothing about.

Before she could read any further, she heard Trinity's footsteps. Trinity was about to greet Hailey when she saw the diary.

Trinity perked up, her curiosity getting the best of her. "What's that?" She quickly came and sat next to Hailey in the other rocking chair, eager to know more.

Hailey didn't know how much she wanted to share with her daughter. She didn't want Trinity to bear the weight of family secrets Hailey had desperately tried to shield her from. Nor did she want her finding out about new ones.

But she also knew Trinity would not stop pestering her if she didn't give her some sort of an answer.

"Not much. Just some of my mother's diaries."

"Read anything juicy?" Trinity lifted a brow and rocked back and forth, wanting to hear more.

If she only knew.

Hailey kept her response short, hoping to keep the questions at bay. "Nothing yet, but I don't think there will be anything interesting in there, anyway."

Trinity gave Hailey a sideways glance. "We tell each other everything, remember? So cut the crap, Mom. I know there's something going on that you're not telling me. When we left Alabama, you claimed to hate this place and now all of a sudden you need to go get coffee with people?" She rolled her eyes. "Give me a break. What are you *really* doing?"

Hailey squared her shoulders. "There's a lot of bad things that happened here and I don't want you knowing about certain people or situations. When you're old enough, I'll tell you about it, but now is not the time."

"When I'm old enough? When's that, when I'm eighteen?" Trinity crossed her arms. "Does it have to do with my father?" It didn't take much to get Trinity worked up and her attitude was a force to be reckoned with, compliments of Hailey.

Though Hailey was blindsided by the question, she shouldn't have been since Trinity knew her father lived in Auburndale. She definitely couldn't tell her about Trey until she at least told Trey...*if* she told Trey.

Hailey considered her daughter for a moment and sighed. "No, it doesn't have to do with your father."

Trinity threw up her arms. "Then why are you being so secretive? I'm not going to leave it alone. I swear I'll start climbing out windows and hiding in your car if I have to."

Hailey stared at Trinity. It both amazed and aggravated Hailey how much her daughter mirrored her...how much she mirrored Trey.

"Mom, please. You can trust me," Trinity pleaded. Hailey's heart softened to the hurt in her daughter's eyes. She was no longer simply curious but was now feeling like Hailey was lying and being secretive, something Hailey tried not to do since she had kept her paternity a secret.

Weighing her options, Hailey reluctantly said, "It has nothing to do with your father. I think your Aunt Sara was wrongly convicted." She paused and then said, "Listen, that's all I'm going to say until I get this mess sorted out so don't keep asking."

"Are you serious right now? My whole life you said she murdered my grand-mother and treated you like crap. Now all of a sudden you think she's innocent? What's with you? This place makes you freaking weird."

"Whoa, lose the attitude. Did it ever occur to you that maybe I was wrong?"

Trinity shook her head in disbelief. "Well, that sucks. If she didn't do it, she just spent thirteen years locked up for no reason." Trinity asked, "So what are you going to do, go to the police?"

Hailey hadn't even considered it. Was it possible Trey could help her? Did she even want his help? Her daughter had unknowingly given her an idea that may or may not have dire repercussions.

"I have an old...friend who is the Chief now. I'm going to see what he thinks. If he doesn't think it's a good idea, we're going home. There won't be much more we can do anyway."

"And what if he does?" Trinity raised a brow, eager to play detective.

Then Hailey would soon find herself in the exact situation she wanted to avoid. She didn't even want to see Trey, let alone talk to him. Funny how he may be the one person who can help her clear Sara's name. She just hoped he didn't hate her as much as she hated him. If he did, she'd be wasting her time trying to hunt down an elusive killer.

Hailey shook her head. "I'm going to take it one step at a time. But I do know you *won't* be helping."

Trinity crossed her arms and pouted. "That's not fair. What are you gonna do, ship me back home? I can help."

"If you don't reel in the sass, I might. Go hang out with Cecilia while I make some phone calls," Hailey said, signaling the conversation was over.

Trinity huffed back inside, and Hailey fetched her phone. She gripped it, steeling herself for the ripple effect this one call could have for her. If Trey didn't want to help, she wasn't sure she had the capability to prove Sara's innocence on her own. Her sister would be forever branded a murderer.

But if he agreed, she would have to put her own feelings aside and trust him. She would have to tuck the past away like he didn't single handedly rip her heart into a million pieces. If he agreed, she would have to prepare herself for the inevitable conversation they would have about Trinity.

But she would have a better chance at finding out who killed her mother. Sara would finally be free from the past Hailey knew haunted her. And that was enough to convince Hailey to punch in the number for the police station.

"Auburndale PD, this is Belinda. How can I direct your call?"

"Hi, Belinda," Hailey said. "I need to speak to Chief Harbor, please."

"I'm so sorry, but he's out of the office today for training. Can I leave a message?"

Hailey hesitated. "Yes, just tell him Hailey Gallagher called." She rattled off her cell phone number.

She hung up the phone and let out a deep breath then instinctively placed her hand over her chest to steady her heartbeat. She wasn't sure how she'd be able to get through a face-to-face conversation if she was this anxious about a phone call. *Grow up and stop being dramatic.*

Hailey hoped he'd call back before dinner so she could have an excuse to miss it.

When she left Auburndale, she was glad to never dine with her father again. The last time they had a family dinner was a few weeks before Morgan died, when Hailey had told her parents she loved Trey and wanted to marry him.

An argument had ensued as David told Hailey she couldn't see Trey anymore. And, for the first time, she had defied him outright, saying she didn't care what he said. It had escalated the more Hailey refused to back down and eventually her father had smacked her so hard she fell off her chair. David had then slammed Hailey into the wall, knocking family photos to the ground.

Hailey touched her palms, vividly recalling the sting as shards of glass penetrated her skin when he had thrown her to the floor.

David had loomed over her. *"Don't you ever defy me! I am God in this house, and you* will *do whatever I say."*

At that point, Sara had jumped up to defend Hailey, only to be shoved away. The drink glasses had crashed to the floor as she collided with the table. Though

Morgan rarely defended the twins from David's blows, she had that night and paid for it with a split lip and black eye.

Hailey had continued getting punished as he beat her with his belt. Through tears and screams, she had refused to stop seeing Trey. Eventually, David had grown tired and stopped tormenting his daughter and retreated to his study, leaving Hailey, Sara, and Morgan to clean up the aftermath of his violence.

Of course, he had always made it a point to hide his rage from the world, only hurting them where the bruises and caked blood could be hidden. But not that night. That night, he had lost control and all three of the Gallagher women conjured up stares from those who were nosey enough to gawk but not kind enough to intervene.

After that night, Hailey swore she'd never sit at a table with him again.

Yet here she was. Trying to give him the benefit of the doubt. Because, as much as she hated it, she still longed for her father's love and affection.

Hailey just hoped she wouldn't have to wash blood off her body like she did thirteen years ago.

Chapter 7

June 26, 2011
12:37 pm

The restaurant Nicole worked at is busy; it's lunch hour, after all. I wait for my order, the crowd roaring with conversation. No one even realizes I'm eavesdropping. You don't become sufficient at blackmail without an intricate understanding of how to gain information. It's amazing what people say when they think no one is listening.

Lana Hill accidentally backed into someone's vehicle in the grocery store parking lot. She simply left as she didn't think she should have to pay for the damages.

The man next to me is talking on the phone. From the sound of it, he and his wife are doing well. However, he failed to mention the pretty brunette that walked in with him and now kissed him deeply.

Finally, my order is up. A young girl waves from behind the counter. She's always excited to see me. She seems to be an odd girl, the other employees not paying her much attention. I assume her home life is similar and so she latches on to anyone who gives her even the slightest bit of attention.

That can be used to my advantage. So, I come into the pizzeria enough so that she's comfortable with me. The more comfortable someone is, the more open they'll be.

People share things in daily conversation without even realizing it. Over the last month, I've learned she has a dog named Toby. She doesn't know her father and she's never had a boyfriend. Her favorite color is pink and she's saving money for college.

Those things may not matter in the moment, but the more you know about someone, the more you can leverage.

I walk to the counter and pay. We have small talk as we usually do, but this time it's quick as the restaurant is filling up and she doesn't have time to talk today.

That's fine. I only came for one thing: to find out what people are saying about Nicole.

"I heard about that woman who went missing. Has she turned up yet?" I ask, concern in my voice.

Her eyes soften. She's touched that I would show such concern for a stranger. Then, her eyes fill with worry. "No, the police haven't found her yet. I just hope she's okay. She's such a sweet lady and a really great boss."

I push her a little. "Do you think someone might have hurt her? People are crazy now-a-days."

"I can't imagine anyone would want to. She's so genuine and nice."

I nod, acting as if I don't know the real Nicole.

A tramp. A loose end. The nail in my freaking coffin.

I hated her. But this girl doesn't even know it. She thinks I'm simply some heartfelt stranger.

"Well, I hope they find her soon."

She smiles and I take my order to my car and begin my ride home.

The grape vine had been hard at work over the last few days. The news about Nicole's disappearance has the whole town on edge. One of their own is missing and no one feels safe.

If only they knew her dirty little secrets. If only they knew who she really was as they all worried about her. She may have this town wrapped around her pretty little finger, but I know better. I know her secrets. And if anyone found out, they'd burn her at the stake. Normally I would have marveled at the thought of Nicole being publicly shamed, but then I would be too.

Her secrets intertwine with mine.

So, I'll keep my mouth shut while people mourn and worry over her, wondering if she's dead or alive.

Little do they know I'm the one to blame.

Fools.

Truthfully, I didn't want *to do it. I didn't want to draw attention to the secrets surrounding her, but she got in my way. And she needed to pay for her interference.*

So, I killed her.

And it had been everything I dreamed about.

I wanted to strangle her, but she put up too much of a fight; something I wasn't expecting. So, I grabbed a knife from the kitchen and stabbed her until my hand cramped.

I both enjoyed and detested the blood that oozed around my fingers. The feeling of life leaving the body was exhilarating, an emotional high that nothing else compares to. But it was messy. And I don't like messes; there's too many chances for something to go wrong, to get caught.

But no one suspects a thing. They have yet to find her body. Not that I'm surprised; I'm too clever for that.

I had to give her a little bit of credit, though. She tried her damnedest to fight back, but I was stronger. I was smarter. And I won.

I smile to myself. I always win.

Chapter 8

Like the rest of the house, not much had changed in the dining room except Lauren now sat in the seat that was once Morgan's. The paintings that decorated the navy blue walls were the same paintings Hailey adored as a child. Even the china and place settings were still a deep blue and gold print, compliments of the late Morgan Gallagher.

Hailey made a mental note to ask Lauren if she could have the set.

And, of course, her father's glare remained unchanged with his jaw clenched tight, always in control. His seat was at the head of the table, a reminder both literally and figuratively.

His face was now beginning to wrinkle and though his hair was still the dark brown shade it had always been, it was now dusted with gray specks and thinning.

He was of average height and build, but there was something slightly intimidating about him. Most people never saw the real David, yet they innately understood he wasn't to be trifled with.

It seemed, though, that the years hadn't been so kind to her father. He had clearly lost weight and Hailey couldn't help but compare him to a fragile old man, something she never thought she'd do as he had always been so agile.

Dinner was awkward with casual questions met with short answers. Lauren tried to befriend Trinity, but Trinity was reserved. Hailey couldn't blame her.

Lauren and David were strangers who claimed to be family but never once checked on her and Hailey. Though Lauren seemed sincere, Trinity probably didn't see it that way.

David sat silently through the meal as he read a newspaper, only chiming in when Lauren spoke to him, eager to engage with his wife while he all but ignored Hailey and Trinity.

Which was fine with Hailey. She tried not to make any conversation with him. And Trinity was clearly uncomfortable, shifting in her seat or playing with her food.

Hailey didn't have much of an appetite either.

The poor girl had no idea the fights that had happened at this very table. Many times, there would be complete silence as the Gallagher women hurried to eat so they wouldn't catch the wrath of the man who was supposed to love and protect them.

On one occasion, David grabbed Hailey's cheeks so aggressively that she bruised. She didn't know how many scars marked Sara's back because of David's lack of control or how he would get inches away from Morgan's face daring her to defy him as she cowered in her chair.

And those were the things Hailey would never tell Trinity.

She would take those secrets to the grave because her daughter deserved to remain unscathed by the Gallagher family's sins.

Hailey wondered if Lauren knew the real David. Was he the same violent man he once was, or had she been able to calm him? Did he ever lift a hand to her or belittle her? Did he uphold their marriage vows?

Hailey glanced at Lauren. She didn't seem scared or nervous, as if she was walking on eggshells. She didn't seem to be flashing a beautiful smile in hopes to mask the fear that was floating just below the surface. No, unlike Morgan, the new Mrs. Gallagher seemed content, even happy. She looked at Hailey's father with love in her eyes.

Hailey hoped that was true. Lauren had always been kind to her and Sara when they were teenagers. She may have been a bit dramatic and materialistic, but she was warm and inviting. Even now, as they all sat awkwardly, she still tried to get to know Trinity.

Hailey appreciated the sentiment.

But Hailey was glad this would be the only time Trinity would sit at this table. And she was glad her daughter wouldn't have to be in the presence of a man who didn't want her as a grandchild and who was nothing short of awful.

It had been a blessing when Hailey cut ties with her father.

Initially, she hadn't planned on entirely severing her relationship with David, despite how vicious he was. After all, he was still her father. There was a part of her that had hoped Morgan's death and Sara's arrest would bring them closer, that he would realize life was fleeting and his daughter still desperately needed her father.

But that realization never came, and he continued to be cold toward her. His suggestion of an abortion is what ultimately sealed his fate, though. So, a month after her mother died, Hailey left town to live with her great-aunt.

And as much as she hated herself for it, she still sometimes found herself yearning for his love. Which is why she was even sitting at this table with him.

"So, Hailey, what do you do for work?" Lauren asked.

"Oh, I'm an insurance agent. Nothing fancy."

"If it pays the bills then it's worth being proud of." She smiled and again, Hailey felt at ease.

Finally, her father broke his silence and proceeded to ask Hailey about Trinity as if he hadn't been listening to the exchange between Lauren and Trinity the entire dinner. "How is she in school? Does she play any sports? Is she getting good grades?"

You haven't called to ask about her in thirteen years, but now you want to know about her?

"She gets good grades but isn't into sports. She likes to read a lot."

Trinity looked at David and gave a soft smile, hoping to gain the man's approval. He simply stared at her and she quickly looked away. Hailey's maternal instincts heightened, wanting to protect her daughter from this man. She took Trinity's hand under the table to ease her growing angst.

"So, she's like her mother. You always had your nose stuck in a book, Hailey, even when it wasn't the time nor the place." He chuckled, attempting to soften his backhanded compliment.

She didn't take the bait. He wanted to appeal to her, to act as if he hadn't been a monster to their family for years. But Hailey simply wasn't buying it. She knew better than to think he had shed his snake skin and traded it in for something better.

He continued, "Is she anything like her father? Does she know who he is?"

Caught off guard by the question, Hailey felt her body temperature rise and her lungs constricted. She was nearly transported in time as she remembered the last time she talked about Trey in this very spot.

He smirked at Hailey, knowing his questions further upset her. She wanted to curse at him but didn't play into his emotional game. Instead, she looked directly at him and replied calmly, "We're not talking about this." Then, she looked at Trinity. "I need you to go with Gen."

To Hailey's relief, Trinity immediately left the table to join Genevieve in the kitchen. Though Hailey knew the teen's obedience had less to do with wanting to please Hailey and more to do with how uncomfortable she was.

When Trinity left the room, David raised a brow, amused by Hailey's boldness. He forgot she wasn't a little girl anymore. She was no longer his pawn, nor did she care about his outbursts of anger. She would no longer allow him to bully her.

He continued the conversation, goading her, "Well, isn't that curious since you two were so set on running away together. I'm surprised he didn't run after you when you decided to leave the only family you had left." He chuckled. "I mean, it's comical how infatuated you were with him, ready to throw away your entire life for someone who could hardly afford to take care of himself. You were quick to lay on your back like some two-dollar whore and what do you have to show for it? Nothing.

"You could have done something with your life if you would have let me help you. But no. You were too proud and now look at you: a single mother selling insurance over the phone. My, how the brightest of the Gallagher daughters has fallen."

"David," Lauren hissed.

Ignoring his wife, he sipped from the coffee cup Genevieve had brought minutes earlier. "Honestly, Hailey, you made such a fuss about your undying love for that boy, and you didn't even tell him you were leaving." He shook his head. "You know, it's probably best to keep her paternity a secret. We both know her father is a dead-beat and she's better off without him, just like you were." He scoffed. "I still can't believe he's the Chief of Police of my town."

Lauren looked at her plate, her cheeks red with embarrassment. It was clear she didn't know what to do.

Hailey didn't blame her for being quiet.

When she was younger, she would have done the same thing. She would have allowed fear to paralyze her. But now, it was rage that engulfed Hailey.

David had a knack for malice and manipulation and often used them simply because he could. He enjoyed getting a rise out of people, proving he was in control. Unfortunately for David, Hailey wouldn't be easily intimidated or manipulated.

"You can either stop talking about this or I will leave the table."

Her father laughed. "Please, Hailey. Stop being so dramatic." Then, his smile faded quickly. "You're a guest in this house. Act like it." He gave her a knowing glance. "You know I won't tolerate disrespect."

Hailey kept her face void of emotion as not to show that his previous comments had gotten under her skin. If she engaged in his conversation, he would only feed off her outbursts. Which is exactly what he wanted.

David was an expert at exploiting emotions. He studied people to find what would make them tick, and then would patiently wait for an opportunity to strike. All while never showing his own emotions, never giving the enemy a chance to strike first or strike back.

She decided to take a page right out of his playbook. She calmly took a sip of her coffee and said, "I know you cheated on Mom."

Lauren's eyes rounded. She quickly glanced at Hailey and then at David, anxious to see his reaction. Hailey couldn't tell if Lauren already knew about the affair or if Hailey had just broken the news to her as well.

A vein on David's temple pulsed. "Who told you that?"

"I'm surprised you're not denying it. Usually, you'd rather die than admit to doing something wrong."

"Who told you that, Hailey?" he said sharply. He stood up and placed his hands on the table as he leaned toward her. His breathing intensified as he worked to gather control.

She remained silent, grateful to finally feel in control.

This time, he slammed his fist on the table and Hailey and Lauren jumped. "Who told you that?! I want their name right now!"

So, her hunch was correct; the tyrant had a kryptonite.

Hailey smiled at Lauren and gently touched her hand from across the table, hoping she could read the apology in Hailey's eyes. Taking a deep breath to steady her heart rate, she tossed her napkin on the table and walked out of the room.

Hailey wouldn't give him the satisfaction of knowing how she found out about his skeleton in the closet. She'd keep her little secret just to spite him.

***

Hailey was irate. She couldn't fathom why her father felt the need to deliberately cause tension and angst. Would it kill him to have just *one* nice dinner?

She had been shocked when he didn't follow her to her room like he had many times when she was a teenager. Though, she might have Lauren to thank for that. The woman seemed to have some such sorcery that calmed her father in a way Hailey had never seen before.

From what Hailey could gather from the brief moments she'd spent around the two of them at dinner, Lauren was gentle with David, and he seemed to be enthralled with her. Though he all but ignored Hailey and Trinity, he happily engaged with Lauren, eager to ask her about her day or listen to one of her stories.

Hailey found their interactions completely bizarre in comparison to how David had communicated with her mother.

Still fuming over how the conversation ended, Hailey had left to tell Sara about the diaries. Hailey wasn't sure the affair had anything to do with Morgan's death, but it was intriguing none-the-less. And she hoped her sister had a change of heart about the videotape after having time to cool off.

Thankfully, Trinity was spending the night with Cecilia at Genevieve's house, so Hailey had no responsibilities for the evening. Hailey was slightly dumbfounded when Trinity requested a sleepover. The teen didn't always take kindly to people. To see her getting close to the girl, and to Gen, was a nice change of pace.

Walking up the porch steps, Hailey saw light filtering through the blinds. She knocked and soft footsteps creaked across the floor just before Sara slowly opened it.

Sara was clearly on edge, her eyes darting around as she took in her surroundings. Was Sara always on edge or had Hailey startled her by showing up unannounced?

Sara huffed and rolled her eyes as soon as she saw her sister. "Go away, Hailey," she said as she slammed the door closed.

How mature.

Well, Sara would be irritated to find that Hailey had no intentions of leaving until Sara at least listened to her. The problem with Hailey and Sara was they were both stubborn. And because Sara was trapped inside and Hailey wasn't, Hailey guessed she would be the clear winner of this battle of wills.

Hailey was on a roll pissing everyone off tonight, so why stop now? She pounded on the door loudly. "I'm not leaving until you talk to me."

"Or I can call the cops."

Hailey laughed. "We both know you're not going to call the cops. So, you can either open the door and hear what I have to say and then I'll leave, or I can stand here all night and annoy the hell out of you like the good 'ole days."

Hailey waited, eager to know if Sara would call her bluff.

Finally, Sara groaned. "It's too late to be dealing with your bullshit."

As if it was her very own victory song, the locks clicked, and the knob turned. Sara cracked the door and peered out. Not waiting for an invitation, Hailey shoved her way past Sara. "First of all, it's only nine-thirty. Second, I had 'family dinner' with Dad and Lauren, which was awful, and I needed to get out of the house."

Sara stood at the door, glaring at Hailey. Hailey was trying to keep the conversation light. She didn't want a repeat of their previous spat, but Sara was in no mood for it.

Hailey sighed. "Look, I know I really messed up over the years, but I want to make it right."

It was clear Sara wasn't convinced by Hailey's pleas of redemption, but Hailey was being honest. And maybe it wasn't fair to ask Sara to forgive her after all this time, but Hailey couldn't walk away until she at least tried. It was a measly olive branch, but Hailey hoped Sara would accept it.

Sara didn't respond, she simply stood near the door, far from Hailey. Not knowing what else to do, Hailey sat on the couch. The two became silent, retreating into their own memories as they avoided eye contact.

Finally, Sara said, "Why are you here, Hailey?"

"I want to talk to you about the video..."

Sara rolled her eyes so Hailey quickly continued, "You didn't kill Mom, and the world should know that. Everything you went through could have been avoided if I wasn't so focused on myself."

"See, there you go again!"

"There I go again with what?"

"Making everything about you! I'm not interested in your pity or becoming your project so you can feel better about yourself."

Hailey wanted to protest. She wanted to yell at her sister for not understanding. But it wouldn't help clear the tension they both felt; it would only keep them at odds and Sara would remain distant and cold.

Taking a breath to calm herself, Hailey gently said, "I love you. You were my other half and my best friend. There was a time when we were inseparable, and now it's like we're strangers."

Sara stayed silent, her face void of emotions, and Hailey couldn't gauge what her sister was thinking, something she hated. She used to know Sara better than Sara knew herself. Now, Hailey didn't know her at all, something she never imagined would happen.

"I want my sister back and Trinity needs her aunt. I'm not making amends and proving your innocence because I feel guilty. I want to do it for Trinity and Mom, and most importantly, for you. I may not deserve your forgiveness, but I still want you in my life. And Trinity deserves to make memories with you. Mom deserves justice. And *you* deserve a second chance." Hailey looked Sara in the eyes and Sara held her gaze. "Please, trust me," Hailey pleaded.

Sara chuckled cynically and shoved her finger at Hailey. "Why should I trust you? You haven't exactly given me a reason to."

Hailey quietly eyed the scar on Sara's neck she noticed the day before. Sara didn't have to confide in Hailey for her to know the scar was a daily reminder of what she'd been through. It was a symbol of her vulnerability. And Sara's vulnerability landed her in the middle of a nightmare, her entire life torn apart.

Hailey stood and began to pace slowly, Sara intensely observing her as she did.

Hailey said, "I almost died the night Mom was killed. I found out I was pregnant that morning." Hailey smiled. "I waited the whole day to tell Trey." Her smile fell. "But I never got the chance to tell him because he broke up with me."

Sara grunted, not understanding the vulnerability Hailey was about to share with her. "I ran off and my car broke down. Next thing I know, Ryan pulled over behind me. He was drunk, as always."

Sara stilled, understanding the magnitude that Ryan's name carried. She had seen first-hand how cruel Ryan had been to Hailey over the years. Though he had harassed Sara, he had tormented Hailey.

Hailey finally had Sara's undivided attention.

"He nearly beat me to death, and I was black and blue for months. Initially they thought I would have to get surgery, but thankfully I didn't have to. I was on bed rest for most of my pregnancy because the doctors weren't sure if Trinity would make it."

Hailey lifted her shirt and turned around to reveal a jagged scar that was on her back near her hip. "When he climbed on top of me and started punching me, a stick lodged in my back." Hailey became quiet and then said, "I didn't even feel it. I was fighting for my life so I couldn't focus on the pain. Not that he would have been sorry about it."

Sara's jaw was set as she fought against the rage Hailey could clearly see in her gaze.

Hailey sat back down on the couch. "No one came for me, no one helped me. I'm not even sure how I survived, let alone how Trinity survived." She paused and looked back at Sara. "Aside from Dad and my therapist, I've never told anyone about it. Of course, Dad did absolutely nothing when he heard what happened."

She shrugged. "I hated feeling like a victim. I was vulnerable and someone preyed on that, and I never want to feel that way again."

When Sara didn't say anything, Hailey stood and walked to the door. She didn't feel right pushing Sara to make amends if she wasn't ready.

Her hand was on the doorknob when Sara said, "I almost died twice. The first time," she pointed to the scar on her neck, "was two months in and some lady didn't like how pretty I was. She was aiming for my face, but I turned my head at the last second."

She continued, "The second time was years later and much worse. Someone tried to hurt my cellmate." She lifted her sweatshirt to reveal six scars that sat above her hip where her liver would be. "And that's not counting all of the fights I was in just trying to protect myself."

Hailey couldn't imagine the trauma her sister had been through. She wanted to cry for her but knew Sara wouldn't appreciate it. Crying wouldn't change what happened. So, she simply said, "I'm so sorry."

Sara nodded slowly and the room fell quiet again.

Sara walked to the couch and sat down as Hailey followed suit. Sara said, "Look, I don't know what I want right now. I'm just trying to survive and it's terrifying to think about opening up the case again. No one believed me the first time, so why would they believe me now?"

"Because we'll *make* them."

Sara shook her head. "I don't know. It seems pointless."

"Well, take some time to think about it. I know it's a hard decision." Hailey quickly added, "But you have until Trey calls me back to decide because I already asked for his help." Hailey closed her eyes, ready for Sara's harsh reaction.

Sara stood and threw up her arms. "You what?! Have you lost your mind?"

"I don't exactly want to talk to him either, but he kind of needs to be on our side to get the D.A. to even look at your case again."

"Well since he hates you, my chances are slim to none."

Hailey rolled her eyes. "Don't be dramatic. And besides, there's something else I came to tell you." Hailey blurted out, "Dad cheated on Mom and had a kid with his mistress."

Sara's mouth gaped open. "Who told you that?"

"Gen gave me Mom's diaries. Apparently, Mom suspected he'd been cheating but it didn't come out until the mistress got pregnant. I guess Mom said he had to cut ties from them if he wanted to stay married."

"When did this happen?" Sara asked, shaking her head in disbelief.

"A few years before we were born."

"Who was he cheating with? Did she say who the baby was?"

Hailey shook her head. "She never said, at least not what I've read so far. And since we've never been told about a half sibling, I'm assuming Dad won't give us any answers either."

Sara sunk into the couch and picked at a loose thread. "I'm not surprised. He wasn't exactly man of the year. At least not to us, anyway."

Hailey stared at a stain on the carpet as she thought about the months leading up to her mother's murder. Though there was always tension between her parents, it seemed to be more prominent about a month before Morgan died. They had both been acting strange. David had spent a lot of time at work and was more hostile than usual. Morgan had disappeared into herself and was distant from everyone.

Her once bubbly and confident mother seemed to have closed herself off from the world. Did David start another affair? Maybe he resumed the one that ended in a pregnancy.

"What if the affair has to do with her death?" Hailey asked

"I mean, it's pretty far-fetched. From what you said, Mom was clear that if he kept seeing the other woman or the baby, she would divorce him. They didn't get a divorce, so he clearly stopped."

"What if the baby sought him out and it caused a rift? I can't imagine the kid was happy to find out Mom made Dad abandon them. He or she would have been twenty at that point, it's not out of the ordinary for a kid to look for their biological parents once they reach adulthood."

"I guess...but why would that get her killed? It seems like a stretch." Sara ran her hand through her hair. "I think you're jumping at shadows."

Hailey said, "I think we need to look at all the angles. Even the affair. If we're wrong, we'll just rule it out and move on to the next thing."

"Who's "we"? I haven't agreed to anything."

"Can you seriously look me in the eye and say you don't want to know the truth? That you don't want justice for Mom or for people to know you're innocent?"

Sara's shoulders slumped slightly. "I don't know. I just don't want to make my life more miserable than it already is."

"You deserve better. And if you don't do it for yourself, do it for Mom."

Sara shot Hailey a look and then sighed. "Do you really think an affair could be the reason she was killed?"

"I could be completely wrong, but people have been killed for less. Besides," Hailey stared at Sara intently, "don't you want to know who our half sibling is?"

Hailey had always been too curious for her own good and it had gotten her into a lot of trouble as a kid: eavesdropping on conversations, inviting herself places she wasn't allowed to be, snooping around room's she had no business being in.

Sara rolled her eyes. "Who cares? We've gone thirty-one years without knowing we even had a sibling. How are we going to find out who it is if Dad won't admit to the affair?" Sara pulled her legs up onto the couch, trying to get comfortable. "It's not like he would have confided in someone about it."

Hailey thought for a moment and then perked up. "If anything was happening in that house, I bet Gen would know about it."

It wasn't a secret that David trusted Genevieve. The two had a long history and it was clear the woman was loyal to him, even if he was no longer the boy she had once played with all those years ago. And Hailey knew Genevieve must have heard something with as much time as she spent working at the Gallagher Estate. Genevieve likely knew more secrets than the walls of that house.

And if Genevieve didn't know who the other woman was, Uncle Eli would.

"I don't know," Sara said slowly. "Do you think she'd actually tell us anything?"

Hailey shrugged. "There's only one way to find out."

Sara didn't answer Hailey immediately. When Hailey had come blazing in on her white horse, Sara was furious. It was yet another reminder that Sara was the failure while Hailey was the savior. Sara always got herself into trouble and Hailey would bail her out.

At first, it had been comforting and had even brought them closer. Then, as time went on, Sara began to resent Hailey for it, even though Sara refused to stop asking for help. Hailey would get doted on by their parents for doing the right thing while Sara would get scolded.

As an adult, Sara knew it wasn't anyone's fault but her own, just like every other situation she found herself in. But that knowledge didn't make her hate her twin any less.

She probably shouldn't be so hard on Hailey. After all, she had always been there for Sara because she loved her, not because she wanted their parents' approval.

If anyone had ever been loyal to her, it was Hailey.

Until she wasn't. And that made Sara question everything.

Yet here her sister was: telling Sara what seemed to be her darkest secret.

It had taken Sara by surprise. And, if she was being honest with herself, it made Sara hate her sister a lot less. Hailey running away made sense now. Not that Sara was excusing it, but she understood it.

Though Sara didn't completely trust Hailey, Hailey's willingness to share that part of her meant more to Sara than Hailey would ever know. But Sara still wasn't sold on re-opening her case, though she was considering it. Albeit for her own selfish reasons.

If they could figure out who killed Morgan, she could finally get her revenge. Right now, David was at the very top of her list, but once she uncovered this faceless killer, he'd be next.

And if she cleared her name while doing it, well, that was just icing on the cake.

Besides, it's what she always wanted: for people to know the truth. She may be an addict, liar, and manipulator, but she wasn't a murderer. She had been framed, and no one cared enough to question it.

Innocence always felt like a far-off dream. One that tickled the edges of your mind, but you could never quite grasp once you woke from your slumber. After a while, she stopped dreaming altogether.

Sara hadn't even realized she zoned out. Hailey's quiet voice pulled her from her thoughts. "What happened that night?"

She had shut the door on that chapter of her life and had no intentions of reopening it. But if she wanted to clear her name, she needed to prove her innocence, yell it from the rooftops. She just wasn't sure she had the resilience to do it anymore. Now, it was Sara's turn to be vulnerable, despite her instincts screaming at her not to be.

Sara walked to the window and looked outside, studying the moon. She took in a deep breath as she said, "That week, Chase and I got into a huge fight, and we broke up. So, I had been out drinking almost every night.

"I was at a party earlier, I think. With Thomas, Donna, and Jake. By the time I got home, I was so drunk and high I couldn't even walk. Thomas had to drop me in the yard." She closed her eyes for a moment, trying to remember. When she couldn't, she shook her head. "It's all a blur but I remember waking up to see Mom next to me. I didn't even know she was dead. Then I woke up the next morning to cops pounding on our front door, dragging me out of bed, and arresting me." She put a hand up. "That's the short of it."

Sara didn't want to get into every single detail, didn't want to relive that trauma, but Hailey needed to know the basics. And she truthfully didn't remember most of it.

"So why did you plead guilty? You're the most stubborn person I know, you fought for anything you wanted. Why didn't you fight it?"

Sara shrugged. "I couldn't. If I did, Dad was going to seek a longer sentence. He had already helped the prosecutors paint an ugly picture of me by bringing up my minor arrests and my addiction. Not to mention he's pretty prestigious and a master manipulator. The jury was eating it up and I didn't want to risk it. There's no way they would have believed me over Dad."

Hailey nodded slowly. "Well, now's your chance to prove him wrong, to prove everyone wrong."

Sara nearly laughed. No one believed in her then and she doubted much would change. She came back to Auburndale wanting revenge, but could she also prove her innocence? Could God be so good as to give her both?

She turned around and looked at Hailey. Sara had become a good judge of character, something you learned quickly in prison, or you ended up dead. Trust no one and learn how to read people...and exploit them if the situation called for it.

Manipulation was a tool. And it was something she learned from her father. Funny how he was the one who put her behind bars and yet he would be what helped her survive. Likely to his dismay, if she had to guess.

She studied her twin and saw that Hailey was genuine. As much as Sara wanted to continue hating her, it was becoming difficult. Her sister truly wanted to make amends and wanted to help her. Sara supposed it was better late than never.

And Sara figured getting revenge was enough reason for her to find whoever was responsible for turning her life upside down, along with everyone who watched her slowly fade into the darkness. She sighed. "What's your plan anyway? You have the tape but that doesn't equal exoneration."

Hailey ran her hand through her hair. "I haven't gotten that far yet, honestly. I called Trey but he hasn't returned my call."

"Seriously?" Sara said dryly. "So, you want me to proclaim my innocence with a video tape from thirteen years ago with no plan of how to do it and hope everyone believes me? No thank you. That sounds like the worst idea ever. Plus, I don't know who to trust anyway. We both know Dad has blackmailed plenty of people."

"Not Trey," Hailey said. Sara saw the flash of fire in her sister's eyes. Sara was intrigued by her reaction. Was Hailey still in love with him?

Sara wasn't sold on the idea of Trey helping them. He may be the new Chief, but things hadn't exactly ended well between him and Hailey. She wasn't sure she wanted to involve a man who could very well use her as a weapon to hurt her sister, destroying Sara's reputation even more.

She had come to accept she would forever be the girl who killed her mother, despite the lack of evidence.

Now she had the chance to change that.

But at what cost? Trey might screw her over. The media would likely catch wind of it and all her past sins would be plastered for the world to see. That in-and-of-itself would cause a stir and her father would be out for blood.

Was it worth it?

Sara said, "I don't know, Hailey..."

"I don't exactly want to talk to him either, but I'm not a detective and I don't know anyone else we can trust without it backfiring on us. We both know Dad is going to start threatening us when he finds out, but if Trey is involved and it's on the books, there's nothing he can do about it."

Much to Sara's dismay, Hailey was right. They didn't have many options and they had even fewer leads. And it would be nice to watch her old man sweat a little while they dug into his past and put a spotlight on his secrets.

It was time for the truth to come out. Sara owed it to herself.

For most of her life, she didn't see herself as worthy of anything good. And maybe for a long time she wasn't. Even that little girl who had been so broken she turned to drugs and alcohol deserved justice.

And while Hailey searched for a killer, Sara would plot her revenge.

She had nothing left to lose, but the same couldn't be said for those who hurt her. And Sara would make it her life's mission to destroy them. There would be nothing left but a whispered ghost story about a woman named revenge, taking no prisoners as she destroyed those who had wronged her.

But her sister couldn't know the truth. Hailey would never let her do it. So, for now, she would play Hailey's little detective game until she was able to burn down the world, watching her father go right along with it.

Chapter 9

June 26, 2011
10:32 pm

The drive back to the estate had been filled with thoughts about the past and the many what-if's and could-have-beens. Hailey was only two miles from her father's house when blue and red lights blinded her, and a siren pierced her ears.

Wonderful.

She slowly pulled over and grabbed the vehicle registration and her driver's license. Pink flooded her cheeks as the officer tapped on her window. But irritation quickly replaced her embarrassment when she glanced at the man. She rolled down her window and crossed her arms, fuming, as Trey Harbor smiled down at her.

"Seriously, Trey? You pulled me over because I didn't talk to you at the wedding? Grow up."

Trey laughed at her accusation and she was appalled to find the sound sexy. "Really, Princess? You think I have nothing better to do than pull you over because I felt jilted?" He pointed to her dashboard. "You were speeding."

His pet-name of 'princess' grated her ears. She seethed, no longer happy to hear it roll off his tongue like she once had been.

"Don't call me that," she said.

She blushed at how childish she sounded. Part of it was shock since she hadn't expected to see him. Plus, she was still angry at him despite needing his help, something she really ought to get over.

However, the real cause for her outburst was the secret she was keeping from him.

"Why not? You're acting like an entitled princess. Always have."

"How dare you!" She cringed as soon as the words left her mouth.

She knew he was provoking her. The trouble was, she couldn't help but engage. It was something that had always marked their relationship. He would goad her, and she would let him. She would piss him off, and he would irritate her. A never-ending cycle of fights followed by laughs and kissing because they never could stay mad at each other for very long.

Funny how quickly that had changed.

Yet, here she was again, falling right into the games he enjoyed playing with her.

He lifted a brow as if to say 'I told you so.' "I'll give you a warning this time, but don't let me catch you speeding again."

Hailey rolled her eyes and waved him off.

"I thought you'd be gone by now, anyway," he said as he leaned closer to her window, invading her personal space.

"Not that it's any of your concern, but I ran into some family issues that I need to sort through." She desperately wanted to keep the conversation short so she wouldn't have to speak to him anymore, not when she was so unprepared. He didn't seem to catch the hint.

He put up his hands. "I was just making conversation." He paused for a moment and then said, "How's life been since you left?"

"It's...fine." She shifted slightly, finding it hard to breathe around him.

Trey said, "Are you still so upset that you can't even talk to me?"

Fire burned behind her eyes. "You never said a word to me after that night so why do you care now?"

Trey winced. "Okay, we're really doing this then?"

"You started it."

Trey chuckled cynically. "Wow, I see you haven't stopped being dramatic."

Hailey shot him a look. "And you're still an ass."

"Right," he said curtly. "And for the record, I've always cared about how you're doing. But since you've never been back, I haven't exactly been able to ask."

Hailey balked at him. "Oh, yeah, you really care, seeing as how you've never tried to contact me. It's been thirteen years, and the only time I hear from you is when you happen to pull me over? If I hadn't come back, would you have even tried to check on me?"

He didn't answer.

"I didn't think so."

He stared at her for a moment, and she felt as if he were peering into her soul. As much as she wanted to look away, she didn't.

He sighed and said, "Well I'm here if you need anything. See ya 'round, *Princess*."

She wanted to yell at him for being so irritating and charming at the same time. She was mad as hell at him but still found herself soothed by his calmness, even in the middle of an argument.

He started to walk away but she stopped him. "Trey, wait."

He paused and turned back to face her.

Despite not wanting to talk to him at the moment, Hailey knew she was only prolonging the inevitable. Swallowing her pride, she said, "I need your help."

A sly smile crept on his face. He knew first-hand she would rather eat dirt than ask for help.

"Does this have to do with why you haven't left yet? Because, from where I'm standing, you don't tell people goodbye before you leave."

Ouch.

As much as she wanted to get out of her car and berate him, she took a deep breath and ignored his slight. "Get in."

She regretted her request as soon as the words left her lips, but still motioned to her passenger side. He hesitated for a moment then climbed into her car, the smell of his cologne filling the small space.

He still smelled the same as he did thirteen years ago, a scent that conjured up both good and painful memories. She wanted to run away, but Hailey steadied her breathing and wondered if he could hear her heartbeat.

At the wedding, she had been too angry to pay much attention to him. Now, though, she studied every part of him. She was surprised by the beard that covered his jawline. She found it rather sexy, much like everything else about him.

She wanted to crawl in a hole at those thoughts.

Lines had begun to form at his eyes. His once boyish face was now replaced with that of a man. She also couldn't help but notice the contour of the fabric as his t-shirt pulled taut around his muscles.

A breath caught in her throat, and she chastised herself for even allowing her eyes to wander.

Focusing, Hailey swallowed and said, "This is going to sound crazy, but Sara didn't kill my mother."

Trey whipped his head toward her, brows raised.

She held up her hand. "Let me finish before you say anything."

Trey slowly nodded and she proceeded, "At the wedding, Angie mentioned leaving me a video that would give Sara an alibi. I watched it and it's time stamped. Sara says she was basically railroaded into a guilty plea because my father was going to get the judge to extend sentencing if she didn't."

Hailey shifted in her seat. The whole thing sounded asinine after saying it out loud.

Trey shook his head. "Stop. What is it you want me to do, exactly?"

"I want you to reopen my mother's case."

"Based on a video, Hailey?" Trey demanded. "You're telling me a convicted murderer claims she's innocent and you believe her because of some tape?"

Hailey glared at him. "Don't patronize me. I'm serious. I know it sounds like something out of a movie, but at least watch it. It even shows them parked at a gas station. You could interview people who worked there, maybe help strengthen her alibi?"

Trey shook his head. "This is crazy. I can't exactly open a closed case- where someone has already been convicted and served time, I might add- without some solid evidence to at least suggest otherwise. I need more than Sara's claims of innocence and a tape. And why is this coming up all of a sudden? Where has the tape been this whole time?"

A car drove by slowly, trying to see if anything exciting was happening. Once they were satisfied it was a regular traffic stop, they sped back up and their taillights disappeared into the darkness.

Hailey sighed. "After my mother died, I didn't want to see anyone, talk to anyone, accept any condolences...my whole world had been flipped upside down between her death, our breakup, and Sara being arrested. Angie gave me a package with the tape inside but because I was so upset, I never opened it. She mentioned it at the wedding and when I got home, it was still in the box, so I watched it. And it's pretty convincing, especially because of the time stamp."

"I just don't think a video is going to get the district attorney to reopen the case."

Hailey's heart sank but she pushed harder, "Gen gave me some of my mother's old diaries. Apparently, my father had an affair and has a kid with someone else. That's a possible motive, isn't it?" She quickly added, "And Sara said my father was manipulating the trial. We've all heard the rumors. We know what kind of a man he is; he's not exactly above blackmail and manipulation. "

Trey looked at her and she saw the pity in his eyes. She didn't want his pity; she wanted his help. Though, to be fair, she wouldn't blame him for refusing to help after the way they had left things.

"It could be a motive if someone else actually killed your mother. But at this point, everything is a theory. And closed investigations don't get reopened on theories."

"Please, Trey?" she said softly. "I know it's a stretch, but I need you to help me. I need to know the truth and both Sara and my mother deserve justice."

Trey rubbed his jaw, mulling over everything Hailey had said. She hated that she had to depend on him for this, that Sara's innocence was ultimately in his hands. It annoyed her to her core.

But even though Hailey would much rather ask someone else, she couldn't deny the fact that Trey could remain unbiased, already having stated he wouldn't believe Sara to be innocent until evidence proved otherwise.

Not only that, Trey wouldn't let David stonewall him, manipulate him, or threaten him. That would likely be one of the biggest challenges they'd face once her father inevitably found out what they were doing. If her father had manipulated the trial in order to put Sara behind bars, there was no doubt he would do the same to Trey if he reopened the case.

"I can admit I'm curious to see the tape, but what if you're wrong? Do you really want to bring all this up again? You left town when everything initially happened. Are you prepared to go down that road? Because if this gets reopened, that's it. You don't get to close it if you don't like the way the investigation is going."

Despite the obvious friction between the two of them, Hailey appreciated Trey's honesty. Even through all the heartache, he still had her best interest at heart, despite how cold she'd been toward him. She would have thanked him if she knew it wouldn't have inflated his ego.

"If there's even a slight chance Sara didn't kill my mother, she lost thirteen years of her life. I lost out on time I could have spent with her. Not to mention everything she missed with my daughter." Hailey sighed and looked at her hands that were placed in her lap. "And a killer has been free while my sister paid for his crime."

She could see Trey calculating everything, weighing the pros and cons and the likelihood and solidity of what she'd told him. There was a big possibility for this to blow up in his face. It would be easy for him to deny her request and Hailey couldn't blame him if he did.

She still hoped he'd say yes.

"I want to see the tape and talk to Sara tomorrow. Then I'll decide if this is worth pursuing. Bring the tape to my office and we'll go from there."

She smiled at him as a gust of wind from the open window blew her hair in her face. Without a thought, he brushed it away, his fingertips caressing her cheek. She sucked in a breath as she leaned into his touch instinctively.

It reminded her of a night they shared so long ago, the night she knew she loved him and wanted to spend the rest of her life with him. Hailey felt those same butterflies in her stomach she had years before.

Realizing what she was doing, she quickly pulled away and ran her fingers through her hair in an attempt to hide the shade of pink that colored her cheeks.

Before anything else occurred, Trey quickly opened the door and got out.

He bent over, his arms resting on top of the car door and the roof. Her eyes wandered to the skin that peeked out just above his jeans. Heat coursed through her body, and it took all of her willpower not to blast the air.

He said, "I'll see you tomorrow, Princess. In the meantime, stay safe. Because if you're right, there's a killer still out there and I'm not saving you again." He winked at her and they both knew he was lying. He may be giving her the benefit of the doubt about Sara's innocence, but he would save her. Even if she didn't want him to.

Just as he had done when they first met.

Him saving her life had been a running joke during their relationship, one that echoed through her mind the night she almost died, and Trey was nowhere to be found.

She shook the memories from her mind.

They were going to have to lay some ground rules if they were going to work together. He had to stop calling her 'princess,' and he had to stop flirting with her. Not that he would listen; he never had. She had been drawn to his defiance and bullheadedness, despite the trouble they had brought.

And as much as she had loved him, Trey Harbor had gotten under her skin like no one else in the world, even before they started their whirlwind romance. He had a knack for messing with her and Angie had always claimed it was his way of flirting. Hailey had just thought he was an ass.

But she had found him charming the more she got to know him. Then she fell in love with him and the rest is history.

Unfortunately for Hailey, they say history always repeats itself. But she would be damned before she let it happen again.

Chapter 10

Trey had led the twins to an interrogation room where a TV and VHS player were located so they could watch the tape together. Sara hated being in the lifeless concrete room. She rubbed her arms in an attempt to warm herself. She felt vulnerable and small, as if everyone was watching her every move, agreeing with the already guilty ruling. It's how she felt thirteen years ago when she was being questioned about her mother's murder.

After going through a biased interrogation without a lawyer present, a public trial that named her guilty without even hearing the evidence, and a prison sentence with some of the worst offenders, Sara had promised to never let herself feel vulnerable again.

For the first few years of her incarceration, she had been constantly bullied and pushed around. Other inmates would steal her blankets or food or even her menstrual items. It wasn't until an older inmate took pity on her and taught her prison politics that she had been able to fight off those who wanted to harass her.

The choice to stand up for herself had resulted in a few stints in solitary confinement and some scars to show she wasn't to be messed with, but it was worth it. It had taught her that no one could take advantage of her vulnerability as long as she never allowed herself to be vulnerable.

Sara began pacing as she waited for Trey to come back with Hailey's coffee. She didn't understand why her sister insisted on getting a drink; it wasn't the time or the place.

Sara cursed under her breath, desperate to get out of the tiny room.

She thought back to the night her mother died. It wasn't a secret she could only remember bits and pieces of that night. However, she *knew* there was no way she could have killed her mother, even with how much coke she'd done and how much alcohol she'd consumed.

She remembered being upset about her breakup with Chase. She had wanted to forget about her problems, so she had tracked down her drug dealer turned ex-boyfriend, Thomas Smith, and the rest was a blur.

She and Thomas had met when she was fifteen. He had been a senior in high school, and she had been a freshman, eager to try anything to impress the troubled bad-boy. He had been the one who introduced her to drugs and alcohol, the substances that had slowly taken over her life. The so-called "solution" to her family problems had slowly begun killing her and she hadn't even known it.

Eventually, they broke things off romantically, but she had never completely cut ties with him. Truthfully, she hadn't known what to do without him in her life. He had been her source to the drugs her body craved; especially the night her mother died.

She had flashes of memories, but they were fleeting. It was as if she was reaching for something only for it to disintegrate before her fingers even grasped it. Her memories were there, but she could never pull them forward.

The house party Donna had taken her to was wild, even for Sara. She had danced with some guy that may or may not have been Thomas. She had even slept with him…whoever *he* was. Possibly even a few times. Or had it been a few different people?

At some point she had done coke…maybe Xanax, too? No, maybe it had been Ecstasy?

She knew for certain she had been more than above the legal limit of alcohol consumption, not to mention the fact she had been underage and shouldn't have been drinking at all.

Honestly, she wasn't sure how she hadn't overdosed. That was a freaking miracle in-and-of-itself.

She didn't remember getting into Thomas' car, but vaguely remembered stopping at the corner store. Her anxiety skyrocketed as it always did when she tried to remember what happened next.

She had woken up at one point, staring at her mother's lifeless body. At the time, she had simply wondered why she was in her mother's bed. Warmth had flooded around her arm. She had touched her sleeve, red staining her fingertips. Sara had giggled, wondering why she was bleeding.

Except now she knew it wasn't her blood at all.

She took in a breath, forcing the nausea to leave her body.

She always wanted to vomit when she recalled touching the blood. It had drenched her sleeve, irritating her. And if she focused hard enough, she could still smell the copper scent. Even now, she hated the sight of blood.

The next morning, she had woken up to her father pounding on her bedroom door, having no memory of how she got there, the police ready to escort her to the station. A guilty verdict was tattooed on her forehead before ever being asked a single question.

Sighing, she caught her reflection in the two-way mirror and was repulsed by what she saw. At eighteen, she had been a beautiful girl, with platinum blonde hair, flawless makeup, and pristine clothes. A model in the making, a girl made for the runways of New York. Now, though, she was an ordinary woman with mousy brown hair that needed to be brushed, deep bags under her eyes, and a simple shirt and jeans.

The girl who was once convinced she could take on the world was now looking at a woman who was nearly defeated by it. She missed who she once was, but that girl no longer existed.

She sensed someone looking at her through the glass, though she knew it was all in her mind. She felt as if she was back in a jail cell, being watched like a caged animal. Instead of looking away or turning her back to the mirror, she thrusted her chin up and held her gaze, not wanting to appear weak and intimidated.

Lost in thought, Hailey startled Sara when she quietly said, "Can you sit down? You're making me nervous."

After having a staring contest with her own reflection, Sara took in a breath to calm herself and sat down next to Hailey.

For a moment, Sara considered fleeing. Maybe trying to reopen this case was a bad idea?

Before she could bolt, the door opened and Trey stepped in, handing Hailey her coffee. "Sorry, I got caught up in a conversation about a case. Let's see this video."

Trey then pressed play and the three of them watched the tape. Sara slinked down in her chair and squeezed her eyes closed, not wanting to watch her younger self.

She still couldn't believe how drunk and irresponsible she'd been as a teen. She had spent most of her high school days hanging with a bad crowd just to get back at her father. And her father was going to ship her off to New York that fall, ready to be rid of her.

Instead, she had found herself sporting a blue jumpsuit and shackles.

Once the video ended, Trey didn't say anything at first. He stared at the black screen for what felt like ages. Sara wanted to scream. She needed to leave this room, this building, this town.

He then turned to Sara. "Why wasn't this admitted into evidence, and why didn't your friends speak up when you were arrested? You didn't tell your lawyer about this? Seems a little suspicious, don't you think?"

Sara stood and placed her hands on the table as she leaned toward him. "Despite what you may think, I don't have an ulterior motive here. Like you told Hailey, I've already done my time so why the hell would I try to get this case reopened unless I was innocent? Stop pointing fingers without having all the facts. You're just like every other cop that's been involved in this case."

She crossed her arms. "I didn't know about the video until Hailey showed it to me. I was so wasted that I don't remember anything on that tape, and I don't know why my so-called friends didn't come forward." She threw her hands up. "It would have been nice if they had."

Gently touching Sara's arm, Hailey looked at Trey. "Angie told me that Thomas and Jake didn't think it was their problem. Donna wanted to help Sara but didn't want to be pulled into it either. She figured if she gave someone the video anonymously, it would get Sara off the hook. When it didn't, no one wanted to get into trouble, so they didn't come forward."

Trey looked from Hailey to Sara. He tapped his finger on the table, gathering his thoughts. "I think the tape is a start, but I need more evidence to convince the D.A. you're innocent." He looked at Sara. "I want to talk to your friends and see if I can find the guy who worked at the corner store that night, but I doubt he's still around." He sighed and rubbed the back of his neck. "I'm sorry you weren't given a fair trial. I promise I'll do what I can to fix it, but I'm not sure anything will come of it."

Shocker.

Sara didn't think she stood a chance. She should have left well enough alone. Then again, she'd never get revenge if she kept thinking like that.

Hailey opened her mouth but closed it quickly, narrowing her eyes at him as she studied his face.

As if sensing her reservation, Trey said, "Hailey, I'm not going to manipulate whatever *'this'* is. And I'm assuming that's why you came to me in the first place. You might not like me all that much anymore, but you do trust me. I'll look at the facts, not everyone's feelings; including yours."

Sara raised a brow, amused by his straightforwardness. There had been a time when the cowboy wouldn't dare piss off the princess intentionally. And he most certainly would have considered her feelings before anyone else's.

Hailey was quiet for a moment and then sighed. "I do trust you, that is why I came to you."

Trey nodded and then looked at Sara. "What do you want to do? Ultimately, it's your name on the line. Right now, you've paid your debt to society. Plus, whatever story that's been running in the press will be gone when the next one pops up. In a few weeks, you'll be invisible, and everyone will forget about your past."

He walked to the TV and pushed the eject button. The video popped out and he grabbed it, setting it on the table in between the three of them. "Or you can fight to clear your name with no promise that you will be successful in that fight."

Hailey seethed. "Why would you say that to her?"

Trey motioned to Sara. "*She* has to make this decision. It's her life, and she has the right to make that choice knowing the possible outcomes."

Sara nearly smiled at the irony. Funny, she always wanted to forget about what had happened to her and now she was nearly *choosing* to relive it.

Again, a battle inside her soul began to rage. She desperately wanted revenge, and she desperately wanted to prove she wasn't who everyone believed her to be. But she couldn't have both. She couldn't have her innocence *and* her revenge because once she got her revenge, that innocence would disintegrate. You don't get retribution without losing yourself, without giving up your morality.

So, it was simply a matter of which one she wanted more.

Innocence or vengeance.

"Sara?" Hailey said.

She turned to look at herself in the mirror once more, studying her hardened jaw and dark eyes. What she wouldn't give to do her life over again. To not have chosen Thomas or the drugs or the alcohol. To not have been so consumed by selfishness that it quite literally ravaged her life.

But she couldn't. This is who she was now, for better or for worse. Probably for worse.

She sighed. They wanted an answer, and she wasn't sure it would be the right one. "Do it. Find out who killed my mother."

As much as Sara wanted to forget about that night and everything that followed, she couldn't. She needed to free herself from her past and the only way to do that was by revisiting it.

Maybe it would make things worse. But, honestly, how much worse could it get?

Sara spent thirteen years being silent, allowing someone else's secrets to remain concealed.

Now the secrets that were buried along with Morgan Gallagher would soon surface.

And Sara would be the one holding the shovel.

The receptionist led her into David's office. He sat behind a large wooden box that was just as expensive as it looked. The man was anything but subtle.

"Sir, your daughter is here to see you."

The woman left as David glanced up from his paperwork. His eyes rounded and his smug grin fell from his face when he realized it wasn't Hailey standing in his doorway.

His perfectly crafted facade faltered, and for once in his life, David was speechless. Sara hadn't quite expected that, though she hadn't known what to expect.

"*Daddy*, I'm home," Sara sneered. "We haven't seen each other since you had me thrown in prison for a crime I didn't commit, so I thought I'd stop by and see how you were doing. You know, see if karma caught up with you yet."

After rewatching the video in the interrogation room, she knew she wanted answers. And if she burned down her father's legacy while she searched, well, that would be the pinnacle of her life's work.

"I'm calling the police," David said as he picked up the phone.

Sara laughed cynically. "I wouldn't do that. I'll tell them about how you manipulated the trial. Plus, we just found evidence that gives me an alibi. I'm sure the D.A. will be interested to learn why you lied all those years ago, telling them I was home when my mother was killed."

Sara slowly paced the room and began looking at the accolades that lined the walls, his eyes trailing her as she did. Unlike her, he couldn't contain his need for information so he wouldn't dare kick her out until he was satisfied.

It was laughable how predictable her father was. His attempt to stay in control would ultimately be his downfall.

He set the phone down. "What proof do you even have? If I had to guess, you're lying about that too."

Sara smirked. "Wouldn't you like to know?"

David leaned back in his chair, attempting to appear unbothered. "Enough with your games, Sara. What is it you want? Money? Drugs?"

"Oh, you can't get rid of me that easily. I'm here to burn your legacy to the ground."

Sara knew there was no use in hiding her motives. It wouldn't be long before he realized Sara was coming for him. She'd play David's game if she had to, but she'd rather play her own. And she was starting off by letting him squirm a little.

"Don't play with fire, Sara. You might get burned," he sneered.

"Nothing a little Aloe can't heal," she said with a wink as she turned back to face him.

Though she was inwardly shaking, she wouldn't give him the satisfaction of intimidating her. She was no longer the little girl he had spent years towering over as he beat her repeatedly while yelling obscenities.

Funny, she'd faced scarier monsters in prison and yet he somehow managed to unnerve her more than anyone else. And he would move heaven and hell to make sure he continued being her worst nightmare.

"I see you're still just as crazy as you were before prison. Maybe I should have pushed to have you committed instead of incarcerated. You killed your mother. I don't know if this is guilt talking or if you're just losing what little grip on reality you have left, but you did kill her."

"No. I didn't."

David raised a brow. "That's not what you said at your trial. Who's the liar now?"

Sara tilted her head. "It takes one to know one."

He smirked. And for a split second she wondered if she'd be able to prove her innocence. Like he said, she had lied: she pleaded guilty. Why would anyone believe her now?

Except now she had proof. And she had help. She wasn't fighting off monsters alone anymore. And David Gallagher would soon be enraged to find he couldn't stalk her nightmares anymore.

"You know, what's interesting about being a liar is that secrets come with a price." She shrugged. "The difference between me and you is that *I've* already paid mine. You on the other hand..." She clucked her tongue. "Well, you're going to pay a high price for what you've done."

"You're not getting a cent from me."

Sara scoffed. "You think this is about money? Figures. No, this is about retribution. You ruined my life and now I'm going to ruin yours."

David shifted slightly but didn't break eye contact with Sara. "No one will believe you. You killed your mother, and I'll make sure everyone remembers it. I'll dig up every transgression, every offense. Prison will look like child's play when I'm done with you."

Sara walked to the desk and glared down at him. For years, he had stood over her, threatening and hurting her. As a little girl, she was terrified of him. Even when she was a teenager, deliberately defying him, there was always a voice in the back of her head that warned she may not make it out of that house alive.

But in this moment, she wasn't scared anymore. She was no longer a little girl cowering away from her angry father. She had been to hell and back in spite of the man who put her there. If David wanted compliance, this time he'd have to kill her. Because she wouldn't stop until she made him pay.

Sara smiled. "Oh, David, you're forgetting that I've already lost everything. So unfortunately for you, I'll willingly go up in flames if it means I get to burn you to the ground."

He clenched his jaw. "I suggest you watch yourself, Sara. You might end up like your mother."

She'd rattled him a bit. *Good.*

She just couldn't let him know he'd rattled her too.

Sara sighed and rolled her eyes. "Promises, promises."

She turned to walk away when he said, "And I'll make sure your sister isn't exempt from my fury."

Sara stopped in her tracks for a brief moment. He always knew how to get under her skin, something she detested. But this time, she wasn't going to be intimidated. Hailey could take care of herself, and Sara wouldn't let her sister stand in her way. If Hailey had to burn alongside David, so be it.

Chapter 11

Much to Hailey's irritation, Sara refused to tell her where she'd disappeared to after they watched the video in the interrogation room, only to reappear nearly forty minutes later. Hailey was selfishly curious as to the whereabouts of her twin's mysterious disappearance, but Sara was a vault.

Figures.

Of course, lunch was awkward as Hailey, Trey, and Sara tried and failed at making conversation. Trinity would be annoyed to find out Hailey went to lunch without her, but maybe tonight's sleepover with Cecilia would make the sting of betrayal less painful.

Hailey was thankful Genevieve brought her granddaughter around. It kept Trinity occupied while Hailey did...whatever it was she was doing. Even though her daughter was busy spending time with her friend, Trinity was becoming suspicious of Hailey's whereabouts and had tried to convince Hailey to let her tag along.

No surprise there.

Trinity thought she was a private investigator and didn't know the meaning of 'mind your own business'...not that Hailey did either. The poor girl was just too curious for her own good. Hailey prayed it didn't get Trinity into too much trouble, much like it did Hailey and Trey.

Another knot found its way to the pit of her stomach.

She needed to tell Trey about their daughter. She was actually surprised he hadn't said anything at the wedding or in the car. It was obvious Trinity was his. Hailey wondered if he was too dense to put two and two together or if he just didn't want to overstep.

Hailey guessed he was too dense because Trey wouldn't know a boundary even if it hit him in the face.

They were waiting on their refills when Sara became rigid, and her eyes widened. From Sara's seat, she had a direct line of view of anyone who came into the restaurant, a fight Trey begrudgingly avoided despite wanting a seat facing the door. He noticed the change in her body movements and instinctively placed a hand on his holster as he turned to look at who walked through the door.

Alarmed, Hailey glanced, too.

She wasn't prepared to see the man who walked through the door and apparently neither was Sara.

Her sister sat motionless, making eye contact with the man who stood in the entrance of the restaurant, his body mirroring Sara's. But instead of shock, it was rage that burned in his eyes.

Before Sara could muster the courage to say something, she watched in silence as Chase Renner turned around and left.

"What was that about?" Trey demanded. No doubt he hadn't appreciated Sara's reaction to seeing Chase, as if he was somehow dangerous.

Sara didn't respond. She simply looked away, and picked at her food, content to keep her secrets.

Trey looked at Hailey for answers. She put her hands up in front of her. "She wouldn't tell me anything when they broke up and I don't think she's going to now."

Not knowing what else to do, he grumbled and went back to eating his tacos while Sara pushed her plate away. Hailey nibbled at hers, ready for lunch to be over.

The three continued to eat alone until a group of teenagers came in toward the end of their meal. The bunch stared briefly at Sara, probably wondering if they were seeing the woman who killed her mother. Sara stared back and they quickly turned their heads, whispering as they did.

Hailey's heart hurt for Sara. She was still a person. A person with trauma and demons and pain that went far deeper than the cuts she had received during her time in prison. She was a person who needed to be reminded of what it felt like to be loved and cared for.

Had she ever been truly loved or cared for? Hailey didn't think so. They lived in the same home where love was nearly nonexistent and the only care you got was materialistic. Even Hailey and Morgan were reluctant to love her unconditionally, both afraid of the havoc Sara always created.

As Trey was waiting for the check, Hailey reached for her wallet as well. She glanced down to see it wasn't with her. Sighing, she said, "I think I left my wallet in your truck. Can I have your keys?"

Trey shook his head. "I can get lunch."

"No, that's okay." She awkwardly added, "Thanks, though."

Hailey could see that he wanted to argue, but instead, pulled out his keys and handed them to her.

Once inside the truck, she quickly found her wallet between the seat and the middle console. She ran her hands through her hair and tossed her head back, annoyed with her absent mindedness. The fact that Trey still made her feel like she couldn't think straight really bugged her.

She turned around to walk back into the restaurant when she saw Ryan standing on the sidewalk near the door, arms crossed, staring at her. "Must be my lucky day, running into you here."

Hailey froze.

He sensed her fear and smiled. It was the same wicked grin plastered on his face when he taunted her, harassed her...hurt her.

She tried to command her body to walk to the safety in the restaurant, but he was in front of her before she could make it to the door. He invaded her personal space, his presence reminding her that he was much bigger and stronger than she was; that he was in control now.

Hailey took a step back and nearly tripped on a crack in the sidewalk. Every alarm in her body was going off, telling her to run. She looked around for Trey and Sara, neither having exited the restaurant yet, nor seeing her through the window.

Suddenly, adrenaline kicked in and she felt the urge to defend herself. She refused to give him what he wanted. She wouldn't cower away, and she damn sure wouldn't go down without a fight.

Hailey jutted her chin, looking him directly in the eye. She ignored the panic that was surging through her as her body recalled the day he tried to kill her. "Get away from me," she demanded.

"Awe, come on, Princess. Don't you want to have a little fun again? It was cut short at the wedding."

"Get away from me or else-"

"Or else what, Hailey? You're gonna tell Trey?" He laughed. "I don't recall him saving you thirteen years ago."

Fear gripped her. Every alarm in her body was screaming at her to get away from him. But as she moved past him, he grabbed her upper arm and slammed her into the brick wall of the restaurant. She let out a yelp as the wind was knocked from her lungs, her heart racing as her body responded to the impending danger. She tried to control the panic that was rising inside her, but she knew it would soon be a losing battle.

She heard a siren in the distance and hoped it was for her, but it quickly disappeared.

He smiled again as he got within inches of her face. Just like all those years ago, the sharp scents of liquor and nicotine were on his breath. She fought hard against the nausea that was now worsening as the smell nearly transported her back in time to her worst nightmare.

"Let go of me!" Instinctively, Hailey's hand connected with his cheek.

Rage flickered behind his dark eyes.

Before she could bolt, he let go of her arm and grabbed her by the hair. She screamed, as he yelled, "You stupid bitch!"

Then, he jerked back, his body hitting the ground with a loud thud as Trey tackled him.

Shaking off the impact, Ryan stood quickly and returned with a punch to Trey's jaw. Trey stumbled back but ducked as Ryan's fist barreled at him. Trey swung hard, aiming at Ryan's eye.

Ryan threw an uppercut, blood gushing from Trey's nose. He came back, his first landing a blow to Ryan's stomach. As Ryan crumpled to the ground, Trey climbed on top of him, blow after blow connecting with Ryan's face.

Restaurant staff and onlookers crowded around the scene as Hailey screamed, "Trey, stop! You're going to kill him!"

With a raised fist, he looked from Hailey to Ryan. Panting, Trey stood as blood dripped from his nose and above his left brow. He rolled Ryan to his stomach and quickly placed handcuffs around his wrists. Trey pulled Ryan to his feet. "I'm going to enjoy putting you behind bars."

"You know, the last time this happened you threatened to kill me." Ryan chuckled. "Look at that, Trey Harbor's gone soft."

Trey clenched his jaw and started dragging him toward the truck, but Ryan stopped and turned to Hailey. "This isn't the last time you'll see me, Hailey. I'm coming for you."

Trey opened his mouth to reply, but it was Sara who responded. "I just got out of prison for killing my own mother. If you so much as look at my sister the wrong way, I'll kill you."

With that, Trey shoved him into the truck and dispatched another patrol car to come take Ryan to the station.

After she had a chance to calm down, Hailey said to Sara, "You probably shouldn't have said that since you're trying to convince people you're *not* a murderer."

"He doesn't have to know that."

Hailey smiled and shook her head, thankful for Sara's protective instincts and dark humor.

A few moments later, another police cruiser pulled into the parking lot. The officer parked on the opposite side, hoping for some privacy from the crowd.

After assessing Trey's wounds, the officer retrieved an icepack and gauze from the trunk of his car and handed it to Trey. Though Trey didn't look nearly as hurt as Ryan, he still sported a gash on his left cheek and a bloody lip, nose, and brow. Trey winced at the cold that stung the lacerations now decorating his handsome face.

Hailey felt the need to run to him, to make sure he was okay. But instead, she held his gaze, stunned and scared.

Then the two men exchanged words as the officer took note of Trey's recollection of what happened. No doubt they'd have to give a statement later. Satisfied for the moment, the officer climbed in his car and drove off with Ryan.

Once they were out of sight, Trey quickly made his way to Hailey and wrapped his arms around her. Though she tried her hardest not to, tears streamed down her face.

"You're okay. I've got you," he said.

Sara ignored Hailey's tears, awkwardly looking at the sidewalk.

After a moment, she was able to compose herself and quickly pulled away from his embrace.

Trey said, "I meant what I said all those years ago about protecting you from him. If I ever see Ryan even look at you wrong, it will be the last thing he ever does."

Hailey wanted to cry again but held her breath.

"Why did he attack you?" Trey asked.

"I don't know," Hailey said. She looked at Sara, pleading with her to not tell Trey about Ryan.

Sara raised a brow, surprised by Hailey's secrecy. "Don't lie to him, Hailey." She said it as if to warn Hailey, as if to protect her. Hailey found that rather curious.

"What is she talking about?" Trey asked.

Hailey looked from Sara to Trey. Despite the kindness in her sister's eyes, Hailey felt betrayed. Out of everyone, Sara knew what it was like to have your vulnerability used against you and the fact that Sara would corner Hailey into telling Trey her secret had Hailey seeing red.

"Nothing. Sara thinks Ryan has to have a reason to attack me, but we all know he doesn't." She looked away. "He's been harassing me without a damn reason since I was a teenager."

She prayed Trey didn't ask any more questions. She didn't want to be humiliated all over again and relive that nightmare as she told her story.

Hailey just hoped Ryan didn't make good on his threat like he had last time.

Because if he did, Trey wouldn't be around to stop him.

And this time, they'd bury her next to her mother.

Chapter 12

Too uneasy to drive, Hailey asked Trey to take them to Genevieve's. Though Hailey was nervous to bring Trey around Trinity, she needed to see her daughter after what happened with Ryan, to be reminded of her own survival.

The ride was silent, shock still gripping all of them. Trey tried to clean up his face the best he could, but dried blood still caked his brow. Hailey hoped he wouldn't need stitches.

"You need to tell him about Ryan," Sara said to Hailey.

"Tell me what? What the hell is going on?"

Hailey said through gritted teeth, "Shut up, Sara."

Sara narrowed her eyes. "I don't get why you won't tell him after what just happened."

Hailey whipped around in her seat. "Because it's none of his business. That's why."

Hailey couldn't believe the audacity of her sister. Sara was the queen of keeping secrets, but Hailey was somehow the bad guy for not spilling her guts just because Sara thought she should? Screw that.

"Give me a break," Sara said. "It *is* his business now that he almost killed a guy to protect you."

Hailey's mouth fell open. "I didn't ask him to!"

Sara's words cut deep. She knew Hailey didn't want to be seen as the woman who needed a man to save her. The fact that her sister would throw it in her face proved to Hailey that Sara was still the manipulator she'd always been.

Sara rolled her eyes. "That's irrelevant, don't you think? You don't get to keep secrets when they put other people's lives in danger. It's the right thing to do and you know it."

Right. Like Hailey was about to take morality advice from the girl who had just been locked up for the last decade. Hailey snorted. "That's rich coming from you."

Sara quickly leaned forward. "What's that supposed to mean?"

"It means-"

"That's enough," Trey interjected. "I know you two have your own issues to work through, but I don't want it happening in my truck."

Hailey turned back around in her seat, crossing her arms as she scowled. Sara sat back and did the same.

Hailey hated that Sara wouldn't mind her own business. If she wanted Trey to know what happened, she would have told him. She felt like she'd just been tattled on to her parents.

She wanted the terror of that night erased from her memory. She hoped it would slowly fade into darkness if she pretended it never happened.

Sighing inwardly, she pushed those thoughts aside as they pulled into Genevieve's driveway. Both Sara and Hailey slammed the truck doors as they got out, Trey shaking his head at their childish behavior.

Hailey took in the white farm-house style home and its beautiful wrap-around porch. It had been one of Hailey's favorite places to go as a child; an escape from her own house of horrors. She noticed that Sara didn't move toward the house either, both reminiscing.

Finally, Hailey walked up the steps and Trey and Sara followed. She didn't bother knocking. "Gen? It's Hailey. I have visitors," she yelled.

The older woman appeared and when Genevieve saw Trey at the door, her face lit up and she smiled ear to ear. It was apparent they hadn't seen each other in a long time, which made Hailey a little sad.

"Trey, what a pleasant surprise!" Genevieve greeted him with a kiss on the cheek as if she was his own mother. She waved for him to come inside. "Sit at the table and I'll make coffee."

Genevieve then looked at Hailey and raised a brow, eager to hear the juicy story of the possible rekindling of their relationship.

When Trey moved out of the doorway, Genevieve saw Sara standing behind him. Genevieve stilled. Sara awkwardly played with her hair, unsure if she would be welcomed with open arms.

Genevieve slowly walked to Sara and cupped her face, studying every detail. And then Genevieve cried and embraced the woman she had once taken care of as a little girl.

Sara stiffened. At that moment, Hailey realized her sister hadn't been hugged in the last thirteen years. Not even Hailey had hugged her yet.

Genevieve then traced the scar on Sara's neck. "What happened?"

Sara shrugged. "It's a long story, but I'm okay."

She held Sara at arm's length. "I'm so sorry, Sara."

Sara tried to hide the tears, but when Genevieve pulled her close again, Sara let out a sob and cried into the woman's neck.

Hailey nearly cried herself. She glanced at Trey who nodded her toward the kitchen. She followed him, giving Sara and Genevieve some privacy.

Hailey went to find Trinity as Trey helped himself to the coffee and brewed a fresh pot. Though Trinity didn't need to know the details of what Hailey was doing, she needed to know her aunt was innocent; especially because she was about to meet Sara.

Hailey gently knocked on Cecilia's bedroom door. She heard giggles as the doorknob turned. Cecilia answered the door but Trinity, sitting on the bed, said, "Mom, what are you doing here?"

"I came to check on you, but I also need to talk to you." Hailey looked at Cecilia. "Can I have a minute with Trinity?"

The girl nodded, her dark curls bouncing, and left Hailey and Trinity alone.

Hailey sat on the bed with Trinity, facing her. The two teens must have been doing each other's makeup, Trinity sporting a red lip and blush much too bright. Hailey inwardly chuckled, remembering when she and Sara used to do the same.

"What's up?"

"I need to talk to you about my sister."

Trinity raised a brow. "Okay?"

"Since you were born, I've made her out to be this awful person. I was selfish to do that. And I was wrong about her guilt, too. She didn't kill my mother. And the friend I mentioned the other day said he would help us."

Trinity threw up her arms, her eyes wide, as she said, "Are you serious right now? You come back to this place and now all of a sudden you think she's innocent?" She rolled her eyes. "You were right, this town does make you crazy."

Hailey narrowed her eyes. "First of all: lose the attitude, Trinity Rae. Second of all: This has nothing to do with being back in town."

Trinity let out a huff, annoyed that her mother reprimanded her.

Hailey couldn't blame her daughter for feeling jaded about Sara. After all, Hailey hadn't painted her sister in the kindest light over the years.

Hailey sighed. "Look, I've always tried to do what I thought was best, but your Aunt Sara-"

"She's not my aunt," Trinity spat out and crossed her arms.

Hailey let out a deep breath, trying to gain patience with her teenager. She ignored the comment. "Your Aunt Sara and I have a really complicated relationship. We had our issues growing up and I let those things dictate the way I talked about her to you."

"But Mom, she *killed* your mother. *Her* mother. She doesn't exactly sound like a nice person."

"I *thought* she killed my mother. I was wrong, Trinity. And that breaks my heart."

"Well, you must have been pretty convinced since you let her rot for all those years." Trinity quipped.

Trinity was right, but she had said it to hurt Hailey.

Trinity wiggled a finger at Hailey. "You spent my whole life convincing me she was a bad person and now all of a sudden, I'm supposed to forget everything? I don't think so."

Trinity crossed her arms and turned around on the bed, no longer wanting to talk to Hailey.

A pang of guilt rippled through Hailey. Leave it to her thirteen-year-old to unknowingly put life into perspective. Her daughter was right. It wasn't fair for Hailey to expect Trinity to forget the last thirteen years of Hailey's claims that Sara was guilty.

Hailey said, "You're right, I'm sorry. This is a lot to take in and I shouldn't expect you to change your mind at the snap of a finger. Honestly, even I'm having a hard time making sense of everything. But she's my sister and I owe this to her."

"You told me she wasn't a good sister, so why do you even care?" Trinity snapped.

Hailey calmly got up and walked to the other side of the bed. She kneeled down on the floor, looking into her daughter's eyes. "Honey, there's a lot of stuff that happened between Sara and I that really strained our relationship. And maybe she wasn't always a good sister, but I wasn't either. There were plenty of times I was awful to her. But the fact of the matter is that I love her, and she needs me right now. She needs *us*."

Trinity looked away and scowled. "Yeah, well, I don't like her."

Hailey smiled at Trinity and cupped her face. "I don't expect you to understand everything that's going on, but I *do* expect you to be respectful. Sara is downstairs and I'd like for you to meet her."

Trinity pulled her face from Hailey's grasp. "No way! I don't want to meet her!"

Hailey tilted her head. "How about we talk about this again when you're ready and we'll see how you feel then." She added, "Just give her a chance, okay?"

"Yeah, whatever," Trinity said as she rolled her eyes.

Hailey simply nodded, not wanting to rush her daughter's decision. And really, at the end of the day, she couldn't make Trinity love Sara. To the naked eye, Trinity appeared to be a rebellious teenager who didn't want to listen to her mother, but Hailey knew better. She was being protective of Hailey. She appreciated the sentiment, but it was time for the two of them to move forward.

Hailey left the room and joined everyone in the kitchen.

Sara was telling Genevieve a story, making the woman and Trey laugh. Hailey smiled, happy to hear laughter. Never in her wildest dreams would she have thought she'd ever hear such a beautiful sound. Nor did she think she and Sara would make amends, or that she and Trey would be able to be in the same room together.

But as much as she wanted time to stand still and live in this moment for a little while longer, Hailey knew she needed to address her mother's diaries. She hadn't planned to ask Genevieve about her father's affair, but now that they were all together, the opportunity was right in front of her. They needed answers.

Once the laughter died down, Hailey said, "Gen, did you know about my father's affair?"

Everyone at the table stopped and looked at her, caught off guard. Genevieve almost spit out her coffee. "Excuse me?" She shifted nervously in her chair.

"In the diaries you gave me, my mother said he had an affair with someone, and they had a baby together. She never said who it was."

Genevieve stood up. "I don't know what you're talking about." She went back into the kitchen to get creamer.

When the woman sat back down, Hailey gently touched her hand. "Sara is innocent and that means we have to look at every angle to figure out who really killed my mother. I know you love my father like a brother, but if you want to help Sara, you'll be honest with us."

Genevieve looked at Trey for confirmation. He nodded, despite not fully believing Sara to be innocent.

Sara was holding her breath.

Hailey heard the soft beat of a song as Trinity and Cecilia listened to music, not realizing the depth of the conversation that was happening below them.

Genevieve glanced at Hailey, then at Sara, studying their faces for a few moments before saying, "Your mother was a week past her due date. We were out getting some last-minute outfits when her water broke."

Genevieve's smile slowly faded away. "No one could get a hold of your father, so I rushed over to his office and when I opened the door, I found him kissing another woman." She shook her head. "I've never been so angry in my life."

She paused and put more cream in her coffee. "While we were in the waiting room at the hospital, he begged me not to tell your mother about the affair. And he did it while we waited for the doctor to tell us if your mother was going to live or die. She was dying on the table, and he was more concerned with me keeping my mouth shut." She shrugged. "I half expected him to threaten me, but he didn't. He just...begged."

"Did you tell Morgan?" Trey asked.

A single tear escaped Genevieve's eye and fell to the table, the weight of a decades long secret finally lifting off her shoulders. Genevieve quickly wiped her eyes and took a deep breath. "I couldn't be the one to break up their marriage, I couldn't do that to you two girls. He told me Morgan already knew and had threatened to leave if he ever saw the woman again. He promised to end things, and we never spoke about it again."

Genevieve looked at Hailey and Sara and took each of their hands. "I have regretted that choice for the last thirty-one years. I should have told your mother." She looked away. "Maybe it would have changed what happened to you girls in that house."

Sara's eyes darted up to Genevieve as she pulled her hand away. "You knew?"

The woman began crying again. "Yes. I never saw it first-hand, but I had a feeling he might have been hurting you."

Hailey furrowed her brows. "Why didn't you say anything? Why didn't you help us?"

"Does it matter?" Sara snapped. She stood and began pacing the dining room. "The bottom line is she knew and didn't do anything about it."

Genevieve shrunk at Sara's words but then nodded. "She's right." She wiped her face. "There isn't an excuse in the world that will make it okay."

Hailey angrily pointed to herself. "*I* need to know. You at least owe me that truth."

Genevieve looked away and shrugged. "I didn't want it to be true. I saw a different side of David that no one else saw and I wanted to believe that's who he was. So, I pretended it was. And I didn't want to betray him. It's so stupid now, but we had been so close growing up and I couldn't betray that friendship. It was easier to stick my head in the sand, especially when it came to his affair."

The room fell silent as everyone retreated to their thoughts. Sara was seething and Hailey was trying to make sense of all that Genevieve had confessed to.

Then, Trey asked the question that was hanging over everyone. "Gen, who was he seeing?"

"It was that Nicole House woman. The waitress at the pizza place." Genevieve spoke her name as if it tasted like vinegar.

Hailey froze, her breath caught in her lungs. "What did you say?"

"Nicole House. The waitress."

That wasn't right. It couldn't be Nicole House.

That would mean Ryan was her half-brother.

She recalled the way Ryan's eyes had darkened that night and she was instantly transported in time. He hated her and now she understood why.

Ryan had made good on his threat, his fists pounding on her body. She had tried to fight back but it had only fueled his anger, giving him a sick satisfaction with every punch she landed. It was as if he welcomed her fear, fed off her terror.

She had somehow managed to guard her stomach, aware she would likely lose her baby. He had continued to rain down his fury as he kicked and punched her. And then he had wrapped his hands around her neck and squeezed, watching her life slowly dissipate.

Her own brother had tried to kill her, and their father swept it under the rug to keep his own secrets hidden. How could her father turn a blind eye to all of the torment she'd endured over the years? She found it hard to breathe.

"No. No, no, no." Hailey stood abruptly and began pacing. Heat rushed over her as darkness threatened to take her under. Her heart pounded and she wondered if everyone else could hear it. The room swayed as her body fought off panic and she tried and failed to fill her lungs.

Trey stood up, alarmed by her reaction. He called her name, but his voice was muffled. She tried reaching for him, her hands grasping at the air.

Why couldn't she get to him?

Before she could say anything more, she hit the floor.

"Hailey?"

Why was Sara so far away?

"Momma! Wake up!"

Trinity?

Hailey's head throbbed. As she came to, she slowly opened her eyes, squinting against the light. Trey was holding her and blotting her forehead with a wet towel as Trinity, Sara, Cecilia, and Genevieve gathered around her. She steadied herself against Trey, but a jolt of pain ricocheted through her skull, and she winced.

"You okay, Princess?" She looked up to see Trey, his brows furrowed in worry.

"Don't call me that," she muttered.

Trey chuckled. "Glad you're back in full force."

Hailey immediately sat up once she realized Trey was holding her in front of Trinity. Her body swayed and he gently placed his hand on the small of her back. "Whoa, slow down. You're gonna pass out again. Do you need to go to the hospital?"

"Seriously, Mom, what happened?" Trinity asked.

"Nothing, I think I just haven't eaten enough the last few days."

Trey eyed her and she looked away. Hailey was running out of excuses. "I think I was just in shock. I mean, we ate at that place all the time...it's just weird to think about."

Genevieve was the only one buying Hailey's story, but neither Trey nor Sara called her on it. Finally, the dizziness subsided, and Trey helped her off the floor.

Sara opened her mouth to say something, but Trinity looked directly at Trey and said, "You must be my father."

Genevieve's eyes widened. "Oh, my heavens."

Hailey's face paled as she watched Trey glance from her to Trinity. She wondered if she should feign passing out again.

"Well, this is awkward," Sara said.

"Hush, Sara," Genevieve chastised.

Hailey shot Sara a look. Normally, Hailey would have berated her, but she was too focused on holding her breath.

"What did you just say?" Trey asked Trinity.

"You must be my dad," she said slowly, mocking him. "You're my mom's old fling, right?"

Hailey cut in quickly, "That's enough, Trinity." She wanted to strangle her daughter for saying such a thing. How did she even know Trey was her father?

This time he was looking directly at Hailey, that old fire burning behind his eyes. "No, I think I want to hear more, Hailey," Trey said sternly. He was livid and wasn't trying to hide it, though Trinity didn't seem to notice. Or if she did, she didn't care.

Hailey hung her head and sighed. "Why don't we talk outside."

"Yes. Why don't we?" he said through gritted teeth.

Sara lifted a brow but thankfully held her tongue.

Genevieve intervened with Trinity and told her they would make some sandwiches. Trinity wanted to protest but then nodded in agreement.

Hailey and Trey walked out the front door together. Hailey sat on the porch swing, the one she had sat on many times as a child. Trey stood in front of her, legs spread, arms folded across his chest. His anger was almost tangible.

She thought she might feel the heat come off him if she got close enough. She couldn't blame him, though. He had every right to be infuriated.

"Is there something you need to tell me?" he demanded.

Hailey let out a breath. Not knowing how to tell him the truth, she simply blurted out, "Trinity is your daughter."

"When were you going to tell me?"

"I don't know-"

He threw his arms in the air. "You don't know?! What do you mean 'you don't know?'"

Hailey stood as her own anger began to rise. "I didn't know when I was going to tell you because I was protecting her. I didn't want her to get hurt."

"Protecting her from what? A father who would love her? A father who loved her mother so much it hurt? *You* left *me*, remember? And you have the audacity to say you didn't want *her* to get hurt?"

Hailey tried to calm down, but his last comment had her seeing red. How dare he act like he hadn't betrayed her and broken his vow to love her forever. How dare he act like a hero when he never rescued her, never came for her.

She now stood toe-to-toe with him. "I left *because* of you. You hurt me and I wasn't going to let you do that to *her*! You promised to love me, and you broke that promise."

Hailey paused, trying to compose herself but was instead met with a flow of tears. "You didn't come for me. You didn't come for *us*. You were supposed to be there, and you weren't. You let me leave without so much as a fight and I hated you for it."

"How was I supposed to know that? I had no idea what the right choice was. I thought giving you your space was the best thing for you." Trey sighed and ran his hand through his hair. "I figured you'd come back when you were ready. And when you didn't, I thought you moved on. All I ever wanted was the best for you, whether that was with or without me. So, when you didn't come back, I thought it was the universe telling me you found something better."

Hailey wiped at her tears and sat back down on the swing. She was outraged at how cruel the universe was. They had both loved each other so deeply and endlessly. Yet, here they were, trying to mend their shattered relationship and broken hearts.

She shook her head. "I'm sorry. I should have told you about Trinity. I mean, I was going to but then everything happened with my mother...I just couldn't bring myself to face you. We had just broken up and I didn't want you to feel trapped and resent me years later." She shrugged. "Honestly, I was angry at you. And when I finally wasn't, so much time had passed I didn't think I should bring it up."

A vein throbbed on Trey's temple. He sat next to her then took a breath as he gently said, "I only broke things off because your father convinced me you deserved better than I could give you and I knew he was right. It just wasn't in the cards for me. I loved you too much to hold you back, so I let you go. And you left without ever looking back."

"I couldn't be here anymore," she cried out. "I felt like every piece of me had been broken and I didn't think I would be able to make it out alive." She paused for a moment and then quietly said, "I just never thought you wouldn't come for me."

As an olive branch of sorts, Trey took her hand. Hailey laid her head on his shoulder as Trey began rocking the swing. The two sat silently, neither knowing what else to say.

As much as she felt like her whole life had gone up in flames since coming back to Auburndale, Hailey had to admit it seemed as if something good may come out of it. Not that it would be easy, but maybe it was time for her to deal with her many demons that haunted her from this place.

Soon after, Trinity came out of the house to join them. She stood tall with her arms crossed, pushing out her hip. "It's about time y'all worked it out. The neighbors could hear you screaming at each other."

"Hush, Trinity," Hailey said. Then she scooted over and patted the space in between her and Trey. "Sit."

Trinity hesitated, then complied.

"How did you know?" Hailey asked.

Trinity shrugged. "At first, I didn't. I noticed the way you two looked at each other at the wedding...or were trying to avoid looking at each other. I thought he looked like me but didn't read too much into it. It was also weird that some guy seemed extra protective over you when that jerk-off was threatening you. What a creep. Then Lauren mentioned it was someone you really loved. So when I saw the way he held you inside, I just knew."

"What else did Lauren say?" Hailey was irritated that the woman would overstep. She had no business telling Trinity anything.

Not noticing her mother's concern, Trinity said, "Nothing. I asked her if she knew who he was, and she said you loved him. She wouldn't tell me anything else."

Hailey nodded and the three of them let the silence fall between them as the sounds of summer echoed in the distance.

"So- uh- what now?" Trey finally asked.

"I don't know. We'll figure it out as we go, I guess," Hailey replied. She honestly hadn't thought much about what would happen if Trey found out about Trinity. She supposed that's because she never actually planned on telling him. Though she told herself she would, she never thought she'd have to.

"How about dinner or something?" Trinity suggested. "Mom made this super awkward by not telling us about each other, so we have a lot of catching up to do."

Trey chuckled. "I see she got your attitude."

Hailey made a face at him. "She got your bullheadedness."

Trey smiled. "Dinner sounds like a great idea. My place tonight?"

"Fine," Trinity said. She wanted everyone to think she didn't care about meeting her father, but Hailey knew she was trying to hide a smile and her excitement.

"Unfortunately, I have to go get an update on an investigation, but I will see you ladies later."

The three stood up, staring at each other, not knowing how to say goodbye.

Finally, Trinity wrapped her arms around Trey. But as quickly as she held on, she released her grip and then hurried inside.

Chapter 13

June 27, 2011
4:17 pm

Trey couldn't help but smile when Trinity hugged him. He held on tight, but not too tight; he didn't want to make her uncomfortable.

He also didn't want to let go.

This was his kid…who he knew nothing about.

The shock of that revelation was soon followed by worry as he realized he didn't know the first thing about teenagers or parenting. He had no idea how to talk to Trinity, how to discipline her, or even how to take care of her. About the only thing he knew how to do was love her. He just hoped that would be enough for now.

But somehow, none of that mattered. He had a daughter with the woman he loved. A daughter who was beautiful and sassy and full of life. A daughter he loved more than life itself despite having just met her.

He was still livid with Hailey for not telling him about Trinity. The fact that she had kept him from his daughter for thirteen years both pained and angered him. Though both emotions seemed to be fighting for center stage, it was pain that overtook him at the moment.

Even still, he wanted to understand where Hailey was coming from. If he didn't, he feared he'd grow to resent her.

He tried to put himself in her shoes as an eighteen-year-old who just found out she was pregnant only to have the father of her child break things off, followed by the loss of her mother and the arrest of her sister. He couldn't blame her for not initially telling him, but she should have told him after things calmed down. She owed it to him *and* Trinity.

And as much as he wanted to stew over past hurts and old scars, it wouldn't help them. It especially wouldn't help Trinity. There was a lot that he and Hailey needed to discuss, but becoming a family was all that mattered, whether as a couple or as co-parents.

But for the moment, he needed to bring his focus back to Morgan's case.

While at Genevieve's, one of his deputies texted to tell him they'd tracked down the clerk who was at the corner store the night Morgan was killed. Apparently, the guy still worked there so Trey was heading over to interview him.

Trey walked into the store, welcoming the cool air. The Florida heat was brutal despite the rain clouds that were rolling in. He could hardly walk from the car to a building without soaking his t-shirt in sweat.

A woman was checking out at the counter, so he browsed the aisles until she was finished. Trey snagged a pack of sunflower seeds, some boiled peanuts, and a sweet tea and brought them up to the clerk.

"Are you Arthur Reed?" Trey asked.

"That's me. You the police chief who's 'posed to talk to me?" He sounded as if he smoked ten packs of cigarettes a day. The man yanked a handkerchief from the pocket of his plaid button down and wiped his bald head, sunspots covering his wrinkled hands.

"Yes, sir. I need to ask you about something that occurred about thirteen years ago."

The man scanned the items for Trey and placed them in a bag. "That's a long time ago. I can't promise I'll be much help." He glanced at the cash register. "$5.50."

Trey pulled out his wallet and handed the man some cash. "Thirteen years ago, there was a group of teens who had been parked in your lot. There were four of them and they were pretty drunk."

"Oh yeah, I 'member them. I was getting ready to close and I didn't want to get into no trouble if somethin' happened, so I told 'em to leave. One of 'em girls, she was blonde, stuck her head out the window and threw up all over my parking lot." The man shook his head, still irritated.

Trey assumed he was talking about Sara as Donna had black hair. Trey nodded, confirming they were talking about the same group of kids. "Do you remember what time that was?"

"It would have been around ten-thirty or so because that's when I close."

"Did they leave right away?"

The man shook his head. "Naw, they stayed about thirty more minutes before I told 'em I'd call the cops. After that, they squealed outta here."

So, Sara was *innocent.*

What the hell happened with this case?

Trey asked the man a few more standard questions before leaving the store. Then he walked back to his truck where he quickly blasted the air. Trey drove back to the station to catch up on paperwork and touch base with the crime scene techs investigating Nicole's case.

The whole situation was curious now that there was a connection between Nicole House and Morgan Gallagher. It definitely could be a coincidence, but Trey wasn't so sure.

It also opened up the possibility of Ryan being a suspect in one or both murders. Ryan always had it out for the Gallagher twins when they were younger, and at the time, Trey never understood why. But after finding out Ryan's paternity, it made sense that Ryan would hate them if he knew David was his father. The twins were flaunted by the man while Ryan had been banished to the shadows.

The question was: had Ryan known David was his father and, if he did, how angry was he about it? Could it have caused him to lash out at Morgan? Or even Nicole?

At this point, Nicole could be a suspect. If she became tired of being the mistress, she could have killed Morgan in hopes that David would marry her, and her disappearance could have nothing to do with Morgan's murder.

Could the two crimes be connected by more than just a tangled web of lies, deceit, and lust? Could the same person have killed both women? The timing was especially odd, with Sara getting out of prison.

It was all theories, but it opened up a lot of doors for both cases and added new players that weren't even a thought before. He wasn't sure what to make of it all.

Trey shook his head as he turned into his parking spot at the station. A few days ago, he was giving long talks to teenagers about graffitiing old buildings. Now he had a thirteen-year-old closed case that needed to be reopened and a missing woman who was loosely connected to that case.

He parked his truck and strolled into the station. He eyed Deputy Rodriguez at his desk and beckoned the officer to his office.

"Do you have any updates on Nicole House's disappearance?"

"No sir," he said, shaking his head. Marcus Rodriguez had been in the police academy with Trey. He was a great cop and had a sense of humor that put everyone at ease. The man was a talker and a looker, and Trey valued his friendship as well as his dedication to the law and the people of Auburndale.

He continued, "We're still tracking down her son to see if he's heard from her. And the crime lab is backed up so it may be a while before we hear about DNA results from the crime scene."

"What do you mean you haven't tracked down Ryan? I just arrested him. He should still be in jail."

"They released him, sir."

Trey cursed. "How did that happen?"

The deputy shifted uncomfortably. "I don't have the details, but I can get them for you."

Trey nodded and said, "Do we currently have any reason to suspect him?"

"Not that we've found. I mean, he has a pretty thick record but surprisingly hasn't done much time. From the interviews we did with Nicole's co-workers, they all seemed to think the two were on good terms. Though the ladies said Ryan gave them the creeps."

Trey agreed with that assessment. But now he was curious as to how Ryan was released so quickly. Trey knew he hadn't bonded out as he likely hadn't even been fully processed yet. How the hell had Ryan managed to skirt the law?

Then it dawned on Trey. David Gallagher had the power and the connections to make sure Ryan didn't see the inside of a jail cell.

Would he manipulate his way into getting Ryan out of serving time? If he did, it would surely raise flags for Ryan if he didn't already know about his paternity.

It was peculiar that David Gallagher seemed to land in the middle of these two investigations. First, his wife is killed and now his ex-mistress goes missing thirteen years later.

That's a little too coincidental for Trey's taste.

He made a mental note to track down Ryan after he talked to David.

Maybe the Mayor of Auburndale knew more than he was saying.

***

Hailey wasn't sure how much Lauren knew about her father's affair. Lauren had been David's secretary when Morgan died so she would have been privy to his schedule and meetings. And Hailey wasn't naive enough to believe Lauren hadn't made it her business to know what went on with the influential people in town. She had often worked alongside Morgan to help David get ahead in his politics because she had always been well-informed on local policies and the politicians who wrote them.

Did Lauren and Morgan ever have whispered conversations about David? Did Morgan ask Lauren about his affair? Did Lauren even know about it?

Once back at her father's house, she found Lauren eating lunch on the back porch.

Since Genevieve had the day off and David was working, Lauren had the house to herself. Hailey wondered if the woman enjoyed the peace and quiet or if she was lonely. She felt bad about not spending time with her, but Hailey wasn't sure how to move past the awkwardness.

Lauren patted the table, encouraging Hailey to sit with her. "Hi, Sugar. I thought you'd be out most of the day."

Not to Hailey's surprise, Lauren was well-dressed, donning a name-brand red blouse paired with white shorts that showed off her tan legs. She wore a cute pair of heels to match.

Hailey fidgeted with her hair. "I was planning on it, but something came up."

Lauren eyed Hailey. "Are you okay? You seem a little distracted."

"I need to talk to you about Trinity. I didn't appreciate you telling her anything about Trey."

Red slowly colored Lauren's cheeks. "Oh, I'm so sorry. I didn't realize I did anything wrong. I really didn't mean any harm, she just seemed so sad."

"I know, but there was a reason I didn't tell her anything. She figured out Trey was her father and told him before I was ready to talk to him about it."

Lauren sat up. "Hailey, I had no idea she would even be able to figure it out. It's not like she would ever see him." After the words left her mouth, her eyes rounded. "You've been seeing him again, haven't you? Oh, gosh, if I'd known he was around I wouldn't have opened up my big mouth."

She was genuinely mortified, and Hailey felt guilty for coming on so strong.

"I hadn't planned on it," Hailey said. "But...well, that's actually the other reason I came to talk to you. I have some questions about my mother."

Lauen's brow lifted behind her sunglasses. "Is this the real reason you're staying in town? Not that I don't want you to, but..." Lauren paused for a moment and sighed. "I don't mean this offensively, but we both know you're not out getting coffee with people. Plus, I know Trinity has been staying with Genevieve while you do...whatever it is you're doing."

Hailey contemplated starting this conversation with her. Once she admitted to reopening her mother's case, Lauren would no doubt share that information with David. That is, if he didn't already know. The grapevine was both a blessing and a curse depending on which side you were on.

But, she supposed, the truth had stayed buried for far too long.

"Did you know my father had an affair before my mother died?"

Lauren blinked quickly, surprised by the question, but she didn't hesitate to answer. "Yes. I knew about it...after the fact, anyway." She paused and took a sip of her sweet tea then continued, "And I'd assume that if you know about the affair then you know about your half-brother."

"Yes, no thanks to my father. I found out about it in my mother's diaries," Hailey said.

Lauren nodded slowly. "He's not a very honest man, but you already know that. I found out about it a year after I started working for him. I overheard a conversation between David and Nicole mentioning a son, so it wasn't hard to put two and two together."

"So clearly he and Nicole were still talking, if not seeing each other." Hailey couldn't believe her father would do that to her mother, after all he had put her through. "Does Ryan know?"

"Ryan grew up knowing David was his father, so there was a lot of tension between the two families." Lauren shook her head. "I don't know why Nicole would do that to him. It probably wasn't healthy for a boy to know that his father deliberately abandoned him and then went on to have two more children he obviously loved more."

Lauren fidgeted with her fingers. "I love your father, even for his faults, but he put himself in an awful situation, something I think he secretly still feels guilty about."

Hailey held her breath to keep herself from laughing at Lauren's words. What love? David Gallagher hadn't loved them; he had hated them. He wasn't capable of love. Hailey had learned that the hard way.

"Why didn't he tell us? Ryan was awful to us, and my father did nothing about it."

Lauren smiled sadly. "You know exactly why, Hailey. I love that man more than he knows, but even I can see that his reputation is everything to him. Ryan would ruin what David had spent years building."

Hailey had always wondered why David hadn't pressed charges against Ryan after he attacked her that night. She thought he hadn't wanted to add to the trauma of Morgan's death, but that clearly wasn't his motive at all. The fact that he swept her attempted murder under the rug just to save his own reputation, to keep his secrets, infuriated her. It made her hate him even more.

Lauren gently touched Hailey's hand and tilted her head to the side. "What's really going on?"

"What do you mean?"

Lauren smiled. "I mean, why are you asking about your mother? And why are you asking *me* about her?"

Hailey debated on how much to tell Lauren. She didn't want her father finding out about the tape or that they were looking into her mother's death, but she knew the news would spread eventually.

"My mother's case may get re-investigated."

Short and sweet, not giving too many details.

"I don't understand why," Lauren said flatly. "Sara was already tried and convicted. I don't see a point in opening a case that's already been solved."

"We may have found some evidence that exonerates her, and Trey is looking into things."

"I guess I'm just confused." Lauren sat back in her chair. "For the last thirteen years you've not so much as stepped foot in this town. You haven't called to check on your heartbroken father and you've never said anything about Sara being innocent. Now all of a sudden you think the police got it wrong?"

Hailey knew it sounded crazy. And she couldn't blame Lauren for being hesitant. No doubt David only spewed *his* narrative to her. Plus, love could be blinding when something threatened it. It would only be natural for Lauren to feel the need to protect David from the pain of old wounds should the case be reopened.

"I know, and that was wrong of me. But I can't ignore what I've found out."

Lauren scrunched her brows together. "I don't understand how you think an entire investigative team could have gotten it wrong. They're not incompetent. Whatever information you were given is wrong."

Hailey gently said, "I don't expect you to be okay with this, but we're going to look into it. And I'd really appreciate anything you can tell us that might help us find who really killed my mother."

Lauren bit her bottom lip, contemplating what Hailey said. "You really believe Sara is innocent?"

"Yes, we have proof. She had an alibi."

Lauren nodded slowly. "I wasn't around your family much before your mother died, aside from work engagements, so I don't know how much help I can be." Lauren frowned. "I assume you've been in contact with your sister since all this has come about?"

"Yes, she's staying with an old friend."

Lauren searched Hailey's eyes. "I don't know you or your sister very well, but I can tell this is important to you."

Hailey nodded. "I need to make sure the real murderer is brought to justice. He ripped my family apart and he deserves to pay for that."

Lauren took Hailey's hand. "Then I'll help however I can, but your father isn't going to like this. He believes Sara is guilty and so did a judge and the D.A. Trying to prove her innocence may be next to impossible."

"I know, but it's the right thing to do."

"Well, I suppose that settles it then. And once your father gets home, I'll have him come find you. He owes you an apology for his outburst at dinner." Lauren rolled her eyes and shook her head.

Hailey wondered how an angel like Lauren could fall in love with a snake like David.

Love is blind, she supposed.

Hailey thought about what Lauren said as she drove back to Genevieve's house. Lauren was right, it would be nearly impossible to get the D.A. to reopen the case, let alone get a second conviction. Part of her wanted to let it go, to forget the past, but another part of her told her to fight.

So, fight she would.

———

Trey waited outside David Gallagher's office. Once the secretary was off the phone, she ushered him inside the room. David sat at his wooden desk; paperwork strewn in front of him. His suit jacket hung on the back of his chair and the sleeves of his button down were rolled.

Not surprisingly, his office had very little personal effects. There was a single picture of him and Lauren on the shelf behind him and a few other photos of David shaking hands with what Trey assumed were important politicians.

No photos of Hailey or Sara or his late wife.

Not even Trinity's beautiful face graced the room, something that irked Trey to his core.

Was it because David had no relationship with the teen or was it because she was Trey's daughter? Though Trinity likely didn't know she was like a ghost to this man, Trey's instinct to protect her nearly overtook him. He wanted to tell David how special his granddaughter was and how much he was missing out on because he was a narcissistic bastard.

He inwardly huffed. Trinity was better off without this monster in her life. Something he and Hailey would actually agree upon.

David eyed him suspiciously. He didn't bother hiding his hatred for Trey. "What do you want, Trey?"

Trey didn't bother with pleasantries either. "Do you know where Nicole House is?"

David furrowed his brow as he shook his head. "What?"

"Nicole House. Have you seen her?"

He shrugged and looked back down at the paperwork that lay on his desk. "I don't know who that is."

Trey was in no mood to be jerked around. A woman was missing, and David had a history with her. "Don't lie to me. You spent years sleeping with her until she got pregnant and then you had to cut ties to save your marriage." Trey smiled. "Well, let's be honest: you weren't saving your marriage as much as you were saving your own ass. Except, I don't think you actually stopped seeing her. If I had to guess, you're probably still seeing her. And now she's missing."

David clenched his jaw. "Who told you that? And what do you mean she's missing?"

"So, it's true?"

"I never said that."

"You didn't have to. I have proof of the affair and the baby who was a result of it."

David narrowed his eyes at Trey, but Trey wouldn't be intimidated. He stepped closer. "Ryan, right?"

David clenched his jaw. Then he opened up the bottom drawer and pulled out a single glass and a bottle of aged bourbon.

That was David's sophisticated way of telling Trey to screw off. Men like David displayed their allegiance by sharing a shot of expensive alcohol together. Except this wasn't a social call and he wasn't drinking to celebrate or seal a deal. He was drinking because he was nervous. And he was drinking *alone* because he hated Trey.

Trey didn't care. He hated David more.

David quickly downed the amber liquid and grimaced, coughing forcefully as he did. Trey studied the man who once stood over him, telling him he'd be nothing in life. Who convinced him he could never give Hailey the life she deserved.

Now he looked tired and frail, something Trey hadn't been expecting. He was shocked this was the same man who had intimidated him all those years ago.

It had been two weeks before all hell broke loose that summer. David had found Trey at work, loading horse feed onto a truck at the local feed store. Trey had been working overtime for months, finally earning enough to buy Hailey a ring. Trey had been nervous and wanted to impress the man who would be his future father-in-law.

Mustering up his courage, Trey had marched over to David and extended his hand. He had wanted David's respect. But David had simply stared at Trey's hand. Without missing a beat, David had said, *"Do you love my daughter?"*

"More than anything in the world, sir."

"Anything?"

"Sir, I would die for your daughter. I want to give her the world and more. She deserves nothing less."

David had laughed then, catching Trey off guard. *"You can't even afford to feed yourself, boy, let alone provide for her. You're right, she deserves nothing less than the world and you will never be able to give that to her."*

"Sir, I-"

David didn't let him speak. *"If you love my daughter as much as you say you do, then you won't stand in her way of finishing school and making a life for herself. You won't stand in the way of her living a happy life with a man who can provide for her and take care of her in a way she deserves. A man who truly loves a woman will do what's best for her, not what's convenient for himself."*

David had been right. Trey would never be the man who could give her the world. So, he had broken things off. And it had been the biggest mistake he'd ever made.

Trey found David's last words quite ironic now. The hypocrisy was laughable.

As David lifted the empty glass, Trey saw the worry etched on his aging face. Though, Trey wasn't sure if he was more worried about Nicole's safety or about his secrets coming to light.

Realizing his lies wouldn't help him, David sighed. "If you know Ryan is my son, then you're not bluffing about the affair. So, yes, it's true. Except I stopped seeing her after Morgan died. Now what do you mean she's missing?"

Trey wasn't sure he believed that last part, but he wouldn't call him on it. "We went by for a wellness check and found her door open. There appears to have been a struggle and we can't locate her. So, what do you know about it?"

David poured another glass and swirled the liquid. "I don't know anything about it. I haven't talked to her in years."

Trey was irritated. Nicole was missing and he was running out of time to find her alive, *if* she was alive. And since David wanted to waste time by lying, he was also risking Nicole's life.

"Cut the shit, David. First your wife is murdered and then your mistress ends up missing thirteen years later? That doesn't seem a little odd to you?" Trey tilted his head. "And let's not forget we both know you're capable of hurting the women you claim to love. I seem to recall quite a few bruises on Hailey and Sara back in the day. They say murder isn't a far jump from abuse."

David chuckled. "And what man sees bruises on his woman and does nothing about it? You couldn't even keep her safe from Ryan."

Trey's stomach knotted, knowing that something sinister had happened to Hailey. Rage erupted within Trey as David taunted him with his own daughter's pain. Trey clenched his jaw and glared at the old man.

David continued, "Morgan's killer was already convicted, so I don't know why you think it's odd. Unless you think Sara killed Nicole too."

Trey was done letting David jerk him around. Trey was determined to get to the truth.

"Well, new evidence shows she didn't. Now I'm going to revisit your deceased wife's case *and* investigate your missing mistress." Trey smiled, trying once again to get under the man's skin. "And all your dirty little secrets are about to come out for the world to see."

David stood and leaned over his desk, placing his hands on either side of the wooden box. "Don't threaten me, Harbor. I promise, you will regret it."

Trey stepped to the desk and mirrored David. "I'm not a scared little kid anymore. It looks like you're losing all the control you've spent years building, and I can't wait to watch you go up in flames."

Fear flashed behind his eyes, then fury. David smiled. "And it looks like you can speak to my lawyer."

"I look forward to it," Trey said as he walked out the door.

Trey wasn't sure if David was involved directly, but he was definitely hiding something.

Luckily for Trey, there was someone who hated David more than Trey did, and Trey guessed he would be more than happy to spill all he knew.

With that, Trey knew he needed to hunt down Ryan House.

Chapter 14

Hailey stood on the porch with Trinity, fidgeting with her hair as they waited for Trey to open the door.

"Mom, chill. Dinner is going to be fine," Trinity said. "I'm the one that should be nervous. You already know the guy."

Hailey gave a half smile. "You're right."

Trey opened the door, interrupting their conversation. He beamed at the sight of Trinity and stood to the side, motioning them into the house. "The pizza is almost here."

"Pizza? Here I thought we'd get a home cooked meal," Hailey quipped.

Trey smiled slyly. "I only cook for the girls I'm dating."

"Ew," the teen said. "Can you not flirt in front of me?"

Hailey slightly blushed and made her way to the couch as Trinity followed. Trey sat in his recliner, giving the two their space.

Hailey subtly eyed Trey. He still wore his t-shirt and jeans from earlier but had traded his boots for plain white socks. She felt like an idiot for wearing a dress. He clearly didn't see this dinner as a big deal like she did. He probably wasn't even thinking about his clothes, meanwhile Hailey's emotions got the better of her and she put on a stupid dress wanting to impress him.

She was annoyed with herself for even feeling the need to impress him. There were much bigger issues at hand than her love life.

She then studied the living room. His home was surprisingly cozy and well-kempt. Hailey expected it to be a disaster since he was a bachelor.

Hailey could make out the faint scent of Jasmine, which surprised her. She eyed the coffee table and found the source of the smell, smiling to herself. She didn't peg Trey as being a man who would have candles in his home.

Trinity started to wander around the room to look at photos that hung on the walls. Hailey continued to twirl her hair, not making eye contact with Trey.

Finally, he spoke up. "So uhm... I know this is kind of weird for all of us, but I'm really happy you're both here."

Trinity smiled. "Me, too. I've always wanted to know who my father is."

Hailey stiffened slightly as Trey locked eyes with her. But instead of hatred or anger, she saw sympathy. Thankfully, they were interrupted by a knock at the door.

"Ooh! Pizza!" Trinity ran to the door and swung it open as Trey followed her. The woman carrying the boxes handed them to Trinity and then accepted the cash Trey offered her. Trinity put them on the counter in the kitchen and immediately helped herself.

"Trinity," Hailey scolded.

Trinity looked at Hailey, wide eyed, a piece of pizza halfway in her mouth. Trey stood behind her doing the same and Hailey couldn't help but laugh.

"What?" Trinity said through a mouthful.

"Don't help yourself without asking; it's rude."

Trey finished his bite of pizza and said, "No, it's fine. This is her house now, too."

Hailey's stomach plummeted. Was that his way of telling her that he was going to ask for custody?

Hailey suddenly felt lightheaded. She quickly went back to the living room and sat on the couch.

"Where's the bathroom?" Trinity asked Trey.

"It's down the hall, first door on the left."

Hailey heard Trinity's footsteps pitter across the floor followed by the thump of a door closing.

Trey came into the living room carrying two plates of pizza. "Here, Princess."

She sat the plate down on the coffee table and eyed him, still annoyed by the pet name. "Don't-"

"Yeah, yeah. Don't call you that." He waved her off as he sat down next to her, placing his plate on the table. "I didn't mean to overstep."

"What do you mean?"

"I didn't mean to step on your toes. I just meant that since she's my daughter, this is her home too. Nothing more than that."

Hailey nodded silently and stared at her hands that she placed in her lap.

"Hailey, look at me."

She did and he took one of her hands. "I'm not going to take her from you. As angry as I am that you kept her from me, I wouldn't do that to you or her. She deserves to have two happy parents, however that looks. If it means I fly out to visit every weekend, then I'll do it. If it means I move there, I'll find a house close to you. Or," he shrugged, "if we can work things out, maybe..." He roughly ran his other hand through his hair. "I don't know, but I don't want you to be scared that I'm going to take her from you."

Hailey gently clutched his hand. "I don't know what this looks like either, but I don't want us to be bitter. You're right, Trinity deserves to have happy parents."

"Once things settle after your mother's case and this other case I'm working on, we can sit down and figure out what we think will be best. And if it doesn't work, we can always change it. I just don't want you to be worried. I know I just met her a few hours ago, but I love her more than anything in this world and she will always come first."

Hailey closed her eyes and let out a breath. "Good. No matter what, she needs to be our priority."

"Deal," Trey said.

There was an awkward pause before Hailey said, "So it seems like you've reinvented yourself. Do you like being Chief?"

"It has its ups and downs like any other job, but yeah, I like it for the most part. It's pretty quiet around here, so I usually go out and help the guys who are on call, or I make rounds to the schools and check on the kids."

"Trying to keep them from following in your footsteps?" she teased.

"Make jokes all you want, Princess, but if I remember correctly, you were quite fond of my bad-boy reputation. It wasn't too long ago that we found ourselves in some trouble and you were having the time of your life."

She looked down at her hands and smiled. "We did have fun, didn't we? My parents were furious the night we played Ding-Dong-Ditch around town."

He laughed. "I didn't mean to get you into trouble, but it's one of my favorite memories of you."

She playfully swiped at his arm. "I was grounded for a week after that. I wasn't even allowed to leave the house, no thanks to you."

Trey smiled and pointed at her. "You didn't exactly do as you were told, anyway. The next day we were in my bed making plans to elope after a steamy love making session."

Hailey giggled and looked away. God, they had been naive. They truly believed they would run away and get married and live happily ever after. A part of her wished she still held on to that innocence.

"Are y'all done talking?" Trinity asked, poking her head around the corner.

Hailey jumped a little. "Were you eavesdropping?"

She prayed Trinity hadn't heard Trey's comment about their sex life.

Trinity sat in Trey's recliner. "No, but I wanted to."

"I see you're nosey like your mother." Trey winked at Trinity.

"I'm better at it than she is."

Hailey chuckled and Trey eyed her, looking at her the way he used to. There was a part of Hailey that hoped they could fix their relationship after all these years, maybe have a second chance.

They spent the next three hours trying to condense the last thirteen years into a single dinner conversation. Trinity shared about her hobbies and the latest school drama, which Trey seemed to find quite juicy.

He shared stories of arrests and criminals, and Trinity was on the edge of her seat with each one. Hailey tried to keep quiet, not wanting to interrupt their bonding, something that should have happened long ago.

It was nearly nine-thirty and as much as Hailey didn't want to end the night, they all needed some sleep. "I hate to be the one to break this up, but we probably need to head back."

"Awe, but Mom!" Trinity threw her head back.

"Hey, Kid, listen to your momma," Trey said gently.

Trinity put her arm up. "Are you seriously going to take her side?"

"I might not know how to parent yet, but your mother and I are a team."

Trinity stuck her finger in her mouth and made a gagging noise. "Fine. But I'm not happy about it." She turned to Hailey. "Can I have the keys? I'll wait in the car."

Hailey started digging in her purse when Trey said, "Hold on, I have something for you as long as your mother is okay that you have it."

Both girls raised a brow at him. He went back into the kitchen and came out carrying his wallet and retrieved a necklace out of the fold. He held it up and let it dangle in front of Trinity and Hailey.

Hailey's eyes rounded.

He said to Trinity, "This used to be your mother's. I, uh, never really knew what to do with it. Maybe you should have it...as long as she doesn't want it back."

He glanced at Hailey, but she didn't move.

He kept it all these years?

She always wondered what he'd done with it.

Hailey looked at Trey and he sheepishly looked away as if he was caught doing something wrong. Then she slowly reached out to take it, studying it as she did. "You kept my locket?"

He shrugged. "Never felt right to throw it out or give it away."

She looked back at him again. "Why?"

"It was yours. I couldn't bring myself to get rid of it."

Trinity looked from Hailey to Trey, not knowing what to do. She clutched the car keys and said, "Listen, the locket is nice or whatever, but I don't want my mom's hand-me-downs." She eyed Trey. "Keep it until you can buy her a ring."

Hailey shot her daughter a look, but Trinity ignored her and let herself out the front door.

Hailey studied the necklace again. The night she'd given it to him, he had planned a picnic in a secluded spot by the lake and the sunset had been breathtaking. Trey had held her close as they spent hours talking, sharing things about themselves they hadn't shared with anyone else. They had planned and dreamed together, all while the stars gleamed above them.

He had brushed her hair back as he thumbed her lips. Then he had kissed her. It had started innocently enough, until they had found themselves intertwined on the blanket, the moon the only source of light.

She had known that night she wanted to spend the rest of her life with him. She couldn't imagine living in a world where he wasn't the one who loved her. So, she had given him the only thing she still had on: her locket.

It was her way of promising herself to him. That night they planned to run away together, but they never got the chance before chaos ensued.

He had ripped her heart out a few weeks later. Then her mother died, and her sister went to jail, and she was pregnant and alone. Her whole life had fallen apart and, stuck in her own pit of anger and bitterness, she never asked for the necklace back.

Trey drew her from her memories, though she knew he was remembering the night by the lake too. "I hated myself for letting you go. It was a piece of you I could keep since I couldn't have you. I kept telling myself that if I ever met the right woman, I'd toss the locket, but I never found anyone that came close to what you were to me."

Hailey hadn't realized how close she was standing to Trey. She inhaled, trying to slow her racing heart, but it only beat faster when his scent invaded her. She took a step back, wanting to distance herself. She clutched the locket and scowled. "You kept this stupid locket for thirteen years, but never came for me?

Trey furrowed his brows. "I didn't think-"

"Yeah, I know. You let my father get in your head and instead of talking to me about it, you ended our relationship. And then had the audacity to keep my locket instead of trying to work things out?"

"I tried." He put his hands in front of him. "I came to your house every day until you left, and you refused to see me."

Hailey threw her hands in the air. "I never once saw you!"

"Your father told me you didn't want to see anyone, and you were going off to college like you originally planned. I begged him to let me see you, Hailey. Begged. But he refused and told me you never wanted to see me again."

Hailey had all but fallen apart during the month following her mother's death. She could hardly eat or sleep. She refused to see anyone or take phone calls or condolences. She almost didn't go to the funeral but somehow managed to make herself go even though she felt like she'd throw up the entire time.

But her father never mentioned Trey coming to see her. If he had, she would have talked to him. She still would have agreed to run away with him. But he never came and so she moved on with her life.

Grief tore through her body at what she lost by her father's manipulation and lies. He destroyed so much of her life.

Irritated, she said, "I never knew you came to see me. And why did you all of a sudden start listening to my father, anyway? We spent so many nights sneaking out, never caring what he thought. But all of a sudden, you couldn't climb up my balcony like you'd done plenty of times before?"

Her voice wavered, "I *needed* you, but you were nowhere to be found. I had to learn to be a mother at eighteen all while grieving over everything I'd lost. And I had to do it alone because you left me."

Trey rubbed his hand over his face. "I was twenty, Hailey! I was a kid. I hardly knew what being in love meant. I was terrified of ruining you. And then when shit hit the fan, I didn't know how to be there for you through all of that. I thought I should give you your space, but you never came back."

"I never came back because I thought you didn't love me anymore!" Hailey wanted to pick a fight and make him angry, but she quickly clamped her mouth shut and, instead, inhaled deeply. "I lost everything that summer. I had nothing left for me here except you. And I thought I didn't even have that anymore."

He shook his head. "I loved you so much I let you go. Maybe it wasn't right, but it felt right at the time." He stepped closer to her. Heat crept through her body, and she wasn't sure if it was because she was angry or because she wanted to make love to him.

"I *still* love you, Hailey. I always have and I always will." He looked down at her and stared into the depths of her soul. He gently cradled her face as he thumbed her lips, much like he'd done all those years ago.

When she didn't pull away, he kissed her softly, his hands caressing her cheeks. She returned the kiss, wanting more. She wrapped her arms around his neck, and he traced her spine. She let herself get lost in his kiss, in his touch. It was as if they were young again, loving each other for the first time.

He broke their kiss but kept his lips on hers as he whispered, "I want nothing more than to take you to bed right now, but Trinity is waiting for you."

Hailey smiled as her fingertips traced his jaw and then his lips. He kissed her fingers.

She wanted Trey in her life. She wanted them to be the family they never got the chance to be. After all these years, he still held her heart and she didn't want it back.

She kissed him again. "I want to see where this goes. I want us to try to make things work. I don't know what that looks like, but I want to at least try."

Trey put his forehead on hers and took her hands. "So, are you taking the locket back?"

She pulled away and placed it back in his hand. Then, Hailey smiled as she winked at him and walked out the door.

Chapter 15

June 28, 2011
11:05 am

Trey hated when he had to wear a button down and tie. But despite his hatred of the politics of his job, he was good at it. He knew how to make others feel at ease, how to get them to open up to him, how to make them feel seen and heard. Part of that was dressing the part. And today he was dressed as a distinguished Police Chief instead of a rugged cowboy who couldn't submit to authority and refused to wear anything but jeans and a t-shirt to work even though he should be wearing his uniform.

He still donned his jeans, but they were his good jeans...or so he told himself.

Not that Daniel Whitaker would care. He had seen Trey in tattered, oil-stained t-shirts and didn't think much of it. But, since he was visiting D.A. Whitaker at the office, today's attire called for a nice shirt and tie.

Though Daniel was an older man, he and Trey had a respectable friendship. Daniel hadn't liked Trey all that much when Trey became Chief. But when Daniel's wife, Lyn, found out Trey didn't have family around, she cooed over him as if he was one of their own children. It drove Daniel crazy, and Trey initially obliged just to irritate the man. But, over time, the two found they quite enjoyed each other's company.

Trey walked into the office as Daniel was finishing a phone call with someone Trey couldn't name. While he waited for the conversation to end, Trey walked across the room to the window that overlooked the city. He watched as people hustled the streets trying to get to where they needed to go on their lunch hour. A couple stopped to kiss and then walk their separate ways. A car honked at the man as he didn't pay attention to oncoming traffic, still euphoric from the woman's touch.

It reminded him of the day he met Hailey.

He smiled to himself. She had been in a hurry as she walked downtown, accidently dropping her keys. He happened to be exiting a store when he had first noticed her; her beauty breathtaking, even at sixteen. He had smiled at her and she ignored him, which intrigued him even more.

Hailey had been so focused on looking at her watch, that she hadn't noticed the car that sped around the corner. She had taken a step into the road and, without thinking, he had grabbed her arm and pulled her to safety. She had spun around, her face in a scowl.

She had ripped her arm from his grip. *"Let go of me. I saw the car."*

He had smirked. *"Clearly you didn't. I just saved your life, Princess. You should be thanking me."*

Hailey had rolled her eyes but couldn't quite hide the smile that had tugged at her lips. *"Don't call me that."*

"Okay, then what's your name?"

"Hailey."

"I'm Trey." He had stuck out his hand and she had stared at it.

She had lifted a brow. *"I didn't ask for your name."*

He couldn't help but notice the playful twinkle in her eye.

"Hailey!" Someone had yelled from across the street. Trey had turned and saw a boy waving at her. Later he would learn that the boy was Gavin O'Dell and the two of them would grow to nearly hate each other as they pined for Hailey.

She had smiled and waved back at Gavin, then had turned to Trey. *"That's my boyfriend and I'm late for our date."*

Trey had a hard time containing his disappointment, but he couldn't deny the fire he felt after first meeting her. And even though he knew she'd never admit it, she had felt the same surge.

Trey had nodded. *"I'll see you around, Princess."*

Again, she had rolled her eyes and started to walk away before turning back around. *"Maybe, maybe not."*

She had smiled at him, and he had known right then he needed to make her his. Over the following weeks, he had flirted some more and had gotten her number. Eventually, her fling with Gavin had ended and then the two of them had fallen in love.

And apparently had a daughter together.

Life was full of surprises.

Now he was in the middle of two murder investigations while trying to juggle being a father and fanning an old flame that had come barreling in, taking his breath away like she had the first time he saw her.

He wished life were as simple as it was back then.

Daniel finally hung up the phone and smiled at Trey. "What's going on today, Cowboy? I heard about the missing woman. Did you find something?"

Trey sat down across from the man's desk. "Unfortunately, no. I'm actually here about an old case."

Daniel lifted a brow. "Do tell..."

"Do you remember the case involving Mayor Gallagher's wife and daughter?"

He rubbed his clean-shaven face as he leaned back in his chair. "The daughter killed the mother, right? That was a tough case, to say the least. The girl ended up getting thirteen years. I believe she got out recently."

Trey nodded. "Yeah, she was released two weeks ago."

"What about it?" Daniel's eyes widened. "Did she kill someone else?"

"No, nothing like that." Trey took a moment to gather his thoughts. This case needed to be reopened but in doing so, a lot of people would have to admit they botched the investigation either accidentally or purposefully, including Daniel's office. "Listen, Daniel, I'm not trying to step on toes, but we have evidence suggesting the daughter is innocent."

"What evidence? And why am I just now hearing about it?"

"It's a video tape plus an eyewitness. The tape was in storage until a few days ago."

Daniel nodded. "Do you have it?"

"I left it with your secretary."

"I'll look at it, but I make no promises, Trey. This case is already closed, and there's been a conviction. I don't foresee that changing without compelling evidence. And aside from that, you'll basically be claiming the investigating officers got it wrong. Do you really want to start a war within your police force? Not to mention how it might affect me and my office."

Trey rubbed his face and shook his head. He didn't know what to do about the Morgan Gallagher case. He knew the right thing to do was to reopen the investigation, but was it still the right thing when so many people would be affected?

If he reopened this case, Washington, Whitaker, and potentially a few police officers would be investigated. Not to mention how it would affect the Gallagher family as a whole. Then, of course, the entire town would be up in arms as news outlets ran with asinine theories and half-truths.

It would be a shit-show, no doubt.

He could potentially lose his job if anything went sideways.

Right now, Sara was the only one who was significantly affected by the outcome of the case. But sometimes life just isn't fair and you get the short end of the shit stick. That's life.

Right?

Trey wasn't so sure.

Because at the end of the day, someone got away with murder and Sara had paid the price for it. And no matter how you spun that, it wasn't right.

Sighing, Trey said, "Daniel, I know reopening this case will make waves, but it's the right thing to do. You and I both know that. An innocent woman spent thirteen years in prison for a crime she didn't commit, and a killer has been walking free. Sara Gallagher deserves for her conviction to be overturned, and for her name to be cleared."

Daniel rubbed his jaw, contemplating Trey's words. After a few moments, the man finally said, "For now, I'll watch the video. But again, I make no promises. If it's not enough to reopen the case, you'll have to work to bring me more."

Trey looked at him. "Thanks, Daniel. I-"

He put his hand up. "I'm only giving you two weeks to bring me something substantial or it stays closed. Especially with that missing woman. We can't devote all of your resources to an old case that already has a conviction."

Not wanting to try his luck, Trey nodded and extended his hand. "I'll be in touch."

Daniel shook Trey's hand. "I'm actually glad you dropped in; I was going to call you. Lyn wants to have dinner next Thursday."

"Will she let me bring a date?"

Daniel raised a row. "A date? You've never mentioned a girlfriend. Who's the lucky lady you'd bring out for everyone to meet?"

Trey chuckled. "It's actually my daughter and her mother."

Daniel's eyes widened and his mouth fell open. "Daughter? I didn't know you had a daughter."

"I didn't either until yesterday."

"Now there's a story I want to hear. Well, Lyn will love to have all of you there."

Trey smiled and stood. But before he walked out the door, Daniel quietly said, "You better be sure about this Trey. It could end both of our careers."

Trey turned back to Daniel. "Trust me, I know."

Then Trey made his way back to the station to see what he could uncover about Morgan Gallagher's murder.

Hailey was on her way to meet Trey and Sara for lunch when she decided to make a detour to Elijah Washington's house. She knew Eli would have a better chance at opening up about her mother's case if it was just the two of them.

Though Elijah had been Chief at the time of her mother's death, he was also a close family friend. He and David had grown up together and had been friends for most of their lives. Eli was like an uncle to the twins and had been a confidant for both her father and mother. From what she saw, Eli took Morgan's death just as hard as the rest of them did, as did his wife.

Hailey found it hard to believe he would miss evidence when Sara's life hung in the balance. But she knew accidents happened and many innocent men and women went to jail for crimes they didn't commit. Sara might just be another statistic.

Still, the evidence was weak and Hailey found it unlikely that a seasoned police officer, let alone the Chief of Police, would arrest their first suspect without looking at other possible suspects.

It didn't make sense.

Hailey hoped Eli could shed some light on what happened that night. Maybe after thirteen years, something would jog his memory.

Eli opened the door a minute after Hailey knocked. He was in a pale blue striped shirt and navy slacks. It reminded Hailey of something her dad's golf buddies would wear.

His hair was thinning and gray, and his dark skin was beginning to wrinkle. She was reminded of how much time had passed since she'd last seen him.

The man smiled ear to ear, lines fanning his eyes. "Well, I'll be. What do I owe the pleasure, Hailey?"

He wrapped her in a hug, and she accepted the gesture. "Hi, Uncle Eli. I was in the neighborhood and wanted to drop by. Is Aunt Loretta here?"

"She's napping right now, but come in." He led her through the living room and into the dining room. "Would you like some coffee?"

Hailey declined, "No, that's okay."

He sat across from her at the table. "I gotta admit, I thought you'd be outta town already."

She smiled softly, used to the comment. "Something came up to keep me here longer, which is actually another reason why I stopped by."

"Are you moving back?" The sparkle in his eye fed her guilt.

She chuckled and shook her head. "Uncle Eli, I have a whole life in Alabama."

"And you can pick this one back up, Hailey girl." He held up a hand before Hailey could protest. "All I'm sayin' is that you ought to think about it."

"Okay, I'll think about it," she said, winking at him. "I actually need to ask you about my mother...about the night she died."

He shifted slightly and looked down at the floor. "What about it?"

Hailey looked down at the table for a moment and then looked back at Eli. "Do you honestly think Sara did it? I know the evidence was circumstantial at best and I just..." She sighed. "I don't know. As an eighteen year old, it was easy to believe she did it. But now, I just don't think the evidence was there and I want to know what you saw when you investigated."

Washington visibly tensed and the happiness in his eyes turned to anger...or was it guilt?

He narrowed his eyes at her. "You're right, the evidence wasn't much, but it was enough to get a plea deal. Why are you bringing this up now? She served her time and now she's free."

"We found evidence that has the potential to prove she's innocent."

He stood abruptly, startling Hailey. "You think I didn't do my job? That I put away an innocent woman?"

His agitation wasn't something Hailey had been expecting. Regaining her composure, Hailey placed her hand on his. "Uncle Eli, I don't think that at all. I just want to hear your side before we start looking into my mother's case again."

"Who's 'we?' What do you mean you're looking into her case?"

"Like I said, I found something that could prove Sara is innocent, so Trey is working on getting the case reopened."

A beat.

He clenched his jaw and removed his hand from hers. "Everything is in my report for Trey to read. I need to wake up Loretta for our afternoon walk. You can see yourself out."

With that, he walked away from the table and up the stairs.

<hr>

"Hello?" David coughed out as he clutched the phone. He hadn't expected the bourbon to burn so much. He dabbed his mouth with a handkerchief and ignored the blood that stained the fabric.

Fuck.

He really should listen to his doctor and stop drinking, but he didn't want to give up this one pleasure.

"Hailey came by my house. She's asking questions."

"What did she say?" David poured himself another drink, welcoming the burn as it slithered down his throat. It reminded him he was still alive.

He hadn't planned on spending the day drinking, but after his talk with Trey and Sara's little visit, he couldn't seem to stop himself. He was on edge, and he hoped the liquor might help, despite his doctor's protests against it.

Eli's voice went up an octave. "She said she's got evidence that Sara is innocent, and now Trey is snooping around."

"I'm aware. What else did she say?"

"You already knew? Why didn't you warn me?" he demanded.

"Because they will never get this case reopened. And if you give them a reason to snoop, they will." David said.

Trey didn't need any more of a reason. The fact that he hated David was enough force to drive the cowboy to ruin all he built. It was hardly shocking to find that his own flesh and blood were the ones pulling the strings.

Eli was panicking. "What am I supposed to do, David? You promised no one would find out."

David rubbed his face. "Just shut up and stay away from them. It's really not that difficult."

David hung up, no longer wanting to deal with Eli.

Truth was, David was antsy. He worked decades trying to keep his affair a secret and now even Trey Harbor knew about it.

He figured once Hailey was back in town the two would somehow manage to find one another, he just hadn't anticipated the trouble that may cause for him. Though, he shouldn't be surprised. It's all they had ever done together.

When the girls were teenagers, it was always Sara who he needed to keep an eye on. She was constantly getting into trouble with drugs and boys. It was a damned miracle she hadn't died from an overdose or gotten pregnant before she was eighteen.

Hailey had always been his golden child. When she wasn't helping Sara, that is. And then Trey weaseled his way into her heart and head, and eventually her bed. Hailey was worse than Sara when it came to Trey.

He had so much hope for Hailey. She was bright and beautiful. She had wanted nothing more than to please him and Morgan, though he had to beat her a few times before she understood that he wasn't to be disrespected nor disobeyed.

Like he had to do to Morgan when they were first married.

He would never admit it, but he had gotten off on Morgan's screams and cries as he smacked her and pulled her hair. She had begged him to stop, promising to do whatever he wished. Unfortunately for her, that wasn't good enough. He needed to make sure she *knew* never to cross him.

He had shoved her to the ground and told her to never disrespect him again.

And she hadn't. Until Nicole.

Then she had the audacity to threaten him like he couldn't take the very breath from her lungs. She'd forgotten about his lesson; forgotten she shouldn't cross him.

But he was Mayor by that time and didn't want his reputation ruined. He tried to leave Nicole but couldn't. She was his other half, his heart and soul. Though they could never be together, they were content with secrecy.

And now that secret seemed to be out. Or at least was soon to be out.

Desperate times call for desperate measures. Much like thirteen years ago.

He hurled his glass across his office. It smashed against the wall, shards raining down over the floor, a glimpse of what his life would soon look like if he wasn't careful.

There was one person who could undo the kingdom he built by pulling a single thread.

Which meant he would have to get to them before they began pulling.

Chapter 16

June 28, 2011
1:07 pm

Hailey and Sara had missed the lunch crowd as they waited for Trey at a local sports bar and grill. After talking with Eli, Hailey picked up Sara for lunch where they were now waiting on Trey.

Still irritated with her sister, Hailey quietly said, "Listen, I don't want to fight, but I need you to stop trying to manipulate me into telling Trey about Ryan. It's none of your business."

Sara snorted. "Maybe not, but it's Trey's business."

"And since when do you care about Trey?"

She shrugged. "I don't."

Hailey shook her head. "Then why won't you leave it alone?"

Sara leaned in. "You're going to get yourself killed because you're being a pretentious bitch about it. Stop acting like it doesn't affect the rest of us."

Hailey's mouth hung open. "Screw you. It doesn't affect anyone else. Were you the one who had nightmares about being beaten to death? Were you the one who held your breath at the doctor, praying they found a heartbeat? Were you the one who scrubbed dried blood off your body?"

Sara clenched her jaw and anger sparked behind her eye. Before Sara could respond, their waitress came over and introduced herself.

They had placed an appetizer order when Hailey noticed a man staring in their direction. She immediately noticed the dog tags that hung around his neck, standing out against the black fabric that hugged his arms. She nearly blushed as she assessed him, taking in his muscular build, blonde hair, and beard. The tattoos that covered his arms intrigued her more than she cared to admit.

"That guy keeps staring at us," Hailey quietly said to Sara.

Sara turned around before Hailey could protest.

The man smiled and waved, and Sara turned back around and rolled her eyes. "Creep."

Hailey lifted a brow. There was a time when Sara would have relished in any attention from the male species. This new Sara was both entertaining and peculiar.

Much to her dismay, though, the man walked up to their table. "Hi, Hailey."

Hailey was startled that the stranger knew her name.

He chuckled. "It's Gavin O'Dell from high school."

A grin slowly grew on her face as she stood to hug him. "I didn't even recognize you!"

Gavin laughed deeply. "The Marines change a man."

"Still trying to be a womanizer, I see," Sara said.

"Nice to see you, too, Sara."

"I'm sure it is," she said dryly as she made her way to the bar across the restaurant.

Hailey immediately wanted to strangle her sister for being so rude. "Sorry, she's a little irritable."

He smirked. "A little?"

Hailey smiled. "Okay, a lot. So how have you been?"

"I've been doing pretty good. Opened my own private security firm three years ago with my friend, Carter Anguilar."

"I thought you were going to Harvard to study law?" she said.

Gavin sat in Sara's seat. "I was, but halfway through my freshman year I realized I hated it. Carter was already talking about leaving and enlisting in the Marines, so I did too."

"I would have never pegged you as someone who would enlist and then work in private security."

"Me either. But it was the best decision I ever made. So, what brought you back to town?" he asked.

Hailey shrugged. "Just visiting for Angie's wedding and then heading back home in a few days."

He nodded and glanced at her ring finger. "You know, I'm honestly surprised you and Trey didn't end up hitched. I always knew he was in love with you." He laughed. "And I was pissed as hell about it."

Gavin had always made her feel guilty when it came to Trey. But looking back now, he was right to feel threatened. She had feelings for Trey, despite her protests against them.

Actually, Trey had been a big reason as to why they broke up. That and the fact that Gavin wanted to sleep with every other girl in their class.

While Gavin was calculated and ambitious, standing to inherit a small fortune, Trey had been wild and adventurous, not a dime to his name. Yet, despite Gavin being the safest option, Hailey fell in love with Trey.

She often wondered what her life would have been like if she hadn't.

Hailey sighed. "It just didn't work, unfortunately. After my mother died, I couldn't stay here anymore so I left and lived with my great-aunt in Alabama."

"I'm sorry about that. Your Ma was a nice lady."

"Thanks."

"So, what happened with Sara? I was pretty shocked to find out she killed your mother. I'm even more shocked to see you two together."

Hailey shook her head. "This is going to sound crazy, but she didn't do it. We're trying to get Trey to reopen the investigation."

He lifted his brow. "Sounds like there's more to that story."

Hailey nodded. "There is, but it's too much to get into."

"And what about you and Trey?" he asked.

"We're...friendly."

Gavin chuckled. "No, you don't get to do that. Spill it, Hailey. You clearly have a lot going on in that head of yours."

Hailey smiled. "It's really complicated. Like, *really* complicated."

"Now I'm even more curious."

"We actually have a daughter that he didn't know about until yesterday," she said, looking down at the table. "We're trying to figure out what co-parenting looks like and what that means for us."

Gavin raised his brows, and the waitress came and brought Hailey's appetizer to the table. Not wanting to talk about her past anymore, she leaned back in her seat and asked, "What about you? Is there a Mrs. O'Dell?"

He smiled, showing off a dimple on his right cheek. "Other than my mother, no. I try to keep myself away from the ladies. They're trouble, you know." He winked. "I was actually engaged a few years back, but she wanted me to leave the Marines, and I just couldn't do it. It didn't seem fair to ask her to settle and give up her own dreams. It was amicable but still sad. Last I heard, she was happily married with a baby on the way."

"I'm sorry. I'm sure that was hard for both of you." Hailey gently touched his hand.

Gavin shrugged. "Yeah, but it was for the best. Now I've just decided to stop looking and let love find me...or not."

"I'm sure you won't have any trouble with that."

The two smiled at each other. Then Hailey noticed the restaurant door open and saw Trey looking for her. She waved him down and he immediately noticed Gavin. He instinctively bowed up, much like he had when they were teenagers. Hailey laughed to herself.

Sara, too, came back to the table and Gavin stood to give her back her seat.

"Trey, you remember Gavin," Hailey said as Trey walked up to the table.

"I do," he growled.

"I heard you were the new Police Chief, Harbor. That's shocking, to say the least."

Hailey eyed the two men, amused, as they exchanged a silent pissing match.

"I'm glad we got to catch up," Hailey said to Gavin, trying to ease the tension.

"Me too. See ya 'round," he said. Gavin smiled, then walked off, sneaking one last glance at Sara before walking back to his table.

Hailey was glad she bumped into Gavin. He had always been a good friend, even if he was a lousy boyfriend. As much as Hailey hated to admit it, this little town did hold fond memories for her.

Trey on the other hand, didn't look pleased

Chapter 17

June 28, 2011
2:46 pm

As they walked back toward the police station that was only a few streets away, Hailey could nearly feel heat coming off of Trey. Though, if she didn't know any better, she would have assumed it was the summer sun.

He was irritated, but he shouldn't be. Gavin was part of her past and she planned to keep him there. And honestly, she and Trey weren't necessarily official, so he had no claims to her anyway.

Or were they official? The way they left things at dinner last night may say otherwise.

God, she'd give herself a headache if she thought about it too hard.

Sara caught up with them, shoving her phone into her pocket after ending a call. She glanced at Trey. "What's wrong with you?"

"Hailey was pretty buddy-buddy with Gavin earlier," Trey grumbled.

"Oh, here we go." Sara rolled her eyes.

Hailey giggled at Trey's remark. "You're jealous. That's cute."

Trey scowled. "No, I'm not. I just don't like him. He treated you like shit."

"That was more than a decade ago. I think he's fine now. We actually might go see a movie later."

Trey whipped his head to look at Hailey, who was grinning ear to ear, trying to contain her laughter. For once, *she* was baiting *him,* and he was walking right into it.

"Come on, Trey. You know I'm only kidding."

"Whatever," he said, sulking.

"How manly of you." Sara said dryly.

Trey shook his head at Sara. "Who were you on the phone with anyway?"

She shrugged. "Someone."

Hailey was curious. Sara was up to something. "Someone *who*?"

"If I wanted you to know, I'd tell you." Sara eyed Hailey. "I'll spill my secret if you spill yours, though."

Hailey narrowed her eyes at Sara. Hailey didn't understand why she was so set on Hailey spilling her secrets. She felt like a teenager all over again, wanting to pull her sister's hair and start a fight.

Why did Sara have to be so vindictive? Hailey was going out of her way to help clear her name and all Sara could manage to do was start fights, keep secrets, and have a bad attitude.

Trey eyed her, but she quickly changed the subject. "I went and talked to Eli today."

Trey stopped walking and turned to her. "About what?"

"My mother's case. I told him that we had evidence that proved Sara didn't do it and wanted to hear what he remembered."

"And?" Trey asked, eager to hear what she had to say.

"He was pretty mad that I asked. He accused me of saying he botched the investigation- which I didn't. Then he told me to leave."

"I gotta admit, that makes me curious," Trey said.

Hailey continued, "That's what I thought, too. It was definitely weird, like he was hiding something..."

"Is that it?" Trey asked.

They started walking again. "Yeah, basically. He said everything is in the report."

He nodded. "Something's off and I don't like it. Now I want to triple check every file, every piece of evidence, every interview. "

Sara chimed in, "I've always thought he was working for Dad. I don't know what Dad has on him, but it must be juicy for him to help frame me for murder.

I kept telling him I was innocent and all he did was apologize and say he wished he didn't have to arrest me. Plus, he never looked at other possible suspects. Ever."

Hailey had never considered the fact that David could have manipulated or blackmailed Washington. They all assumed he swayed the D.A. or the judge, but not the investigation itself.

"I don't think we should jump to conclusions just yet. That's a steep accusation against a former police chief and a mayor. And I'm not going to do anything with it unless I have solid proof."

"Whatever," Sara said curtly. "Just don't be mad when I say I told you so."

Trey shook his head. "I've got some other news. I talked to the D.A. and he's willing to at least watch the tape. He said he couldn't make any promises to reopen the case officially, but he gave me the okay to poke around a bit."

Sara's head shot up. "Are you serious? Could this case really get reopened?"

"I'm not promising anything, but at least D.A. Whitaker is willing to look at it if we bring him sufficient evidence."

"That's amazing news!" Hailey hugged Sara, unable to contain her excitement. Sara tensed, and Hailey immediately pulled away. It felt odd hugging her sister after all this time, especially given the tension between them. But it somehow still felt natural to want to celebrate with her.

"Yeah, but that's not all." Trey shifted. "Nicole House has been missing for a few days now. It looks like there was a struggle."

Hailey's mouth gaped open, and Sara scrunched her brows.

"Are the cases connected?" Hailey asked.

Trey shook his head. "I honestly don't know. Right now, it doesn't look like it, but I do think it's interesting your father is right in the middle. First, your mother is killed and then Nicole goes missing and your father was involved with both of them?"

"He probably did it, that bastard," Sara said.

Hailey wasn't sure if Sara was blowing off steam or if she meant it.

"When I first pressed him about Nicole, he stonewalled me. But then he admitted to the affair and that Ryan is his son. He denied having seen her recently, though. I mentioned your mother too, so the cat's out of the bag to some degree."

Hailey said, "This whole thing is weird, Trey. You can't tell me those cop instincts of yours aren't buzzing."

"They definitely are, I just haven't connected all the dots yet. But all we need is one person to blow these cases wide open. You're just not going to like who we're going to talk to."

Hailey stopped abruptly. "No. We're not talking to Ryan."

"*You* don't have to. I will." Trey sighed. "We all know he's probably the only person who would be willing to tell us anything."

Sara said, "How do you know he won't lie?"

A truck honked as another car lulled too long at a stop sign. The driver stuck her hand out the window and gave the truck driver the middle finger and sped off.

Trey waited for an older couple to walk around them before continuing the conversation. "I don't. But with as much as he terrorized you both growing up, I'd be willing to bet he hates David. And if that's true, he might be willing to tell us what he knows."

Hailey inwardly shivered. If Trey talked to Ryan about that night, there was no doubt he would goad Trey with what he'd done to her. Then, she'd have no choice but to face Trey about her own worst nightmare.

Sara said, "Talk to him. We all know my father isn't going to help us and apparently Eli won't either."

"Please don't," Hailey said, hanging her head.

Sara shifted slightly but Hailey couldn't read her thoughts. She had honed her skills of secrecy and Hailey often couldn't figure out what Sara was thinking or feeling.

Trey looked at Hailey. "I'm sorry, but I don't need your permission to talk to him. I have an entire case that involves him directly."

Hailey took a step back and tilted her head at Trey, scowling at him. "*Excuse me?*"

"I can't do my job unless I have all the facts, Hailey."

Hailey felt heat rising through her body. She didn't want Trey to know. She didn't want him to look at her differently, to see her as a victim. Even though that's what she was. And that fact pissed her off more than she cared to admit.

Sara quietly said, "I know this is hard for you to talk about, but you need to tell him what happened."

"No," Hailey said through clenched teeth. "And why do you care, anyway? It's not like you were sober enough to know what was going on."

Hailey wasn't going to be strong-armed into spilling her secret. She hadn't done that to Sara. She had given her sister the space to open up when she felt comfortable. The fact that Sara was so adamant about Hailey being vulnerable with Trey irked her to the nth degree.

Sara glared at Hailey.

"I'm sorry. I shouldn't have-"

"If he has information that could clear my name then I want to know what it is." Sara pointed at Hailey. "*You're* the one who brought me the tape and told me to go to the cops with it. So, excuse me for getting annoyed with your little secret. Quit being so dramatic."

Trey stood silently, watching the exchange. Another pedestrian walked around them, eyeing them curiously. Sara stomped away, leaving Hailey to deal with yet another mess.

"Where are you going?" Hailey yelled.

Sara didn't answer and Hailey let her go.

Maybe that was for the best. Hailey wasn't sure she could be around Sara without a fight breaking out. Hailey needed a break from Sara's incessant miserable attitude.

Sweat beaded on Hailey's hairline. The summer heat was beating down despite the impending rain clouds that were rolling in, causing the sky to darken.

She was hurt that Sara felt she was being dramatic. Maybe she was. But what she went through that night was traumatic in its own right, though maybe it paled in comparison to what Sara had been through.

Trey took Hailey's hand. "Please tell me what happened to you. Not knowing is killing me."

Hailey's eyes filled with tears. She didn't owe anyone an explanation of her trauma. She felt betrayed that he would ask her to tell him something she wanted to keep private.

"No. We're not doing this, Trey." She turned to walk away but he gently grabbed her arm, and she spun around. With fire in her eyes, she tore her arm from his grasp and began walking away.

"Hailey!" Trey called after her. She felt childish walking away and was both embarrassed and angry with her display of emotions. She wished she could turn them off like Sara did.

Trey finally caught up to her. "Talk to me. What happened to you?"

She spun to face him, her chest rising and falling rapidly. "Why do you care? Because of your investigations? You never cared until now."

Stunned, he stammered, "No. I mean, yes, but that's not the only reason. I love you and clearly something awful happened to you."

Hailey smiled angrily. "Oh, that's priceless. You haven't given a damn about me since I left but now that I'm back, you're somehow entitled to my secrets? I didn't ask for your help because I wanted to rekindle things. Believe me, if I could do this on my own I would."

She saw the hurt in his eyes as he said, "That's not fair and you know it."

"Yeah, well, I've done just fine without you for the last thirteen years so maybe I should plan to keep it that way. I don't owe you anything, Trey. You broke things off with me, remember?" She was shaking now. Unable to contain her anger, she blurted out, "You're the reason Ryan almost killed me that night!"

Trey froze.

Hailey covered her mouth, stunned by her own admission.

She hated that Ryan was still controlling her. After years of living in fear, she had found safety in having a *choice* to share her trauma. But now that choice was gone, along with any control she'd had over her emotions. She probably sounded like a lunatic to Trey, but no one understood how horrific that night had been and how traumatic it was to talk about.

It had been nearly ten years since she recounted that night. Her therapist tried to dig it out of her, but Hailey refused to talk about it. The woman didn't prod too much, but kept reminding Hailey she couldn't heal if she didn't talk about it.

The only reason she divulged the information was because her nightmares had become so frequent she wasn't sleeping. All she could see when she closed her eyes was her bloody body and Ryan's evil smile as she looked up at him.

She never talked about it again and she hadn't told anyone else since that day in therapy...until she told Sara. And Sara had betrayed her trust.

And now she'd have to relive it again.

Hailey beelined for a secluded bench tucked into the corner of the park. Trey followed close behind, confused by her actions. She sat down, thankful to be away from listening ears and prying eyes. Trey sat next to her, putting space between them.

In the distance, thunder echoed through the sky. The park was nearly empty, aside from two families that were playing. A little girl was swinging, her legs dangling as she tried to heave herself into the air. A little boy who looked to be the girl's brother was chasing a lizard as their mother yelled at him to stop. The other family sat close by as two twin girls raced through the jungle gym, their shrieks of laughter ringing through the park.

She watched the families for a minute or so, though it felt like an eternity. They were making memories, and she envied their happiness. She had never gotten that as a child. Her family was broken long before she was ever born.

Maybe it was time to break that cycle. How could her own little family be whole if she never let herself heal? Despite not wanting it to be true, she knew a part of her would feel relief by confiding in Trey.

Taking in a deep breath, she picked at her nail polish. "I had just found out I was pregnant with Trinity that morning." She smiled and looked at Trey. "I had been so excited to tell you. I mean, I was scared but I just knew it would all work out. We had our date planned for that night, but then you started saying we shouldn't be together and that I was better off without you." Hailey furrowed her brow. "I was so angry because I thought we would have this happy ending that happens in movies..."

Hailey paused for a moment, steadying herself. "When I left, I drove aimlessly for a while, just stewing over everything and crying. I was a wreck, and the hormones probably weren't helping. I was scared of what my parents would say, too. I knew my father was going to lose it."

She rubbed her arms, despite the heat of the afternoon. "I was on Bolender Road when my car gave out. It was dark by then and I didn't know what else to do..."

The first parts of her story were relatively easy to recount but now she needed to mentally prepare herself. She began fidgeting with her hair to keep her anxiety at bay. She stared at the grass, getting lost in memory as she told him what happened that night...

Chapter 18

Thirteen Years Ago
June 3, 1998
9:45 pm

Hailey sobbed harder as she turned the key in the ignition only for it to sputter yet again. She glanced at the moon that hung in the darkness, accompanied by the flashes of heat lightning that lit up the sky. Normally she'd admire its beauty, but tonight it gave her the creeps. She was only a few miles from home and now she was stranded.

Mascara streaked her cheeks, and her lips were red and puffy. She wiped at her face as she climbed out of her car, locking it as she did. She'd figure out what to do about the worthless piece of metal tomorrow after she had time to calm down.

She began walking home when headlights illuminated the road in front of her. The vehicle pulled over and parked behind her car. She was curious who the good samaritan might be, but the beams of light made it difficult to see. She was standing a few feet from her car when Ryan got out, a wicked grin splayed on his face.

Panic raced through her body.

Hailey bolted back to her car and struggled to get her key into the lock. She fumbled them and they bounced onto the pavement and under her car. Ryan made his way toward her, and her body screeched at her to run.

Ryan grabbed her arm, and a scream escaped her lips, but it was useless. No one would hear her.

He pulled her close to him and the smell of whiskey and cigarettes filled her nostrils. Her stomach soured but she willed herself not to throw up.

"I told you I'd find you when Trey wasn't around to protect you," he slurred.

Hailey wondered how he was able to drive. She tried to free herself, but she wasn't strong enough to break his grip. "Let me go! I swear if my father finds out-"

Smack!

Her cheek stung and she tasted blood on her lip.

"Your father is a coward!"

Hailey wasn't sure how to get out of this situation.

She tried to soothe him. "Okay, I'm sorry. Whatever he's done to make you upset, I'm sure he can fix it."

Ryan laughed. "Oh, Princess, you have no idea what he's done. But I'm going to make him pay. And I'm going to use you to do it."

Her eyes rounded as her heartbeat quickened. Hailey instinctively touched her stomach, afraid of what might happen.

She hadn't been expecting his first blow. His fist connected with her cheek and her head struck the car. She shrieked in pain and brought her hand to her face.

He swayed slightly and she shoved him away from her. He stumbled back and laughed as he hit the ground with a thud. Her body recognized the danger before her mind registered it and she darted into the orange groves on the other side of the road, trying to find cover within the trees. Ryan ran after her.

"Hailey," he cooed. "Come out, Hailey."

She covered her mouth, trying to muffle her sob.

He popped out from behind a tree. "I found you."

Hailey screamed and jumped back, stumbling on a root. She fell into the dirt and leaves, the distinct acrid smell of oranges overwhelming her. She tried to pull herself up, but the trees were spinning, and she collapsed.

Ryan grabbed her foot and pulled her toward him. She kicked at his stomach, and he hunched over. She tried to turn away, but pain exploded in her back as he landed a blow. He was on top of her as she smacked and clawed at his face. He laughed at her terror, enjoyed her rage.

She was waiting for Trey to rescue her, just as he'd done at the festival; just like he promised. But she knew he wouldn't come. He didn't love her anymore.

Ryans fists continued to rain down on her face and shoulders. Hailey shrieked, her voice cracking, as she punched at him wildly.

Ryan laughed again as he aggressively gripped her wrists and straddled her, pinning her hands above her head.

She closed her eyes, bracing for what would come next.

Then, he wrapped his hands around her throat and squeezed. He snarled, "I can't wait to watch the life drain from your eyes, knowing I'll be the last face you ever see."

Her lungs constricted as she tried to gasp for air. Her nails dug into his hands, but he didn't release his grip. He smiled as she slowly faded into the darkness.

At first, she was scared of it, but the more palpable it became, the more she welcomed it. It seemed so peaceful compared to the pain that tormented her body. She could taste the blood as she tried to spit it out. Every breath was labored, and she couldn't help but cough, spattering blood all down her blouse.

She thought of how horrific it would be for someone to find her body like this; covered in blood, beaten so badly she couldn't be identified. Her baby would still be safe within her womb, except, like Hailey, there would be no heartbeat.

A guttural instinct surged through her. If she didn't do something, she was going to die and so would her baby.

She let go of him and felt her surroundings, darkness threatening to overtake her. Her hands grasped a rock, and she slammed it into his head. He yelped and fell off of her as his blood leaked all over Hailey and dripped down his face.

Rage engulfed Ryan.

She rolled onto her stomach and crawled away, still not moving fast enough. He stood and pain exploded through her head as he grabbed a fistful of her hair. He slammed her body into the dirt.

She wasn't going to get away.

She would die here.

The darkness was luring her in, promising an end to the pain. So, she curled up into the fetal position, protecting her unborn child, as he punched and kicked her body. Hailey's screams of terror were trapped within the trees that hid the horror that was happening to her as her pleading sobs echoed through the night.

But no one heard them.

She finally gave into the darkness as the moon smiled down at her and the stars watched her bleed, unaware of the violence that was happening below their beauty.

***

Hailey limped toward her house, holding her stomach protectively. When she came to, Ryan had been long gone. So, she walked the few miles back to the Gallagher Estate, her body on autopilot as she did.

Flashing red and blue lights in the distance grabbed her attention.

Had they arrested Ryan? Had her father called the police to come find her?

Dazed, she pushed past the ache of her body and the stabbing pain in her lungs and guided herself to the safety that was now only a few yards away. But with each step, the crime scene tape and police officers blurred together as her body fought off exhaustion and shock.

The hairs on the nape of her neck stood at attention and she innately knew something awful had happened. She wanted to sprint toward her home, to see the atrocity that had surely been left behind by whatever evil had been there before her. But after what she'd been through, she didn't have the energy or the strength. Yet, despite her body's protests, she was instinctively drawn to the scene of the crime, every step becoming harder than the last.

She was nearing the estate when she stopped abruptly, realizing she was a mess. She wondered if she should change. Her mother would have a heart attack if Hailey came home like this.

Her clothes were torn, and she was missing a shoe. Where was her shoe? She brushed away the grass that clung to her jeans, the green streaks irking her. She pulled a stray leaf from her hair.

Assessing herself, she grasped at the locket she always wore and nearly cried out when it wasn't there. She quickly remembered she'd given it to Trey weeks ago.

However, it was the blood that startled her. She was still covered in the crimson stains that mixed with dirt, though at that point it caked her skin. She aggressively scraped at her arms and hands, trying to erase the terror her body had just endured. When it wouldn't come off, she nearly screamed.

Her heart raced and she looked to see if anyone had noticed her yet. There would be so many questions. And she wouldn't give them answers. She didn't want to relive the horror she so narrowly escaped.

What if Ryan came back to finish the job?

Where was Trey? Why hadn't he saved her? He promised to always save her.

But that promise had been broken, just like his vow to love her forever.

Again, she ordered her legs to walk forward, toward whatever violence occurred on such a warm summer's night. Every step was heavy, as if her body was trying to protect her from the monsters that lurked in the shadows. Tears flowed down her cheeks, attempting to wash away the dirt and horror that stained her face.

Her eyes darted to the fountain where her father and Uncle Eli stood, both in deep discussion. Her body swayed and she attempted to steady herself. The sound of crime scene techs and police officers all seemed to fade into one another.

Eli noticed her first and immediately jogged over to her, David following much more slowly.

Eli cupped her face. "Oh my god! Hailey, what happened?" He yelled to the other officers, "I need a medic!"

An officer came over to her, carrying a first aid kit. "I'm Officer Young but you can call me Bobby. Can you tell me what happened to you?"

Her head swam and she couldn't make sense of his words. Her body swayed once more and she reached out, putting her hand against his chest.

Where was Trey? She needed to see Trey.

When she didn't answer Bobby, David said, "Your mother died. Sara killed her."

Hailey's eyes flickered to the grand French doors of her home just as the coroner carried out a black body bag on a stretcher.

She heard what her father said, but her brain lagged, a fog threatening her consciousness.

Sara had killed their mother? No, her mother was inside sleeping, and Sara was partying.

Hailey could hear Bobby talking to her father and Eli. She could feel his cold hands as he gently assessed her injuries, but it was as if she was frozen, her mind muddled.

"She needs a doctor, Chief. These lacerations are deep and there's so much blood, I can't tell what's a flesh wound and what needs stitches."

"Call one. I'm not taking her to the hospital," David's voice boomed.

"Shit," Bobby said, "she's got a stick lodged into her back. She needs medical attention. Now."

God, she felt so tired. All she wanted to do was lay on the ground and sleep.

Their voices faded as she walked to the middle of her yard, a few feet from the fountain that her mother hated so much. Then she laid in the grass and screamed, her shrieks of grief and sorrow sending everyone running in a direction other than her own, even Eli. And especially her father.

But not Bobby. He sat next to her as she screamed and cried out. He took out antiseptic wipes and gently- and silently- cleaned the blood off her wounds. She winced as the sting of the medication bit her skin and he paused until she was calm again.

She found that his kindness was a safe place. He didn't even know what had happened to her just hours before, how much she desperately needed to feel safe and protected. And he gave that to her. A stranger made her feel more loved and cared for than her own father ever did. David Gallagher simply ignored his daughter's outrage and grief and continued to watch the police work, allowing a perfect stranger to console and care for his daughter.

Bobby thought she had been screaming only for the loss of her mother, but she had been mourning so much more. She sobbed again and he held her hand until she finally passed out in the grass, her voice hoarse from grief and her body broken and bloody, just like her soul.

Chapter 19

The family with the twin girls were no longer at the park and another mother rushed her kids to the car as the storm winds picked up.

Trey touched Hailey's hand, and she jumped but didn't pull away. She hadn't even noticed he had inched closer to her. His presence reminded her she wasn't eighteen anymore and she wasn't hidden in the orange groves. She was safe and had survived.

The morning after the attack, Hailey had woken to a splitting headache, a broken rib, a dead mother, and a guilty sister. Not to mention the bruises, stitches, and blood that had still caked the crevices of her body, despite nearly scrubbing her skin raw.

She had left town a month later.

A single tear tried to escape but she blinked it away as she turned her head. She hated that she still cried about it, that it still haunted her so deeply.

"I'm so sorry," Trey said.

"It's not your fault. You couldn't have known," she said.

Hailey couldn't bring herself to look at him. Shame dug its claws in, taunting her.

"No, I should have been there to protect you. I should have been a better man and gone after you when you left. There's a lot of things I should have done differently. I promised to be there for you, and I wasn't. That's on me."

She pulled her hand away from his and picked at a leaf that had fallen on the bench next to her. She didn't know what to say. Part of her wanted to yell at him again. He *should* have been there. But the other part of her knew it wasn't his fault, she was only looking for someone to blame.

And that someone was Ryan.

"Look at me, Hailey," Trey said.

"I can't. I shouldn't have needed you to save me, and I hate myself for it. I hate that you'll only see me as this girl who couldn't save herself." She closed her eyes and sighed, calming herself.

Trey gently touched her chin with his finger, turning her head to look at him. His jaw was set, and his brown eyes were now darker.

He said firmly, "You're a *survivor. You* did that. You made it out alive. You didn't need me, and you saved our daughter because you refused to be a victim."

She cried then, soft sobs. Trey pulled her close and kissed her hair. She allowed herself to melt into his chest, her body shaking as she did. She felt safe in his arms, and he stroked her hair as her tears stained his shirt. She took in a breath, his scent calming her.

Finally, she pulled away and placed a hand on his cheek. "Somehow, we've been given a second chance, and I don't want to mess that up. I want to make this work."

Trey kissed her then. Deep but gentle. His hands cupped her face and hers rested on his chest as she took him in.

Then, she pulled away and smiled. "Slow down, cowboy. We've got stuff to do."

He kissed her nose. "We'll pick up where we left off later." He winked at her and she giggled.

She hoped they could make things work between them not only for Trinity, but because she and Trey deserved to be happy. Because she loved him. And she wanted to spend the rest of her life with him.

"Twice in one day," Gavin said.

Sara turned around, surprised to see him.

She always thought Gavin was a prick for the way he treated Hailey. He was snotty, entitled, and a womanizer, even as a teenager. She hated to think how seductive he was now, especially given the way he looked. His beard and tattoos made him appear daring, maybe even dangerous. To her horror, she found him quite attractive as he smiled at her, eyeing her up and down.

"Wow, how could I be so lucky?" Sara said dryly.

"You look good, Sara."

Sara could feel the heat on her cheeks. She nearly shriveled up on the ground, equally embarrassed and intrigued by his straightforwardness. Ever the ladies' man, she didn't trust him at all. And that somehow made him even sexier.

Typical.

"Can't say the same for you," she quipped.

He smiled. They both knew she was lying.

"I'll walk with you."

She eyed him suspiciously. "I'll pass."

Gavin was the last person she wanted to spend time with. The fact he thought she was even approachable was slightly alarming.

He put his hands up. "I just wanted to catch up, see how you were doing."

She raised a brow. "You mean get the inside scoop on my life's story and how I spent the last thirteen years locked up for a crime I didn't commit?"

His lip turned upward, showing a dimple. She wanted to scream at the flip her stomach did.

He said, "Yeah. But for what it's worth, I think there's more to you and I'm curious."

She eyed him, trying and failing to hide a smirk. She was both irritated and intrigued by this man. His straightforwardness was a relief while everyone else tiptoed around her as if she was a bomb waiting to go off. And maybe she was. But she didn't need to be handled with care, and he somehow knew that.

Sticking her nose up at him, she said, "Fine. You can walk with me. But I'm not great company."

He chuckled. "You look like great company to me."

A smile tugged at her lips, but she pushed it away. "You realize I'm a convicted felon, right?"

"And? You're innocent, aren't you?" He shrugged. "Hailey told me."

She nodded slowly. "Good to know she's got a big mouth."

He laughed again and she found herself loving the sound. They began walking around downtown, the shadows of palm trees covering them every few feet. Sara had forgotten how beautiful it was here, with the palm trees lining the sidewalks, bright flowers, and brick sidewalks.

If she wasn't so miserable, she might actually enjoy it.

"So, tell me about yourself," she said.

Ugh. She sounded lame. As a teenager, she would have never said something like that.

"Obviously, I was in the Marines." He held up his dog tags, proud of his service. "I met my business partner in college and we both decided to drop out of law school and serve. Then we opened a private security firm."

"Was being a Marine as hard as they make it out to be on TV?"

Gavin smiled. "Harder. What about you?"

She tensed. "Not much to know, other than the obvious."

"That's not true. You went to prison for something you didn't do and now look at you. You're a fighter. Plus, you've got a scar on your neck that I'm sure has one helluva story."

She started, alarm racing through her body. She was beginning to regret letting him walk with her. Regret seemed to be in high numbers these days.

"You don't have to tell me. I was just making conversation," he said.

Sara looked away. "Like I said, there's nothing to tell."

He grinned mischievously. "Whatever you say."

Gavin didn't push her for details and instead changed the subject. It had been such a long time since she'd truly connected with anyone, something he quickly picked up on. But he didn't seem to mind and made it easy to laugh at his jokes. She even allowed herself to flirt for a minute.

As they walked, he shared stories about what he'd seen while overseas, most of which was very traumatic. Much like what she felt.

"I still have nightmares from time to time. It's hard to make sense of feeling like you did something good, even if it cost people their lives." He pulled down the collar of his shirt, revealing a round scar on his pectoral. "I was shot and almost died. We were taking fire, and my buddy had been hit. I went back to drag his body behind a building and was hit in the process. Don't remember much after that, but I woke up in the hospital and was told I almost didn't make it."

She studied the raised flesh and nearly reached out to touch it but caught herself. Instead, she traced the one on her neck, memories flooding her.

"Did your friend make it?" she asked.

Gavin slumped slightly. "No. He left behind a wife and newborn. That was rough. I don't really have any family and yet he was the one to die."

"I'm glad you didn't."

He smiled sadly and nodded.

For the first time, she felt safe enough to share her story. Funny it was with someone she didn't much care for, though her hardness for him was softening. Sure, he was still flirtatious and arrogant, but there was a quiet gentleness about him that hadn't been there years before.

She found herself drawn to tell him about her life, her secrets, her thoughts. She'd tell him about her hopes and dreams if she had any.

She sighed. "I almost died twice."

Gavin arched a brow. "I wasn't expecting that. I had hoped prison wasn't that bad for you."

"I wish."

He eyed her neck. "Is that where you got the scar?"

"Yes, and I've got a lot more." She pointed to her side but didn't show him the jagged marks that lay just underneath the thin cotton. "Long story short, a girl hated how pretty I was. And after that, my cellmate was jumped and I helped her."

He studied her for a moment, and she looked away, ashamed of her past.

"That explains why you're always on edge. I get that. We may have different reasons for it, but we're both a little high strung."

Sara smiled. "You're not judging me for being an ex-con?"

"You said you didn't do it."

She tilted her head. "How do you know I'm not lying?"

"Because, you wouldn't have told me about the scar." He gently traced the jagged edges on her neck, and she sucked in a breath, quickly jumping back from his touch.

Sara's heart pounded and she wondered if Gavin could hear it. Her palms began to sweat as heat crept through her body. Her voice caught in her throat, and she realized they had stopped walking.

He nodded toward a door behind him. "Well, this is my office. Thanks for letting me walk with you."

"You didn't give me much of a choice," she said.

They stared at each other for a moment, and she wondered if he'd kiss her. A part of her hoped he would. Another part of her felt foolish for even entertaining the thought. The last thing she needed in her life was a relationship. Her last one went up in smoke and almost took her with it.

"I'd like to see you again."

She furrowed her brows, taken aback by his comment. "I don't know, Gavin. I've got a lot going on. Plus, I'm not the type of girl you bring home to your mother. I guarantee you deserve someone a lot better than me." She smiled. "Even though you're cocky and arrogant."

He laughed. "It's a good thing my parents disowned me then."

"I'll think about it," she said, a twinkle in her eye. She turned and walked away, feeling like she was on cloud nine.

Gavin called out, "I'll call you!"

"You don't have my number," she called back.

She locked eyes with him again and that same reaction from earlier simmered.

Sara didn't know what to do or how to feel. She had once been a magnet for boys, even as a teenager. She could easily suck them in and spit them back out, the male brain and body something she understood well.

Not now, though. Now she felt awkward and almost uncomfortable.

But the butterflies in her stomach were undeniable.

Sara was surprised to find herself feeling so alive again. Maybe there was hope for her after all.

Trey was glad to be back in the air conditioning. He sat at his desk, filling out a form to request the files from Morgan Gallagher's investigation. Hailey and Sara sat in the chairs across from him, eager to see what he might find in the decade old files, their tiff from earlier at an impasse.

He thought back to seeing Hailey and Gavin together at lunch. It had taken him by surprise and old feelings seemed to float back to the surface. Even thirteen years ago he felt like he had to fight for Hailey, that he wasn't good enough to simply have her. Gavin was a man who had everything, and Hailey had truly cared for him.

Part of him was jealous. She hadn't been that happy to see him when she came back. To be fair, though, he had also ripped her heart out and stepped on it.

Still, he didn't like Gavin getting cozy with Hailey now any more than he liked it thirteen years ago.

A light tap on his door caused him to look up. Deputy Rodriguez stood in his doorway and said, "Chief, we tracked down Ryan House. He's at a bar in Lakeland."

Hailey's face paled slightly at the mention of Ryan's name. Trey's heart raced knowing what that SOB had done to her. As much as he didn't want to talk to Ryan, he knew the monster may be able to give them new leads to follow. And if he was lucky enough, maybe he'd get to toss him in jail. Plus, Nicole's case still had no updates. So, with any luck, Ryan may be able to shed some light on who may have wanted to harm her.

"Okay, I'll head up there in a few minutes. Call Lakeland PD and see if a squad car can sit on him until I get there."

The officer nodded and smiled at Hailey and Sara as he exited the room.

Trey said, "Why don't you two head back to Gen's. I don't know how long it'll take me to interview Ryan."

Sara lifted a brow. "Do you really think *you* should do the interview after what Hailey just told you? I'm quite sure having the Chief of Police arrested on murder charges isn't a good look for the department."

Sara had held her tongue to keep from gloating when Hailey had mentioned that she finally told Trey about Ryan. But Hailey had seen the glimmer of cockiness in her sister's eye and Trey had to quickly intervene to keep them from fighting again.

Trey rolled his eyes. "Thanks for the concern. I'll be fine."

That was a lie. Though he might not kill Ryan, he was considering hurting him at the very least. If he found him alone, he might actually do it. It wasn't a secret that Trey went searching for trouble, but he still had a moral code he lived by; his own rules and boundaries he wouldn't step over. But maybe it was time to break them.

He glanced at Hailey and pictured her curled up on the ground, screaming and crying as Ryan hurt her. Rage boiled deep inside him. It was a rage he had never felt before. He wanted Ryan to beg for his life like Hailey begged for hers. He wanted Ryan to feel his life slipping away as he gasped for breath, just as he'd done to Hailey.

Hailey stood to leave, pulling him from his dark thoughts. "Please be careful," she said.

"I will, I promise."

He thought about their kiss earlier. He found himself getting lost in her scent and he craved the way she melted into him, as if nothing had ever changed over the years.

He never thought he'd get a second chance and now that he might, he wasn't going to let her go again. If he had to move to Alabama to be with her and Trinity, he'd drop everything in a heartbeat.

He walked over to her and took her hands in his as he kissed her on the forehead. "Maybe we can do something tonight. Go get ice cream or dinner?"

Hailey wrapped her arms around his neck and kissed him. "I'd like that."

"Get a room," Sara scoffed.

Wasn't that the pot calling the kettle black? Sara had been anything but modest years ago. Clearly so much had changed since then.

Hailey's phone chirped and she quickly pulled it out of her pocket. She scowled and answered the call, putting it on speaker. "Hello?"

"Hailey, why did you tell Trey about Nicole? It's none of his business," David said.

"Hello to you too," she said dryly.

"I'm serious."

Trey and Sara exchanged glances with Hailey.

Hailey said, "Because I can prove Sara didn't kill Mom which means someone else had a motive to do it. And where better to look than at the woman who destroyed her marriage."

He cursed at her. "You know damn well your sister is a murderer. I did everything in my power to put her away and now you're trying to undo everything. She deserved to be behind bars, and I made sure that's where she ended up."

Trey shook his head. David was anything but a victim, though he would use that ruse if it suited his needs. Having your daughter kill your wife definitely fell into that category.

Sara clenched her jaw, willing herself to stay quiet. Trey could see the fire behind her eyes, fury burning within. He didn't blame her.

David continued, "I'm assuming your sister is with you? Put me on speaker, I'd like to talk to her too."

Hailey said, "She doesn't have anything to say to you."

"I didn't ask if she did. I said 'put me on speaker.'"

Trey nodded. There was no use in denying it. David knew they were all together and Trey was curious as to what he wanted to say.

"You are. She can hear you, so can Trey."

David chuckled cynically. "Of course he's there, too. Sara, it's nice to see you haven't changed since you were a teenager, dragging your sister into your mess. I warned you that if you didn't drop it, I'd come after you."

"And *I* warned *you* that I was going to destroy you. So, you can do what I did thirteen years ago and just roll over and take it, or we can make this a blood bath."

Trey didn't like the way the conversation was turning. And he really didn't like that Sara had clearly been in contact with David, threatening him, no less.

"For someone who claims to not be a murderer, you sure sound like one," David replied.

Sara wanted to defend herself, but Hailey beat her to it. "We all know you're lying, Dad. So go ahead and prepare your news speech about how *you* screwed up. I'm sure you'll come out looking like the victim as always."

Trey lifted a brow. There was a time when Hailey would have nearly cowered in a corner if her father was upset with her. Now, she was bold and outspoken, something he found incredibly sexy.

"Why are you two trying to ruin everything I've built, destroy everything I've done for you?" David said.

Trey nearly cursed the man, as if putting a roof over Hailey and Sara's heads somehow absolved him of his abuse. They all knew better than to believe that crock of shit. David Gallagher did everything in his own self-interest, never out of the goodness of his heart.

Sara said, "Let me be very clear: I will tear down your entire kingdom brick by brick if I have to. I'm not interested in cradling your ego or worrying about your reputation. I'm going to find out who really killed Mom and if that means I have to burn down the world to figure it out, so be it."

David inhaled slowly, regaining his composure. It was another part of his game, another way to make you think he was in control. "I will give you both one chance to let things be. Sara, you served your time, but I can make sure you go back if you don't leave well-enough alone."

Trey tried to speak, but Sara cut him off. She sneered, "You tried to bury me thirteen years ago, but I clawed my way out of the dirt. You don't get to threaten me. You don't get to control me. And you damn sure don't get to manipulate me. If you want to try to bury me again, be my guest, but I'll come bringing a shovel for you, too."

David chuckled wickedly. "You talk a big game for someone who signed a guilty plea deal."

Sara didn't say anything, she didn't want to engage with him any longer. When she didn't respond he said, "And Hailey, don't go looking for trouble because you might just find it."

"I'm sure I will."

"You'll both regret this," he said. The line went dead, and Hailey put her phone back in her pocket.

The fictional kingdom David built had been for his ego and his need for control. And it seemed the twins were done letting David play the part of king. The princesses were going to overthrow their father from his throne and David hated them for it.

Trey instinctively stepped closer to Hailey, wanting to protect her. He remembered the last time she defied her father, the beating she had gotten. When he found out, Trey had wanted to kill David and had even started driving toward the Gallagher Estate. Then, he had found himself too scared to challenge the devil who had left bruises all over Hailey's body.

But Trey was no longer a kid. He was a man who wasn't afraid of the repercussions when it came to his family.

Hailey quickly said, "He's hiding something, and I want to know what it is."

"You and me, both," Trey said.

This wasn't just about David's image and reputation, there was something else going on.

"Well, that was fun," Sara said to break the tension.

Hailey shook her head and raised an arm. "What did you do, anyway? He was pissed at you."

Sara shrugged. "I went and saw him after we watched the tape with Trey. I wanted answers. Instead, I got under his skin. Which is exactly what we want."

Trey said, "You need to be careful. He's clearly agitated and he's grasping for control. People who are used to being in control will go to great lengths to keep it."

"He's not actually going to hurt us," Hailey said.

Trey threw an arm up. "Hailey, he literally threw you into your dining room wall when you refused to break things off with me."

Sara said, "He's right. Dad is effing crazy so be careful because you royally pissed him off this time. I mean, nice it's not me for a change." She quickly added, "Don't get me wrong, he's mad at me, but he's pissed at you."

Trey glared at Sara and Hailey ran her hand through her hair. "At least we know we're doing something right. He wouldn't have called if he wasn't worried."

Trey nodded. "His whole world is being threatened between Nicole going missing and us looking into your mother's death. News of the affair itself is likely enough to cause him to panic. He's starting to unravel and that makes me nervous."

"Yeah, but why?" Sara said. "Why is he so nervous about us finding out the truth about either of these cases if he isn't involved?"

Sara was right. An innocent man didn't care if you snooped around because he had nothing to hide.

David Gallagher was guilty; Trey just didn't know of what.

But he'd find out.

"You two need to watch your backs for now. People are unpredictable when their livelihood is threatened," Trey said.

If David was capable of abusing his daughters, what else could he be capable of? Most abusers escalated and murder wasn't out of the realm of possibilities. And even if he didn't murder Morgan, Trey couldn't be sure he wouldn't kill Hailey or Sara to keep his secrets hidden.

Sara said, "Well, it looks like the devil wants to come out and play."

Hailey clenched her jaw. "He's not the devil. I faced the devil and lived to tell about it."

Trey shuddered. He used to think David was the devil, but he was sadly mistaken. Trey hadn't stared into eyes so dark even monsters were afraid of what lies behind them. But Hailey had.

And Trey knew the devil would be the one to unravel David Gallagher's kingdom.

I watch as Hailey and Sara walk with the cowboy to Hailey's car. They can't see me though. I've parked far enough away to keep an eye on them, but not close enough to attract attention. Even if I did, no one would think anything of it.

Hailey tilted her head back and laughed at something Trey said. I clench my jaw, disgusted with the flirtation. The two girls get into Hailey's car and drive off as the Chief goes back inside his precinct.

What a joke.

How is it that Trey Harbor is the Chief? What shitty luck.

I wait a few seconds to pull out of my parking spot and follow Hailey. I'm angry she's still here, stirring up trouble. If she left like she'd planned, I wouldn't have to watch her. And if she would simply leave well enough alone, I wouldn't have to kill her.

But here we are. I'm waiting for the right moment to do what needs to be done. Most people wouldn't be this driven. Most people won't do the dirty work. They would rather wither away than fight against an enemy coming to take what is rightfully theirs. They would rather die than shed blood. Not me. I've spent my life shedding the blood of my enemies.

At first it was daunting, doing things that are against your instincts. Yet, the more I did it, the easier it became. And now it's in my nature to do what most people won't.

Even Morgan Gallagher wasn't my first victim, though no one even knows I'm the one who killed her. Nor do they know of the other bodies I so cleverly disposed of. People would be shocked to know my secret life; the life of a manipulator, a liar.

A murderer.

The Beast that lurks within doesn't come out often, only when it needs to be satisfied. Only when someone must be silenced. The Beast has become innate to me, working alongside my instincts, so quietly that no one even knows it's lurking just under the surface.

Sometimes even I forget The Beast is there.

And then it hungers for bloodshed, and it must be released.

It must be fed.

It must be satisfied.

And it wants Hailey. Maybe even Sara.

Hell, the cowboy may serve a purpose too.

But Hailey and Sara will have to wait.

The Beast has decided that it's Elijah Washington's time to die.

Chapter 20

June 28, 2011
5:21 pm

"Ice cream sounds really good right about now," Sara said.

Hailey shook her head, "After everything that just happened, you want ice cream? I still can't believe you talked to Dad. The last thing we need is for him to get involved. And thanks to you, he's going to make it so much more difficult for us to open Mom's case."

"I'm fully aware of the situation, Hailey. I'm just done letting him control everything I do. And plus, I haven't had ice cream in thirteen years."

Despite being angry at Sara, Hailey had to admit ice cream sounded like a nice treat on such a hot day. The storm had since passed and the sun was now shining bright, drying up the water that had poured out of the sky.

Hailey took a right and drove back past the park toward a little ice cream shop that had been a favorite spot for them as teenagers. Shocked that it was still standing, Hailey found herself reminiscing.

The restaurant was a quaint, mom-and-pop shop that served savory foods but was famous for their sweet treats. It was an outdoor eatery with tables lined under a pavilion. They walked up to the window, ordered their snack and sat at one of the tables.

The sound of cars passing by filled the silence as they waited for their order, not knowing what to say to each other. It was clear they were at odds, though Hailey didn't understand why. After they had connected about their battle wounds, she believed they had patched things up. Well, maybe not entirely, but enough to start mending their broken relationship.

Hailey was trying to help her sister, but all Sara seemed to want to do was fight and argue. She had known it would take a lot of work to fix the relationship, but it wouldn't go anywhere if Sara was constantly destroying what little progress they made.

"Why are you trying so hard to get back at me? I'm trying to help you, and you keep throwing it in my face. I thought I could trust you with my secret and all you've done is try to manipulate me into telling Trey."

Sara leaned in close to Hailey's face, her voice just above a whisper, "Despite what you might think, I was actually trying to help you."

Hailey balked. "Ugh! Don't act so self-righteous. We all know ninety percent of what you do is for your own selfish gain."

An employee from the shop called out their order and they both collected their ice cream and sat back down.

Sara sighed. "Look, I've seen the way you and Trey look at each other, it makes me want to puke." She waved away a bee and continued. "I've lived the consequences of people keeping secrets. All you would have done was ruin the second chance you have with him. If you're comfortable keeping a secret from someone you love, it's never going to work."

Hailey looked at her ice cream, unsure if she could trust her sister's claims. "Is that what happened with Chase? You kept a secret from him?"

Sara shook her head. "No. I told him the truth."

Hailey tilted her head. "That doesn't really help your pep-talk."

"Whatever, Hailey. It doesn't matter what you say, you know I'm right. Trey knew something happened with Ryan and it would have eaten away at him. And if you refused to tell him, it would have strained your already fragile relationship. You can't trust people who keep secrets from you. Trinity doesn't need parents like that."

Hailey winced. She hadn't expected Sara to be so honed in on her shortcomings.

She nodded. "You're right. I'm sorry for accusing you of being selfish."

Sara lifted a shoulder. "Well, I am selfish about ninety percent of the time."

"Like that stunt with Dad? You don't think you should have warned us?" Hailey said.

"I'm done cowering in a corner. I'm not a little girl anymore and I want him to pay for what he did to me."

Hailey shook her head. "Well, pulling the lion's tail isn't all that smart. We both know we have to figure out how to play his game better than him. All you did was piss him off more than he was before."

"Good. People slip up when they're pissed, which is why I did it," Sara replied.

That much was true. And David was already starting to get nervous. He wouldn't have called to threaten them if he wasn't concerned about them poking around. Hailey wondered if there was any truth to Sara's claims that he was involved with Morgan's death. It certainly looked that way. "Just promise me you'll stay away from Dad and let Trey handle him," Hailey said.

Sara scowled. "Not a chance."

"Sara, let Trey handle it. You're going to get one of us hurt."

"Do you not understand that I *have* to do this?" Sara leaned in toward Hailey and pointed to herself. "I need to prove to myself that he can't control me anymore."

Hailey furrowed her brows. "You don't need to prove anything-"

"You don't get it!" Sara snapped. "I used to think I could take on the world. Even though I was terrified of Dad, I refused to let him dwindle my fire." She looked away. "Now I don't even have a spark left, thanks to him. It's pathetic. The part of me that was so wild and free, he took that from me. So yeah, I do have something to prove. He needs to know my fire isn't gone." She sighed and shook her head. "And I need to find that part of me again, the part of me that was resilient and that couldn't be tamed."

Hailey was surprised by Sara's words. Even when they were kids, Hailey always saw her sister as the strong and tenacious one. She was confident and fearless, always going after what she wanted. She refused to let anyone bully her or boss her around. It was clear those parts of her were still there.

But Sara didn't see herself the way Hailey did. Hailey knew her sister was still strong and resilient, probably more so now. She may be a little rigid, but then she had always had a chip on her shoulder about one thing or another.

"You haven't lost that fire," Hailey said.

"Don't do that. Don't patronize me."

"I'm not." Hailey leaned in closer to Sara. "You're still strong and fearless. You still refuse to take shit from anyone. You're a survivor. You lived through thirteen years of prison, not to mention what you went through at home before any of this happened. You're more ready to take on the world than you ever were before."

Sara sighed. "Then why do I feel so defeated?"

"Because it's exhausting trying to keep a fire going when you've hardly got a spark."

Sara paused, and then said, "What if this is all for nothing?"

Hailey shrugged. "Then we'll figure it out. But you're not alone anymore, Sara. You just have to learn to trust me."

Hailey stuck her pinky up in the air and Sara laughed. "Are you serious? A pinky-promise?"

Hailey chuckled. "It worked when we were kids."

"Yeah, because we were both sneaking out and had dirt on each other."

"Still, I mean it. I've got your back." Hailey said.

Sara smiled and shook her head as she looped her finger around Hailey's. "Then I guess I've got yours."

Music blasted over the speakers and conversation filled the room as glasses clinked together, the familiar anthem of the run-down bar. A man who sat in a booth tucked away in the corner eyed Trey as he walked inside, curious as to what the cop was doing there.

Trey nodded to him, but the man ignored him.

Trey sat next to Ryan at the bar top and the bartender came to take his order. "I'm on duty so just a Coke for me."

She smiled and left. Ryan glared at Trey. "Surprised to see I'm not behind bars?" His lip was still slightly swollen, and the black eye was now a bluish-purple shade and fading.

"I'm not here looking for trouble, even though you're full of it."

The girl brought Trey his drink and he took a sip.

"What do you want, Harbor? Is Hailey being a little pest and you want me to take her off your hands?"

It took every ounce of self-control Trey had not to grab Ryan by his collar and beat the life out of him. He took a deep breath to slow his racing pulse.

Ryan smiled, knowing he got under Trey's skin.

"It's about Nicole," Trey said.

Ryan took a swig of his whiskey and slammed it down. He yelled at the bartender, "I'm empty."

She looked uncomfortable as she came to fill his glass again, her eyes darting from Ryan to Trey. He cat-called her and she hurried away.

"I told that other cop I haven't seen her."

"That's interesting since it's your mother we're talking about."

Ryan chuckled. "Not everyone likes their parents."

"You would know."

Ryan whipped his head to look at Trey. "What's that supposed to mean?"

Trey waved him off. "Maybe not everyone does, but I heard you were on good terms with her. Is that true?"

Ryan shook his head and took a drink. "No."

Treys' curiosity piqued. "Why?"

"Why would I tell you?"

Again, Trey ignored Ryan's questions. "What do you know about Morgan Gallagher?"

Ryan clenched his fist. "Nothing."

"We both know that's a lie." Trey sighed. "Nicole is missing, and we have evidence to suggest Sara didn't kill Morgan."

Confused, Ryan said, "And? What's that got to do with me?"

"I want to know what you know about your father. We know it's David."

Ryan flinched and Trey took another drink as Ryan did. Ryan nursed his whiskey, studying the precipitation on the glass. "I aint got nothin' to say."

"You tried to kill Hailey just to get back at your old man for abandoning you." Trey shrugged. "A therapist would say that's some serious daddy issues."

Ryan narrowed his eyes. "You little-"

"Call me whatever name you want, but right now our interests align: to spill David's secrets to the world. You want revenge and I need to figure out what he's hiding. We both know he's not lily white in your mother's disappearance or his late wife's death."

Ryan thought over what Trey said. "What makes you think I know anything?"

"A little birdie told me."

Ryan eyed him suspiciously, but Trey wasn't going to give away his sources. Both Lauren and Genevieve could be in danger if Ryan decided he wanted revenge for their willingness to talk.

"All I want to know," Trey continued, "is any dirt you've got on David and the names of anyone who may have had it out for your mother or even Morgan."

The bartender came by again to fill Ryan's empty glass and cast a worried glance toward him. Trey would bet Ryan either threatened or harassed the girl when he had one too many.

Ryan looked at Trey. "What's in it for me?"

"Knowing you got to stick it to David if the info you tell me pans out. Plus, you may be able to help us find your mother. That seems like more than enough for a piece of shit like you."

Ryan chuckled and took a gulp. "You're funny." He sighed. "I'll tell you what I know, but I want you to make sure I get an exclusive with every reporter in the city. I want everyone to see David for what he is."

Trey nodded. "Deal, but not until after my investigation is done."

Ryan clenched his jaw but didn't put up a fight. "I found out David was my father when I was ten. My mother let it slip one night and told me how he didn't want us, how he refused to leave Morgan. I was curious about him, so when I got older, I confronted him. He flipped his shit and told me to never contact him again and that he wanted nothing to do with me." He lifted a brow and smiled. "Dad of the year."

"What about Morgan?"

"I don't know who I hated more: her or my father. He wanted nothing to do with me because of her. As a kid I would listen to my mother cry herself to sleep at night, empty bottles of booze left all over the house while random naked men scavenged through our empty fridge at three in the morning, using her like the trash she is."

Ryan threw back another glass of the brown liquid, slamming it down with a thud. Trey thought it might shatter.

"Everyone loved Morgan. They swooned over her, and people thought she was all sunshine and rainbows when she was really a wolf in sheep's clothing, just like David. But no one was allowed to know our secret, or my mother wouldn't get a dime."

Trey prompted him. "What about the girls? They didn't even know."

"Oh, spare me the victim card. Hailey and Sara sat up in their mansion, looking down their nose at the rest of us, even you. We struggled to eat while Sara and Hailey didn't have to want for anything. It's disgusting."

Trey had a lot of questions but held his tongue. Ryan was finally talking, and Trey didn't want him to stop. He hadn't understood the degree in which Ryan's disdain stemmed. Even in the way he said their names permeated hatred and resentment.

"Shortly before I turned eighteen, I started blackmailing them. I told David and Morgan I'd go public with a paternity test if they didn't give me money whenever I needed it and get me out of trouble whenever I called. At the time, it seemed like the best way to get what I wanted."

"Can't imagine that went over well with David."

"Such great detective skills," he said as he rolled his eyes. "He threatened me, but he didn't realize I had proof he'd been seeing my mother again, so he shut his mouth pretty quick and did what I said."

Trey wasn't shocked to hear that David had been seeing Nicole again. He'd assumed as much.

"Did he stop seeing Nicole after that?"

Ryan shrugged. Trey wanted to keep him talking. "Are you still blackmailing him?"

"You tell me. I'm not in jail right now for assault and battery against a cop." He smiled as he recalled their tussle.

Trey ignored the comment. "What else do you know about David?"

"Not much else. Morgan hated me and my mother, and she made it obvious. But my mother hated her just as much, if not more, so it was always a pissing match if we ran into each other."

Trey nodded. Could Nicole have killed Morgan? It didn't explain why she was missing now, but it was plausible, though he had no evidence to support that theory. And as much as he didn't like coincidences, they still existed.

"Aside from Morgan, did your mother have any enemies? Had she gotten into trouble recently?"

Ryan didn't answer at first as he considered Trey's question. "Not really. Everyone liked her. I heard a rumor that she got into it with some lady at work in the parking lot, but I didn't care enough to get details."

Could be something. Could be nothing.

It wasn't much to go on, but Trey wanted to run down the lead with other employees and see if the restaurant had cameras to help identify the lady.

"And what about you? Did you hate her enough to hurt her?"

Ryan laughed. "She was a mediocre mother at best. I think she secretly hated me. If I hadn't come along, she probably could have kept seeing David. But I ruined that for her."

If Ryan wasn't so deplorable, Trey might actually feel sorry for him.

Ryan threw down some cash on the counter and whistled at the bartender. "One of these days, Rita." He winked at her and she visibly tensed. Trey made a mental note to speak to the owner about getting a bouncer to keep the bartenders safe.

Trey laid down his cash as well and followed Ryan out the back door. Trey welcomed the fresh air. The stench of cigarettes and alcohol was bringing on a headache.

Before Ryan walked away, Trey asked, "Did you have anything to do with your mother's disappearance?"

Ryan turned around. "No. But I wish I would have."

The hair on Trey's nape stood upright. Ryan was a creep.

Trey had one last question, "Where were you the night Morgan Gallagher was killed?"

Ryan grinned ear to ear. "I was with our little Princess."

Flashes of Ryan hurting Hailey raced through Trey's mind. Rage filled him as he envisioned her screams, body bleeding at the hands of the man who stood in front of him. He could have lost Trinity.

He looked around and saw they were alone. He pulled his fist back and connected with Ryan's jaw. Blood spattered all over Trey but he didn't care. Ryan was startled, but then quickly threw a punch at Trey. This time, Trey was ready, and he ducked. He knocked Ryan in the stomach and brought him to his knees. He smacked Ryan, Ryan's head lopping to the side as blood dripped from his lip.

"That was for Hailey," Trey hissed as he wiped Ryan's blood from his hands.

Ryan's breathing was labored as he sat hunched over, blood dripping to the ground. "Like I said, you've gone soft. You better keep your word and kill me, because I'm coming for your whole family."

Trey grabbed Ryan by the collar and slammed him into the brick building. Ryan let out a huff of air and Trey got inches from his face. "This is my only warning, Ryan. I will kill you if you hurt my family again. Right now, you're not worth my time. I have too much to live for. Which is more than I can say for you."

Trey shoved him away and Ryan fell into a heap on the sidewalk. Trey walked away and climbed into his truck.

His gaze never left Ryan as Ryan stood and spat blood onto the concrete. He glanced at Trey and smiled as he climbed into his red pickup truck, waving at Trey as he did.

Chapter 21

Sara studied Gavin as they all sat around Genevieve's table playing UNO. Hailey was losing while Gavin and Carter cheated their way to each only having two cards. Sara held a single card, causing the tension in the room to heighten.

Genevieve was in the kitchen baking cookies while her husband, Carl, watched football in the living room. Every time the four of them shouted in triumph or defeat, Carl would tell them to keep it down and then would laugh at their groans.

Trinity and Cecilia had eaten and darted back up the stairs to Cecilia's room, snickering as they gossiped and told secrets. Sara ached to be young again, to redo her life.

She hadn't yet gotten into drugs when she was Trinity's age. She had been boy crazy, but she was still innocent. She hoped her niece didn't give into peer pressure like Sara had.

Pulling her from her thoughts, Gavin laid down his card and called out, "Uno!"

Then, Sara slammed hers down with a sly smile, winning the game. "Sucks to suck."

"I thought we were working together?" Gavin exclaimed.

Sara laughed. "No, you and Carter were *cheating* together."

He gasped and placed a hand over his heart. "I would never do such a thing."

"You totally would," Hailey said as she pointed at Gavin.

"Don't throw me under the bus," Gavin said.

Sara hadn't laughed this much in a long time.

When Gavin had called, she had found herself pleasantly surprised to hear his voice. Sara hadn't expected him to actually go out of his way to get her number, something she secretly found endearing. And her twin clearly wanted to play matchmaker since she was the one who had given Gavin her number. Hailey claimed Sara needed to live a little. Maybe she was right.

Sara was so focused on the past that she hadn't given herself permission to live in the present. She was allowing her need for revenge to consume her, and she was uneasy with the person she found herself becoming. Though she wasn't ready to lay down the torch completely, she would let the fire dwindle a bit and she would try to have fun while it lasted. Something she used to do often as a teenager.

Maybe she would find a piece of herself she'd long since lost.

At first, she had been nervous to be around Gavin again. And, sensing her pause, he had offered a night of card games with Hailey and Carter; even Trey if he'd actually show up. She just wasn't sure what to make of his flirting and boldness. It confused her how he could be so straightforward yet gentle.

Despite her reservations about the man, she couldn't deny how much she liked the attention he gave her. It made her feel like herself again, the Sara she had been before her life was flipped upside down.

There was a light tap on the back door and Trey poked his head in. "Gen, can I come in?"

Genevieve came out of the kitchen. "You know you never have to knock, Honey. Just let yourself in. And you're just in time for cookies, too." She winked.

Trey came through the door and scanned the room, his gaze falling on Hailey. Jealousy colored his eyes as he spied Gavin.

Sara inwardly rolled her eyes. Men were so predictable.

Sensing the tension, Gavin stood and greeted Trey with a handshake while Carter pulled up an empty chair and sat it next to Hailey. Trey paused for a split second and Sara thought he might sit down and pout. But instead, he shook Gavin and Carter's hands. A silent peace offering.

Before he sat down, he leaned in to give Hailey a kiss on her head. Then, he sat next to her, and she took his hand.

"Who won?" he asked.

Gavin eyed Sara. "The traitor."

She lifted a brow. "I'm no such thing." She smiled widely. "But I *am* a winner."

Genevieve called for Trinity and Cecilia, "Girls, come get some cookies!"

Seconds later, thumping filled the staircase as they trotted down. The two giggled uncontrollably, sharing a knowing glance between them. It reminded Sara of all the inside jokes she and Hailey had growing up. How they could share one glance and know what the other was thinking.

That had changed when Sara got into trouble, though. Her drug use had only worsened the more she hung out with Thomas and his group of friends. Then she had started lying and manipulating everyone, mostly just for fun.

Just like her father. That thought turned her stomach.

Eventually, Hailey would become distant, putting up her own walls to keep Sara's chaos out. Unfortunately for Hailey, Sara had still somehow managed to seep into the cracks and break them down piece by piece.

As much as Sara wanted to blame David or Thomas for her misfortune, she was really the one at fault. She chose drugs and alcohol and a rebellious lifestyle to retaliate against her father and it completely backfired, disastrously so.

But somehow, she'd gotten a second chance to rebuild the life she'd so utterly destroyed, and she wouldn't take that for granted. She didn't want to be selfish and self-centered anymore. Living like that had caused so much heartache. She wanted to love herself enough to say no to things that could hurt her, even if she desperately wanted them. Even now, she knew Gavin was too good for her and she'd be damned if she tainted yet another person with her destruction. She liked Gavin, but she would say no to his advances if she thought it would end in chaos and heartache.

And though she wanted to be a better person, she wasn't so sure that person could even exist right now. Not until David got what he deserved. Not until she made everyone pay for what they did to her.

Coming into the room, Trinity said, "Hey, Dad," She walked over and wrapped Trey in a hug.

"What's up, Kid?"

"I'm not a kid," she said matter-of-factly.

Trey put his hands up and she giggled as she ran off with Cecilia.

"So how did your talk with Ryan go?" Hailey asked Trey.

Trey eyed Gavin and Carter and then looked at Sara.

"They know what's going on," Sara said. She didn't share every detail, but they knew the basics. She needed people in her corner and her instincts told her both of the men could be trusted.

Trey took a cookie from the dish that Genevieve put in the middle of the table. "He said he blackmailed your parents for money and wanted David to bail him out of trouble whenever he needed the help."

"Like father, like son," Sara said.

Trey nodded. "He told them he would go public with a paternity test, but I think him having proof that David and Nicole were seeing each other again was probably the driving factor behind David complying."

Grabbing a cookie himself, Carter said, "Whoa, back up. Why would he care about a paternity test?'

"My father had a long-term affair with Ryan's mother," Sara explained. "Ryan was the very unfortunate result of that affair, and my mother told my father she would leave him if he didn't break things off."

"Sounds like a bad soap opera," Carter said.

"You have no idea," Sara said as she recalled the terror of that house.

It truly had gotten worse the older she got. As a child, she saw very little of David. But when she became a teenager, his expectations were more than Sara cared to achieve, so she stopped trying. And when she didn't bend to his rules and commands...well, she was hated by her own father. She was his constant reminder that he didn't have complete control and he loathed her for it.

"So was he still seeing Nicole when my mother was killed?" Hailey asked.

Trey shrugged. "He wasn't sure...or just didn't want to say. Again, I'm taking everything he said with a grain of salt until I can confirm what he told me. But at least it's a starting point."

"Did he say anything else?" Sara asked.

"Not really. I could tell he hates your whole family which could make him a suspect."

"*Could*?" Gavin said.

Trey sighed and eyed Hailey. "He kind of has an alibi."

Her eyes rounded. "Me?"

Gavin and Carter looked at Hailey curiously. Though Sara wanted to clue them in, it wasn't her story to tell. She had learned her lesson earlier. Her sister was clearly traumatized from the incident and Sara understood that feeling more than anyone. She wouldn't betray her again like she had with Trey, even if it had been for Hailey's own good.

Trey nodded. "He said he was with you when your mother was killed."

"I thought he hated you?" Carter said. "Why would he be with you?"

Hailey looked at the table and inhaled. "Long story short, the night my mother died, my car broke down and Ryan saw I was alone. He attacked me and nearly beat me to death."

Trey clenched a fist instinctively.

Gavin's eyes round. "I had no idea."

Hailey shrugged. "I've tried my best to keep it a secret."

"That's rough shit. I'm sorry," Carter said. Hailey simply nodded.

Sara wanted to kill Ryan, but she didn't think that would be a good idea seeing as how she was trying to prove she *wasn't* a murderer, though the night was still young. However, it looked like Trey might have beaten her to it. She didn't notice the blood on his knuckles until now, which hadn't been there earlier. She hoped Trey got Ryan good.

"But he wasn't with me when my mother died," Hailey said quickly. "Her time of death was 10:42 pm and Ryan found me around 9:45 pm. I remember the time because I was planning to walk home, and it was almost past curfew."

"How did no one see you being attacked?" Carter asked.

"I ran into the orange groves across the street to hide. If anyone drove past, they probably would have assumed it was just two broken-down cars parked on the side of the road."

Sara scrunched her brow. "So, Ryan wasn't with you when Mom died?"

Hailey shook her head. "No. My car broke down around 9:35 pm and Ryan got to me around 9:45 pm. The whole thing wasn't long, maybe ten minutes, so he would have left around 10:15 pm at the latest. Mom died around 10:40 pm."

Sara hadn't even considered Ryan as a suspect. But he definitely had motive and opportunity since, according to their father, no one was home with Morgan when she was killed. Except Sara, he claimed. She always thought it was peculiar that he had that knowledge since he said he wasn't home either.

"What do you think, Trey?" Gavin asked.

Trey didn't answer immediately. When he did, he said, "I think we have reason to suspect him, but I'm not completely sure. He's really erratic and that makes it hard for me to know what's true and what's a lie."

No surprise there.

"What if he had help?" Carter asked.

The room fell silent as everyone turned to Carter. He said, "What if David helped him? Or maybe even his mother? It could explain another link between the two cases."

Trey tilted his head, thinking, and then said, "It's worth looking into."

Sara rubbed her temples, feeling a headache coming on. Gavin reached out and took her hand. Her internal alarm shrieked, and she quickly pulled away, embarrassed. Again, Gavin wasn't bothered by her reservations.

"What now?" Gavin asked.

Trey looked at Sara. "I called your friends that were with you that night but could only get a hold of Thomas. I want to see if they saw anything when they dropped you off and why none of them came forward when you were arrested."

She picked at a spot on the table. "What did he say?"

"He agreed to talk with us tomorrow afternoon."

Sara wanted to vomit. She wasn't sure she could even look at Thomas again. Though she had been sober for the last thirteen years, she didn't know if she could keep her demons at bay if she saw him again.

But she would go.

Because there was a killer lurking in the shadows.

And she needed to find him before he found her.

Sara was tense as they headed to Thomas Smith's house. All of them were eager to talk to the man who may hold the answers they were looking for.

"Do you think Thomas has anything that could help?" Sara said from the back seat.

"I think he's a good start. Donna moved out of state and I couldn't get Jake to return my phone calls so Thomas is who we're talking to first." Trey paused as he switched lanes on the highway. "I also want to know why he was never a witness at the trial."

"I'll be surprised if he remembers anything from that night. He was far worse an addict than I was."

Carter said, "Since he's gone to rehab and is sober, maybe he wants to get something off his chest. You know, the twelve steps or whatever."

Sara didn't say anything else. Her mother taught her what every mother taught their children: if you don't have something nice to say, don't say anything at all. Problem was, Sara never listened to that advice. This would be a rare occasion when she did.

She just didn't believe Thomas was actually sober, despite what he had told Trey when Trey spoke to him last night. Apparently he was married with a kid, which was even more bizarre. He always seemed too much of a free spirit to settle down. Not to mention he didn't know how to be faithful to save his life.

She began tapping her foot the closer they got to his house, a nervous gesture she'd gotten from her addiction. Would she be pulled back into that life when she saw Thomas again? Would he be able to help her?

Sara heard the sirens before she saw the flashing lights coming behind them. She silently gasped for air and steadied herself against the window. She took deep breaths in and out. Though logically she knew the sirens weren't for her, her body recalled the distress she'd been in as the police hauled her away, screaming for her father to help her, only for him to ignore her pleas.

Trey directed his truck into the other lane, making space for the police cruiser to pass them. Traffic was slow and now she knew why. There was likely an accident up ahead, making their hour drive just a little longer.

Once at Thomas' house, the five of them walked up the driveway and knocked. A 'welcome' wreath hung on the door, a nod to Mrs. Thomas Smith. A little pink tricycle was parked in the yard.

According to Trey, Thomas had gotten clean when his parents sent him to rehab. Sara was curious how that happened because his family hardly had two nickels to rub together. After getting clean, he started working at that same facility for some time, which is where he met his wife.

By all accounts, Thomas seemed to be thriving.

And Sara wanted to scream at the unfairness of it all. She should be the one thriving but instead, she jumps at the sound of police sirens and can never seem to relax because she's too paranoid.

Thomas opened the door and greeted them and Sara took in a sharp breath. He looked the same, but healthier now. Older too. He had gained a little weight and was clean shaven, wearing a button down and trousers with a tie. If you didn't know about his past, you would never guess he used to be into the drug scene.

"Do you mind if we talk out here?" Thomas asked.

Trey nodded and Thomas closed the door behind him. Hailey and Sara stood behind Trey, and Gavin and Carter stood behind them.

He took in the five of them, uneasy. Then his eyes met Sara's. "Hi, Sara."

"Hi," she said, shifting a bit. Her legs felt unsteady, but Gavin put an arm around her waist. She wanted to protest, to pull away from him, but she found she couldn't. She wasn't certain she could stand without him, something she wasn't sure if she loved or hated.

"Thanks for talking to us," Trey said. "There's a lot that doesn't make sense and people either don't know anything or aren't willing to tell us what they do know."

Thomas ran a hand through his hair as he picked at his arm. Like Sara, it was a tick from his drug use, no doubt. He said, "I figured it's the least I can do."

He looked back to Sara and gave a soft smile. It was clear he felt guilty about what had happened that night. Not that Sara cared about his feelings. She hoped the guilt ate him alive.

"Why don't you start by telling me what you remember," Trey said.

Thomas shook his head. "Not much. I was pretty drunk and high. I definitely shouldn't have been driving. I remember Sara coming to my house with Donna earlier." He looked at Sara. "You were really upset about Chase. We all started drinking and doing coke and other drugs."

Thomas looked around to make sure no one was around to hear him. "At some point we went to the corner store and then I took Sara home. I don't remember a lot of details, just flashes of memories. Like when Donna was videotaping or when the clerk came out and said something to us."

"What happened next?"

Thomas thought for a moment. "We, uh...we ended up taking Sara home, but I don't remember why because we were going to go back to my house again."

"I was pretty hysterical while we were at the store. I wouldn't stop crying so I'm assuming you just didn't want to deal with it," Sara said, her cheeks flush.

Thomas nodded but didn't say anything, not wanting to further embarrass her.

This time, she was thankful for his silence.

Gavin had tightened his grip on her waist slightly, signaling he was there to protect her, though she wasn't sure what he thought she needed protection from. Sara simply wanted to crawl in a hole, so she pulled away from his grasp.

"When did you leave the corner store?" Trey asked. "The video tape cut off at 10:45 pm, about the time Morgan was killed."

Thomas closed his eyes and thought for a moment, "I think..." He sighed heavily. "I don't know, man. I wish I could tell you. I don't think we were at the store that much longer after the clerk came out and told us to leave.

"I took Sara home and was being a jerk to her." He eyed Sara who looked at the ground. "I kept telling her to get out, but she was too incapacitated. I parked near the side of the house and got out to open the door for her because she was fumbling with the door handle.

"She literally fell out of the car. She tried to get up but kept falling...she was in really bad shape. Then she threw up all over herself and passed out in the grass. I was over it at that point so I left. Donna and Jake were pissed, but we were all too inebriated to think straight."

Hearing Thomas' recollection brought back flashes of memories for Sara. She remembered the drive home and fumbling for the door handle. She thought she remembered someone dragging her into the house but wasn't sure.

This time Hailey spoke up, "Did you see anyone at the house when you dropped her off? See anything suspicious?"

"No, but I was too messed up to pay much attention. I dropped her off and left. I didn't hear about Mrs. Gallagher until a few days later. After that, I got out of town and my family put me in rehab and I've been clean ever since."

No one said anything for a few moments. Trey was trying to piece together the information and Hailey's eyes were daggers as she glared at Thomas. Even Carter seemed to straighten a bit after hearing what Thomas had done.

Sara couldn't help but be angry with her friends for not coming to her aid. But, if Sara was honest with herself, it was no one's fault but her own. If she hadn't been an alcoholic and drug addict, if she hadn't been so selfish and self-centered, if she hadn't felt the need to rebel against her father, then maybe she wouldn't be in this mess.

But here she was, and nothing could change it.

"Just one last question and then we'll be out of your way," Trey said. "Why weren't you a witness at the trial? Why weren't any of you witnesses?"

Thomas started looking around and fidgeting with his tie. He ran a hand through his hair nervously. "I, uh...I don't know."

Sara closed the space between them and jutted up her chin at him. "You dumped me in my yard and never checked on me again. I'm tired of being called a murderer when you know damn well I didn't kill my mother. So, whatever you're hiding, spill it. I'm done suffering because you're a coward. I lost thirteen years of my life because of *your* secrecy."

Thomas paled slightly and stilled. He didn't speak at first, just searched Sara's eyes. Then, he hung his head. "I was paid not to say anything and to disappear. So was everyone else. I had been wanting to get clean for a long time, but never had the resources. That deal made it possible for me."

"Who paid you off?" Sara asked.

He hesitated before saying, "Your father."

Sara felt dizzy and her lungs constricted. She started pacing as she gasped for air and clawed at her throat, wondering if she might die right in Thomas' yard.

"Get her some water!" Carter yelled to Thomas.

Hailey was quickly by her side. "Sara, breathe."

Gavin took her by the hand and had her sit down in a lawn chair that was in the yard. "Put your head between your knees and breathe with me."

Once she calmed herself, she squared her shoulders as if nothing happened. Thomas came out of the house holding a glass of water. He offered it to her, and she accepted the drink.

Sara always believed she had been set up, but because she lacked proof, she never told anyone. Plus, the first year of her sentence was filled with tremors, cold sweats, fevers, and hallucinations as she detoxed from the drugs and alcohol. At the time, she wasn't sure if she could even trust herself to know the truth.

But she had been right. And it was her father who had done it.

It grieved her to *think* David could be so vindictive, but to have confirmation of his hatred...that brought on wounds she'd never felt before. Wounds that cut deeper than the physical ones he'd left on her body as a teenager.

Sara's head was swimming as she tried to make sense of it all. Hailey hadn't left her side, clutching Sara's hand.

"What did David say to you?" Gavin asked as he took a step toward Thomas. Sara could see the vein that bulged at his temple.

Thomas' eyes rounded. "He said if I didn't leave town and accept his demands, then he would have Chief Washington arrest me for drunk driving, drugs, serving alcohol to minors...I'd be put away for life! So, I could keep my mouth shut and have freedom, or I could tell what I knew and spend the rest of my life in prison."

He shrugged and looked away. "I didn't actually think it would go to trial, so I took the money and got clean. I've never had any reason to go back or to open my mouth."

The idea that his hands were somehow clean of this mess was infuriating. Sara hurled the glass cup at Thomas. It shattered at his feet and his eyes darted between Sara and Trey, begging the Chief to step in. Gavin stood in front of her and put an arm around her waist, a wall between her and Thomas. Hailey walked toward Thomas, but Carter gently put a hand on her shoulder as Trey tried to defuse the situation, "Let's all take a break-"

"Me being convicted of murder wasn't enough to convince you to come forward?" Sara sneered as she fought Gavin off of her.

Thomas put his hands up in defense and took a step back, almost tripping over a toy that lay on the porch. "You pleaded guilty. I didn't want to mess up my life."

"Right, you were just okay destroying mine." She shook her head and started to walk toward the car but then turned around. "You know what? I'm only in this mess because of you. Drugs and alcohol weren't even on my radar until *you* introduced me to them. You might be able to run from your past and act like nothing happened, but I'm still paying for *your* sins. So, during your next session with your little recovering addicts, why don't you tell them about the girl whose life you completely ruined because you're a selfish prick."

She couldn't stand to look at him after knowing what he had done to her. Despite him being an ass, she never thought he would stoop so low as to do something that would send her away to prison. His betrayal stung and added to the growing number of lashes she'd gotten from those who claimed to care for her.

It was clear no one could be trusted. They were all hiding something, trying to keep their secrets buried. All while she paid the price for their silence.

So, she would make it her life's work to unveil those secrets, and she would burn down the whole damn world if she had to in order to do it.

Trey, Gavin, Hailey, and Carter followed Sara to the car, Sara seething with every step. Just before they closed the doors, Thomas called out, "Sara, I'm really sorry. If I could take it back, I would."

Sara let out a throaty laugh. "Well, it's a little late for that now. Don't you think?"

With that, she slammed the door.

Chapter 22

June 29, 2011
2:13 pm

If what Thomas said was true, then Eli knew more than he was saying. And Trey wanted to know what it was. So, armed with fury and determination, Hailey and Trey went to talk to Eli while Gavin stayed with Sara at Genevieve's, hoping to calm her down. Carter had tagged along, trying to convince the housekeeper to bake more cookies.

At first, Trey had fought with Hailey, not wanting her to get involved. But after hearing Thomas' admission, she refused to be sidelined. Plus, Trey knew she would do it on her own if he didn't include her.

"Looks like they're home," Trey said as they pulled up to the house. Both vehicles sat in the driveway, catching the sun's rays.

The two of them climbed out of the truck and walked up to the door and knocked. There was no movement on the other side of the wood barrier, so Trey knocked again.

Silence.

"Maybe they're taking a nap?" Hailey said.

Trey shook his head. "I'm gonna see if they're in the backyard."

Trey walked around the side of the house and through the back gate. When he didn't see them in the yard, he walked up the porch steps and peered inside through the sliding glass door.

That's when he noticed the smoke.

"Shit," he said as he jumped off the porch and ran around to the front of the house. Hailey's hand was already pushing the door open as he yelled, "Hailey, no!"

Before he could stop her, she darted into danger.

He swore under his breath as he quickly went to his truck and dispatched fire and rescue. Then, he ran into the house toward the flames, hearing sirens in the distance.

Once inside, Trey called out for her but was only met with the roar of flames as they fanned up the walls and ceiling. He immediately had to crawl on his hands and knees, the smoke thick and hot. He began coughing so hard he nearly gagged.

He tried to call out for Hailey, but she didn't answer. Neither did Eli nor Loretta. All he heard was the crackling of the fire as it burned toward him.

He rounded the corner and saw a figure, arm raised, a weapon in his hand. Then, Hailey fell to the ground at the assailant's feet. Fear gripping him, Trey tried to move quickly to protect her from the man. But the faster he moved, the more his lungs constricted, and the room spun.

He crouched close to the floor, attempting to get away from the smoke. But there was no point, it was growing and becoming wild. The fire's flames were closing in on them.

Then, the figure raced out the back door. The cop in him wanted to run after the masked man, but he couldn't leave Hailey. So, he let the assailant get away as he picked up her limp body and ran toward safety, pain searing through his lungs as he did.

Please don't be dead. Please don't be dead.

He desperately needed fresh air and water, but his body moved much slower than he wanted it to. He was so thirsty, and his chest burned terribly. He could hardly see as smoke clouded his vision and stung his eyes. He cried out as he pushed through the black cloud, each movement bringing nothing but pain.

The bright summer sun blinded him as he emerged from the darkness. Once in the yard, he dropped to the ground and clung to Hailey as firefighters ran past him and paramedics surrounded them. He called her name, desperation filling his voice. A single tear fell down his cheek as he fought off a paramedic who was trying to help.

"Sir, please. We need to get you both to a hospital."

He thought they may have to restrain him. He was distraught as he fought their hands away. He didn't want anyone else to touch her, despite knowing they wanted to save her. His heart and body wouldn't comply with his brain.

"Hailey, please wake up," Trey's voice cracked as he held her, gently shaking her.

The paramedic moved to take her from him when Hailey began coughing loudly and harshly, unaware of what was going on. Trey held her tight, afraid he would lose her if he let go. He kissed her face and silently cried as she was assessed.

Then he carried her into the ambulance and laid her on the gurney, forgetting about all protocols. "I'm going with her," he demanded.

The EMT opened her mouth to object but decided against it. Trey quietly held Hailey's hand as they began placing wires on her body and IVs in her veins. He gently stroked her hair and whispered, "I'm right here, Princess. I'm not leaving."

And that was a promise he intended to keep.

I swear aloud as I hang up the phone. No one else was supposed to be at Washington's house. It was only supposed to be Eli. Loretta had her book club, but for some reason she was home. The woman walked in as I stabbed Eli, so she met her demise as well.

There had been so much blood.

I don't normally resort to such brutality with my kills, but sometimes The Beast is uncontrollable.

I wanted to stay and savor my handiwork, to touch the redness of the stains and smell the copper scent that lingered in the house. But I couldn't. I had to take care of the mess. So, Ryan doused everything in gasoline and lit a match. I was long gone by then.

But then Hailey showed up. I should have known she would come to see Eli again. Just my effing luck; always sticking her nose where it doesn't belong. So, Ryan bashed her over the head and slipped out the back door, making Trey choose between pursuing the shadowed figure or saving the love of his life.

Anyone with half a brain knew he would save Hailey.

She's quickly becoming a threat. I may have to kill her; not that I'm upset by the thought.

I drive to my lover's home and carefully pull into the garage. I wait until it closes to get out and go inside. Once I'm in the house, I assess myself.

Blood has seeped into my clothes and stained my body, the color bringing me joy. I feel a smile creeping back on my cheeks as I remember their last moments: their screams, the crimson that flowed so effortlessly, the final breath leaving their butchered bodies...my heart leaps.

Unfortunately, Eli knew too much, and I wasn't taking any chances for the old man to croak about all he knew.

Thankfully, my secrets died with him. Just like they died with Nicole.

I step into the shower, removing the soiled clothes as the hot water cascades over me. I exhale as the steam wraps around me. I watch intently as the blood mixes with the water and swirls down the drain. Too bad. I enjoyed it staining my skin, a reminder of what I'm capable of.

Everything I do, everything I've done, is to protect all that I've built and the secrets that I want to keep buried.

And I'll kill anyone who gets in the way of that.

Chapter 23

June 29, 2011
9:32 pm

A car horn rustled Hailey from her sleep. She'd been napping on and off since she left the hospital, but this was the first time she felt strong enough to stay awake.

She squinted against the hall light as she slowly opened her eyes. Though her room was dark, its brightness seeped through the cracked door, pain igniting behind her eyelids.

Ugh. My head.

She peeked through one eye and saw Sara and Trey. Her sister's eyes were sunken in, and her face was drained of color. Trey simply looked like he might have a panic attack, bouncing his leg as he roughly ran his hand through his hair and let out a breath.

Hailey's eyes fluttered open and she smiled. "Bust me out of here, please. Bedrest is no fun." Her voice was hoarse from the smoke and her throat burned when she spoke.

Sara smiled but the concern in her eyes remained. "Not yet. Doctor's orders. They want you to rest for a few days. You're lucky Trey has a great nurse-friend who owed him a favor, or you'd be having to rest at the hospital instead of at Trey's."

Hailey shook her head and quickly stopped when pain rippled through her skull. "Ow! Oh, gosh."

"What's wrong?" Trey took her hand and gripped it tightly. She thought he might break it.

"Relax, my head just hurts." She eyed her hand. "You're going to break my hand if you're not careful."

He let her go. "Sorry, Princess."

Hailey gave a soft smile as she rubbed her temples, wishing her headache would go away.

Gosh, her lungs burned.

Her eyes did too, though not as much.

After a few moments, she quietly asked, "Are they both dead?" She looked down and picked at a loose thread on the blanket that lay across her, terrified of Trey's answer.

Trey said, "Loretta is. Eli is in the ICU right now and it's been touch-and-go."

Hailey sunk back into the pillows even more. She wished this nightmare would end. All she wanted was to find the truth. And clearly, someone else had different plans.

Hailey closed her eyes, trying to recall details of the man who'd been in the house. Nothing came, though. It had been so dark from the smoke and her body was beginning to panic from lack of oxygen. Her senses had been working overtime, but they offered no details about the shadowed figure.

Hailey continued, "I bet I startled him when I ran inside."

Trey bristled and his face contorted in pain. But it was the anger in his eyes Hailey took note of.

He said, "Which you shouldn't have done. How could you be so stupid?"

She turned her head away from him as if she were a teenager getting reprimanded by her parents. She couldn't blame him for being angry, though. What she did *was* stupid. But as much as she hated that he was angry with her, she also knew he was scared.

And truth be told, she was scared too. Someone tried to kill her and would have succeeded if Trey hadn't saved her.

Trinity threw open the door, grabbing everyone's attention. To Hailey's surprise, she was followed by Gavin and Carter.

Hailey smiled at the sight of her daughter. "Hey, Sunshine-"

"Mom, how could you do that? Why would you run into a burning building?!" Trinity yelled as she threw herself into Hailey's arms.

Hailey winced as she pulled herself up to sit. She really didn't have much of an answer, at least none that would suffice her daughter. She looked to Sara who had a brow raised, anxious to hear Hailey's excuse as well.

"I don't know. I just saw the smoke and knew they were inside. It wasn't my brightest moment, but I just wanted to save Mr. and Mrs. Washington."

"Too bad he didn't burn," Sara said as she sat back in her chair, arms crossed over her chest.

Hailey rolled her eyes. "I didn't ask for your opinion."

Hailey knew she shouldn't be too hard on Sara for her feelings toward Eli. After all, the man who claimed to be family had taken away thirteen years of her life.

"Nice to see you two getting along so well," Carter quipped. Trinity giggled, pleased by the man's sarcasm. He gave her a fist bump.

Sara eyed Gavin and Carter. "I see Trey called in reinforcements. Or are y'all just glorified babysitters now?"

Gavin smiled at Sara's remark. "I don't care what I'm doing as long as I get to see you."

Sara blushed and quickly looked away, but not before Hailey noticed.

Trinity spoke up, "Yeah, Dad hired them as security. Kinda cool, if ya ask me. Makes me feel like I'm in a movie."

Trey put his hands up when Hailey shot him a look. "I'm not taking any chances after today."

Trinity peeped up again, "I just think it's funny that Dad asked your ex-boyfriend to keep an eye on *y'all's* kid."

Gavin's eyes rounded in horror and Trey shook his head.

Carter smiled. "The kid has jokes. Trinity: twenty points, Mom and Dad: zero. You two better get it together or she'll be the boss around here."

"You're telling me." Trey said.

Hailey looked at Trinity. "Who told you that?"

Trinity shrugged. "Lauren."

Hailey inwardly groaned. Hadn't Lauren gotten the hint the first time Hailey talked to her about sharing details of Hailey's past?

Trey looked at Trinity. "Listen, Kid, I trust both of these guys." He pointed toward Gavin and Carter. "So, you listen to whatever they tell you, understand? If they tell you to run, you run. No questions asked."

Trinity nodded, sensing the severity of the situation.

"How are you feeling?" Gavin asked Hailey, changing the subject.

She sighed. "I've been better, but I'm doing okay."

Gavin stared at Hailey, his eyes narrowed, and his lips turned down at the corners.

"What is it?" Hailey asked.

"Nothing. It's not my place to say."

"Just say it."

Gavin paused before saying, "What you did was really stupid."

"Thank you, ex-boyfriend!" Trinity said as she threw her arms up in the air.

Carter laughed as Gavin rubbed his face. Sara raised a brow at Trey who shook his head. Hailey simply looked annoyed.

Gavin continued, "You need to be careful. Something is clearly going on, so use your brain and trust your gut. Believe me, my gut has gotten me out of a lot of tough situations. It's usually right, so listen to it."

"He's right, Hailey," Carter added. "I know we just met, but I'd hate to see something happen to you that could have been avoided. Someone is killing people, and you seem to be right in their sights. That's serious."

Trey took her hand, and she looked at him. "Listen, Princess, I know you don't like being told what to do, but you almost died today. You've got to stop being so impulsive. Stop trying to be a hero."

Hailey looked away, eager for everyone to leave the room. She was a grown woman, and she hated that everyone was treating her like a child...even if they were right.

Trinity chimed in with a fierce attitude and a wiggling finger. "Yeah! I know you clearly don't care about dying, but I do. So don't be dumb."

Trey put his hands on Trinity's shoulders. "Whoa, Kid. Cut your mother some slack. She was trying to do the right thing."

Trinity huffed at being scolded.

When everyone fell silent, Trey looked at Gavin and Carter. "Keep a close eye on David. You can't trust anything that comes out of his mouth. Not to mention his track record with putting his hands on his daughters."

Carter lifted a brow but didn't comment, something Hailey was thankful for. Gavin glanced at Sara who looked away.

It was painful to know your father hated you enough to hurt you. It tore through her heart on a level she had no intention of visiting. Hailey would rather ignore it all together.

Trey's phone vibrated and he pulled it out of his pocket. "Chief Harbor."

There was a long pause accompanied by muffled inflections of a voice on the other line. Whatever they were saying was serious and they had Trey's complete attention.

"Are you sure?" he asked.

Another pause.

"Okay, I'll be there in twenty."

He hung up the phone. "That was one of my officers. They found Nicole House's car."

Hailey's eyes widened. "Is she alive?"

Trey shook his head. "I don't know, she wasn't there. I've got to go check it out."

"Now do you think Nicole's disappearance is related to my mother's case?" Sara asked.

Trey sighed. "At first, I wasn't sure, but there's too many coincidences for me to believe they're not connected. It just seems suspicious. Especially because she could potentially have a lot of information that would ruin David."

Gavin asked, "Could they all be in on it?"

Hailey hadn't even considered that. If Morgan was the one standing in the way of Nicole and David being together, it would give both of them motive. And Ryan, well, if he was jealous of the life Hailey and Sara lived, Morgan would be a good target for that rage. Plus, it wasn't out of the realm of possibilities for there to have been a recent tiff between Nicole and one, or both, of the men. Which would explain her disappearance.

Trey clenched his jaw. "I guess we better find out, and fast. Because if I had to guess, Nicole likely isn't the only liability. Which means I'm probably going to find some bodies if I don't figure this out soon."

He kissed Hailey on the lips and then kissed Trinity on the forehead and said his goodbyes.

Gavin and Carter followed Trey out to the living room. It was somehow eerie to know the three of them were discussing a plan that would keep them all safe from this faceless killer. Hailey just hoped they would catch him before he killed again.

Not long after, Hailey fell into a deep sleep, plagued by nightmares of sticky blood, scorching fire, and the dead body of her mother crying for Hailey to help her.

⁂

Sara looked around the bar for Jasmine Johnson. She spied her sitting in the back corner, eyes already trained on Sara. She could tell the woman didn't miss a beat, just like Sara.

Jasmine was stunningly beautiful, her skin a warm golden brown that accentuated her striking amber eyes and curls that highlighted her high cheekbones.

Sara walked toward her, clutching her mother's diaries as she did. Stealing them out of Hailey's car had been easy since she was on bedrest, and everyone was completely focused on her. Not that Sara didn't feel a little bad about that, but it's what needed to be done.

When Sara contacted the reporter a few days ago, Jasmine had requested that Sara bring proof of her father's affair, or she'd never run the story. So, Sara took them from Hailey's car. And now she was here to tell her side of the story and burn her father at the stake.

Jasmine stood and extended her hand. "Hi, Miss. Gallagher."

Sara took her hand. "It's Sara."

The woman nodded. "I've got to say, I was surprised to receive that phone call from you. Why did you call *me*?"

"You're not afraid to get your hands dirty in order to get the truth out. I didn't kill my mother, my father set me up. And now I want revenge. He ruined me so it's time I return the favor."

Jasmine smiled. "So, the princess gets revenge on the king who locked her in the tower. Okay, I like that. So, what's your story and why should I believe a convicted murderer?"

Sara appreciated that Jasmine didn't shy away from speaking her mind. Her bluntness was a breath of fresh air.

Sara said, "If I was guilty, why would I want to bring all of this up again? It would be easier to act like it never happened- for people to naturally forget about it- than it would be for me to lie about my innocence."

Jasmine considered Sara for a moment, then said, "Okay, I'll bite. Give me the summary of what story you're wanting to sell."

Sara sat back. "Everyone loves Mayor Gallagher. But what they don't realize is that he's an abusive narcissist who would beat his wife and daughters, all while claiming to love them as we posed for the cameras. He had me tossed in jail for killing my mother when he knew for a fact I had an alibi. He even paid off the witness so there would be no proof. And, to top it off, he had a years-long affair that resulted in a baby."

Jasmine raised a brow and took a sip of her margarita as Sara began flipping through the pages of one of the diaries. If she hadn't learned how to be so detached from her emotions, she may have burst into tears at the sight of her mother's handwriting.

Instead, she pointed to the entry that detailed the affair and the pregnancy.

Jasmine pointed to the book. "May I?"

Sara nodded and Jasmine picked it up and began reading. "Shit. Do you know who the son is?"

"Ryan House." Sara smiled slyly.

Jasmine's eyes widened. "The son of the missing woman?"

"One and the same."

"Sounds like I might have just found myself in the middle of a crime piece," Jasmine said as she sat back and smirked.

"Sounds like it."

Sara's phone buzzed and her breath caught in her throat when Gavin's name popped up on her screen. She knew it wouldn't be long before he called to check on her. She had left abruptly, and he had been curious about her secrecy, but didn't press her.

Thankfully he gave her space when she needed it, but he had already been suspicious when she left. Plus, they were all walking on eggshells since Hailey had been hurt.

She ignored the call but knew she had to cut the meeting short. "Look, I gotta go. Is this enough proof for you to run a story?"

"A beloved Mayor who's actually a monster? The public will eat it up. But I have to have more proof to run anything other than the affair or I can be sued for defamation. Get me something irrefutable and I'll greenlight it. For now, the story of the affair will run in about a week or two, maybe sooner."

Sara nodded. "Thanks. I'll be in touch."

Sara ducked out of the bar and made her way back to Angie's. Now, it was time to watch David Gallagher's kingdom crumble right out from under him.

Chapter 24

Hailey sat on the couch next to Trey. The box that held the case files was small and the reports were even smaller. Dust from the box riddled his coffee table but neither of them cared.

Despite Hailey's invitation, Sara stayed behind to help Genevieve with Trinity, though Hailey figured it had more to do with spending time with Gavin and not being re-traumatized. Truth be told, Hailey hoped something developed between the two of them.

She and Trey had been looking over crime scene photos for nearly thirty minutes, studying each photo carefully. Hailey would look at the image as a whole then she would look from left to right, carefully examining each pixel.

Hailey almost missed the slight change in color of the dirt in the photo, but the light caught it just right. At the time, her father was having their yard relandscaped and there were marks running through the dirt that covered part of the yard.

Hailey showed Trey the photo. "What is this from?"

Trey took the photo from her and looked at it for a few moments. Finally, he raised a brow and said, "They're drag marks. I bet someone dragged your sister inside."

Hailey shook her head and furrowed her brows. "Wait, why would they do that? That doesn't make any sense."

Trey said, "Think about it: your mother is killed, and your sister is passed out in the yard. The killer waits for Thomas to leave and then gets an idea to move her body next to your mother's, making it look like she may have had something to do with it."

"That sounds like the killer is counting on luck and that's a huge liability for someone who just killed a mayor's wife. Plus, they're running a huge risk of her waking up."

Trey nodded. "True, but not if you're someone who can control the narrative."

Hailey knew he was referring to her father. Truthfully, he was looking guiltier by the minute.

"But why wouldn't he carry her? She wasn't that heavy," Hailey asked.

"She vomited when Thomas dropped her off. He probably didn't want the added mess."

Hailey closed her eyes and exhaled. Sara was in the wrong place at the wrong time, and it had altered her entire life. Hailey felt anger surge through her as she pictured her father deliberately setting up his own daughter.

Trey gave her back the photo and picked up the one he had set down. After a moment, he asked, "Were any of you going on vacation when your mother died?"

Hailey tilted her head and furrowed her brows. "No, we were about to head off to college, so she was doing last minute stuff to prepare for that."

"Was your dad going on a business trip or coming back from one?"

Hailey shook her head in confusion. "No. Why?"

Trey slid the photo over to her and pointed to the upper left corner. "There are suitcases sitting near the front door. Why are they out if no one was leaving and no one was returning?"

Hailey studied the photo. "Those are definitely my mother's." After a moment, Hailey's eyes widened. "She was leaving him, Trey."

He nodded. "And your father wouldn't take too kindly to that."

"No, he wouldn't. He would have been humiliated." Hailey's voice trailed off as she realized the likelihood that her father had killed her mother. She had seen first-hand the rage that overtook her father when he was disobeyed or disrespected. She couldn't imagine how he would have reacted to her mother leaving him.

Morgan was finally standing up for herself after being manipulated, lied to, and abused by the man who claimed to love her. And she had died trying. And Sara was framed for it.

Hailey stood and started pacing, grief consuming her. After a moment, she stopped abruptly. "Do you really think he did it?"

"I uh-"

"Please, Trey. I can't keep thinking in circles," she said quietly.

He let out a breath and nodded slowly. "Yes, I think he killed her."

Hailey squeezed her eyes shut. "We have to make sure he never sees the outside of a prison."

Trey stood and wrapped her in an embrace. "Yeah, we do. But we have to find proof first."

"This feels impossible," she groaned.

"I know. Whoever helped investigate didn't do their job. There's hardly any evidence, there's no eye-witness statements, not even from you. It's like they botched the investigation on purpose right along with Eli. And that thought scares me."

Hailey didn't want to believe the police would intentionally ruin a homicide investigation, but she knew better. There were countless stories of police deliberately derailing investigations for one reason or another. It was infuriating. She especially hated that it happened to her sister.

Hailey wanted to scream at the injustice of it all.

She buried her face in Trey's chest, inhaling his scent. She wished time would stop. She felt safe in his arms but knew that tonight the nightmares would come back, and she'd have to face her monsters alone.

Trey kissed her crown. "We're going to figure this out. I'm going to talk to the investigating officers, and I'll likely have Internal Affairs open an investigation. If I.A. finds out they helped cover it up or botched the investigation, it would likely help get this case in front of a judge."

She appreciated his dedication to her mother's case, something he didn't have to do.

Hailey lifted her head and studied Trey's face. She loved him more than she cared to admit. Though she had come back to Auburndale full of anger toward this man, it had entirely melted away.

She didn't dare tell him she was considering moving back so that they could rekindle their relationship. Well, likely not Auburndale because she wasn't sure she wanted to live in a place that held so much anguish, but somewhere close by.

She kissed him then, long and hard as she wrapped her arms around his neck, and he pulled her close. His hands traced her figure and she found herself running her fingers through his hair. It was as if they were making up for lost time.

She allowed herself to get lost in his kiss, to forget reality. She wanted to stay in this moment forever.

"I love you, Hailey," he said, "but I want to make sure this is right. I don't want either of us getting hurt if things don't work out again, especially with Trinity."

She closed her eyes for a moment. "I love you too."

He stilled, not expecting her response. She giggled. "I mean it, Trey. I love you."

"So does this mean we're done acting like we don't like each other?"

She threw her head back and laughed. "I think so. Unless you do something to piss me off again."

"Well, that's pretty easy to do so..."

He laughed when she playfully smacked at his chest.

He kissed her again as they blindly made their way to his bedroom. Hailey kicked the door closed and melted into him, hoping that when this was all over, she wouldn't regret it.

Unfortunately, Hailey and Trey didn't find anything else of importance in the case files. As much as he wanted to sit in his cozy home on this rainy day and kiss her for hours, he needed to catch a killer. And he'd bet his entire career that person was David.

Though his gut told him David murdered Morgan, he couldn't shake the feeling that Ryan was still somehow involved. The whole damn case was complicated. It was infuriating.

But despite who killed Morgan, it was evident Sara had been exploited. Everything Trey found out about the investigation thus far should have already been looked into. And from what he'd gathered, hardly anything had been thoroughly investigated.

No one checked alibis, potential eyewitnesses, or even possible suspects. Genevieve and Hailey should have been interviewed since they had the most involvement with Morgan. Nicole, Ryan, and David should have been questioned. But Washington bypassed any protocol and went straight to arresting and detaining Sara.

The problem with this case was they investigated Sara, but they didn't investigate Morgan's death. They went into the case with a biased opinion that Sara was guilty, and, because of that bias, they didn't bother to chase down any other potential leads or suspects.

Trey just couldn't figure out why.

Why would Eli not make sure this was an air-tight case since, according to Hailey, the Gallaghers were like family to him?

He needed someone who could tell him exactly what happened with the investigation that night. So, he dropped Hailey off at Genevieve's while he went back to the station to talk to the one man, he thought might actually tell him something.

Once inside, he beelined for Sargent Williams' desk. Lucious was an older man, in his mid-sixties, with long salt and pepper hair that he kept pulled into a ponytail, his beard and mustache matching. Not a style Trey would wear but the ladies loved the Sargent, despite him being married for nearly forty years.

He was one of Trey's favorite, and best, officers. Lucious was a wise man who spent his career taking the time to train other officers. He was fantastic at his job; fair and just, but he was also merciful when the circumstances called for it. He was no-nonsense and didn't mind calling other officers to the carpet, including Trey. Trey actually respected him for it.

Lucious saw him approaching and smiled. "Afternoon," Lucious said with a nod.

"My office."

He quickly followed Trey and took a seat across from the desk as Trey closed the door and sat down himself.

"How can I help, Chief?"

"This is off the record so we can drop the formality," Trey said.

Lucious shifted slightly. "Okay."

Trey tried to keep his temper at bay, but he was slowly losing control. This case was driving him crazy, and he was furious to know his own officers potentially covered up a murder. Especially Lucious.

"Do you know anything about a cover-up concerning the Morgan Gallagher case?" Trey saw fear flash behind the man's eyes. Or was he being paranoid and seeing things that weren't there?

When Lucious didn't respond, Trey continued, "There's a lot of missing paperwork. You were one of the responding officers and I want you to tell me why protocol wasn't followed. Walk me through the investigation."

"I don't know why reports aren't there. I, uh, gotta get back to my desk. I'm trying to finish up some paperwork." Lucious stood quickly and tried to exit.

Trey's voice boomed, "Sit down."

The older man's hand rested on the knob, his back to Trey.

Trey said, "I know something went on with this investigation and I want to know what it was. I'm going to make a phone call to I.A. and this will be your only chance to come clean before I involve them."

The man shook his head. "Oh, hell." Sighing, Lucious sat back down and rubbed his face. "We were blackmailed into incriminating Sara."

"What are you talking about? What blackmail?"

Lucious looked at the floor, embarrassed. "David blackmailed me."

"Are you kidding me, Lucious?" Trey was livid. If Lucious was capable of being blackmailed and altering reports, anyone was. And that thought had Trey feeling nauseous.

Lucious said, "A few years before Morgan died, he approached me about my son. Said he had been hooking up with Sara. David told me he would let it go but that I would owe him."

Trey shook his head. "Why didn't you go to Washington?"

"My son was eighteen and Sara was only fifteen."

No wonder the man did as he was told. If Trey was in Lucious' shoes, he likely wouldn't risk his son being arrested for statutory rape and possibly even pedophilia. Especially if it had been consensual.

Trey made a mental note to ask Sara about it.

"Why didn't you go to the higher ups?" Trey asked.

Lucious snorted. "You and I both know where their loyalty lies. And it wouldn't have mattered anyway. David had pictures of my boy and Sara- which is pretty sick if you ask me- so there would have been an investigation regardless."

For years, Trey heard rumors that David paid off a number of people for a number of things, from keeping his family out of trouble to gaining votes. But blackmailing cops into helping him frame his daughter for the murder of his wife...that seemed low even for David.

When Trey didn't respond, Lucious said, "I don't have proof, but Eli and David go way back, and I know Eli would have done just about anything to stay in the mayor's good graces."

"Would *you*?" Trey asked plainly.

"Would I what?"

"Do anything to stay in David's good graces? Or was this the only favor you did for him?"

Trey saw the pain in his friend's eyes. It was clear Lucious felt guilty about the ordeal, but Trey couldn't simply forget about all that the man had confessed to, as much as he wished he could. It was one thing to extend mercy to someone who had broken the law, but to willingly screw up an investigation was inexcusable.

Lucious shook his head. "No, I never took any calls if I thought his family was involved."

"Did Washington know about the blackmail?" Trey asked.

Lucious shrugged. "I never told him but that doesn't mean David didn't."

"Had anyone else at the scene been blackmailed?"

Lucious rubbed his hand together, not making eye contact with Trey. No one wanted to rat on a fellow officer, but Trey could tell that all of this weighed heavily on the man.

Lucious sighed. "Yes. All five officers at Morgan's crime scene had accepted a bribe or had been blackmailed...except Bobby Young. He was new which is why I think Washington had him there; easier to control and manipulate. He was thrown off the force shortly after, so he wasn't as easy to manipulate as Washington and David thought. Serves them right, honestly."

If Bobby was fired because he wouldn't follow orders, he may be their best witness as to what happened with the investigation that night.

"And, if I were you," Lucious continued, "I'd also check with the Medical Examiner. The report that's in the file isn't the original. I heard Eli telling the M.E. to change it."

Trey perked up. He hadn't expected the M.E. to be involved, but that wasn't surprising if they wanted to doctor an outcome.

Trey studied his friend. Lucious was a great cop and an even better friend. He was a deacon at his church and was a wonderful father and husband. Trey had a hard time believing all of this was true.

Yet, here Lucious was, admitting it all.

This job taught Trey that no matter how good someone is, there's always a breaking point. And there's almost always a secret to be uncovered.

Trey said, "I'll make a call to I.A. For now, I'll need your gun and badge. You're suspended until further notice."

Every case Lucious had been a part of would be investigated, as would the cases of the other officers. He didn't doubt that many criminals were about to go free because of technicalities and that made Trey even more angry with David and Washington and the involved officers.

He had a serious clusterfuck on his hands. No doubt people would be coming out of the woodwork to file misconduct charges against his precinct, many of which would be fabricated. Not to mention the press was going to have a field day once news broke. Of course, he couldn't forget how quickly the rumor mill worked. He got a headache just thinking about it. Their P.R. specialist was going to have her work cut out for her.

Lucious stood and placed his gun and badge on Trey's desk, his hand lingering for a painful moment. However, despite being saddened by the news, he shook Trey's hand and said, "It's been a pleasure serving under you."

Trey admired the man for his humility. Most cops would likely need to be escorted out of the building. It made this decision even harder for Trey. He didn't want to fire or suspend Lucious because Trey knew that one bad moment doesn't define your character. But he also knew that if the police couldn't uphold the law, then they sure as hell couldn't enforce it.

Before Lucious left, Trey said, "Be careful. Someone is killing people involved in this case and I don't want to see you hurt or have to stand over your dead body."

Lucious simply gave him a nod. With that, he left the building, gaining stares from other officers as he did.

I've been watching Trey since he got back to the police department. I know he's getting much too close to the truth. Enough to keep me tossing and turning at night.

I try to calm myself. Even if he knows the truth, he can't do anything about it, not without proof. I smile at that. He must be going crazy trying to put the pieces together.

Unfortunately for him, I'm too smart for that. I have eluded the police for thirteen years, and not by luck. It's taken planning and cleverness. I've had to be cunning and calculating, leaving nothing up to chance.

I turn my attention to the door, movement catching my gaze. I was hoping it was Trey coming out, but instead it's Lucious. I saw him on patrol earlier so his shift shouldn't be over yet. He's now back in street clothes, no gun or badge visible.

That's concerning. Lucious always wears his gun and badge on his belt, even when off duty. Part of me wants to approach him and ask why it's gone, but that would raise suspicion.

However, I don't need to ask. I already know the answer. It only makes sense that the cowboy would question him about Morgan's murder. And if he is without a gun and badge...well, it means he told Trey what he knew.

Which is fine. For now.

He doesn't know enough to make me worry, though I'll keep an eye on him.

The Beast beacons for Lucious as he climbs into his car. My gaze follows him until he's out of sight.

Today is Lucious' lucky day. Today, I won't kill him.

But the Beast is clawing at the surface again, begging to be released. I feel myself losing control. Not that I mind, I love The Beast. Because of him, I'm able to let out the darkest part of me. The part that society would love to slaughter.

They would be surprised to know I'm the monster found in nightmares, the kind that lurks in the sunlight, waiting for darkness to fall. I'm the creature you let into your home, not realizing you should have locked your doors instead. I'm the beast you trust...and by the time you realize the truth, you're already dead.

As children, we're taught to bury the darkness, to ignore the monsters that live within us. But what they don't understand is how satisfying it is to succumb to the yearning that beckons us. Everyone likes to pretend evil doesn't exist within them, but it's those who embrace it that are completely satisfied.

We understand there's a euphoria that comes when our monsters are released. When we're on the hunt and catch our prey, there's nothing more fulfilling than that of the whimpers of the weak. And when our hands are covered in the blood of our victims, that's when we're most alive.

Now The Beast is tearing through, his force much too strong for me to stop. It's painful, a stabbing in the pit of my stomach. It's an aching desire, one that will need to be satisfied in order to stop the pain.

And Trey Harbor will be the one to fulfill it.

Chapter 25

July 1, 2011
8:05 pm

After Lucious left, Trey spent a few hours catching up on paperwork before heading to Genevieve's to get Hailey and take her to get ice cream. She needed a pick-me-up, and he knew the way to her heart was sweets. Unfortunately, his plan wasn't going as well as he'd hoped.

The two were now on their way to talk to Bobby Young, and Hailey was giving him the silent treatment. Trey hadn't wanted to involve her in the conversation he had with Lucious. He could lose his job if he talked to her about an ongoing Internal Affairs investigation.

So, despite her pouting, he kept matters to himself.

When Trey told her he was going to talk to Bobby, though, she had begged to come with him. And it was something he wholeheartedly disapproved of since she had a knack for getting herself into trouble and not minding her own business. But, she wanted to thank the man who had helped her the night her mother died and Trey couldn't tell her no. He didn't think it was fair to take that from her after everything she'd been through.

"I know you're mad at me because I'm shutting you out, but I need you to understand why. The last thing we need is to jeopardize this case or for you to get hurt or killed. I need you to stay in the car while I talk to him."

"Fine," Hailey said, crossing her arms over her chest.

Trey smiled to himself. He had always been amused by her attitude, as aggravating as it could be sometimes. She had no problem letting him know when she was displeased.

The sky was painted beautiful hues of pink, purple, and orange as the sun had nearly set. If there wasn't a murderer on the loose, he might actually enjoy the view. However, with bodies turning up and Hailey's life being in danger, it was a painful reminder that another day was passing without being any closer to arresting the murderer that was wreaking havoc on his city and his family.

"Is this how you're going to be the rest of the night?' he asked.

Silence.

He'd take that as a yes.

Shaking his head, Trey focused on the road and let Hailey pout.

He took notice of a car that had been following them through a stretch of town. Though not completely abnormal, he was now being extra careful since Hailey had been hurt. He clenched his teeth as he remembered holding her limp body in his arms, soot dusting her face and clothes. It wasn't until they had gotten into the ambulance that he noticed her blood on his hands.

Anger boiled below the surface and then guilt followed. He should have protected her. She should have never gotten hurt while he was there.

He turned down a side road, driving slowly to see if the car would follow.

It didn't.

Once he was satisfied, they weren't being followed, he took another side street and circled around to the main road where he continued toward Bobby's house. He felt paranoid but wasn't willing to take a chance with Hailey's life.

Once there, Trey turned to Hailey before getting out. "I don't want to do this with you. You can be mad, but we're not going to ignore each other."

Hailey side-eyed him, holding on to her pride which slowly dissipated when she realized he was right. She sighed. "I'm sorry. I just don't like that you're keeping things from me. I get why you're doing it, but I don't like it."

"If I.A. wasn't opening an investigation, I would tell you," Trey said.

"Doesn't mean I have to like it."

Trey chuckled. "You're right." He kissed her on the nose and climbed out of the truck.

He knocked hard and waited, hearing faint footsteps as someone came to the door. Dusk was approaching and the pink streaks of the sunset would soon be replaced by darkness. Even the crickets and frogs were beginning their lullabies.

Trey studied his surroundings. They were far more secluded on this stretch of land than he had anticipated. The small farmhouse was enclosed by woods. He turned back toward the door when he heard the knob jingle as it opened.

Bobby Young stood at the door, a dish towel in his hand. He wore a t-shirt and basketball shorts that made him look much younger than he was. His brown hair was now graying and, despite being in his fifties, he was still in great shape.

"Can I help you?"

"I hope so. I'm Chief Harbor with Auburndale PD. I have some questions concerning the night Morgan Gallagher died. I'm not sure if you remember that case or not."

"How could I not? It's the case that got me thrown off the force," Bobby replied.

Trey nodded. "So, I've been told. Do you mind if we talk inside?"

"I guess." He stepped aside and ushered Trey into his home. The living room was just off to the left of the front door. Trey sat down on the couch and Bobby sat adjacent to him in a recliner that was upright.

Trey said, "I'm actually investigating Morgan's death again. We have reason to believe Sara didn't kill her and that the investigating officers obstructed the investigation."

Bobby snorted. "You're a little late to the party, Chief. I tried to tell people, but no one would listen. The cops who investigated were dirty."

Trey nodded. "What do you remember from that night?"

Bobby closed his eyes. "We got there shortly after 11:30 pm. Morgan's blood was nearly dry which was my first red flag seeing as how David claimed to have called us right away. Sara was laying next to her, unconscious.

"David told us she was under the influence and had killed Morgan, but there wasn't any evidence to prove that theory. It was clear from some of her wounds that Morgan had fallen down the stairs, and later the M.E. said the cause of death was blunt force trauma. But there was no evidence linking Sara to the crime. The only reason her involvement was even considered was because she was laying next to Morgan and because David told us she was guilty, despite claiming he wasn't home at the time.

"I mean, it wasn't out of the realm of possibilities, but David was so adamant that Sara had done it. It didn't sit right with me. Most parents would do anything to keep their kids out of trouble, not purposefully throw them into it."

He paused for a moment, gathering his thoughts, and then continued, "And besides that, she was so heavily under the influence that I don't think she could even walk. Nothing made sense to me. Yet, all the other guys had no problem pointing the finger at Sara."

He shook his head in disgust. "I tried talking to Washington about it but then David got involved. Next thing I know, I'm out of a job and had a 'cease and desist' letter along with a restraining order."

"Did you ever believe Sara could have killed Morgan?"

Bobby vehemently shook his head. "Not a chance. She was unconscious by the time we got to her. If she had that much drugs and alcohol in her system, she wouldn't have been able to get up the stairs. And she damn sure wouldn't have been able to get back down the stairs either; especially without falling. She didn't get to the crime scene until after Morgan was dead. I'd bet my life on it."

Trey hadn't thought about Sara having to go up and down the stairs for David's story to make sense. Bobby was right. There was no way Sara could have gone up and down the stairs with how incapacitated she was that night. That alone should have been enough for the cops to look at other suspects.

"Who do you think killed Morgan?"

Bobby opened his mouth but quickly closed it.

"I know you don't want to point the finger, but whoever killed her has killed someone else and attempted to kill two other people, including Hailey Gallagher. I have one man fighting for his life in the ICU, a terrified lady who was nearly killed, and a missing woman who may be connected to this case." Trey pleaded, "I need *something* before someone else gets hurt or killed."

Bobby looked at the floor, placing his elbows on his knees. He sighed and said, "I've always thought it was David. I have absolutely no proof, but the way he conducted himself and how he was so hell bent on Sara being guilty...it never sat right with me."

Trey nodded. "Yeah, David seems to be right in the middle of all of it."

He stood and Bobby followed. "I'll be in touch if we can get the D.A. to officially reopen the case. We would need you to testify if you're willing."

They walked toward the door and Bobby said, "Of course, just let me know what you need from me."

Once at the door, Trey handed him his card and Bobby took it. "Thanks for talking with me. If you think of anything, call me."

As Trey stepped onto the sidewalk, Hailey got out of the car and waved at Bobby, making her way up the walkway.

Bobby squinted. "Is that Hailey Gallagher?"

"It is. She wanted to say thank you," Trey said.

As Trey turned around to face her, gunshots echoed through the sky and Hailey started screaming.

Bobby yelled, "Put pressure on the wound, I'll call 911!"

Trey tried to shield Hailey from the impending danger, but his body wouldn't obey.

Why was he on the ground?

Excruciating pain ripped through his abdomen. He touched his stomach, water soaking his fingertips as it seeped onto his shirt and the sidewalk.

It wasn't rain, it was blood. Why was he bleeding?

A dark pool of red filled each crack and crevice of the concrete.

Hailey knelt beside him, her voice far away as tears streamed down her face. "I'm sorry, Baby, this is going to hurt."

She placed her hands on top of his stomach, putting pressure on the wound and he cried out in pain. She screamed and cried as she tried to help him, assuring him she wasn't going to leave his side. Bobby was yelling that the ambulance was on its way.

Hailey kept crying, begging him to stay with her.

Trey tried to laugh but no sound passed his lips.

Why did she think he was leaving? He would never leave her.

But the darkness was threatening him. He felt sleepy.

Two more shots thundered in the distance.

Hailey was screaming again, high pitched shrieks of terror. But this time she was screaming for Bobby. Trey wanted to keep her safe, but he couldn't find her. Everything was blurring together as darkness came for him.

Where was Bobby?

He only needed a few minutes of sleep and then he could get up. Hailey's cries were growing farther and farther away as he slipped into the darkness.

That's when he realized he had been shot.

And then, Trey Harbor took his last breath.

Chapter 26

Hailey studied her reflection in the mirror, distressed by what she saw. Her cheeks were blotchy from crying and stained with makeup she had yet to wash off. Her eyes were red and puffy- much like her lips- and her hair desperately needed to be brushed.

Every time she closed her eyes, her mind replayed that horrific night at Bobby's. The gunshots, Trey collapsing to the ground, blood seeping from his abdomen and all over her hands as she tried to save him. She had heard screaming and later realized it was her own cries of terror.

And then Bobby had gone down in a huff, bleeding from his chest, vacant eyes staring into her soul.

She physically shivered and rushed to the toilet where she dry heaved, her body trying to rid her of the horrific memories that haunted her.

She would never forget seeing Trey slip away, his eyes slowly closing as she watched him slip from consciousness.

Hailey sobbed into her hand. There was so much left to say, and she hadn't said it. They were getting a second chance to love each other...

A voice on the other side of the bathroom door drew Hailey from her thoughts. She rubbed water on her face and wiped it with a paper towel, put her hair into a clip that Sara had brought, and walked out of the bathroom.

The nurse was checking Trey's vitals and Hailey smiled at her. "Do we have an update?"

She shook her head, black curls bouncing as she did. "Not yet. We're just waiting for him to wake up. His vitals have been stable so it should be any day now."

"Hasn't it been too long, though? Don't people usually wake up quickly after surgery?" Hailey pleaded. She wanted to pretend she wasn't scared, but the nurse saw through her facade. They both knew Hailey was terrified of losing the love of her life.

Trey's surgery had been hours long. And though the surgeon was able to remove the bullet, they hadn't been completely out of the woods until early this morning. And now it was simply a waiting game, something Hailey wasn't good at.

The nurse looked at her sympathetically. "Mrs. Harbor, please don't worry yourself just yet. His body is recovering from a serious trauma. If the doctor isn't worried, you don't need to be either. Why don't you go get breakfast in the cafeteria?"

Hailey almost protested the name but stopped herself. It somehow brought her comfort that the nurse assumed she was Trey's wife.

She knew one thing for certain, if and when Trey woke up, she was marrying him. No doubt about it. She knew she needed to spend the rest of her life with him.

"No, I'm fine. I want to be here when he wakes up," Hailey said.

The nurse nodded simply to appease Hailey and left the room. Hailey sighed and stood in front of the chair she had been sitting in since Trey got out of surgery. She had pulled it up to his bedside so she could hold his hand. She would lay her head on his arm, hoping to get some sleep, but sleep never came. All she could do was worry.

Not to mention the nightmares that plagued her.

She could still hear the explosion of the gunshots that had pierced her ears. Trey had collapsed and it was only a moment later that blood had pooled around him, staining the pavement. Somehow, in all the panic, she had been able to apply pressure to his wound. Then he had passed out, sending her into near hysteria as she called out for him over and over, trying to wake him.

Her cries of grief had echoed into the night sky as they collided with the sirens that wailed in the distance, her very own lullaby of anguish. Even the animals and crickets had stopped their song, allowing for Hailey's to be the only one heard.

She had laid across his body, begging him to come back to her but he hadn't. He had remained lifeless and all she could do was think about the second chance they never got, and the father Trinity would no longer have.

Her heart had shattered, pain tearing through her body as tears had fallen to the ground, mixing with his blood. Her heart was trying to die along with him. Even her lungs had refused to gather breath. Her body didn't want to live if he was no longer in this world.

The paramedics had jumped out of the ambulance, one of them dragging her away from his body as she shrieked and fought against him. She had hated that they were taking her away from Trey. All she had wanted to do was be with the love of her life. To hold him and kiss him one last time, even if he was no longer there to feel her touch.

An EMT had held her upright as her knees buckled. She had gasped for air and clung to the man, terrified she may die right alongside Trey. Part of her wished she did.

"I've got a pulse! It's faint, but it's there," someone had yelled.

Hailey's heart had nearly stopped. "What did she say?"

Then everything blurred together. She had ended up at the hospital and was now standing by his bedside after surgery, praying he woke up.

Hailey studied his face as she caressed his cheek, a lump forming in her throat. She gently kissed him and sat down, taking his hand as she laid her head on his arm. Her shoulders shook with each muffled cry.

"I didn't realize being called Mrs. Harbor would be so bad you'd cry about it, Princess," Trey croaked.

Hailey's head shot up. It took her a moment to realize Trey was awake and talking to her. She laughed through her tears when she realized what he'd said. Then she kissed him, his fingers wiping her tears away.

She said, "I thought I lost you. I can't imagine my life without you."

He gave her a side smile and kissed her head. "That's the trauma talking. You'll be back to being pissed at me as soon as we leave the hospital."

She laid her head on his chest and listened to his heartbeat; a melody she'd never take for granted again. He hugged her tight, wincing as he did.

She said, "Probably, but it's what we do."

Hailey got up to get the nurse when he grabbed her hand. "Don't get the nurse yet. I just want to hold you for a little longer."

She smiled, climbed into the bed with him, and put her head back onto his chest. Then, she quietly said, "I thought you were dead."

Trey pulled her close. "Me too. I tried to jump in front of you to protect you, but I couldn't move. And then there was this darkness I just couldn't fight anymore..."

Her eyes filled with tears again, but she blinked them away, grateful to finally hear his voice. "The ambulance happened to be a mile out and thankfully they were able to life-flight you or you wouldn't have made it."

He said, "Did they find who did it?"

Hailey shook her head. "No. They have no idea who it was. They found a shell casing along the tree line so they're running ballistics, but it'll be a while before they have anything conclusive."

"How's Bobby?"

Hailey's face contorted. "He was shot after he called 911. He didn't make it." Hailey started sobbing uncontrollably, his lifeless green eyes still haunting her. She wished she could have done something more, but she knew he was dead as soon as his body hit the ground. She needed to stay with Trey and stop the bleeding. So, she did.

And now Bobby was dead.

He wiped at the tears that were streaming down her face. "I hate that you're crying."

"Some maniac is trying to kill us, and no one knows who he is! He's not going to stop until he finishes the job."

"That won't happen, I promise."

She wanted to oppose him but was interrupted. "Chief Harbor," the nurse said, "I'm so glad to see you're awake."

Hailey got up as the nurse began taking Trey's vitals and asking him questions about pain and potential side effects. As she did, Hailey called Sara to bring Trinity in from the waiting room.

The nurse continued to assess Trey's wounds, causing him to wince. She finally left the room, telling them the doctor would be in shortly.

A few minutes later, Sara and Trinity walked in, followed by Gavin and Carter. As much as Hailey didn't want Trinity to see Trey like this, she knew it was the right thing to do.

Trinity ran to his side and threw herself into his arms. "I just got you. I don't want to lose you, Dad."

Hailey teared up again and she noticed her sister's eyes trained on her as Sara studied Hailey, worry etched on her face. She was clutching Gavin's hand and then quickly brushed it away when she realized Hailey had noticed. Gavin smiled, amused by Sara's charade.

"Damn, Harbor, you look like death," Carter said.

"Yeah," Gavin said, "I don't know who you pissed off, but tell them to knock it off. I'm trying to work on my love life, and you keep interrupting."

Sara gasped and smacked the back of her hand into his abdomen. Gavin huffed out air and laughed. He then kissed her temple, and she gave him a look that could kill.

Brave man. Hailey arched a brow at Sara and smiled.

Carter beamed with happiness for his friend. "I'm just glad she can keep you in line."

"I'll be sure to let them know," Trey replied with a chuckle. He pushed himself to sit up and flinched, trying not to let anyone see his discomfort. "On a serious note, though, I need you and Carter to keep an eye on the girls for me.

We have no idea who the shooter is, which means he could go after Hailey or even Sara."

"We assumed as much," Gavin said.

Trey took Hailey's hand. "Listen, Princess, you and Trinity are staying at my place until we figure out what the hell is going on."

Hailey nodded. "Okay, but where are we staying while you're in the hospital?" She looked at Sara. "What about you? Where are you going to stay?"

Sara smirked. "No one knows where I am, remember? Plus, I can take care of myself." She pointed to her side where her scars laid beneath her t-shirt.

"Why don't you stay with Sara?" Carter said. "Like she said, no one knows where she's staying."

Gavin added, "Yeah, it would be best to keep everyone together as much as possible. And we can post outside."

Trey nodded. "Stay there until I'm released and then you and Trinity can stay with me. I'm hoping they'll release me in the next day or two."

Hailey gave a soft smile. "You just got shot, Trey. A day or two doesn't seem long enough."

"There's a killer on the loose who's hunting me and my family. I don't have time to stay here." Trey frowned as he looked at Gavin and Carter. "Keep your guard up. This guy shot me from yards away. He's not an excellent marksman, but he's very good."

Hailey's heart dropped as unwanted memories flooded her again.

Trey pointed at Gavin. "Don't let them out of your sight. Do you hear me, Gavin? If anything happens to my girls or Sara, I will kill you myself."

Gavin bowed up slightly. "I know you remember me as the asshole who broke Hailey's heart, but that's not who I am anymore. I will protect them with my life. Count on it."

Carter added, "I've survived things that make nightmares look like daydreams. Your family will be safe with us."

Trey nodded, a silent understanding between the three men.

Then Trey looked at Sara. "This is going to be a weird, and potentially embarrassing, question and I want you to answer me honestly..."

Sara eyed him suspiciously.

"Were you with Lucious Williams' son when you were a teenager?"

Her cheeks turned bright pink as she looked at Gavin then looked at the floor. "Um, yes. I was fifteen."

"Was it consensual?"

Her head snapped up. "Yes. We were at a party. It was the only time it happened with him. Why?"

Trey chose his words carefully, not wanting to reveal too much information, "I have reason to believe David used it as blackmail against Lucious Williams and I needed to confirm if it was true or not."

Sara tossed her head back and cursed. But before she could respond, the doctor came in, indicating that everyone needed to leave. Trinity put up a fight at first, but ultimately understood her father needed to rest. She reluctantly followed her aunt out the door. Hailey stayed behind, wanting to spend time with Trey so Carter offered to pick her up when she was comfortable leaving Trey alone.

When the doctor left, Trey asked for his phone, so Hailey grabbed the bag of belongings off the extra chair but dropped it, its contents spilling out. She cursed as she began putting the items back into the bag as Trey chuckled at her.

Then, her eyes rounded and she froze. She slowly picked up a small box that had tumbled out of the bag, her eyes locking with Trey's. He held her gaze, but she couldn't mistake the worry in his eyes.

"What is this, Trey?"

"Why don't you open it?"

She knew what it was but wasn't ready to say it out loud. Her mind was swimming with so many emotions. Fear, happiness, nervousness, worry...

"No, I...When did you get this? Why do you have it?"

He looked away from her. "I've had it for years, since before you left. It's been in a drawer this whole time but..." He shrugged. "I've been carrying it around the last few days. I don't know what I was planning to do with it, but I felt like it didn't belong in a drawer anymore." Trey looked at her. "I love you, Hailey.

I don't want you to feel pressured to say anything or do anything. You weren't supposed to see it until the time was right. Just know I love you."

She didn't respond. Instead, she opened the velvet box. Hailey hadn't meant to gasp, but she did. The small diamond was embedded on a gold band with three smaller diamonds on either side. The ring was breathtaking.

"I had saved up all my money to buy it. I planned to give it to you a few weeks after you gave me the locket. Then your father talked to me and...well, you know the rest. So, I kept it in a drawer. Until now. That night with Trinity, when you gave me back the locket, I got the ring out of the drawer, and I've kept it on me.

"I think I was hoping there'd be some magical moment or maybe I just thought it could be good luck...I don't know. But this isn't me asking. This isn't me pressuring you into anything. I know we have a lot to work through and I'm okay with that."

Hailey was crying again, and she let out an irritated grunt. She was so tired of crying. But she was glad they were finally happy tears.

Trey immediately put his hands up. "I didn't realize it would upset you so much. I'm sorry."

Hailey laughed through her tears. "That's not why I'm crying. I'm running on fumes, and it's been an emotional last few days and that's the most romantic thing I've ever heard."

And, just as she'd done under the covering of the moon and stars all those years ago, she layed in Trey's arms as they made plans of wedded bliss.

Chapter 27

July 4, 2011

7:30 pm

Hailey had spent the last three days at the hospital with Trey and now that she felt comfortable leaving his side, she was looking forward to having a sense of normalcy. The last few days had been exhausting and Hailey was ready to sleep in a regular bed. After her much needed shower, she relaxed under the covers. She finally stopped long enough to notice that the throbbing in her head had resumed.

Sighing, Hailey got up and padded through the living room to Angie's kitchen. She could hear the TV in the guest room, Sara's laughter carrying through the house. Hailey smiled. She was glad her sister was finding happiness, especially with all that was going on. Sara deserved it, even if it was in a TV sitcom.

And, thankfully, Hailey didn't have to worry about Trinity tonight. After the stress of the last few days, and the trauma of her father being shot, Hailey had agreed to let her stay with Cecilia at Genevieve's for the night.

Hailey got herself a glass of water and brought it back to her room where she took two ibuprofens for the pain. She slid back under the covers and, finally, after three very long days, allowed herself to relax.

She wanted to spend the night combing through what she knew, but instead, Hailey drifted off to sleep and tried to fight off the nightmares that came with it. Some were about the fire, others about her mother, her sister, and, of course,

Trey getting shot. There was always a faceless killer chasing after her. His figure would contort from David's to Ryan's to Sara's. Even her mother became the boogeyman.

She awoke with a jolt, nausea threatening her.

Loud booms and crackles thundered through the sky. Disoriented from her dreams, she nearly screamed, searching for cover from the gunshots.

Hailey breathed a sigh of relief when she realized the sounds were fireworks. She hadn't even realized it was the Fourth of July. She inhaled and sat up quickly, breathing in and out as she calmed her nerves.

The bedside clock showed it was only 9:30 pm.

As she went to lay down again, she heard a noise coming from the other side of the house. She told herself it was Sara getting water or using the bathroom, but her gut told her something was wrong.

She thought about calling Gavin, but didn't want to alarm him if it was nothing. Instead, she grabbed her phone and tucked it into the pocket of her sweatpants and made her way toward the sound.

"Sara?" she whispered.

Nothing.

Heart thudding loudly, palms sweaty, Hailey continued to slowly walk toward the kitchen. She heard something to her left and quickly turned around. She let out a scream as Sara crept around a corner.

Startled, Sara returned the scream and then began laughing, along with Hailey.

"What are you doing up?" Hailey asked.

"I thought I heard something, so I came to investigate."

Hailey stopped. "I came out because *I* heard something."

The two shared a knowing glance.

Sara ran to the kitchen to grab a knife while Hailey tried to quickly pull her phone out of her pocket.

More booms and crackles ricocheted above.

Movement on the other side of the room caught her eye, the flashes of light illuminated a shadow hiding on the other side of the room. Hailey let out a blood curdling scream and ran toward Sara. Hailey was tackled to the ground, her phone clattering across the tile. Pain ruptured through her body as she collided with the floor and her breath was knocked from her lungs.

She struggled to move the fog from her mind. Once again, she felt hands tighten around her throat as Ryan began to squeeze. Flashbacks began flooding her as she recalled the last time he tried to kill her.

Just like before, the black hole threatened to swallow her.

She didn't want to die like this. She didn't want Trey to find her body and have to tell Trinity what happened. She wanted to make things right with Sara. She wanted more time with them.

She had to fight back. She had to get away from this monster.

Then, a force ripped Ryan from her, and he grunted as he crashed to the ground. She sucked in air as quickly as she could, relief filling her.

She knew Trey would save her.

She started calling out to him as she pushed herself off the floor. Disoriented, she shook her head.

No, not Trey. Sara. Sara had saved her.

Sara quickly brought down a knife and sliced his left shoulder blade and Ryan howled in pain. Furious, he went after Sara as she ran toward the front door to get Gavin and Carter. Blood was pouring out of his wound, leaving a trail of violence behind him.

Sara screamed as Ryan grabbed her by the hair and threw her to the ground and the knife slid across the floor and under the couch. Hailey fervently tried to grasp the weapon, but her arms weren't long enough. Not waiting a moment longer, Hailey reached out and grabbed Ryans ankle, causing him to stumble. He cursed at her as she yelled, "Run, Sara!"

Sara hesitated.

"Go! Now!" Hailey screamed as she scurried toward the kitchen to get a weapon. She wasn't sure she'd make it out alive, but she'd die trying if it meant Sara could live.

Sara ran like her life depended on it. She tore through the front door, leaving it open. She darted to the truck that was parked at the edge of the drive, screaming and waving her arms as she did. Gavin and Carter rushed out of the truck when they saw her.

She began crying hysterically. "Ryan is in the house!"

Gavin's eyes widened as he grabbed her upper arms and studied her face. She brought a hand to her mouth and realized she was bleeding, but she didn't care. Her sister's life was in danger.

Carter ran inside, pulling out his pistol as he did.

Gavin handed Sara his phone. "Get in the truck and lock the door. Call 911 and *do not* get out until they're here. No matter what."

She nodded and Gavin followed, gun drawn.

Sara climbed into the driver's side and locked the door. She called 911 and tried to calm herself down. If she was hysterical, it would take them longer to get there.

"911, what's your emergency?"

"Someone broke into my house and my sister has been hurt. He's trying to kill her!" She rattled off the address and quickly hung up. Then she searched the phone for Trey's number.

His voice was groggy, "What's up?"

"Ryan is here! He's got Hailey!" Her voice quivered as she tried to keep from crying.

"I'm on my way," he said and hung up.

She sobbed as she watched red and blue ribbons fill the sky. This was her first Fourth of July being free. But she still felt like she was in prison, shackled and chained to the past that seemed to haunt her and bring chaos and heartache to her family.

Revenge always comes at a price, and she wasn't sure she wanted to pay it. And now her sister might die because of it.

Another boom vibrated through the air and more ribbons danced in the sky as colors fell to the ground.

Three more booms reverberated through the darkness. But this time it wasn't fireworks.

It was gunshots.

Sirens in the distance pierced her ears. She just hoped they made it in time.

Now, all Sara could do was wait to see who had been killed.

Chapter 28

July 5, 2011
1:58 am

It didn't take long for Angie's street to be filled with the sound of sirens and strobes of blue and red lights that nearly blinded them. Yellow ribbon taped off Angie's yard and home, drawing out nosey neighbors who couldn't help but stare and whisper.

Angie was going to be pissed when she got back from her honeymoon.

Sara sat on the tailgate of Gavin's truck; a blanket wrapped around her while a paramedic tried to convince Hailey to go to the hospital. She refused to leave Sara's side, and the man gritted his teeth and narrowed his eyes, but she ignored him.

"Leave her alone. Trey will make sure she gets checked out," Sara said sternly. The man eyed her but then silently walked away.

Thankfully, Hailey's injuries weren't life threatening, but her nose had bled on and off and her lip was split open. According to Hailey, she managed to get a hold of the knife Sara had dropped and had stabbed Ryan in the leg. He had run off as soon as Carter came barreling in and Carter chased Ryan out the back door.

Once Gavin had assessed Hailey and had safely gotten her out of the house, he ran after Ryan and Carter. He had seen the back gate open and had followed suit, thinking Carter had chased Ryan out of the yard.

Gavin had found Carter lying face down on the sidewalk, only feet away from Angie's yard, a single bullet to the skull. From what Trey and Gavin could piece together, Ryan had used the cover of darkness and the fireworks to silence his movements and was able to fire off three shots, one killing Carter.

The Medical Examiner emerged from the house, pushing a body bag on a stretcher. Sara followed it with her gaze until Carter's body had been carefully loaded into the back of a van. She didn't break her stare until the van disappeared into the night.

Guilt swept over Sara. She was putting people in danger, and she didn't know what to do. She wanted revenge, but at what cost?

Sighing to herself, she watched as Trey made his way to the truck. He had discharged himself from the hospital when he heard what had happened and somehow managed to catch a ride with a nurse who had just gotten off shift.

As he walked toward her and Hailey, he winced with every step and clenched his own wound. He had pulled a suture at some point during all the confusion and had to be stitched up again by a paramedic.

Sara was shocked he was still standing, though she knew it was likely due to adrenaline.

He nodded to Gavin who now stood next to him. "Gavin said they didn't see anyone drive down the street, there was no suspicious activity. They think Ryan might have been here earlier today and left the bathroom window unlocked, then came back by going through the neighbor's yards. He was probably watching Gavin and Carter for a few hours, trying to figure out their routine."

Gavin said, "We would walk the perimeter of the house every thirty minutes. I'm guessing he took the opportunity while we were in the truck to jump a few fences and get in through the window."

"Did you arrest him?" Hailey said, her voice shaking.

Trey said, "We don't know where he is. He used the traffic from the fireworks show to get away. We put out a BOLO, but nothing has popped yet."

Trey was trying to contain his anger, but Sara could still see it. She even noticed the fear. She was scared too.

Hailey had stabbed Ryan in the leg and Sara had sliced open his shoulder. *How had he gotten away?*

With a sigh of defeat, Sara asked, "What happens now?"

"I'm going to take Hailey back to my house and we'll get Trinity on the way."

Sara was thankful he didn't bring up the fact Trinity stayed at Genevieve's, though he was likely thankful for it at the moment.

Gavin added, "And I'm going to call Carter's mother and notify her on the way to my house. I need to get a change of clothes before heading to Trey's."

Trey said, "From now on, we all stay together. I also have uniforms patrolling my street around-the-clock until we catch Ryan." He looked at Sara. "You're welcome to come with us or go with Gavin."

"His mother is going to be distraught." Hailey choked out a sob and Trey brought her to his chest. "How could this happen? How does someone like Ryan walk away from this and someone like Carter is about to be buried? A mother should never have to bury her son, Trey!" She pounded his chest, and he held her tighter. "It's not fair!"

Sara held her breath to keep from crying. She wanted to be numb to the pain, to act like she didn't feel anything. But she couldn't. She needed to feel the pain that she brought on...it would be her punishment to bear, and she would feel it fully.

Sara looked at Gavin, whose eyes were red, and face was splotchy. He angrily wiped at the tears that were falling to the ground. She blamed herself for Carter's death and she expected Gavin to as well. After all, it was ultimately her decision to reopen the case that had brought down this fury. But he extended his hand to Sara, and she took it, grateful for his presence.

Gavin looked at her. "I'm not leaving your side until this whole thing is over."

Sara squeezed his hand for a moment but didn't let go.

Trey shook his head. "And neither of you goes anywhere by yourself. You stay with me or with Gavin until I figure out what to do next."

Hailey simply nodded, too exhausted to put up a fight; probably too scared, too. Sara was grateful, she didn't have the energy to fight about Hailey's stubbornness tonight, though it was nearly two in the morning now.

Sara wiped her brow. The sun wasn't even out yet and the heat was still hardly bearable. The buzz of officers moving around on the property had drowned out the sounds of the night. Though it seemed that silence would soon fall as dawn approached and the investigation came to an end.

Another officer walked up to the truck. "I'm so sorry to interrupt, but Chief, we need you and Mr. O'Dell to come take a look at one last thing." She looked at Sara and Hailey, and then back to Trey and Gavin. "I'm sorry for your loss."

Trey nodded. Then he looked at Hailey and Sara and said, "We'll be right back."

Hailey took Sara's hand and moved closer to her, as the two men followed the officer back to the crime scene. Then she laid her head on Sara's shoulder and cried. Sara wanted to cry too, but she held her breath so the mist in her eyes would disappear. But the tears still came streaming down her face and she let them.

Then, soft chirps of her phone had her brushing her tears away. She furrowed her brows. The number was private.

"Hello?" she coughed out.

"I told you to mind your business, Sara; to leave things alone."

"And I told you I was going to bury you," she said matter-of-factly.

How had her father gotten her number? She was using a burner phone and had kept the number a secret aside from Hailey, Gavin, and Trey.

Hailey furrowed her brows and clutched Sara's hand tighter. After what they'd just been through, they were both on edge.

"I saw your little interview in the paper." David didn't bother hiding his disdain.

She was surprised by his straightforwardness. Her father was a textbook narcissist, gaslighting his victims so they wouldn't see his attacks coming. And, once they were vulnerable, he would strike.

But David knew they were no longer playing his game of cat and mouse where he would toy with her before attacking. She had grown accustomed to his deceit and was no longer playing along.

"A gift: from me to you," she mocked.

"You know, Sara, revenge comes at a price. And it's always the innocent who pay it."

Her heart dropped to her stomach. She looked around, trying to find him in the crowd, but David wasn't among the neighbors and the first responders.

"Who told you about Carter?" she demanded.

"The man who killed him. Ryan was supposed to kill Hailey, but of course you had to intervene. And now Carter's blood is on your hands. And your sister's will be too if you don't stop."

"How could you-"

"Did you truly believe I would sit back while you tried to destroy me? I warned you and you didn't listen." He chuckled, "Do I have your attention now, Sara?"

The line beeped and Sara screamed, startling Hailey. Rage engulfed her. She heaved her phone onto the ground, and it smashed onto the pavement.

After tonight, she would make it her life's mission to hunt down Ryan House.

Next, she would find her father.

And then she would become the murderer everyone claimed her to be.

Hailey quickly jumped off the tailgate and followed Sara down the street. "Sara, stop!"

But Sara didn't stop, she ignored her sister's pleas and continued into the darkness of the early morning, dim streetlights their only source of light. Hailey could hardly keep up and was limping, her body still throbbing from the attack.

Finally, Sara stopped and vomited into the grass of a nearby neighbor. Sara wiped at her mouth and stood, putting the palm of her hands over her eyes.

"Shit! Shit! Shit!" Tears fell from her eyes. "I really screwed up, Hailey. I can't fix this."

For the first time, Hailey saw the fear in her sister's eyes and that had alarm racing through Hailey. Which was exactly David's intent. Since he could no longer manipulate Sara, he would intimidate her.

And it was working.

Sara began pacing frantically. "This wasn't supposed to happen. I didn't think anyone would get killed!"

"What are you talking about? What did you do?"

Sara threw her arms in the air. "I stole the diaries out of your car and showed them to a reporter. Dad read the article, which was the point, but now he's out for blood."

Hailey's mouth gaped open. "Why did you do that?"

"Because, Hailey, he ruined my life, and I want to ruin his."

Hailey rubbed her face. "That's why we're trying to clear your name!"

"No. Clearing my name is the justice the world owes me. But revenge...that's what I *deserve*. I meant what I said. I'm going to bury him and if I have to go down with him, so be it." She closed her eyes. "I just didn't think he'd kill people to get back at me for it."

Hailey shook her head, panic sweeping over her. "Who did he kill? What happened?"

How was everything spiraling so out of control?

Sara crossed her arms and looked away. She was shutting down and Hailey hated that Sara still didn't fully trust her. Hailey trusted Sara with her life, she wanted the same in return.

Hailey said, "We're going to get through this, but you have to start trusting me. I know it goes against every instinct you have, but I swear, this is only going to get worse if we don't start trusting each other."

Sara sat on the curb and roughly ran her hands through her hair. "I know, I know. I just..." She began crying. "Ryan was at Angie's because I went to the reporter."

Hailey's heart dropped. Guilt clouded her sister's eyes, as if it was Sara's fault their father was so evil. Sara didn't need to carry his demons; she clearly had her own.

Hailey sat next to her and took her hand. "His death is not your fault. You were trying to do the right thing-"

Sara ripped her hand away. "No, I wasn't! I was trying to get revenge, and I didn't care what it cost me. I just didn't think someone else would pay the price." She hung her head to hide her tears, but Hailey saw them hit the pavement below.

Hailey didn't say anything for a moment. She let the sounds of the early summer morning talk for her. The smell of gunpowder hung in the air even though the fireworks had long since passed.

Hailey tilted her head back and looked at the stars. She wondered how they could shine so bright despite all the horror they'd seen.

Sara looked over at her. "What are you doing?"

"Looking at the stars."

Sara rolled her eyes. "Carter is freaking dead, Hailey! How can you look at the stars after all this?!"

Hailey looked back at her sister and furrowed her brows. "I don't know what else to do right now. I'm devastated about Carter, I'm worried about you, I'm terrified for Trinity and Trey...None of this was supposed to happen."

Sara looked away, her chest rising and falling rapidly as she struggled to calm herself. Hailey didn't blame her. She was angry too.

After a few moments, Sara softly said, "Ryan was supposed to kill you. Dad wanted you dead. He was going to make you pay for what I did."

Rage burned through Hailey, but it was sorrow that splintered her heart. Though David was her father, she'd always known deep down she was expendable to him. He didn't love his family, he used them. And when they no longer served his purpose, he got rid of them.

How could a father hate his children so much?

All she and Sara ever wanted was his love, but he never had any to give. That was saved for Nicole...and Lauren. For some reason, only those two women were worthy enough of the emotion that seemed to evade their father.

Hailey hadn't realized she'd never earn his love until that fateful summer. Sara, however, had quickly figured it out and lived her life in retribution. He demanded control, no matter the cost. Hailey thought she had long since dusted herself of his manipulation. Yet, here he was, still controlling them and he wasn't even near them.

Finally, Hailey said, "Maybe you weren't doing the right thing. And thirteen years ago, I probably would have blamed you, but we're not teenagers anymore. This isn't your fault, even if it feels like it."

Sara shook her head. "If I hadn't been so desperate to get back at Dad, Carter wouldn't be dead." She pointed to herself. "I've been suffering for years because of him. When will it be his turn?!"

Hailey didn't know what to say. She had often wondered the same thing.

Hailey sat silently and Sara kept her gaze on the stars as if they held all the answers. But they didn't, they only held secrets.

Finally, Sara said, "What if I have this darkness inside of me that's just waiting to take over? I feel it. I feel this compulsion to give into what I know is wrong. I hate him so much, but I might be everything I hate about him."

"You're nothing like him. What you hate about him, the parts of him that he used to destroy people, you used to survive."

"How do you know? I'm so scared I won't be able to come back from this dark place."

"Because you're scared of it. Because you know it's darkness." Hailey sighed. "Dad thrives on darkness. It molded him into a monster. But you...it didn't mold you; it broke you. And you survived, despite everything he's done to you."

Sara simply gave a nod as tears silently streamed down her face. They both looked back at the stars, content with each other's company.

Thirteen years ago, these same stars watched as Sara's freedom was stripped from her, a part of her dying right along with their mother.

And thirteen years ago, these same stars watched as Hailey's body and soul bled, her whole world crumbling around her.

Now, these stars would watch the two of them pick up the pieces and rise from the horror they had endured at the hands of their father.

Chapter 29

Sara was hesitant to accept Trinity's invitation to go to the spa. Her niece had all but given her the cold shoulder since they met. But after Trey's shooting and Ryan's attack, the teen seemed to be coming around.

So here she was, her feet in a pedicure bowl, as she, Trinity, Genevieve, and Cecilia got pampered. It had been a long time since Sara had even thought about getting her nails done. She used to look forward to her weekly spa dates with her mother and sister. Now she felt out of place.

Plus, she was still healing from her run-in with Ryan from three days earlier.

Though Hailey had gotten the brunt of Ryan's rage, Sara hadn't gotten away unscathed. Her lip was still healing and the bruise on her cheek beckoned stares from everyone. Trinity and Hailey tried to help cover it with makeup but the dark purple still peeked through.

Sara tried to relax as Trinity shared her life plans, but she found it difficult. She lived in a constant state of paranoia and caution, which was now magnified. It didn't help that she was running on fumes and was nearly depleted both emotionally and physically.

Once again, her gaze swept across the spa as she assessed the building for danger. Gavin was doing the same as he stood near the entrance.

Ryan still hadn't been caught and now David had disappeared. According to Trey, even Lauren didn't know where he was. Sara knew it was only a matter of time before there was more bloodshed.

She prayed Gavin wouldn't be the next body to fall. She was still coming to terms with Carter's death and if something happened to Gavin, she'd never forgive herself. Despite her best efforts, she was quickly falling for the even-tempered man.

Even in his grief, he was aware of her in ways no one else was. His ability to understand her both terrified and thrilled Sara. He knew what she needed long before she ever voiced it to him. And when she had cried over the loss of their friend, he had given her the privacy she desperately needed. He didn't feel the need to fix things as many men did. He was content with her emotions, however erratic or absent they may be.

Trinity's voice brought Sara back to reality. "I want to become a doctor one day, but I don't know what kind. I just want to help people." She shrugged. "It helps that they make a lot of money, too."

Sara was amused by the girl. She was actually more like Sara than she was like Hailey: sarcastic, blunt, and sometimes somber. She wasn't sure if it was simply the hormones of being a teenager, but Sara enjoyed having someone mirror the traits that many didn't understand.

"That's cool. So, what do you do for fun?" Sara rolled her eyes at herself. What a lame question. But truthfully, she didn't know how to hold a conversation with an adult, let alone a teenager.

"I usually read and just hang with friends...dance. Sometimes I'll go to the movies, but Mom doesn't let me do a lot of stuff."

"Your mom sounds lame," Sara teased.

Trinity snickered as Genevieve said, "Sara, stop being ugly."

Sara smiled and winked at Genevieve and the woman giggled alongside them. It reminded Sara of the days when she and Hailey would fight, and Genevieve would make them hold hands until they could get along.

Though Sara was still hurt by Genevieve's choice to stay silent about David's abuse, she couldn't stay angry at the woman. Truthfully, she simply didn't have the energy to hold on to that rage. So, she forgave the woman who had taken care of her as a little girl. Sara loved her too much to hate her.

The four of them finished their pedicures and headed to the pizzeria in town. Sara was hesitant to walk into the doors of the restaurant, uncomfortable knowing Nicole had been the one to rip her family apart, but the girls had wanted pizza. So, Sara pushed aside her angst, and Genevieve placed their order while Sara, Trinity, and Cecilia found a booth to sit at, Gavin following behind.

He held her hand under the table and this time, Sara didn't pull away. It felt strange having feelings for someone after all this time. And it was laughable that it was her sister's ex. Not to mention the fact that Sara hadn't much cared for him when they were teenagers.

"Sara," Genevieve said as she nodded toward the front door, her brow raised.

Immediately, Sara tensed. Chase Renner stood in the doorway. The anger that had been there earlier had dissipated and was replaced with the calmness he had years ago.

He waved her over and walked out the front door.

Sara exchanged a curious glance with Gavin and excused herself, Gavin following suit.

She stopped just outside the front door and turned to Gavin, putting her hand on her forehead to shield her eyes from the sun. She motioned to her bruises and said, "You don't need to follow me, I can take care of myself."

He caressed the cut on her lip and her bruised cheek with his thumb. "I know, but I care about you too much to let anything happen to you again. I won't eavesdrop, I just want to keep you safe. Plus, I have a better view of the front door if I'm standing next to it."

She smiled and gently touched his hand that rested on her face. "No, you need to be in there watching Trinity. I guarantee if something happens to her, Trey will come after you. Go have Trinity's eight or whatever it is you say."

He laughed. "Six. We've got each other's six."

"Whatever." Sara said dryly, but then smiled once she turned around.

Auburndale was quiet, despite it being lunch hour. Only a few people walked the street as everyone tried to stay indoors in order to escape the sweltering heat.

She made her way to Chase who was standing on the sidewalk, a few feet away from the building.

Sara steeled herself for what he might say. She awkwardly said, "Hey."

Chase immediately hugged her, and she stiffened as he said, "I was walking to my car and saw you go into the restaurant. I wanted to make sure you were okay... I heard about what happened."

News of the attack had spread like wildfire along with the fact that Sara Gallagher- murderer- was the victim of said attack. Many people thought she deserved it, something she wondered as well.

He let her go and she simply said, "I'm fine."

The two stared at each other. Sara felt vulnerable and the familiar sensation of panic began to creep in. "Are we just going to stare at each other, or do you have something to say?"

Chase raised a brow. "I see the sarcasm and attitude is still intact."

"Yeah, well, prison will do that to you."

"Sara-"

"Look, someone just tried to kill me and my sister, so I don't really have time for whatever *this* is."

Chase shook his head. "I honestly can't imagine what you've been through."

She shrugged. "It is what it is."

"So, Gavin O'Dell?" he said, nodding toward the door.

She understood the inflection of his voice. His audacity pissed her off. "That's what you wanted to talk to me about?"

Sara was about to leave when Chase quickly said, "We didn't exactly leave things on the best terms. I was really angry at you, but I shouldn't have shut you out."

Sara shifted. She was irked by his need to be her knight in shining armor, as if she needed saving now. She nearly scoffed at that thought. If anything, this was the first time in her life when she didn't need saving. His timing was awful.

He hadn't said a word to her since they broke up that summer, and now all of a sudden, he wanted to make amends? She was the one who had cheated on him. She was the one who had told him to stay in Auburndale while she went off to New York and L.A. to pursue her stardom dreams, even though he begged to come with her and build a life together. And she was the one who had always chosen drugs over him.

And every time, he tried to save her; fix her. But she had needed a man who could handle her, who understood her. Not a knight swooping in to save her.

And if she didn't need one then, she damn sure didn't need one now.

But she couldn't deny that he had been good to her. All Chase had ever done was support her hopes and dreams, even when he didn't like them. He hadn't wanted to leave his hometown, but he had been willing to do it in order to be with her. He had thought she would be a great wife and mother, but he had been willing to give up his dream because she didn't want to have kids and ruin her figure.

Funny, all of that sounded so ridiculous now.

Now she worried about making it through the day, not about her figure or her hair or makeup. *Now* she worried about surviving, not about careers or building a life with someone.

She said, "You don't owe me an apology. Actually, I'm surprised you're talking to me...you know, being a convicted murderer and all."

"I talked to Trey after I heard about the attack. He explained the situation."

Sara chuckled cynically. "You didn't even have the courtesy to ask me yourself? You're unbelievable." She pointed a finger at him. "I bet if Trey wouldn't have told you, you wouldn't be standing here right now."

He stepped closer to her, fire in his eyes. "You're right. I have two kids to protect. I wasn't going to open that door if you weren't innocent."

Annoyed, she threw her head back. "What does that even mean? Why are you talking to me, Chase?"

Chase shifted uncomfortably as he calmed himself. "Seeing you the other day took me by surprise, and I wanted to know how you were."

"Oh, please. You could have asked me that while I was locked up. It's not like I was going anywhere. And that answers your question: I just got out of prison after serving thirteen years for a crime I didn't commit, so how do you think I'm doing? And now, after I'm finally free, I'm being hunted down because there's proof I'm innocent." Sara put her hand up. "Life is freaking great."

She couldn't help but lash out. She felt abandoned by the one person who swore to always love her and protect her. But when push came to shove, and the whole world turned against her, he had too. And she wouldn't forgive him for it.

She was also bewildered by his nerve to ask how she was as if she hadn't just lived a traumatic life thus far. It wasn't as if she went off to New York to actually pursue modeling and was coming back to town. It wasn't as if she was visiting after moving away with a wonderful man that she built a life with.

No. She was, by everyone's account, a murderer, an ex-junkie, and a girl who had so much potential but just couldn't live up to it.

What a joke.

She turned to leave but he gently grabbed her arm. "Sara, wait. I shouldn't have said that. That's not what I meant. I just..."

Sara stood with her back to him and closed her eyes. She spent years learning how to detach from her emotions, because feeling anything got you hurt or killed. But being around Chase, she didn't think she could and that terrified her.

Yet, as much as Sara wanted to run away, she also wanted to stay with him. Even after all these years, after the betrayal and heartache, she couldn't deny the heat that burned within her when he spoke to her.

Sara knew she should push those thoughts from her mind, but she couldn't. After all, she quickly noticed the wedding ring on his finger. She considered living up to the Gallagher namesake and adding homewrecker to the list, but she knew that would only break her even more.

And she really liked Gavin. In the short time he'd known her, he understood her in a way Chase never had. He respected her privacy and secrets, never expecting her to give herself to him completely. He was content with her independence. And he understood that, while she was broken, he couldn't be the one to put her back together.

Chase continued, his voice soft as he said, "I just needed to talk to you. I never wanted to admit it, but I missed you. And seeing you again brought back all of these feelings I thought no longer existed."

Sara quickly spun around. "Ugh! I'm not doing this with you. And I'm sure your wife wouldn't approve either." Sara eyed his ring, and he followed her gaze.

He let go of her arm. "She doesn't have to know."

"You have some nerve-"

"Sara, please." Chase touched her cheek, and she instinctively leaned into his hand, her heart skipping a beat. He paused for a moment and then she pulled away, embarrassed by her reaction.

"We had something special. Even Elizabeth doesn't compare to you."

Sara laughed bitterly. "Do you hear yourself?"

Chase slowly stepped closer. She suddenly found it hard to breathe. She spent most of the last decade grieving their relationship after she royally screwed it up. But he was the one who put the nail in their coffin when he didn't come to her defense while she rotted behind bars.

So much for a love so special...

She was angry at herself for wanting to kiss him in that moment. Because as angry as she was at him, she still missed what they once had. She missed their meaningful conversations, the way he made her feel safe, the way he held her and kissed her. She missed Chase Renner.

But she also knew that was a lifetime ago. And she was no longer the same person.

The fact he was married and pining for her showed that he had changed as well. The Chase she had known would have never betrayed his wife's trust.

Out of the corner of her eye she noticed that Gavin had stepped closer to them, making himself known. Sara didn't know if it was for the sake of his promise to Trey or because he was jealous and concerned. Sara looked at him and smiled gently, trying to put him at ease.

Chase saw the exchange. Gavin stood, arms crossed, glaring at Chase. After a moment, Chase looked back at Sara.

"So, you really are going to move on? We could have a second chance, like Hailey and Trey. Do you really want to throw that away?"

Sara studied his face. She had been heartbroken when their relationship ended. She had been selfish and more concerned with getting drunk and high to even notice the amazing man she had in front of her at such a young age.

But even from the beginning she somehow knew it would never work. Chase was a great man...or had been. He was willing to give up anything and everything for Sara's happiness and, as an adult, Sara could see how toxic that was.

Even as an eighteen-year-old, she would often get annoyed with Chase for being so doting. He wouldn't fight with her or fight for what he wanted. He simply rolled over and did whatever she said. He expected her to spend every waking minute with him, giving him more than she had to offer.

But she needed someone who would challenge her when she needed it. Who would respect her privacy and secrets. She needed someone who was content with what little she had to offer.

Somehow, even then, she had known it wouldn't have worked.

Which is why she slept with her casting director.

She was bored and wanted to spice things up. She was tired of having a yes-man and wanted someone who would make her feel alive (even if it was only for one night). She wanted to feel free, something she'd never truly felt before.

She told Chase about her affair, and he had quickly forgiven her, surprisingly to her dismay. Then he said he would follow her to New York and support her with anything she wanted. It was in that moment she couldn't breathe, much like she couldn't now. Chase suffocated her and she needed freedom.

Yet, she had still loved him so deeply it scared her.

Thirteen years later he was still suffocating her.

And she was still so deeply in love with him it scared her.

But this time, she wasn't calling it quits out of selfishness. This time, she was doing it because she loved herself enough to choose what was best for her. For the first time in her life, she was making the right choice and not the selfish choice.

And maybe that meant she needed to put her revenge to rest. Her sister was right, it would only bring more heartache. Hailey deserved her second chance at having a family. Trinity deserved to have a relationship with her father. Gavin deserved happiness. And Carter...he should still be alive.

And Sara deserved better. She deserved a life of peace.

Sara sighed. "I can't do this, Chase. I don't want to do this. I don't love you anymore." She eyed Gavin. "I'm seeing someone else, and I really like him."

Chase clenched his jaw as she continued, "Go work things out with your wife. You deserve someone who can make you happy and that's not me."

With that, Sara left Chase standing on the sidewalk.

She didn't want to. Selfishly, she wanted to rekindle the fire they once had, to build a life with him, to pretend the last thirteen years had never happened. But she couldn't.

She would always be seen as the villain, even if she was truly the princess who had been left behind in the tower. But instead of being a damsel in distress, she would save herself.

If she had learned anything over the last decade it was that you can't depend on anyone to save you.

Either you saved yourself or you died while you waited for someone else to do it.

Chapter 30

July 7, 2011
12:45 pm

Today was the first day Hailey had gotten out of bed. Her sides and abdomen were sore, and bruises covered her body. It hurt to move. But more than that, her heart was heavy. Their friend was dead, and she was to blame.

Carter had dashed into the house, chasing Ryan out the back door. The sound of gunshots had collided with the thundering of fireworks. She could hardly tell them apart. She had wanted to get up, to see what had happened just beyond the door frame, but she couldn't move.

Then, Gavin had rushed in and carried her outside.

It wasn't until she saw the body bag that she had realized she'd never seen Carter come back inside.

She had laid in bed for the last two days, staring at the ceiling as she wondered if they made the right choice in re-opening her mother's case, Trey's concern growing. Hailey tried to put on a brave face for Trinity, but even that was difficult.

There had been so many casualties. And for what? Nothing. They weren't any closer to figuring out what happened that night any more than they were the day she had watched the video. And now, people were dead.

Early this morning, she had finally dragged herself out of bed and stood in front of the mirror in Trey's room. She had studied her bruises and cuts and scrapes. She hated them, hated what they represented: secrets, lies, pain, death. They were a reminder that Ryan had hurt her again.

But Hailey had held her head high, her reflection gazing back at her. This time, she wore her bruises like a badge of honor. And instead of being a reminder of the horror she survived, they would now be a reminder of the sacrifice Carter made. And she wouldn't let that be in vain.

She was going to get the truth and expose the secrets that caused such turmoil.

Now, she sat in the medical examiner's office with Trey as they sought answers. Hailey rubbed her arms, trying to get warm and steady her nerves.

"I can get you my jacket from the truck," Trey offered.

"No, I'll be fine," she said kindly.

The doctor entered the room and took a seat behind his desk. Trey extended his hand, and the man shook it. "Hey Doc., Sorry to be meeting again."

The M.E. was slightly goofy looking with bush eyebrows and a nose too big for his face. He had kind eyes though, and that put Hailey at ease.

"Yes, well, I'm getting tired of seeing you, Chief. No offense." He said as he lifted his hands as if in surrender.

Trey smiled sadly. "None taken." He then motioned toward Hailey who was sitting next to him. "This is Hailey Gallagher."

Dr. Johnson shifted behind his desk and pursed his lips. "David Gallagher's daughter?"

"Yes, sir," Hailey replied.

He nodded. "You look an awful lot like your mother, may she rest in peace."

Hailey smiled. She found comfort in hearing she resembled her mother. She often worried that one day Morgan's face would disappear from her memories. That she wouldn't be able to recall her beautiful brown hair and bright red lipstick, or the scar near her jaw that she so desperately tried to cover with makeup.

Once again, her heart broke. She wished her mother was here to hold her one more time, to tell her it would all be okay as she brushed Hailey's hair out of her face. But she couldn't, because she was dead. She had been ripped away from the people who loved her, and a deep void took her place.

"We're actually here about Morgan's case," Trey said.

Furrowing his brows, the M.E. said, "What about it?"

"We have some questions concerning the *original* autopsy report."

The man sat back in his chair and sighed. His mouth was turned down at the corners as he hung his head. "I was wondering when someone would figure it out."

"Sir?" Trey said.

Dr. Johnson continued, "You wouldn't be asking for an original report if you thought the one in the file was the original."

"Doc, if you say anything incriminating, I'll have to file a report and arrest you."

The man held up a hand. "Son, I'm dying of liver failure. I have about six months to live. So even if you do arrest me, I won't live long enough to go to jail by the time the trial is over. If I even make it to trial."

"I'm so sorry," Hailey said.

Dr. Johnson shook his head. "It's my punishment for sending an innocent woman to jail." He looked at Hailey. "Your sister is innocent."

Hailey froze. "What did you just say?"

The man held her gaze, shame filling his eyes. "Your sister is innocent. And both Elijah and I knew about it."

Hailey nearly cried. For the first time, someone admitted Sara's innocence. She was both shocked and relieved. For the last week and a half, it felt as if they were chasing a ghost, as if their theories and evidence were meaningless. Now, she *knew* she wasn't chasing something that didn't exist.

But that relief was overcome by anger as she realized this man had been the reason for her sister's strife. How could this man live with himself knowing what he'd done?

Hailey opened her mouth to curse the doctor, but Trey said, "What the hell happened that night?"

Dr. Johnson stood and walked over to a filing cabinet that sat in the far corner of the room. He pulled at the handle and retrieved a manila folder from the back of the metal box. He walked back to his desk and laid it down in front of him as he sat down.

He stared at the folder, getting lost in memory. Finally, he said, "Years ago, before any of this, I lied about something on the stand during a trial. It wasn't anything that would sway a verdict. It was a personal matter that I didn't want on record, so I lied about it. David had proof that I lied and threatened to take it to the board if I didn't do what he said, which mostly consisted of gaining information he could use against people."

He looked at Trey, shame filling his eyes. "You'd be surprised what people divulge when they're grieving over a loved one."

Hailey was disgusted. How could someone manipulate grieving families like that? How could someone exploit them while their hearts were shattered into pieces, likely sobbing in this very room unaware they were being preyed upon.

"As soon as I got the call that night, I knew it would cost me. I got there and looked over the crime scene, did my work, and left. The next day, I had just finished the autopsy when Washington came and asked what the cause of death was. When I told him, he begged me to change the report. He said if we made it look like an accident, as if Sara had accidently killed her mother, then she could potentially get off with a slap on the wrist and very little jail time.

"So, I changed it. Our goal was to either get her off or at least get a reduced charge of manslaughter." He scoffed. "Lot of good that did since she took a plea deal."

Trey shook his head. "Why didn't Eli just refuse to arrest Sara? Why even go through all this trouble if he knew she was innocent?"

"Because David had Eli in his pocket. Eli didn't just bend the rules for David, he completely shattered them. And David kept proof. If Eli ever went against David, he would have been thrown in prison. Plus, Eli is loyal to a fault. I think that's the only time he ever went against David's demands. Not that it mattered." He looked at Hailey. "Your father still got away with it."

"Wait," Hailey interrupted. "What are you saying?"

"Your father killed your mother," he said matter-of-factly. "Then he called Washington to cover it up and blamed it all on Sara. He set your sister up to take the fall for your mother's murder."

Hailey closed her eyes. After all this time, she'd finally found the truth. And she was devastated by it. She'd expected this moment to bring her closure, maybe even peace. But all it did was amplify the turmoil she already felt.

All her father ever did was bring pain to her life. And this moment hurt the worst.

"Do you have proof?" Trey asked.

Dr. Johnson tapped the folder in front of him. "I have the original report. But that's all. I kept it because I figured there may come a time when I needed it."

"Would you testify in court against David?"

Testify? Trey was already thinking of a trial? Hailey could hardly process what was happening in this moment, let alone a future trial.

"Yes, I will. I would like a deal though."

"I'll talk to the D.A."

Hailey wanted to protest, to demand justice, but she knew she would never get it. This doctor was just as bad as her father and deserved to spend the rest of his miserable life in jail. But he would never see the inside of a cell.

Maybe liver failure was karma's justice.

Hailey asked, "Do you know why he killed her?"

Dr. Johnson's eyes softened. "I didn't ask. The less I knew the better."

Trey chimed in, "Is there anything else you can tell us that might help us get some evidence? Everything we have is circumstantial and I doubt it'll hold up in court."

The M.E. shook his head. "No, nothing off the top of my head. Any physical evidence found could easily be tossed because of an unreliable chain of custody. You'll likely need a confession from David himself, along with eyewitness testimony of those who were there that night and whom he blackmailed."

Hailey had suspected her father may have killed her mother, but it was somehow far more distressing to have it confirmed. But what unsettled her the most was how believable it all was.

Hailey needed some fresh air. She felt a migraine coming on and the room seemed to shrink. She stood to leave but Trey took her hand.

"What about the cause of death? What was on the original report?" Trey asked.

"I thought Washington already told you?"

"No sir, he wouldn't divulge any information."

"Well, then I suppose it's time for the truth to come out."

Hailey held her breath.

"Morgan Gallagher was strangled."

Hailey was back at her father's house, but this time Trey was with her. David was still MIA. His lawyers claimed he was away on business and Lauren couldn't shed any light on where he could be. So, if they couldn't talk to him, then they would talk to her.

Of course, Trey was angry when Hailey refused to let him come inside, but she knew Lauren wouldn't tell Hailey anything if Trey was there. Lauren saw Trey as David's enemy and she would treat him as such.

So, Hailey sat in the living room alone with Lauren, eager to see what the woman could tell her. Hailey was certain she knew more than she let on. If Lauren had information about the affair and Ryan, she likely knew about other secrets David was harboring.

"So, you're telling me you have proof the police didn't investigate properly, and Sara is innocent?" Lauren said. The woman didn't bother to hide her frustration and Hailey couldn't blame her.

Hailey said, "Yes. We found evidence and eyewitness statements to corroborate it. We also know my father was blackmailing people."

Hailey let her words permeate between them. She would tell her stepmother about David's guilt, but first she wanted to see how much Lauren knew.

Lauren didn't even blink, confirming Hailey's suspicions. "You knew he was blackmailing people."

Lauren shook her head and looked down at the coffee mug placed between her hands. "I had an...*impression* that he did, but I knew better than to ask questions or make accusations."

Hailey ran a frustrated hand through her hair. "So, letting people suffer is okay? You knew he was hurting people, and you did *nothing*. He may not have physically hurt them, but what he did is inexcusable."

Lauren put a hand up. "I never said it was, Hailey. But I couldn't tell anyone because then everything your father worked for would be gone. His name, his legacy...all of it would be torn to shreds and I refuse to be the one to blame for it. His name is everything to him. So, I'm sorry that people have suffered, but they also made their choice to give into the blackmail."

She was right. Any of those people could have chosen the high road but instead, they went along with it. But it didn't change the fact that what David did was illegal.

The man played dirty.

So, Hailey would too. She said, "You realize I have to tell Trey, right? That means, not only will my father be investigated, but you will be too, for conspiring with him. I think they call it accessory after the fact."

Lauren's mouth gaped open, and Hailey continued, "And when they look into that, they'll have no choice but to arrest him. Eventually, the truth will come out that he killed my mother."

Lauren's color drained from her face, and she tightly grasped Hailey's hand, making her jump. "Hailey, please, you can't do that. Your father may have blackmailed people and manipulated them, but he didn't kill your mother. He's a lot of things, but he's not a murderer."

The fear in the woman's eyes was real. She didn't want her whole world to come crashing down. Hailey felt bad for Lauren. She was being dragged into family drama that had started long before she became a Gallagher. But it didn't change the fact she was waist deep now.

Lauren leaned in closer and peered intently at Hailey. "Your father was with me the night your mother died."

If Hailey hadn't been sitting, her buckling knees may have landed her on the floor. "Were you having an affair with my father?"

Lauren shook her head quickly. "No, not at all. My car had a flat tire and he happened to drive by and helped fix it."

"Why would my father blackmail the police then? That makes no sense if he was innocent."

Lauren hesitated. "I really don't think-"

"If you give me information that can prove he didn't do it, then I won't tell Trey you knew about the blackmail."

Lauren clenched her jaw, angry that Hailey was cornering her. Then she sighed as she said, "He saw it as a fool-proof plan to teach your sister a lesson. I don't agree with it, but it's what he told me. We all know your sister was off the handle by that point and she needed to be brought down a few pegs."

Hailey shook her head. It was just like her father to prey on Sara's vulnerabilities. And it would make sense that Lauren would never bring it up as she wasn't part of the picture until after Sara had gone to jail and Hailey had moved away.

"Why didn't you say something when I first came to you?" Hailey asked.

"Would you have believed me?"

That was fair. Lauren truly had no reason to confide in Hailey.

Now, Hailey didn't know what to believe. Both Lauren and the medical examiner seemed to be telling the truth. Could the doctor be mistaken? For now, she decided to play into Lauren's story, gathering as much information as possible in hopes that it would help bring justice to her mother.

"Is there anything else you can tell me? Anything that might help me figure out who *did* do it?" Hailey asked.

Lauren thought for a moment. "Nicole hated your mother and did everything she could to antagonize her. I think a part of her hated David too, as much as she loved him. You know, 'lovers scorned' and all?"

Lauren's distaste for Nicole was clear, though Hailey felt the same way. The woman had ruined her life and her family.

Lauren continued, "It didn't help that she was constantly getting death threats from another mistress too."

Hailey tilted her head and scrunched her brows. "What are you talking about?"

Lauren bit her lip and looked around, unsure if she should divulge that information. "There was someone else your father was seeing aside from Nicole."

How could this case get any more complex?

Hailey's mouth fell open but Lauren ignored her gesture. "Once your mother found out about Nicole, she was devastated so David stopped seeing her for quite a while. During that time, he saw other women." She shook her head. "One mistress in particular became obsessive and sent your mother death threats."

"What was her name?" Hailey asked.

Lauren hesitated.

"What was her name? You can either tell me or I'll walk out to the car right now and tell Trey about your complacency in my father's crimes." Hailey meant it, too. She was done with all the secrets.

Lauren narrowed her eyes but said, "Her name is Hannah Rowland. She's a local realtor who had fancied your father for years."

Lauren shifted uncomfortably in her chair. Hailey pitied her stepmother. It must be hard picturing your husband with other women. Hailey wondered if Lauren ever suspected David of being unfaithful to her as well.

Lauren poured more coffee into her cup from the pot that had been sitting out. She didn't drink it, though. Instead, she held it in her hands, ushering its warmth to her body.

She continued, "It was just a fling for your father, but Hannah started to get clingy and wanted him to leave his family. At one point she began stalking him. Eventually, he took out a restraining order because she was threatening to harm your mother."

Hailey perked up. "What did she say?"

Lauren shrugged. "I don't know. All he said was that Hannah claimed she would harm Morgan if David didn't leave her."

Hailey nodded, the wheels in her head turning. Lauren may have just handed them the name of their killer. While David definitely had a motive, and the M.E. claimed he was to blame, it sounded like this woman did as well, possibly even stronger than David's. Or perhaps she was simply more willing to act on that motive.

Could the M.E. be wrong about David's involvement? If Hannah killed Morgan and used the affair as blackmail to manipulate David into helping her, David would do it in a heartbeat. He would rather cover up his wife's murder than have his name tarnished.

It was obvious David was pulling strings and Sara happened to be in the wrong place at the wrong time. Now they needed to figure out which strings he was pulling.

"Did my mother ever confront Nicole or this Hannah woman?"

Lauren thought for a moment. "I don't think so. I think your mother just tried to act like she didn't exist, but..." Lauren paused, and Hailey sat silently, on the edge of her seat. "But I think I saw Nicole and Hannah talking one day. Recently, actually. They were outside that little pizza place Nicole works at. They seemed to be in a heated argument, and I thought it odd that two of David's...lovers...were arguing." Lauren spat out the word 'lovers' as if it carried a bitter taste in her mouth. Hailey assumed it did.

"Was my father seeing Nicole when my mother was killed?"

Something flickered behind Lauren's eyes.

"What?" Hailey asked.

"It's nothing."

"Don't stonewall me. If my father is innocent, I need to know all the facts."

Again, Lauren contemplated Hailey's words. Hailey never realized how loyal Lauren was. If she didn't hate her father, Hailey would appreciate it.

"I don't know this for a fact, but I think he and Nicole started seeing each other again shortly before your mother died. He's never outright said it, but there's just something in my gut that tells me he did."

That corroborated their theory that Morgan was leaving David because he'd gotten back with Nicole. And it could also support the theory that Nicole killed Morgan in order to be with David.

"What about Hannah? Did she stay away?"

"I doubt it. I mean, she was obsessed with David so she probably got as close to him as she could without violating the restraining order. I assume she blamed your mother."

"Do you think either of them could be capable of killing my mother?"

Lauren looked at Hailey with sad eyes. "Oh, Sugar, people are capable of anything when it comes to the people they love. I don't know either of them personally, for obvious reasons, but nothing surprises me anymore."

Hailey nodded and the two women sat silently for a moment.

Though she initially thought Lauren had married her father for his money and stability, this conversation proved that she was actually deeply in love with him.

But those who loved David seemed to end up hurt or dead. And that was unnerving.

The question remained: was David to blame for his late wife's death?

It seemed to be the most likely explanation, though Lauren claims he had an alibi. But Nicole and Hannah certainly had a huge motive. And where did that leave Ryan?

She felt as if she was back to square one but had more pieces than she originally started with.

"Listen," Lauren said, "I wasn't around much before your mother died, but if I hear of anything, you'll be my first call." She looked at her watch. "But if we're done, I need to go to the hospital and deliver flowers to Eli."

"Has he come out of his coma yet?" Hailey was hopeful the man would regain consciousness.

"No, but the doctors said he's stable. I feel bad no one is around to check on him now that Loretta is gone."

Hailey nodded. "I really appreciate you talking to me about this. I know it isn't easy for you."

Lauren stood and Hailey followed. Lauren said, "I know you still suspect your father had something to do with your mother's murder."

Hailey opened her mouth to explain, but Lauren held up her hand. "I get it. He can act suspicious sometimes and I know he wasn't always kind to you and your sister when you were kids. But I know he didn't do this. I'm sorry if your sister was wrongly convicted, truly I am. But David isn't guilty either. He loved your mother enough to leave a son behind."

Lauren crossed her arms over her chest as the two walked toward the front door. Trey was already standing at the truck with the passenger door open, assessing their surroundings for any threats.

Lauren waved kindly to Trey, but Hailey didn't miss the disdain that remained in her eyes. It was sad that her father had tainted Lauren's view of Trey all these years. Maybe once all of this had blown over, they could start over. Hailey was really beginning to like Lauren, even for her flaws.

Lauren looked at Hailey with concern and gently touched her arm. "I know we're not close, but be careful, Hailey. It's clear someone doesn't want you finding out the truth."

Hailey didn't respond, just simply nodded. Lauren went to close the door, but Hailey stopped her. "Do you think my mother should have left him? At first, I thought she was a good woman for sticking it out, but now I'm not so sure she was who I thought she was."

"Yes, I do. Your father needed a certain type of woman that your mother couldn't be. She was a good woman, just not for him."

Then, she closed the door.

Chapter 31

Once back at Genevieve's, Sara and Gavin sat outside on the porch swing, listening to the rain beat against the pavement and grass. It was a sound she hadn't realized she missed until now. Years ago, before prison, before her mother's death, and even before the drugs, watching thunderstorms through her balcony windows was something she loved to do.

The sounds of nature's fury somehow brought her peace when she was a little girl. Even then, she understood the darkness and the force and power that accompanied the loud crackling and bright shots of light.

Hailey would always hide under her covers, but not Sara. Sara would stare at it with amazement and envy.

Now, she focused on its sounds, searching with her own fury for the peace rain once brought. Closing her eyes, she gave herself permission to relax and live in the moment. Gavin held her hand, rubbing his thumb on hers as she melted into him, laying her head on his shoulder. As she did, she realized it was the most peaceful thing she'd done since before the drugs. And that had been a lifetime ago.

How pathetic was that? Her life was so destructive that she hadn't had a moment of peace in nearly seventeen years. That was more than half her lifetime.

When she got out of prison, she thought revenge was what her heart craved, to make everyone feel the pain she felt. She wanted to tear them down, piece by piece, like they'd done to her.

But it was in this moment that she realized it wasn't revenge her heart craved. It was peace. And peace was so foreign to her that she set out for blood instead of contentment.

Maybe it was time to lay her revenge to rest.

Gavin pulled her from her thoughts, "Do you want to talk about what happened with Chase today? It looked pretty heated."

She knew he was both curious and slightly worried. Maybe even jealous? She appreciated that he gave her space to choose what she shared.

Sara shrugged. "He wanted to rekindle things."

Gavin tensed but kept his tone kind. "How do you feel about that?"

She lifted her head, looked at him, and smiled. "I told him no. Number one, he's married. Number two...well, I like you."

Gavin lifted a brow and smiled. "Wow, so you admit it?"

She giggled. "I thought laying my head on your shoulder made it obvious."

"Eh, my grandma does that."

Sara rolled her eyes. "Don't compare me to your grandma."

She studied his face, her eyes darting to his lips. He didn't make a move, but she couldn't help but notice his pulse throbbing. She brought herself close to him, her nose nearly touching his. She wanted to kiss him but was scared.

Did she even remember how to kiss? Could she trust him? Would he shatter her heart the way Chase had?

Remembering who she once was, that wild teenager who was unafraid of heartbreak or mistakes, she kissed him gently and he kissed her back. He let her take the lead and she wrapped her arms around his neck, getting lost in him.

He pulled her onto his lap, and she giggled. "Is that better?"

Gavin sat back and grinned, feeling like he'd won the lottery. "For now."

Sara laughed and smacked his shoulder playfully. She put her head on his chest and listened to his heartbeat.

They had known each other for years, their families long-time friends. But neither had said more than two words to one another, their lives too different to close the gap. Gavin had been motivated, driven, and smart. Sara had been lost, broken, and selfish. But now she felt like he understood her more than anyone.

She desperately wanted to open herself up to him, despite the fear that threatened her heart. "You know, I was fifteen when I started doing drugs and drinking. It was weed at first, then it turned into harder stuff. Eventually, my whole world was crumbling. You already know my history with Thomas and how he was an ass to me, but I thought I deserved it." She shrugged. "Then came Chase."

She paused and Gavin didn't interrupt. She was sharing an intimate part of herself, and he respected her choice to share it with him.

Sara smiled sadly. "He loved me in a way no one else had."

"He sounds like he was a good guy. Why didn't it work out? Because you were arrested?"

"Turns out good guys only like bad girls until they're accused of murder," she teased.

Gavin smiled, but there was sadness in his eyes.

"No, we actually broke up a week or so before my mother died. He wanted me to settle down and be a stay-at-home-mom with lots of kids. You know, picture perfect family".

"But you didn't want that?"

"Not at all. I always dreamed of being a model and moving to a big city. Plus, being a stay-at-home-mom and wife sounded like a death sentence."

"So why did you stay with him?" Gavin asked softly.

Sara stood and walked to the railing of the porch, looking over the yard. Genevieve lived in a quaint little neighborhood tucked back behind acres of orange groves. It was the perfect place to have a family. Ironically, Chase would have loved it.

She took a deep breath and said, "He was safe and kind. He supported everything I wanted, even if it wasn't good for me. He'd never say it, but he hated that I wanted to be a model."

She shrugged. "He loved me in his own way, but he didn't love me enough to put his foot down when I needed it. He never told me no, never put up a fight-even when my body was killing itself. He would actually go score drugs for me when I was coming off a really bad high, despite wanting to get clean."

She hadn't realized Gavin was standing behind her until he grasped the railing, his arms surrounding her as he locked her in place. She didn't flinch or move away, though. Instead, she stuck her hand over the railing, feeling the rain as each drop fell over her fingers.

It's funny how rain could be taken for granted. She savored this moment in a way not many could appreciate or understand.

Tears stung her eyes, and she let them fall, mourning with the sky.

"My own father hated me, and I made his life hell. My mother loved me, but I had pretty well worn her down, so she kept her distance. She watched her child all but disintegrate, and there was nothing she could do. I think she thought my inevitable overdose would hurt less if she distanced herself from me. And Hailey...well, Hailey loved me enough to clean up my messes and bail me out of trouble, but even she had her own walls."

"But Chase wasn't like that," Gavin said. It wasn't a question but a statement.

"He was so supportive and caring that I felt like I was suffocating. He was always there, always understanding, never harsh toward me, never fought with me. It was all sunshine and rainbows. And while it was safe, it was *too* safe. He loved me despite how broken I was. And that was the problem: he thought I was something broken that he could fix. But I didn't think I needed fixing."

"So, what happened?"

"My agent reached out and offered me a contract I couldn't pass up. I had a meeting with him, and I realized he expected me to sleep with him and I couldn't lose out on the offer."

She allowed her voice to trail off. She was embarrassed at what she'd done, selling her body. It was degrading and shameful, but back then she didn't care. All she had wanted was to get away from this town and for people to notice her and know her name.

Gavin's jaw clenched and he gently took her hand in his.

She shrugged. "I think a part of me was self-sabotaging my relationship. I told Chase what happened, and he didn't even care that I slept with my agent. He cared more about the fact that I didn't want him to come with me to New York anymore."

Gavin wrapped his arms around her as she continued, "He just kept saying we would work through it, and I couldn't take it anymore. I said I'd be willing to come back and visit or he could visit me, but I wanted to do it on my own first."

"What did he say to that?"

Sara chuckled. "He stormed off. He was heartbroken but I felt so...free. I thought I would feel sad, but I was relieved."

"I'm assuming he didn't visit you once you were in prison?" Gavin asked.

Sara shook her head. "Apparently, 'murderer' isn't a reputation that impresses a potential mother-in-law."

Gavin chuckled, knowing her dark humor was her defense mechanism. She cracked jokes, but they both knew she was still healing from the destruction of her past. And yet, he gave her the space to process her thoughts and traumas the way she wanted to. She loved that about him.

"Do I make you feel like that? Suffocated?" Gavin asked.

Sara turned around and looked up at him. Then she gently cupped his face, her fingers feeling the stubble of his beard. "You make me feel safe and loved and cared for. You don't act like you know what's best for me, even if you disagree with my choices. You let me have my freedom. And that means more to be than you'll ever know."

He smiled at her and she kissed him again.

"Good," he said. "Because you deserve to be free."

Gavin gathered her up in his arms and held her until darkness fell.

Chapter 32

July 7, 2011
8:12 pm

Elijah Washington had been pronounced dead before Hailey and Trey ever made it to the hospital. When Trey had first entered the room, he had been unsettled by the absence of the beeps of the heart machine or the swooshing of the ventilator. Now it was the sound of CSI techs collecting evidence that filled the space. And because the room was a crime scene, Hailey was not allowed to go inside, something she was pouting about.

Shocker.

In the hall, an officer was trying to console Lauren as she cried over the death of her friend. Trey detoured to where the blonde was standing, and gently touched her back. "Lauren, would you like me to call David for you?"

She patted her eyes with a tissue, mascara marking her cheeks and snot running down her nose. "No, I'll be okay. David is in a meeting, so I'll call him later." Her eyes rounded. "David is going to be devastated. How am I going to tell him that Eli is dead?! They were best friends."

Lauren began sobbing again and the officer gently pulled her into his chest and stroked her hair. By the slight grin on the officer's face, he was smitten with the southern belle and was happy to be a shoulder to cry on.

Trey eyed the man and then returned his gaze to Lauren. Once Lauren composed herself, Trey continued, "I know you've already told Officer Montez what happened, but can you go over it again for me?"

Nodding, she inhaled deeply, her voice shaky. "I uh- I was about to come into Eli's room when I saw a man holding a pillow over his face." Her voice cracked and she let out a yelp.

"You're doing great. Were you already in the room or still outside the door?"

"I had just opened the door. It took my brain a minute to figure out what was happening."

Trey nodded. "Okay, what happened next?"

"I screamed and dropped the flowers." She looked over to the puddle of water, red roses, and broken glass that was in the doorway, tagged by a yellow evidence marker. "I startled him, I think. He dropped the pillow and ran off, almost knocking me to the ground."

"Did you get a good look at him?"

She looked at the room full of police then looked at the floor as she twirled her hair. "No."

Trey furrowed his brow. "You know who did it, don't you?"

"He could have killed me! I'm not going to put a target on my back. Look at what happened to Eli, to Loretta. Look at Hailey!"

He glanced at Hailey who was making conversation with a nurse. Though she tried to cover the bruises with makeup, he could still see their shadows. He could hear her cries at night when she would wake up from a nightmare.

Trey felt as if he'd been punched in the gut. He was supposed to keep people safe, but people were dying. And he was not any closer to making it stop.

Lauren started crying again and Trey gave her a moment to stop. "Lauren, we will make sure you're protected, but I need to know who it is in order to do that."

She tore at the tissue in her hands, considering her fate if she told what she saw. Finally, she sniffled and sighed. "It was Ryan House."

Trey stilled. "Are you positive?"

"Yes! I know what he looks like," she chastised

"You're going to need to come down to the station and make an official statement. Can you do that?"

Irritated by the inconvenience, she huffed and nodded her head. She puckered her lips and crossed her arms, a stance in which Trey knew she had done a thousand times to get her way. He was confident no one dared tell this woman no. If they did, they would surely suffer her husband's fury.

Officer Montez quickly chimed in, "Mrs. Gallagher, I'd be happy to drive you to the station and take your statement."

Relishing the attention from the man, Lauren gave him a soft smile while wiping at her tears. "I'd love that, Jimmy." She touched Jimmy's arm softly and Trey thought he might melt right at her feet.

As Lauren began walking down the hallway toward the elevator, Trey warned Jimmy, "Don't forget she's the mayor's wife. Don't do anything stupid."

The young man ran his hand through his hair, debating if a night with Lauren would be worth the ramifications.

Trey brought him back to reality, "Jimmy."

"Yes, sir."

"And don't let her leave the station until we find Ryan. The last thing I need is for her to get hurt or killed."

Jimmy tipped his head and walked away quickly to catch up with the woman.

Trey shook his head and smiled, knowing that if Lauren wasn't married, Jimmy would probably have a shot with the lady.

Hailey was now walking toward him. "What did she say?"

Trey wasn't ready to upset Hailey, but she would just have to deal with it. "I can't tell you because it's an open investigation."

Hailey rolled her eyes. "I figured you'd say that. I overheard some of the cops talking. I know it was Ryan."

Trey shot her a look and then shook his head. "I just can't figure out where he's hiding. No one has seen him since your attack, and they still don't have any leads. How did he get away without being noticed?"

"Well, I was eavesdropping and they're wondering if he had help from someone. They think it may have been a nurse. Or maybe he dressed up as one to get access."

Trey eyed her, annoyed by her incessant need to pry and snoop. But even he couldn't deny her Achilles' heel was also one of her greatest assets.

"Now I need to find him."

"I bet my father knows where he is."

Trey nodded. "I just don't think he'll tell me and he's MIA, too."

"Do what he does: threaten to blackmail him."

Trey smiled. "I don't think that will go over well with a judge or my bosses."

He sighed. Why would Ryan kill Eli? If Ryan wanted to ruin David, he would blackmail Eli into helping him, not kill him.

Trey was even more confused than when they started this investigation. Nothing made sense and so many pieces overlapped and intertwined with one another, yet still didn't make a direct connection to the murder of Morgan Gallagher or Nicole House's disappearance.

He had three working theories, all lacking evidence:

Number one: David killed Morgan and framed Sara, which seemed to be the most likely theory. But it didn't explain Ryan's involvement. And that was assuming Lauren lied about David's alibi.

Number two: Ryan killed Morgan and David was covering for him, as he did for most of his life. It was clear Ryan hated the Gallagher family, especially Morgan. Plus, Ryan had the makings of a killer. It wasn't a far stretch to think he had done it. If he thought Eli would rat him out, it would explain why he had killed the old man.

And lastly: There could be a third person, like Nicole or Hannah. Nicole had a motive, and no doubt David would cover for her. It would also make sense for them to break up after the murder. After all, killing your lover's spouse would cause quite the strain on a relationship.

But after hearing about Hannah, it was safe to assume she may be capable of killing Morgan as well. Stalkers were notorious for escalating. Again, David could be covering for her to save his own ass. But neither of those theories explained Ryan's involvement.

And either way you look at it, David Gallagher was involved. How or how deeply, Trey wasn't sure.

Despite not wanting to even look at the man, they needed to talk to him. He had avoided them the entire two weeks, claiming to be booked up with meetings all over the county, but Trey didn't buy it. What better way to avoid saying something incriminating than to simply avoid the people asking the questions. But sooner or later, he'd have to talk to them.

Trey just wanted it to be sooner, before another body turned up.

"So, what now?" Hailey asked.

"Now, I'm going to go interview Hannah. If she was stalking your family thirteen years ago, she may be able to tell us what happened…as long as *she* isn't the killer." Which Trey wasn't so sure about. "I'll run you to my house so you can be with Trinity and your sister until I'm done."

Before Hailey could protest, her phone buzzed, and she reached into her pocket to retrieve it. "Hello?"

Trey couldn't hear the person on the other end of the call.

Hailey said, "It is. Who am I speaking to?"

A pause as she listened to the other caller.

"What do you mean? Has his wife been contacted?"

Another pause.

Hailey stood completely still. "Cancer treatment? He has cancer?"

Trey was on edge.

"Uh, yes. I'll be there as soon as I can." Hailey hung up the phone and rubbed her face.

Trey didn't wait a moment. "What was that about?"

Hailey shook her head and furrowed her brows. "That was a nurse. My dad was having cancer treatment today and had an adverse reaction to it. I'm the only person listed as a contact."

"Your father has cancer?" Trey couldn't contain his shock either.

"Apparently, he didn't tell anyone. He won't even let them call Lauren and I have to follow strict instructions not to tell her either." Hailey crossed her arms, irritated by her father. Though Trey suspected she was also scared, even if she'd never admit it. Despite Hailey's hatred of David, he was still her father, and she loved him in her own way.

Trey's eyes narrowed.

"What is it?" Hailey asked.

"Your father sent Ryan to kill you and now Ryan just killed Eli."

"Okay, so?"

"We know your father was involved with your mother's death, but we're not sure if or how Ryan was involved. I think Ryan has been helping him take care of anyone he sees as a liability."

Hailey's eyes widened. "He would never have Eli killed. They were best friends."

Trey was angry at her defense of her father. "Hailey, he tried to have you killed! His own daughter. He would have Eli killed if he thought Eli might spill his secrets."

The man had done nothing but terrorize her her entire life and here she was defending him. As much as he wanted to let the anger linger, he couldn't. He knew Hailey had an innate need to protect the people she loved. And he had no doubt Hailey loved her father despite his horrific deeds, at least in her own way.

Though he wasn't fond of her emotions toward David, he loved her for it. She wasn't so jaded she couldn't be bothered with compassion or love. Of course, she knew he was nothing but a monster, but she would still mourn his death when the time came. Because she was a good person. She was kind and gracious. The world needed more people like her.

Trey said, "We need to go talk to him."

Hailey tilted her head. "He's in the hospital, Trey."

"Exactly. He's stuck in a hospital bed. He can't leave. And right now, he's vulnerable. We're going to confront him about your mother. Despite what Lauren said, he either killed her or knows who did. And we both know it wasn't your sister. He wouldn't be telling Ryan to kill people if he wasn't involved. So, let's see if we can get him to tell us what happened."

"Why would Lauren lie?"

"For the same reason as everyone else: blackmail. She lives with him. I'm quite sure it isn't difficult for him to find something he could use to persuade her to lie."

Hailey nodded slowly. "Okay, but what makes you think he's going to tell us anything? He's gotten away with something for thirteen years. Why would he ruin that?"

Trey began walking toward the elevator and Hailey followed. "I don't know. And I don't know if he'll even talk, but I've run out of ideas. We have nothing concrete, and we have no idea what happened that night...but he does."

He pushed a button, and the doors closed. "And we need to know before more bodies hit the floor."

Chapter 33

July 7, 2011
8:37 pm

Sara sat on the couch with Gavin while Trinity watched TV in Trey's room. She saw Hailey's name pop up on her cell phone screen. "Hey."

"Dad's in the hospital. Apparently, he has cancer and had a reaction to his treatment medication."

Sara sunk back into the sofa. "Is he dead?"

"What? No."

Sara sighed. "One could only be so lucky."

She was disappointed he hadn't kicked the bucket, but then found herself on cloud nine knowing his body was slowly killing itself. She shouldn't be so thrilled by the news, but she was.

That man had ruined her life in more ways than one and it was finally catching up with him. She couldn't fathom why Hailey sounded so worried, but then again, Hailey hadn't suffered the way Sara had.

Maybe vengeance was coming disguised as karma.

Gavin stared at her intently, curious about the call.

Hailey said, "We're going to talk to him, and I thought you'd want to come."

Rage boiled within her. Sara hated that Hailey was worried for David, that she still felt any type of love toward their father. The sharp pain of betrayal tore through her heart.

Sara stood, anger flooding her. "Talk to him about what, Hailey? How he set me up? How he ruined my life? Or how I would have to use makeup to cover bruises from him punching me or throwing me against a wall?"

She started pacing. "Right. Let's just forget everything he did and sing kumbaya together. All of a sudden he has cancer and that somehow absolves him of his sins? Fuck that, Hailey."

Hailey said through clenched teeth, "Nothing will ever absolve him of what he's done to us, to you. I risked my life for you, Sara, so don't question my loyalty. Me and Trey are going to see if he'll *confess*. He's stuck in a hospital bed and is likely dying. It might be a long shot, but we're running out of options."

"I don't want to go near that bastard." She slammed the phone closed.

Sara couldn't believe all that was happening. She had been shocked when Gavin had read the text about Eli just a few hours ago. Despite the old chief ruining her life, he had been like family to her. And she couldn't completely discount his attempts to save her, even if he'd gone about, it the wrong way.

And now her father was in the hospital with cancer?

Sara walked back to the couch and sunk into it. Gavin stayed standing, peering out the window. With Ryan's disappearance, Gavin was on edge. He wasn't willing to let his guard down until Ryan was caught.

Sara couldn't help but be on edge too, her anxiety mounting. She was vulnerable. And this time, there wasn't anything she could do about it. That thought nearly crippled her. Over the past few days, she'd had to work hard to keep herself from panicking, something she had trained her body not to do.

"What was that about?" Gavin asked.

"My father has cancer and Hailey and Trey are going to use his deathbed to get him to talk."

Gavin raised a brow. Like everyone else, he hadn't expected that news. "Are you okay?"

Sara didn't immediately answer. She thought about everything she had been through with her father. His torment and hatred for her.

All she'd ever wanted was for her father to love her, for him to notice her and be proud of her. She had been a free spirit and he thought she needed to be tamed. She could still feel the pounding of his fists on her body, the degrading words that passed his lips. He had tried to break her down, but she was too resilient. The drugs hadn't killed her, so he had tried to bury her, and she had dug herself out of the dirt.

How ironic: he wanted her dead, but he was the one dying.

Before she could stop herself, she began laughing uncontrollably; shrieks and cries filling the room. Despite her best efforts to control them, all of her emotions and trauma came roaring to the surface. Tears formed at the edge of her eyes as she laughed and hunched over, wrapping her arms around her waist.

Was she finally having a psychotic break?

Gavin awkwardly sat down next to her, unsure of what was happening.

She finally caught her breath and wiped at the tears. "I'm sorry. I just..." She giggled again but focused enough to stop. "My dad was awful and I'm so glad he got what was coming to him."

"Sara-" Gavin said.

She knew he was worried, but she wasn't going to talk about it. At least not tonight.

"If I wasn't a recovering alcoholic, I'd pop champagne." Sara started laughing again before crying hysterically over all she'd endured.

The monster from her nightmares was finally going to die.

***

Trinity was glad she had turned down the TV in an attempt to eavesdrop on the conversation between Sara and Gavin. Her aunt's high-pitched laughter had alarmed Trinity. Though she didn't know her aunt well, she had never seen her that distressed, and Trinity found it frightening.

Initially, she didn't like the woman who seemed to have caused her mother so much pain. But over the last few days, she grew to really love her. Even if she was prickly and standoff-ish.

She'd been surprised by what she'd found out as Gavin and Sara had talked in hushed tones. As if being related to a convicted murderer wasn't bad enough, she found out that said convicted murderer wasn't even a murderer. It was another family member who had framed the other family member.

How wild! And sick!

And slightly confusing.

She had only met him twice, but her grandfather gave her the creeps. Something about him made her uneasy. Which was weird because he basically ignored her.

She liked her grandma though. Er, step-grandma. Initially, Trinity couldn't believe how young Lauren was, but she had been cool the few times Trinity had run into her around the house with Genevieve.

The woman was a total Barbie too, but Trinity wouldn't hold that against her. If she had Lauren's beauty, boobs, and body, she would probably flaunt what she had without a care, just like Lauren.

Trinity knew she wasn't ugly, but she also didn't think she was pretty either. She wasn't all that curvy and had hardly gotten boobs yet. Her butt was still small, and she had some acne.

Even though she didn't always like the way she looked, she loved her thick black hair. She had been growing it out for a while now and it was almost to the middle of her back. She got compliments on it constantly and she wore it like a crown. She'd always known she got her beautiful hair from her father's side because her mother was a brunette.

Trinity was glad to finally know exactly what he looked like. She also loved that he was kind and protective and a good man. Trinity saw the way he looked at Hailey, as if she was the entire world. She hoped a man would look at her like that someday.

Focusing on the task at hand, Trinity shoved her thoughts aside and looked down the hall for Gavin. Sara had left the house fifteen minutes ago, despite

Gavin's protests. Gavin was sitting on the couch, an old show playing on the TV, the volume low.

Trinity's phone buzzed and a text from Cecilia flashed across the screen. Cecilia had lost her phone earlier in the day, but apparently, she found it again and the two were planning to go skinny dipping with some older boys they had met a few days ago.

> *Rdy? Sneak out the window. We r here.*

Trinity typed quickly:

> *Coming now. Dnt leave w/out me.*

Taking in a deep breath, she tiptoed back to the bedroom. She had to admit, she was a little nervous to sneak out because of the guy who was trying to kill her mother. But since her mother wasn't even here, Trinity's life technically wasn't really in any danger. And besides, she would be with her friends and killers didn't like witnesses.

She went to the window and opened it before she lost her nerve. She scanned the yard but didn't see Cecilia.

She texted again:

> *I dnt c u. Where r u?*

Her phone buzzed a second later:

> *Dwn the st. red truck.*

Trinity looked out the window again and saw the red truck parked a few houses down. She should have known better than to think her friends would park right outside the house. That would be stupid. They would definitely get caught if they did that.

Gosh, she was so lame for never having snuck out before.

Before climbing out the window, she listened one more time for footsteps. When she didn't hear any, she took a deep breath, climbed out the window, and ran toward the vehicle.

Her heartbeat quickened as she ran through the dark, streetlights hardly illuminating the sidewalk or her surroundings. If she wasn't careful, she would trip.

She felt wild and free as she did something daring, but the darkness sent a chill down her spine. You never know what kind of evil could be lurking.

She hurried her pace to a near run, wanting to get to the truck and out of the eerie night. She tugged on the handle before noticing no one was in the car.

What the...

Her brain registered danger, but her body didn't comply. Fear paralyzed her and panic gripped her.

A large hand covered her mouth, and a man whispered in her ear, "If you scream, I'll kill you."

Tears streamed down her face as she let out a soft whimper. She wanted her mother.

Because she knew today would be the day she died.

The hospital floor was quiet, with only faint hums of the air conditioner, beeps of machines, and the occasional squeaking as the staff pushed medical carts down the hall. The stillness was unnerving in contrast to the chaos that was only a few floors away in Eli's room.

It had taken Trey and Hailey nearly forty minutes to convince someone to tell them which room David was in; a nurse had accidentally marked his room as private. But after getting the run-around, Trey had finally flashed his badge and David's room number was magically no longer private.

The door was ajar, and David looked to be sleeping. Hailey lightly tapped on it. "Dad?"

His eyes fluttered open, and he smiled at her. "Hailey, I didn't think you'd come."

He strained to breathe, his body weak from whatever trauma it had been through. He eyed Trey in disgust.

"Didn't expect to see me, though," Trey quipped.

Hailey gave Trey a sharp look and he shrugged.

"Why didn't you tell us you had cancer?" Hailey asked David.

David let out a labored breath and closed his eyes. "I haven't told anyone, not even Lauren. The prognosis wasn't good and it's incurable. The medicine I've been taking only helps with the pain. They gave me two years and I'm in my final months." He opened his eyes to look at Hailey. "The cancer had gotten worse, so I knew my time was coming. I've been running around trying to get my affairs in order, so Lauren isn't stuck with a mess."

Hailey's heart plummeted. She hadn't realized he would be dead soon. She hated the sorrow that swelled in her chest. How could she feel both sadness and hatred for this man? She hated him, no doubt, but he was still her father. And though she had a vast amount of horrific memories of him, she also had a few cherished moments with him.

She had fallen off her bike when she was five and he ran over to help her. He placed a bandage over the scrape and drew a smiley face on it. He had even taken her and Sara on a late-night ice cream run one summer night, all three of them singing along to some song on the radio. She couldn't remember the song to save her life, though.

There were other memories, but she chose not to let them flash through her mind. Because he was a monster and had always been a monster.

And that's what she would remember him as.

At least he was doing one kind thing by getting his affairs in order for Lauren. It also explained the many 'business trips' he had taken over the last week and a half. He wasn't just avoiding Trey, he was getting ready to die.

"Why aren't you telling Lauren? She'll be devastated."

"Because I don't want her to worry I'll drop dead every time we're together. I want to enjoy the time we have left without looks of pity or concern or fear."

Hailey didn't think that was fair to Lauren, but she understood it.

He took another labored breath. "I just took care of my will a few days ago and Lauren will get the majority of my assets, but the rest will be split between you and Trinity's college fund."

"I don't want your blood money."

David didn't look shocked by her response as much as he looked hurt. "Sunshine, this isn't blood money. I'm trying to help you."

His use of her old nickname grated her ears. Hailey Rae, his "ray of sunshine." As a child, she had loved the name and had thought it was his way of showing her affection, even favoritism. But as she'd gotten older, she had quickly realized it was another way to manipulate her.

He would make her feel special and she would do his bidding. And then, as quickly as he had shown his affection, it would be replaced with anger and disdain.

"Nothing you do is ever for the greater good of someone else. And you think giving us money when you're dead is going to make up for everything you put us through?" She pointed at him. "Screw you."

He pinned her with his gaze. David looked from Hailey to Trey, who was standing behind her, legs spread, and arms crossed. He narrowed his eyes at the old man, daring him to threaten her.

David nodded at Trey. "I see you didn't take my advice after all. Maybe if you had, she wouldn't be in danger and people wouldn't be dying."

"Are you still pushing that bullshit? Blaming everyone for your sins?" Sara said from the doorway.

Hailey and Trey turned to her, and she walked over to them. Hailey took Sara's hand and Sara gave it a light squeeze before letting go.

"Well, the murderous daughter returns."

Hailey said, "Just stop. We know you blackmailed the police to frame her."

Sara lifted a brow and smirked. "We might even have reason to believe you killed Mom." She took a step closer. "Let's not forget the death threats and hitman you so graciously sent after us. Though, you really should find better help. Ryan doesn't seem like he's fit for the job seeing as how Hailey and I are both still breathing." Sara pointed at Trey. "Even Trey is still standing."

David didn't respond, he simply glared at them. But they weren't going to be swayed, bullied, or manipulated into leaving.

"What happened the night Morgan died?" Trey asked. He kept his voice steady as he tried to calm the heightened emotions and growing tension. If David was going to tell them anything, he wasn't going to do it with Sara and Hailey lashing out at him.

David reached for the call button the nurse had laid on the tray table. His fingers barely grasped the cord, and it fell onto his bed. Hailey slowly sat on the edge of his bed and pried it from his hands, placing it out of his reach.

"You're going to talk to us," Hailey said.

Sara said, "You can either tell us what we want to know, or we will go public with every theory, every whispered rumor, and every person you blackmailed. I will ruin your name and your legacy. You might walk free, but you will be a pariah and an embarrassment. They may already know about Nicole and Ryan, but they don't know about everything else." She snapped her fingers. "That can change in an instant."

A vein throbbed on his forehead as he tried to contain his rage. "You have no proof."

Hailey shook her head. "We don't need proof. Mom's diaries, Ryan's paternity test, the officer's statements...that's all we need. Who cares about criminal court?" She leaned closer to him, getting inches from his face. "In the eyes of the community, you will no longer be the wonderful mayor. They will finally see you as the tyrant and monster you really are, and you will lose *everything*. I'll make sure of it."

He lunged at her and tried to grab at her neck but his IV restrained him and he quickly brought his hands back to his side as Trey pulled Hailey away from the bed and stood in front of her, shielding her.

"You ungrateful little bitch! I gave you everything and this is how you repay me? I'll kill you just like I killed your mother."

David shook with rage. Sara's mouth hung open. Trey stilled and Hailey audibly gasped as she clutched Trey's arm.

David closed his eyes as he strained to breathe, acting as if nothing happened.

Trey said, "If you tell me exactly what happened that night, I'll see if the D.A. will cut a deal. You're dying and you're well-liked in the community so they will likely try to help you."

"No! He doesn't deserve a deal," Hailey said.

"He deserves the damn death penalty," Sara sneered.

"We need to know what happened and we will never know unless he tells us." He eyed David. "I want to know *everything,* and I want to know who's been helping you. I know you haven't been going around killing people in the condition you're in."

"I'm not telling you shit," David spat.

"Fine, have it your way," Hailey said. "I'm calling Lauren right now and telling her you're on your deathbed."

Her father seethed, glaring at her, murder in his eyes. He had no control here and he hated her because of it.

Finally, David said, "I want my deal drawn up before I leave the hospital, or I'll recant everything."

"Fine," Trey said.

He nodded and began telling them what happened that night, staring at a spot on the wall as if he was transported back in time.

Chapter 34

Thirteen years ago.
June 03, 1998
10:24 pm

David pulled up to his half-million-dollar home. He was proud to say his family had one of the biggest estates in the city, potentially even the county. He came from old southern money, his great-grandparents owning acres of orange groves and the Gallagher estate had been passed down through the generations. They had been pillars in the community for decades, their name carrying weight as if they were royalty.

And because of that weight, no one bothered to dig deep into his financial records. Though he was into real estate by trade, no one knew he was also laundering money through some of his properties. People suspected, but no one cared enough to look.

Plus, he was now the beloved Mayor.

However, his family didn't share that same sentiment. Not that he cared much, he didn't love them either. Especially his wife.

When they had first begun dating, he truly believed Morgan would make the perfect politician's wife. Eventually, though, he became bored of her. And now he'd grown to hate her as she constantly held Nicole and Ryan over his head.

Unfortunately, having a mistress would be distasteful to the public, so he hid Nicole and Ryan away, his own precious secret. One that could destroy his name, his reputation.

But he couldn't end things with Nicole, even if Ryan hated him and Morgan threatened to divorce him. It was different with her. Sure, he had loved Morgan once, but the love he had for Nicole was incomparable. They were soulmates, they were each other's missing half.

When they were together, the world stopped. They laughed together, they had fun together, they understood each other. Nicole was kind and gentle and drop dead gorgeous. Not in a typical way, but she had an exotic beauty about her that was mesmerizing. And she was a seductress. That's what had initially drawn him to her.

They had seen each other at the ribbon cutting of the restaurant she was waitressing in. He had seen her from across the room as he spoke to a few other councilmen. Their eyes had locked and she had smiled seductively. He had immediately needed to claim her, but held himself firm. He had a wife at home who loved him and who was stunningly beautiful.

Yet, he couldn't help but stare at this woman who had kept her eyes on him, almost daring him to talk to her.

So, he had.

Before leaving, he had stopped her as she put away dishes on the shelf in the back. "Ma'am, I'm City Councilman Gallagher." He had extended his hand to her to which she had eyed coyly and had kept stacking dishes, saying nothing to him.

At first he had been confused. No one had ever ignored him before, especially when he told them he was a councilman. He hadn't realized it at the time, but it had all been sport for her. A clever game of cat and mouse in which he would eventually win.

He had gone to that pizzeria once a week for three months before she ever spoke a word to him. Eventually, they had found themselves meeting behind the restaurant on her break to talk, which had then led to rendezvous meetings in his car.

Once he realized how special Nicole was, he didn't want to settle for wild and passionate car sex, he had wanted her to feel special.

She was special.

She gave him something Morgan didn't: Nicole made him feel alive.

Though they had to hide their relationship, he would take her on work trips or they would meet up at a hotel for a long night together where she'd hurry home in the early morning hours. Of course, Morgan eventually began suspecting he was having an affair, but she had never confronted him, so he had kept seeing Nicole.

But when he became mayor, he and Nicole had to be even more careful about seeing each other. That's when they had their first fight.

She was angry they had to be so secretive. She had cried and he had felt awful, but he didn't have a choice. She had paced around the hotel room, not bothering to cover her naked body. He had wanted to claim her again, just as he had a few moments ago, but had contained himself. She was upset and it was his fault.

"I hate being your dirty little secret. Don't I mean more to you?!" She had started sobbing again.

He had somehow managed to calm her down and convince her things were better that way.

A few weeks later, she had found out she was pregnant. He had been ecstatic to be having a child with the woman he loved so much yet was terrified of what would come of it. He knew his secret life may be coming to an end.

He thought he would pick Nicole if it ever came to that. But when Morgan made him choose, he had chosen himself and his reputation. He had promised to take care of Nicole and Ryan, but he knew he had to stop seeing her.

Nicole had screamed at him as she pounded his chest with her fists, two-month-old Ryan screaming in his bassinet as he felt his mother's angst.

Her words still echoed in his mind, "I hate you, David Gallagher! I wish you were dead! I hate you!"

She had smacked him then, and tried to slam the door in his face. Fire had burned through his body at her outburst, and he had shoved her inside her home and into the wall. He had put his hand around her neck and started to squeeze. She had clawed at his grip but he didn't flinch or let go.

His nose had touched hers as he snarled, "Don't you ever disrespect me like that again. You knew this wasn't going to be anything but a secret. It's not my fault you're a whore."

His words had stabbed like a knife, just as he intended. She had cried even harder as she fought him off of her. He had kissed her one last time, a kiss even she didn't protest.

She had welcomed it, knowing it would be their last.

He had left her crying that day, as she screamed his name, distraught.

He had continued to support her and Ryan, even when the twins were born. Though he loved his girls, or rather tolerated them, he was heartbroken that the only son he had would always be a secret. He wanted a boy to carry on the Gallagher legacy and Morgan couldn't even give him that.

Of course, it was Nicole who would give him what he longed for. She was, after all, the one who knew him in the most intricate ways; their bodies completely in sync, even in creating a life together.

As fate would have it, they would meet again. He had been at a hotel out of town on business and she happened to be there with her boyfriend. They hadn't seen each other in five years and he wasn't prepared for the rage that had filled him upon seeing her kiss another man.

Nicole had found herself in his hotel room, though, destiny drawing them together once again. They had spent the rest of the trip entangled under the sheets. He had even missed all of his meetings for that one last fling.

Over the years, they would find themselves in the same place at the same time, fate beckoning them together and they would fall in love all over again. Always believing it would be the last time they would see each other.

That had been a few years ago, and they had continued their affair on and off ever since. She just didn't know about Hannah...his recent ex-girlfriend.

He sounded like a pig but he didn't care. Morgan understood. She might have claimed to leave if he was with Nicole, but she laid her ego aside and understood he was a man with needs she couldn't fill and allowed him to do so in whatever way he wanted.

Hannah was never anything serious, though she thought so. She was simply a means to an end. Initially, he had thought things would be fine, that she would never expect him to be anything more than a fling. But she quickly became too needy and had believed that he'd leave Morgan for her.

Yeah, right.

If he hadn't left Morgan for Nicole, he wouldn't leave her for anyone else.

So, he had called things off and started seeing Nicole exclusively.

Hannah hadn't liked that. She had started sending Morgan death threats and it was causing a rift in his already broken marriage. She had even talked about going public with the affair, but if she knew what was good for her, she would keep her mouth shut.

Honestly, though, he was becoming slightly afraid of her. She would show up at his office unannounced, threatening him. Eli caught her following Morgan and the twins, a gun in her glove box.

David had quickly realized the woman was a lunatic. He took out a restraining order and paid her off in return for her silence. Not like it did any good. She was still lurking in the shadows, even after all this time.

He sighed as he climbed out of his car and slammed the door. He had just left Nicole's, coming home to a woman he no longer loved. He wished he could have stayed with his mistress, but Morgan was getting suspicious again.

He unlocked the door and let himself in.

Morgan was coming down the stairs, suitcases in tow. Heat radiated from her. She knew.

She always said she'd leave him, but he didn't think she would go through with it. Though, now that the girls were going off on their own in a few weeks, there would be nothing left for her here.

He slowly walked toward her. "Morgan..."

She stopped and forcefully put her hand up. "Don't, David. Don't even speak to me."

"Morgan, let me explain."

She walked back up the stairs to retrieve another suitcase. "Explain what? That even after I let you sleep around on me, dirty our wedding vows, you still couldn't stay away from Nicole? I let you cheat on me with whoever you wanted and you still couldn't respect me enough to stop seeing her."

"How did you even find out?" David caught up to her on the top floor where she knelt down to close her last suitcase.

"Are you serious? I'm leaving and you're worried about how I found out?" She stood up again and crossed her arms in front of her chest. "Lauren told me. She said she saw you two together and then it all made sense: you running late again, staying at the office after-hours, late-night phone calls in the den, unnecessary business trips.

"You know, most men would give anything to have a wife that would let them have affairs anytime they wanted. But not you. Not the great David Gallagher."

"Lauren told you?" he mustered.

She forcefully zipped the luggage closed. "Poor girl didn't even realize what she was telling me. She mentioned a meeting from this week and low and behold, Nicole's name came flowing from her lips."

He felt betrayed by Lauren, though it wasn't her fault. She was still young and he hadn't thought to tell her to keep certain matters private. "Lauren is just a receptionist. She must have confused the names on my calendar," David pleaded.

"I hate you," she hissed.

She stood up to leave but David blocked her. "Morgan, please. Think about the girls."

She choked out a laugh. "Do you hear yourself? Maybe you should have thought about that before having an affair and a child with a woman who isn't your wife." Morgan got in his face, her anger burning like a fire he could almost touch. "And let's forgo lying. You're not worried about the girls, you're only worried about your reputation."

She pushed past him and he grabbed her upper arm. "You can't leave me. You promised to love me forever, to stay by my side."

"Guess we're both liars then," Morgan said.

She tried to pull her arm away, but David gripped her arm tighter.

She yelped, "Let go! You're hurting me!"

"No, you're not leaving. You don't get to walk out on this marriage. I didn't leave you for Nicole, you don't get to leave me now."

Morgan spit at him as she tore her arm from his grasp. "Well guess what, you can have your whore and her bastard son."

David shoved her away, appalled that she dared to disrespect him and tarnish Nicole.

Before he realized what he'd done, Morgan's screams echoed through the house. A thud and the cracking of bones reached his ears.

His heart raced as he ran down the stairs. "Morgan!"

Blood pooled around her head. It was bright, and the smell of iron immediately invaded his nostrils. He wanted to vomit, but somehow managed to keep the contents of his stomach in place.

He knelt beside her body. "Morgan! Wake up. I'm sorry. I didn't mean it."

She didn't move or make a noise. Shock flooded him.

He had just killed his wife.

And if he didn't do something, he would find himself locked in a jail cell for the rest of his life.

He climbed to his feet and quickly made his way to his car and began driving around aimlessly. He called Eli. Washington would fix it, the man owed David.

After twenty minutes of driving, he pulled into his driveway to see that Eli hadn't arrived yet. His palms sweating, David gripped the steering wheel and debated staying in the car or going inside.

David calmly climbed out of his car once again and walked up to his home. He froze when he noticed Sara lying in the grass. His heartbeat quickened as panic filled his body.

How much had she witnessed? How long had she been home?

She wasn't moving, so he quietly walked to where she was laying in the yard, only a few feet from the front door. He bent down and felt she was still breathing.

If he didn't need to cover up his own murderous act, he'd wish she was dead with all the foolishness she'd put him through over the years. But he wasn't that lucky, she was just unconscious. And she reeked of vomit.

He stood up again and ran a hand through his hair as he tried to figure out what to do about his worsening situation.

He attempted to wake her up several times, wanting to know if she knew his secret. But she didn't stir.

And then it dawned on him: Sara might not be dead, but he could still get rid of her for good.

He looked around again and when he didn't see anyone coming, he scooped Sara up under her arms and dragged her into the house where he laid her next to Morgan. When Eli showed up, Sara would become a murderer and he would be the grieving widower.

"You lying bastard! I hate you!" Sara lunged for David, but Trey grabbed her and dragged her away. She fell into him and wailed her fists into his chest, the emotional toll of the last thirteen years surfacing.

Hailey erupted with her own rage. "She was just a kid and you took her life from her. Did you know she almost died twice in prison?"

"I'm aware...and a little disappointed to see she's still breathing."

Sara lifted her head abruptly to look at David. Hailey saw the hate in her sister's eyes, could feel the resentment and bitterness that seeped into even the most hidden places of her heart. A chill found its way down Hailey's spine.

Hailey felt like she would be sick.

Hailey walked closer to his bed, her voice just above a whisper, "You're a monster. What you did to Sara-"

"Oh, stop with the self-righteous anger, Hailey. You deserted your sister, too, so don't act like you're beyond betraying her. And your mother was going to ruin everything. All I did was love her and give her the best of everything, and what does she do? She tries to leave me. She throws it all in my face like I'm not the sole reason she was who she was. She should have kissed the damn ground I walked on, but instead she's buried under it. She shouldn't have crossed me."

He had some nerve, as if their life was an amazing fairy tale. He was a horrible father and an even more horrendous husband.

"You're unbelievable." Hailey snorted, shaking her head. "I can't believe you have the audacity to act like the victim after all you've done."

"It was an accident, Sunshine. I didn't mean to push her. And Sara was just the easiest scapegoat. It wasn't right, but it's the truth. She would have destroyed our family if I hadn't done it. I did it for *us*."

"Don't call me that!" Hailey yelled. His ability to effortlessly switch personas was jarring, going from monster to martyr as it suited his needs. He was a narcissist. And at this point, she wondered if she was staring into the eyes of a psychopath.

"Strangulation will be hard to pass as an accident," Trey mocked.

David tilted his head. "What are you talking about?"

Hailey wanted to scream. She was sick of his deception and manipulation. Even after being caught, he still peddled his narrative. She wondered if he truly believed the lies he told.

Hailey said, "Don't act like you don't know what Trey is talking about. We saw the original M.E.'s report. We know she was strangled. Stop lying."

David's face paled. For the first time in his life, David Gallagher was telling the truth. He didn't know about the strangulation.

And if he didn't know about it, he wasn't the one who killed Morgan.

And from the look on his face, he didn't know who had.

Chapter 35

July 7, 2011
10:36 pm

Hailey was speechless. David had truly thought he had killed Morgan and that's why he had worked so hard to cover it up. But if he didn't do it, there was still a killer on the loose.

Panicking, Trey asked, "David, who wanted to kill Morgan? Was anyone there with you or were you expecting someone later?"

David quickly shook his head. The steady beeps of the monitor increased as the rhythmic beating of his heart accelerated. For the first time in his sorry life, he was scared.

"No, no one else was there except Sara. And I don't know of anyone who would want to hurt Morgan."

"Or you're lying. One last ditch effort to save your sorry ass," Sara said.

Sara was right. David was lying again but Hailey didn't know why, though she suspected it was to control what little narrative he had left.

Trey intervened, "We know there were people who wanted to hurt Morgan. Or maybe even hurt you. So, who are they?"

"I don't-"

"You can either tell me the truth or our deal goes away."

Fire burned behind David's eyes. He didn't like being cornered and he hated that Trey was fully in control. The once passive teenager was now a fearless man, hellbent on protecting his family; something David should have done from the beginning.

Sara looked directly at David and pulled out her phone. "Why don't I make a phone call to my journalist friend. I think she'll find all of this quite fascinating." Hailey and Trey exchanged glances as David ignored his daughter.

After a moment, she said, "Fine." Sara punched in the number and waited for the woman to answer.

Before the line connected, David quietly said, "Hang up the damn phone."

She smiled slyly at him. "What's the matter, *Dad*? You don't want her knowing your dirty little secret?"

David's jaw twitched and he clenched his fists. His hate for Sara burned deep within his soul. Hailey found herself terrified for her sister, though Sara didn't even flinch.

Trey said, "Could Ryan have killed Morgan?"

Instead of looking at Trey, David looked at Hailey. "Ryan hated you and your mother."

"No shit," Sara snapped. "An idea *you* perpetuated. He tried to kill Hailey, and you did nothing."

Hailey never forgave her father for what he'd done the night her mother died, or rather what he hadn't done. He had seen the stitches, had watched her cover the bruises. He had handed her towels as she had washed the blood from her body, praying her baby would make it. He had heard her screams as nightmares plagued her sleep.

David had known what Ryan did and he still protected him.

"*Could he have killed Morgan?*" Trey demanded. It was clear that everyone in the room was losing control of their emotions. The tension was mounting, and time was running out. This killer had an end game that was likely already in play, and he was still a ghost.

David snapped, "I don't know! Ryan's the one that's been killing people." He finally looked at Trey. "I told him if he helped me, I would give him a million dollars so he could disappear. He was only supposed to scare people so they wouldn't talk, unless I told him otherwise. Murder complicates things."

"Wow, aren't you just a fucking saint?" Sara said dryly.

"What about Hannah?" Trey asked.

David looked away.

"Answer me."

He shook his head, furious with Trey. "She was definitely crazy enough. But how would she have done it without me knowing?"

Hailey's wheels were spinning. If Hannah was stalking Morgan or David, she would have known about David pushing Morgan down the stairs. She could have come in after David left and finished the job, wanting to make sure Morgan was dead. No one saw any other cars around the estate but there were plenty of places to park on the main road and walk onto the property and never be detected. Not to mention all of the places on the property that offered cover in the nighttime.

And since David *thought* he was guilty, he would still ask Eli to cover it up and make it look like Sara was guilty, never knowing he didn't actually kill his wife.

"Would Nicole kill her?" Trey asked.

David vehemently shook his head. "Nicole may have hated her, but she wouldn't actually hurt Morgan. She loved me too much to do that."

Hailey wasn't completely convinced. Love was blinding. And it was clear that David Gallagher loved his mistress far more than he did his late wife.

David sighed and shook his head. "Talk to Hannah first. But you need to find Ryan. He went AWOL and won't return my calls. He's spiraling and I no longer have control over that situation so there's no telling what he'll do."

Trey nodded, then put his hand on Hailey's back. "Let's talk outside for a minute."

David narrowed his eyes at them, suspicious.

Good. Maybe it will keep him unnerved.

Trey closed the door behind them, leaving Sara in the room with David. "I was already going to talk to Hannah tomorrow, but now I'm even more concerned that she may be, at the very least, a witness, if not the killer. I'm going to talk to her, and I'll push for more manpower to find Ryan."

"Okay, what do you want me to do?" she asked.

"I want you to stay here for now. I'm going to post a security guard outside the door. No one except for ID'd staff will be allowed in and only if it's necessary."

"But I-"

He gently grabbed her arms. "I know you want to come with me, but if Hannah killed your mother, I don't want you near her."

He kissed her on the forehead and took off down the hall.

"I love you," she shouted.

"I love you, too!"

Hailey went back into her father's room and closed the door, hoping the killer didn't come barging in.

Sara awkwardly stood by the door, her eyes burning a hole into David's soul. But all he did was stare at the white walls, ignoring her. She felt like a child again, yearning for his attention and affection only to be met with silence or beatings.

But David Gallagher didn't have affection to give. And what attention he could spare, it was never good attention. He didn't want to be bothered with her or Hailey, they were a nuisance. So, she had acted out.

In the beginning, she was unsure, not knowing what the repercussions would be of her wild outings. And at first, she had liked the attention, even if it was her father yelling at her. At least he noticed her. But then her yearning slowly turned into hate. And everything she had done was to spite the man who should love her more than anything.

She said from the door, "Why do you hate me?"

The beep of the heart machine was his response. A steady rhythm and song of his impending death; one Sara was looking forward to celebrating.

"All I ever wanted was your love, but you looked at me and Hailey as if we were your death sentence." She walked a little closer to his bed. "But you're incapable of love, aren't you? Or at least you're picky about who you give it to."

Silence.

Sara snorted and shook her head. "Even while you're dying you don't have enough decency to answer me."

He narrowed his eyes at her. "You refused to be controlled. Your free spirit needed to be broken but you wouldn't break. You were my reminder that I had one weakness: you. And I'd be damned if I let you get away with it."

Sara stared at the man who had ruined her. She felt a deep hatred, one that darkened her very core. It was an evil that had seeped into every part of her, a cancer that was eating away at her heart.

A wicked grin crept on his face. "Kill me. I know you want to; I can see it in your eyes. I'm dying anyway so you'd be doing me a favor."

At first, she didn't move. She was surprised by his words. Then, she slowly walked to the edge of his bed. She wondered what it would be like to feel his life leave him, to know she had been the one to destroy him. How poetic would it be if she, the one thing he hated most, was ultimately his downfall?

She wondered if she was just as much of a monster as he was.

Then Gavin's face flashed through her mind: his kind eyes and quiet nature. He would hate that she was dancing with the devil, willing to throw everything away. He would hate to see the darkness swallow her, turn her into a monster.

And that's exactly what David wanted. To make her just like him. To take her life from her for good.

Hailey's words echoed in her mind, *"You're a survivor."*

She had survived too much to let David steal one last piece of her before he died.

"I'm not like you," she said.

A laugh wheezed from his lungs. "I see that glint in your eye, the bloodlust. You want to kill me. You have hate flowing through your veins. You are every bad part of me. *You are just like me.*"

"No, I'm not. You think the darkness made you invincible. But your greatest strength is actually your weakness. And at your core, that's what you are: weak. You thought the darkness would make you a bigger monster, but all it did was hide your failure in the shadows. I rose from the grave you tried to bury me in, and I'll be damned if I let you do it one last time."

She stepped closer to him, getting in his face. "I'm not going to give you the satisfaction of killing you." She smiled. "Karma is coming for you, and she's coming with a vengeance."

Chapter 36

July 7, 2011
11:12 pm

It had only taken Trey twenty minutes to make the drive to Hannah Rowland's house and the moon was now high in the sky. If he wasn't high on adrenaline, he might have felt tired.

He winced as he walked up the porch steps. His hand flew to his abdomen, and he gritted his teeth as he squeezed his eye shut, hoping the pain would subside. Once it did, he raised his hand to knock, but the door was ajar.

The hairs on the back of his neck stood up. His instincts heightened as he listened for movement beyond the wooden barrier. He quickly pulled out his service weapon and flashlight and slowly pushed the door with his foot.

He carefully swept through the house, assessing each room, closet, and potential hiding space. After what happened to Carter, he walked with his back to the wall, not taking a chance for Ryan- or someone else- to get the jump on him.

The front door jamb was intact, there were no broken windows, and nothing seemed to be rummaged through.

Maybe she left in a hurry and didn't close the door all the way?

Trey wondered if something had spooked her. After all they'd uncovered, she was likely the one who killed Morgan.

Stalkers usually escalated, and if she realized David wouldn't leave Morgan, that may have pushed her over the edge. Or maybe she thought killing Morgan was the right thing to do: release David from his awful marriage. She even could have done it to get back at David for breaking things off.

People killed for a lot less.

Truthfully, he was glad to see the door was ajar because it gave him probable cause to search the premises. He may not be able to collect evidence, but he could at least look and come back with a warrant.

So, he started in the living room which was tidy and smelled of vanilla. It was obvious a woman lived here. Hannah's home was clean and organized. Everything had a place.

She collected expensive art and had clearly been abroad quite a few times from the many knick-knacks she had on shelves. There was a beautiful chandelier that hung in the middle of the room.

Trey walked to the kitchen, carefully eyeing the floor and walls for any blood, just as they'd found in Nicole's home days earlier.

Nothing in the kitchen was awry so Trey moved to her bedroom. Her bed was made, and she had a water bottle sitting on the bedside table next to a photo of her winning an award. He glanced at the clothes hamper in the corner of the room and almost blushed when he saw her panties and lace bra. He felt uncomfortable seeing her intimate items without her knowing.

Nothing in her room led him to believe there was foul play or that she had been out killing people to cover up Morgan's death.

He slowly opened the closet door. His initial search hadn't indicated someone hiding in the shadows of the small alcove. The darkness, however, had concealed something else.

He ran his hand over the wall as he felt for the light switch. The room illuminated, revealing a chilling discovery.

Photos of David Gallagher covered the back wall of her closet. Some were of him eating lunch or running errands. Others were taken through the window of his home, Lauren's face etched out with what appeared to be black ink.

It was clear the woman was still stalking David, even years after he had ended the relationship with her.

But what really caught his attention was the photo of Morgan and David on their wedding day, except Morgan's face had been replaced with Hannah's. Trey couldn't believe what he was seeing. There were some of the twins and Morgan but, again, Morgan's face was replaced with Hannah's.

Trey's stomach lurched.

This woman was sick.

How long had she been stalking David? How did she get all the photos?

Trey was about to call the D.A.'s office to request a warrant when he noticed crimson droplets staining the carpet. He bent down and studied the trail that led to the back of the closet.

Bracing himself for what he might find, Trey pushed aside the clothes to see what looked like a crawl space door, blood smeared over the white slat.

If he couldn't have gotten a warrant before, he definitely could now.

Heart racing, he took a deep breath and shoved the door open. The smell of decaying flesh assaulted him, and he gagged as he brought up his shirt over his nose and mouth. On the other side of the frame was a small room with enough space for a child to stand. He took out a flashlight and slowly swept the beam around the room.

He cursed and nearly fell back. He was never prepared to see a dead body, let alone find one when he wasn't expecting it. He nearly threw up but regained his composure, slowly breathing in and out.

Nicole House's body glistened as he swept the beam of light across the room one more time. Her skin was gray, almost translucent. His gaze swept over the wounds that covered her. The blood had stopped flowing and was now crusted to her lifeless body.

He may have thought she was simply sleeping if it wasn't for the look of pain that was still etched on her face. Her lips, now blue, were parted as if she'd been screaming when she died. Though her eyes were vacant, Trey couldn't mistake the fear that still lingered.

He gently closed the door, wanting to preserve any evidence and then quickly made his way out of the house to call in a CSI team as well as a judge to get him a warrant. After that, he called his dispatchers and issued a BOLO for Hannah.

In the middle of the chaos, his phone chirped, and he saw he had two missed calls from Gavin. A shiver slid down his spine.

Something wasn't right.

Gavin picked up on the first ring. "Trinity is gone. After Sara left, I went to check on her and her window was open. I found her phone on the sidewalk a few houses down. Apparently, she and Cecilia were planning to meet up. But when I called Gen, she said Cecilia was in bed and the girl's phone had been missing all day." Gavin paused for a moment and then said, "I think Ryan has her."

Trey's heart nearly stopped. Trinity was in danger, and she needed him.

He jumped in his truck and sped out of the neighborhood back toward town. Rage boiled up inside of him. "How did you let this happen? My daughter was supposed to be safe with you!"

"I know, I know," Gavin said quickly, his voice cracking. "I'm sorry. I had no idea she'd sneak out with a freaking maniac on the loose."

Trey rubbed his face. Out of everyone, Gavin understood what it meant to lose someone to Ryan's violence. And the former marine was right. Trinity shouldn't have snuck out.

Nausea threatened him. He couldn't lose his daughter.

"What about Hailey and Sara?" Trey asked.

"I don't know. They're not answering," he said softly.

Trey felt like he was going to come unglued, "Damn it, Gavin!"

Anger consumed him, though, he knew it was actually fear. Fear he would never see his daughter again or that he could lose the love of his life. Fear they would never be able to finally be a family. Fear he wouldn't be able to save them.

Trey took a few seconds to calm himself down. "Meet me at the station." Trey hung up and as he placed his phone in the cupholder, it began ringing and he snatched it up.

Relief flooded over him when he saw Hailey's name on the screen. "Hailey, where are you?"

"He has her, Trey! He has Trinity," she sobbed.

"I know, Baby, I know. Where are you?"

"He told me to go to the cabin in the woods on my father's property. He told me to come alone, or he would kill her."

She was nearly hyperventilating. He could vaguely make out what he thought was Sara's voice as she tried to calm her sister, but Hailey wasn't listening. He desperately needed her to calm down or she wouldn't be able to tell him anything useful. "I know you're scared; I am too. But I need you to stay where you are. I'm coming to get you. Whose car are you in? And is Sara with you? Gavin can't get a hold of her."

"Ryan told me there was a car in the parking garage for me. I think it's Hannah's. Her wallet and keys were in here. And Sara's with me but her phone is dead."

After what he'd just found, he wasn't surprised Hannah was involved.

"Hailey, it's too dangerous. Please go somewhere safe."

"I can't! He will kill her! We both know he will," she pleaded.

Trey could hear the hysteria creeping in behind Hailey's words. He wanted to tell her to wait for him and to stay away, but he knew it was pointless. She wasn't going to listen; she was going to save their little girl.

His heart broke, as he realized the impending doom that awaited him. If Hailey complied, Trey would lose everything. Ryan and Hannah would kill her and Trinity. What he loved most in this world was about to be ripped away from him and he found himself wanting to cry out in rage.

He just hoped he could save them in time.

"Hailey, please be careful."

She tried to respond but static took over her words and the call was dropped.

He cursed, but his phone buzzed again, and he quickly answered, hoping it was Hailey.

"Chief, it's Libby. I have the lab results from the hair found in Nicole's car."

"Did you get a name?"

"Allison Duval. I texted you a photo of her. And, get this, it was linked to a double-homicide cold case. A couple was killed in 1994. Their daughter was the prime suspect and she's been missing for the last seventeen years."

Allison Duval? Who the hell was she?

Trey opened the text to look at the photo of the woman who had been wreaking havoc on his family. His chest constricted.

Trey knew exactly who Allison was.

Except that wasn't her name at all.

Chapter 37

Hailey's call dropped again. Frustrated, she hit her steering wheel.

Pressing on the gas pedal, she sped toward the cabin, hoping she didn't get pulled over in the process. She took a deep breath and wiped away her tears. Trey was right, she needed to get a grip, or she'd end up getting them all killed.

"I don't know what the hell we're walking into, but your sole focus needs to be getting Trinity out alive," Sara said.

"We're all going to get out of this," Hailey said, shaking her head, though she knew it was an empty promise.

"We both know that's not true. Save her and don't even think twice about me. Get out and run as fast and as far away as you can."

Hailey's face contorted in pain. "No! I won't leave you behind. I just got you back."

"Stop trying to save me. You have a daughter who needs her mother. And for the first time in my life, I don't need saving. This is the clearest decision I've ever made."

Hailey didn't respond. She didn't want to have to choose. She didn't want to lose her family. But she knew she would. Ryan hated them too much to let them live.

Sara stuck her pinky in the air. "Promise me."

Hailey tried to blink away the single tear that slid down her cheek as she reluctantly wrapped her pinky around Sara's.

The orange groves pooled together as she raced through the roads. Finally, she came upon a dirt road. If you didn't know it was there, you'd miss it. Most people thought it was just an entry for tractors to get into the field, but it would lead to a cabin if you followed it long enough.

She turned onto the path, and they were quickly secluded as trees surrounded them. The thick branches shielded the moon and darkness loomed around them.

Hailey wondered what monsters may be hiding in the woods, watching them as they drove toward their own terror that waited for them at the end of the path.

"This is something right out of a horror movie," Sara whispered.

The cabin came into view and Hailey had to fight against the panic attack that was threatening her. She breathed in and out, slowly counting to ten. Her daughter's life depended on her to make rational decisions. She could have a mental breakdown after everyone was safe.

Hailey didn't immediately get out of the car. Instead, she sat for a moment, taking in her surroundings, making sure Ryan wasn't lying in wait. She glanced at Sara who was staring intently at the cabin, her gaze slowly following the tree line.

Hailey took one more look around. The dense woods and darkness made it difficult to see far into the brush so if anyone was hiding, she couldn't see them.

Hailey said, "You can leave. I won't blame you if you want to run away and start over. I'm the one who dragged you into this and I don't think we're going to come out of that house alive."

Sara grasped Hailey's hand. "We started this together, we'll finish it together. I'm not leaving your side. Trinity needs us."

Sara got out of the car first and Hailey followed. She wasn't sure how they were going to overpower or outsmart Ryan, but when your child is in danger, most of your common sense and reasoning goes out the window and you're left with a primal instinct to protect- no matter the cost.

Placing her hand on the rusted knob of the front door, she paused. Once they stepped inside, they would not come back out.

Taking a breath, Hailey slowly turned the metal and pushed open the door. The wood barrier gave a sharp squeak. They both tensed at the noise that had alerted Ryan to their presence. She listened for footsteps. Hearing none, she pushed it open a little further and they walked inside.

The smell of whiskey and nicotine filled her, and Hailey wanted to gag. She was beginning to wonder if she would be able to do this, to save her daughter. Every fiber of her being was screaming at her to run, that she was in danger and she needed to flee.

Sara took her hand, leading her forward, reminding her she wasn't alone.

Hailey forced herself to walk through the house, carefully looking for any sign of Trinity. There were no photos on the walls, no knick-knacks displayed, no signs of any human connection. Just a few pieces of furniture, dirty dishes, and trash strewn all over the house.

Hailey could hear Trinity's faint cries coming from a back bedroom. She slowly pushed open the door, holding her breath for what she would find.

The moon, peaking through an opening in the dense woods, casted an eerie glow over the room. The cabin might have made a great romantic getaway if she didn't know about the evil that lurked within its walls.

Trinity's hands were zip tied in front of her, a gag in her mouth. Hailey wanted to cry but remained firm. She could cry when they were safe.

Trinity met her gaze, eyes wide as she shook her head. But before Hailey could say anything, she felt a sharp prick on her back.

"Don't do anything stupid or I'll kill you in front of your kid, *Princess*." Ryan said.

He was mocking her and she hated him for it. Hailey wanted to claw at him for tainting the name Trey had given her. But, despite the fury that surged through her, she let it go. Their lives weren't worth that fight.

Ryan nodded to Sara. "I see I get two for the price of one."

Hailey glanced at Sara whose eyes were a pool of darkness as hatred clouded them. Hailey thought Sara might actually try to kill him. Part of her hoped she would.

"If it isn't the bastard child himself. How does it feel knowing *Daddy* doesn't love you?" Sara seethed.

Ryan's hand connected with her face and she yelped as blood spewed from her lips. "That's rich coming from the daughter he framed for murder. He may not claim me, but he *hates* you."

He nudged Hailey. "Sit by your daughter." He waved the knife at Sara who took in a sharp breath. "Sit on the other side of Trinity."

The two of them complied, though Hailey's body instinctively wanted to fight back. Sara clenched her jaw and balled a fist.

Trinity silently cried and Hailey smiled, hoping to calm her. Trinity hung her head as teardrops fell to the floor. Hailey desperately wanted to reach out and comfort her daughter but refrained. She was terrified that any movement could set Ryan off.

Ryan zip tied Sara's hands in front of her. Then, zip tied Hailey's, his knife still in his grasp. He got inches from her face and sneered, "Say goodbye to your daughter, Hailey. I'm taking her with me, and you'll never see her again." He shrugged. "Or maybe I'll just kill her."

Trinity squealed and sobbed, and Sara lunged toward him. "Leave her alone! She's just a damn kid!"

Hailey's chest constricted. "No, please! Take me instead. She didn't do anything!"

Ryan laughed at their outbursts. "*She's* my prize for helping your father...Well, *our* father."

"What are you talking about? He said your payment was one million dollars."

He stood up and looked down at Hailey. "At first the one-mil sounded great. But then I got to thinking: how can I really stick it to the old man and his Little Princess?" He paused and gently caressed her cheek. She recoiled at his touch, and he reveled in her discomfort. "You know, Hailey, I really, *really* hate you. I've hated you since I found out that David is my father.

"Sitting up there in your castle while my mother and I lived in a trailer with a single AC unit that could hardly keep up. Sure, Dear-Old-Dad sent money, but your wench of a mother made sure it was *just enough* to cover bills."

Hailey didn't respond, she didn't want to escalate his agitation.

He looked at Sara. "And, as luck would have it, you were the black sheep of the family. Even more than I was. Which is quite ironic seeing as how I'm the bastard child. Our father's hatred for you is what saved you from my fury."

He stood over Sara and she clenched her jaw, her eyes like daggers. "But it won't save you today. You should have left when you had the chance, *Sis*."

Sara didn't respond. She was detaching herself, turning off her emotions. She looked at the wall just behind Ryan, eyes nearly glossed over. But Hailey knew Sara was still listening, calculating.

Ryan looked back at Hailey and began walking back toward her, pointing the knife in her direction. "But not you. You were the favorite, the perfect little angel who got whatever she wanted. So I'm going to take something from you that will destroy you. And then I'll tell anyone who'll listen about all our daddy's secrets and ruin his perfectly crafted reputation."

He wasn't bluffing. He meant every word he said.

Sara chuckled. "You're a little late to that party, *Bro*."

Ryan turned to Sara. "I heard about your interview. Too bad you didn't have a big enough pair to tell them *everything*." He slowly walked over to her and bent down, getting inches from her face. She didn't flinch or recoil, she stared at him, her eyes a pool of emptiness.

"I'm honestly disappointed, Sara. I'd always heard you were the wild child, the fearless one out of Gallaghers. The one who hated her father so much she did whatever she could to ruin him...except you didn't. You're all talk."

"You're right, I hate him. Why do you think I came back? I'm out for blood. But unlike you, I'm willing to play the long-game. I'm willing to wait to uncover every secret I can in order to destroy him. I'm not content with just ruining his reputation. I want him to suffer...I want him dead."

Hailey knew Sara wasn't simply telling Ryan what he wanted to hear. Hailey inwardly shuddered.

Ryan smiled. "I see we both inherited his rage. We're like him more than we care to admit. It's what makes us survivors."

"Then let Hailey and Trinity go. I'll kill David for you, and you leave town with your one million. Everyone gets what they want...and what they deserve."

Ryan stood and clucked his tongue. "Unlike you, I hate Hailey as much as I hate David."

He came to Hailey again and grabbed her cheeks. She tried to look away, to remove herself from his grip, but he dug his nails in tighter. "You should have let me kill you that night. If you had, your little girl's life wouldn't be in jeopardy, nor would your sister's. All those other people wouldn't be dead because you started snooping around in something that wasn't your business. But no, you had to live. So now you're going to pay the consequences."

Ryan put his cheek on hers, whispering in her ear, "I'm going to take your daughter and disappear. Maybe I'll kill her...or maybe I'll sell her to the highest bidder."

He laughed as Hailey screamed and pleaded, rage engulfing her whole being. "Don't you dare touch her! I swear I will murder you myself!"

Ryan was getting off on her pain and now Trinity was crying hysterically. Sara struggled to free herself as Hailey shrieked at Ryan, her cries echoing in the tiny room.

He gripped the knife and walked over to Trinity. She began screaming through her gag, trying to fight away from him but he only laughed as he cut her restraints.

Trinity quickly ripped the gag from her mouth as she kicked his groin and he fell back in a heap, dropping the knife. Hailey screamed, and in one swift motion, Sara lifted her arms above her head and brought them down against her stomach, breaking the zip ties.

Ryan pushed himself off the ground, his face contorted with rage. "You little bitch!"

"Run, Trinity! Run!" Sara screamed as she fumbled for the knife.

Trinity froze, terrified.

Ryan stood and charged at Sara. She raised the knife but as she brought it down, he stopped it. He slammed her hands into the wall in an attempt to get her to drop the weapon, but she grasped it tightly. She kneed his groin, and he howled, but the pain only added to his fury. His fist connected with her cheek and Sara screeched.

Hailey bolted toward Ryan and threw herself into him, knocking him away from Sara. The knife clattered across the floor. He shoved Hailey away from him and her body collided against the wall.

Ryan turned to chase after the knife, but Sara tackled him. She brought down blow after blow, his blood spurting all over her face and shirt. He smiled as he grabbed Sara by the hair and dragged her off of him, her screams piercing Hailey's ears.

Hailey saw that Sara was growing increasingly tired as her twin commanded her body to fight, but it lagged with every movement. Hailey tried to get up, but she wasn't fast enough.

Ryan rolled over and quickly crawled toward the knife as Sara scrambled to her feet and ran toward him.

Ryan's fingers gripped the handle.

He pulled his arm back and drove it into her stomach.

Screams rippled through the room as Hailey put herself between Trinity and the horror she was witnessing.

Sara stumbled back into the wall, her hands clutching her stomach. Her eyes rounded and her mouth formed an 'o' as blood flowed from her mouth and around the wound. She slowly crumbled to the floor, her hands reaching behind her to catch herself.

Ryan laughed. "Is that all you've got, Sara? After all the stories I've heard, I expected you to have more fight in you. It's okay, though. I'll enjoy watching the life drain from your eyes. And then I'll kill your sister and your niece."

Slowly, she dragged herself from the ground, using the wall for support as her face contorted in pain.

"There she is," he said with a smile. "The survivor."

But her hands slipped on the blood, and she crashed back to the floor.

Ryan chuckled. "Maybe not a survivor, after all."

Sara slowly lifted her head, her voice strained as she struggled to breathe. "I hope Trey fucking kills you, asshole."

Hailey watched Sara's eyes slowly close and her shoulders slump.

Ryan walked over to Trinity and forcefully grabbed her arm, blood still dripping from his face and hands. Hailey tried to fight him away, screaming as she did, but he threw her to the ground. He brought the knife to Trinity's throat and Hailey immediately stilled.

He shoved Trinity into the corner of the room. "Sit," he commanded. "If you so much as twitch the wrong way, I will kill your mother."

Trinity's eyes widened and looked at Hailey who nodded, trying to keep things from escalating.

He walked back to Hailey and gently poked her in the chest with the knife. Hailey muffled a cry and closed her eyes as Trinity squealed.

"I'm not playing around!" he yelled. "I will kill you if you do anything stupid."

She didn't know how to get them out of this, but she also had to trust that Trey would be there soon. Ryan was already unraveling quickly, and she didn't want to do anything to set him off anymore.

She glanced at Sara who remained perfectly still.

Please don't be dead. Hold on just a little longer.

Hailey wanted to panic, to scream and shout and call for help, but she knew it would only enrage Ryan. And just like thirteen years ago, no one would hear her scream.

Frantically, she stalled, hoping that Trey would get there in time. "Why did you kill my mother?"

He wiped Sara's blood across his shirt. "I didn't kill your mother. I've just been helping the person who did."

"Then why go through all of this? If you didn't do it, who did?"

He enjoyed toying with them. "I'm not telling you, even if I am going to kill you before I leave."

Trinity screamed, "No! Please!"

"Shut up!"

She cowered back, sobbing softly. Hailey didn't know how to calm her down, she was hardly able to keep herself calm.

And now Sara might be dead.

Hailey continued, "Was it my father?"

"Yeah, right, Hailey. He's a mean SOB, but even he's too soft to kill the woman standing in his way. You know he loved my mother more than he loved yours, right?"

Hailey closed her eyes, knowing it was the truth.

He snorted. "What kind of wife lets her husband cheat? And what kind of wife tells her husband to disown his only son?" Ryan was seething now, and Hailey regretted bringing up her mother.

He got inches from her face, her skin crawling as he whispered, "She got what she deserved."

Hailey cursed at him, and he laughed at her angst. All she could see in him was their father, a man who deliberately got off on people's pain. Ryan didn't hold the Gallagher name, but he was every bit a monster just like their father.

He continued, "Like I said, I didn't kill her. But I wish I had. I dreamt about it. Thought about it. Planned it, even. But I never went through with it. Then the Good Lord sent an angel who did the job for me."

He began pacing, letting his guard down as he relived whatever past he was remembering. "It was by pure accident that we met, fate pushing us together. We were both walking downtown, and she ran right into me, spilling her coffee all over me. She was the most beautiful and heavenly thing I had ever seen. She apologized and I stood there speechless."

Hailey tried to slowly loosen the ties around her hands, but they only tightened with her movements.

Ryan said, "We started seeing each other and eventually I told her about David and Morgan, and she could see how much pain I was in. She hated them for hurting me and promised to get revenge. And then she told me her deepest secret and I knew we would forever be joined together. She had killed her parents when she was sixteen."

He smiled proudly. "She was tired of them standing in her way, so she killed them. When Morgan died, I knew my angel had done it. She had done it for me, and I told her I'd forever be in her debt. So, when she needed my help to keep people quiet, I happily agreed."

Hailey was disgusted at how easily Ryan spoke of his heinous crimes, and even more disgusted by the admiration he held for his *angel*. It was creepy how they had bonded over murder, especially her mother's.

Hailey shook her head. "I thought my *father* asked you to help him keep people quiet?"

Irritated, he shook his head. "Helping your father was a means to an end. He and my angel had one common goal. And if helping him meant helping her, then so be it. It was just a bonus that he offered me money to do it."

"Don't move, Ryan," another voice said.

Hailey had been so focused on Ryan that she hadn't even noticed Lauren, her gun shoved into his back.

Relief flooded over Hailey. But then fear slithered down her spine.

How did Lauren know they were here?

"Angel, what are you doing?" Ryan asked.

Chapter 38

July 13, 2011
12:20 pm

"I've worked too hard to keep my secret, to get everything I wanted, just to let you ruin it by kidnapping some kid," Lauren said.

He turned to face her, dropping the knife to his side. She didn't move her gun away from him.

"Don't do this to me, Angel! This is *my* revenge," Ryan yelled.

Lauren waved her gun around the room, causing Hailey and Trinity to flinch. "This was not part of the plan."

How long had this been going on?

Hailey had to give Lauren credit, though. She never suspected a thing. No one did. And that terrified her. This woman so easily pulled the wool over everyone's eyes.

Ryan's face reddened and he was visibly shaking, realizing her betrayal. "How can you do this to me? We were supposed to destroy David together!"

Lauren wasn't fazed by Ryan's outburst. Instead, she smiled. "You were a means to an end, *Angel*. Don't you see, you're supposed to take the fall for this." She tilted her head. "Well, you were until Hannah started poking around."

Ryan threw his arms in the air and began pacing aggressively. "No, no, no. I love you, Lauren, and you love me. We planned to run away, to be together forever."

Lauren laughed. "You can't be serious? You actually believed that?"

He hung his head, and his shoulders slumped, as if he were a little boy who had just been told his dog died. "Angel-"

"Stop calling me that!" Lauren shrieked as she tightened the grip on the gun.

Hailey flinched and Trinity whimpered. Tension filled the room.

Ryan yelled back at Lauren, "You're ruining everything, Angel! I loved you so much I agreed to let you marry that prick so we could end him."

He paused, slowly walked up to her, his nose inches from her. He sneered, "I had to watch the woman I love marry the man I hate. I had to spend my days living in the shadows while he paraded you around like he owned you. I had to sleep in my bed alone every night knowing you shared a bed with my father. I did that all for you. For us."

Lauren rolled her eyes. "You are so dramatic. And stupid. The day we ran into each other was planned. I wasn't in love with you, I was in love with your father. I wanted *him* and I knew I could use you to get what I wanted." An evil grin tugged at her lips. "And I always get what I want."

Bam! Bam! Bam!

Hailey and Trinity screamed and closed their eyes, Hailey moving her body to shield Trinity.

Ryan's body jerked as three bullets entered his chest. He looked at Lauren, eyes wide as he slid down the wall, a trail of blood following him.

Hailey nearly vomited and Trinity began crying hysterically. She fought hard against her restraints, but the ties wouldn't give way.

Lauren slowly walked over to Ryan, her heels clicking against the old hardwood floor. Blood poured out of his mouth as he tried to draw in a breath.

"I love you, Angel," he said, gasping for breath.

"Rot in hell," Lauren responded.

Ryan's chest stilled; his lifeless eyes still focused on her.

"Trinity, look at me, don't look at him," Hailey said, panic rising in her voice. Trinity was crying silently, her petite body shaking.

Lauren stood up and went to Hailey. "Are you ready to die?"

She raised her gun and Trinity screamed.

Suddenly, Lauren crashed to the ground and the gun spun across the floor.

Sara was on top of her and the two were exchanging blows. Hailey knew if she didn't get free soon, Lauren could easily kill Sara. Her sister was on borrowed time and her adrenaline was the only thing keeping her alive.

Hailey rushed toward Ryan's body in search of the knife so she could cut her restraints. But her footing was unsteady, and she came crashing down, her head hitting the floor with a loud *crack*. Her vision blurred and she saw stars but blinked them away.

Bam!

Hailey shrieked, "No!"

Hailey's ears were ringing, and she heard muffled cries.

Lauren was lying on the floor next to Sara, both of them unmoving. Blood was everywhere and Trinity was standing over Lauren, gun in hand, shaking uncontrollably.

A loud thud came from the door as Trey barreled in, gun drawn, followed by Gavin.

Hailey pulled herself up and crawled to Ryan's body, feeling for the knife that had been shoved under his body when he had dropped to the floor. Trey locked eyes with her, and she said, "I'm fine, but Trinity shot Lauren, and I don't know if Sara is dead or alive."

Gavin ran toward Sara as Trey holstered his weapon and slowly made his way to Trinity and gently put his hand on top of the gun that Trinity was holding. "Trinity, it's Dad. Can you give me the gun?"

Her eyes were wide and hollow as she stared down at Lauren's dead body, blood filling the cracks in the old wooden floor. The gun remained pointed at the monster she'd just killed.

"Trinity, look at me," he said gently.

"I didn't help Aunt Sara when Ryan attacked her. I couldn't let Lauren kill her." Trinity finally released her grip on the gun and looked at him as she crumbled into his arms, crying hysterically.

Hailey managed to cut herself free, and she ran to her daughter and held her close, Trey wrapping his arms around both of them.

Only a few feet away, Gavin brought Sara's limp body to his chest and held her tight as he cried into her neck. "Sara, please. Stay with me. I can't lose you, too."

Hailey brought her hand to her mouth and let out a sob. Then, she heard footsteps as other officers raced down the hall. One ran to aid Gavin as he placed two fingers on Sara's neck. "She's got a pulse! Let's go!" Two paramedics were already coming down through the door and they loaded Sara up on a stretcher and quickly rolled her out to the ambulance, Gavin running behind them.

The third officer walked over to Ryan and shook his head, confirming he was deceased.

Then he walked to Lauren to do the same. "Get another medic in here!" he yelled.

Hailey turned around quickly.

Then the medic came and took Lauren's body away on a stretcher and loaded her into the ambulance.

Chapter 39

July 12, 2011
6:37 pm

Sara clung to Gavin as they stood around the gravesite. Funny, she thought rain would be more fitting for such a sad day, but it was the sun that showed it was a force to be reckoned with, though it wouldn't be out much longer. Not a single cloud filled the sky, much like the day when this all began.

A bird perched on a tree branch just above the gathering, as if to signal that Carter was with them.

Sara shifted slightly, trying to ease the pain in her stomach. Though it had been a week since Ryan had stabbed her, she still found herself feeling as if her abdomen had been ripped to shreds. The doctor tried to prescribe her something for the pain, but she refused. She'd rather writhe in pain than become addicted to painkillers.

Hailey and Gavin had been nothing short of amazing during her recovery, both of them taking turns to help her clean her wounds and change out her bandages or drive her around. Even Trinity helped her get dressed or would make Sara lunch.

At first, she had fought with them. She didn't need them to take care of her. But she quickly realized she did, in fact, need them. And, to her surprise, she found herself thankful she didn't have to recover on her own.

For the first time, Sara wasn't alone. She had people who loved her and who *wanted* to take care of her, who didn't see her as a burden. She wasn't quite sure how to process that. So, for now, she simply let them dote on her; something her younger self would appreciate.

Breathing slowly to ease the pain, she brought her attention back to the preacher who spoke of Carter's strength and kindness. Sara found herself mourning the man she'd hardly known. She was grieved she had only gotten to spend a few days with him before he was tragically taken from his friends and family.

His mother, father, and three sisters clung to one another as they cried in agony. Life was cruel. The good die young but the monsters seem to live forever. While Carter would be lowered into the ground, Lauren was living and breathing. She may be behind bars, but even that was too good for her.

Both Sara and Hailey had been livid when they found out the D.A. made a deal with her. After all she'd done, they were willing to give her a life sentence with the possibility of parole after only fifteen years if she told them everything about her crimes.

What a freaking joke the system was.

Finally, the preacher finished the service with a touching prayer and then invited everyone to place a rose on the casket and give their condolences to the family.

Gavin gently pulled himself from her grasp and looked at her. She gave a soft smile. "Go. They need you right now."

He kissed her. "I'll be back in a few."

Sara watched him walk away as Hailey came and stood next to her. "I can't believe this is real. It feels like a dream."

"More like a nightmare," Sara said.

Hailey nodded.

Sara sighed. "So, have you decided if you're staying in town?"

"For now. I can't leave you unattended. We both know you attract trouble like a damn magnet."

Sara smiled inwardly. She didn't dare tell her sister she was happy Hailey had decided to stay. Their relationship still needed a lot of work, but after all they'd been through, it was safe to say they were doing better than when they'd started.

"So where are you staying now that Angie is back in town?"

Sara chuckled. "Miraculously, she didn't kick me out. But Gavin asked me to stay with him."

Hailey raised a brow. "What did you say?"

"I needed to think about it." She shrugged. "It feels really fast and part of me wonders if it's just some type of trauma-bond or something."

"Sounds like you're making excuses."

"Maybe. But I think I need to be on my own for a while, at least in that aspect. I like having him around, but I know I'll need my space."

Sara watched as Gavin talked to Carter's mother across the yard. She hugged him and kissed his cheek. Then, he pointed to Sara and the woman beamed and waved at her.

Sara awkwardly waved back and looked at the ground.

Hailey shook her head and smiled. "He's smitten."

"He's not half bad."

Genevieve walked up to Hailey and Sara and hugged each of them. "That was a beautiful service for such a kind man."

Hailey nodded. "Yeah, it was. I still can't believe he's gone."

Genevieve smiled sadly. "You know, he called me earlier that day and asked me to make them cookies, but I accidentally burnt the batch." She giggled. "He still ate six of them."

Sara smiled. "He's going to be missed."

Genevieve kissed Sara and Hailey on the cheek and took their hands. "I'm so proud of you both, for being there for one another and for finding the truth." She looked at the ground. "I'm sorry I didn't help you when you were kids. Maybe things would have been different if I had."

A tear slid down the woman's cheek and Hailey said, "Gen, you did what you thought was best."

"No, I did what was convenient. And both of you paid the price for it and I'll forever carry that with me."

Sara clutched Genevieve's hand. "You don't have to carry that. We forgive you. And now we all have a fresh start, so don't be too hard on yourself."

Genevieve smiled. "You both have grown into such beautiful women. Your mother would be proud."

Trinity called to Genevieve from across the cemetery, waving at her to come back as Trey tried to quiet her down. Genevieve looked at Hailey and chuckled. "She's my new slave driver now. She wants me to take her home to make cookies with Cecilia. Go figure."

Hailey smiled. "You better go, then. She's not very patient."

"I wonder where she gets it from," Sara quipped.

Hailey rolled her eyes. "From her father, obviously."

Trey winked at Hailey as he waited for Genevieve to walk back over to him and Trinity.

"I better go. I've got wedding planning to do," Hailey said.

Sara nodded but before Hailey walked away, she said, "Hailey…"

Hailey turned around and looked at Sara.

"Thanks…for having my back."

Hailey smiled. "Always."

Sara squeezed Hailey's hand for a brief moment before Hailey walked away. Sara turned around to see Gavin walking toward her.

He said, "I tried to keep busy talking to people while you were with Hailey. It looked like a serious conversation."

Sara shrugged. "Just sister stuff."

"Is everything okay?"

"For once, yes."

He took her hand and led her to the truck. "Let's go grab some dinner."

"Are you sure you don't want to go be with Carter's family?"

"Momma A. blatantly told me life is too short and I better not screw this up with you." He chuckled. "Obviously, she's devastated that Carter is gone, but she also knows life doesn't stop and we should live it to the fullest…at least that's the gist of what she said."

Sara smiled. "Well, then let's go live a little- in memory of Carter."

He kissed her and she opened the door to the truck. As he walked to the driver's side, a flock of birds flew across the sky as the sun's rays beamed down on her. She closed her eyes and took in a breath.

Freedom.

Except this time, she had everything to lose. And that was somehow far more liberating.

And with that, she climbed into the truck.

Hailey kicked off her shoes near the front door. It wasn't until she sat on the couch that she realized how much her feet ached from the heels she'd been wearing all evening.

The funeral had been beautiful, but she couldn't help but feel such anger about the injustice of it all. Even her father wasn't going to be charged since he wouldn't be alive much longer. Hailey still wasn't sure how she felt about that, nor did she think she would ever be able to make sense of the conflicting emotions she felt toward the man.

But at least she knew the truth.

Hailey sighed as Trey extended a hand to her. She placed her hand in his and he gently pulled her to her feet. She groaned. "My feet are killing me."

He laughed. "You'll be fine. Come on."

He led her to the front porch where he stood behind her near the railing, his arms wrapped around her waist. The setting sun painted the sky beautiful shades of pink, orange, and purple. The same sunset they'd watched together as love-struck teenagers.

Life had changed so much in such a short amount of time.

She was finally home with Trey, watching the sunset with him while their daughter baked cookies at a friend's house.

Hailey smiled. *Home.*

She laughed at the sentiment. He had always been home to her, even when they thought they hated each other.

They hadn't talked much about the future. The last few days had been far too crazy to even think about it. But she wore the ring Trey had bought her, a promise she intended to keep this time. She couldn't help but stare at it. As a teenager, she had dreamed of becoming Mrs. Trey Harbor. She wanted nothing more than to be his wife, to love him forever. And now, after thirteen years, it was becoming reality.

That night all those years ago, as they lay entangled together under the moonlight and the glow of the stars, she had meant what she'd said when she claimed to love him forever. And even through the worst of the worst, their love somehow lasted.

And now, they would raise their beautiful daughter together.

She sighed inwardly. Hailey's heart broke for Trinity. Her daughter had been in shock the night they'd been held hostage, needing to be sedated once they had gotten to the hospital. She had screamed and sobbed hysterically as the doctors attempted to assess her. Hailey and Trey had slept at the hospital while they waited for her to calm down, neither one actually sleeping as they kept a watchful eye over her.

Finally, she had calmed down enough for them to take her home, though she was still timid and jumped at the slightest noise, worried that Lauren managed to escape and was coming after her. Of course, the nightmares had her waking up screaming and crying at all hours of the night. The three of them had been sleeping in the living room together because that seemed to be the only place Trinity felt safe.

Thankfully, Trey was taking a leave of absence until he felt he could leave Hailey and Trinity alone. Hailey knew he blamed himself for what happened, despite never voicing as much. She innately knew as much by the way he looked at Hailey and Trinity, or by the way he would hover or reach for his service weapon during the night.

"She'll be okay," Trey said quietly, pulling her from her thoughts.

Hailey turned around and wrapped her arms around his neck. "I know. I just hate that she's so scared."

"Me too." He kissed her forehead. "But she's a survivor, just like her mother."

He was right. Ryan had nearly killed her twice, and both times she had defied his attempts. Trinity was a force to be reckoned with and Hailey knew she would take the world by storm one day.

Much like Hailey once thought Sara would.

Seeing her sister hooked up to a ventilator had been difficult and Hailey hadn't left her side until she was stable. Thankfully, Sara had pulled through and seemed to be healing quickly. Though, in pure Sara fashion, she had discharged herself against medical advice, making everyone upset. Hailey couldn't blame her though. Sara had felt confined to the hospital room, and she needed her freedom...something she hoped Lauren would never know again.

Of course, the police were still piecing together Lauren's crimes, but the FBI was now involved and would be taking over her case. One of the agents who interviewed Trinity had gone above and beyond to help her feel safe. He promised to be there every step of the way and when it came time to testify, he wouldn't leave her side. He'd given Trinity his card and the teenager had clung to it like a lifeline.

Hailey didn't blame her daughter for being so scared. Upon hearing some of the FBI's findings, Hailey was realizing that Lauren shouldn't be underestimated.

Apparently, she had killed her parents and eluded police for decades. Plus, she had been arrested for killing Nicole, Ryan, Hannah, Bobby, Loretta, Eli, and, of course, Morgan. Not to mention conspiracy and fraud and her attempt on Trey's life. And there were whispers that she may have been involved in the disappearances of other people, but nothing had come of those rumors yet.

And, unsurprisingly, all of the investigating agencies were having a hard time sorting through the truth and her lies.

Even Trey managed to find holes in her statements. When he finally viewed the footage from Nicole's restaurant, he was shocked to find that it was actually Lauren whom Nicole had been fighting with. From what he gathered, Hannah had seen the two women fighting and confronted Lauren about it. Ryan was supposed to be the fall-guy, but when Hannah started poking around, she became a liability and Lauren had killed her.

And Hailey hadn't been prepared to learn it was actually Lauren who had killed Eli. The hospital surveillance showed she had been the only person to enter his room in the two-hour window of when he died. She could be seen walking into the room, holding a vase of flowers. She was inside for nearly ten minutes before walking back out, turning back toward the door and opening it where she proceeded to scream and drop the vase, acting as if she'd seen Ryan kill Eli.

She had even used Hannah's car to drive herself to the hospital, knowing the police likely wouldn't notice it for days, possibly even weeks. She knew they would escort her, the weeping witness, to the station for a statement and no one would bat an eye at the inconsistency.

Unfortunately for her, Ryan used Lauren's plan to his advantage when he kidnapped Trinity and demanded that Hailey come for her. Hailey vomited when she found out Hannah's body had been in the trunk the whole time.

Despite Ryan being absolutely heinous, Lauren was likely the most cunning person Hailey had ever met. Even David paled in comparison to his wife in that regard.

That thought sent chills slithering down Hailey's spine. But Hailey took solace in the fact that the secrets Lauren kept in the dark for so long were now coming to light.

She studied Trey's face, memories flashing through her mind. Funny, she had hated this place so much when she first came back to town. But now, it felt like home. And maybe that's because it was always home, even for all the bad memories it held.

"What are you thinking about, Princess?"

Hailey smiled. "Everything. Our past, our future. Me and you."

"I like the sound of that."

"I'm sure you do," she giggled.

"I love you, Hailey," he said

"And I love you."

He kissed her and then twirled her around, causing her to laugh. He pulled her close and they slow-danced together as dusk turned to darkness.

Once night had fallen, Hailey wrapped her arms around his neck and kissed him as they made their way to the bedroom. Trey shut the door and Hailey melted into him, knowing she'd love him forever.

Chapter 40

August 5, 2011
11:32 am

The alarm buzzed loudly indicating Lauren could enter the room. She hated the piercing sound that now controlled her. But she hated the blue jumpsuit even more. And the shackles she wore on her wrists and ankles would not be her first choice in accessories.

The corrections officer took her by the upper arm and led her into the room where she sat at the lonely table. It was a cold room, dirty and void of color. The walls that were once white had yellowed from the grime that had accumulated over time.

A spider scurried across the floor, and she clenched her teeth. With the lift of her foot, she stomped on the creature, releasing her rage.

One last kill.

The guard then brought her arms up in front of her and chained her wrist restraints to the table.

Clearly, they weren't taking any chances with her.

She should feel flattered that they believed her to be cunning enough to harm someone while in chains, but she was merely irritated by the notion. She hated being restricted. She hated being controlled.

The alarm buzzed again, ringing through her ears. She gritted her teeth.

However, her anger subsided, and her heart skipped a beat as David walked in the room. Much like it had when she first saw him.

He had been at a luncheon with the city's representatives and Lauren happened to be dining there too. She hadn't noticed him until he had nearly collided with her as they both stood to leave. She had dropped her purse and its contents had spilled out. Her cheeks had turned red as he bent down to help her clean it up.

He had apologized profusely, his charm captivating.

She knew a snake when she saw one, she just wasn't afraid of them. She was drawn to them. And, as fate would have it, he was drawn to monsters.

She had known right then that they were made for each other. Darkness entangling with one another.

They had started talking, her mentioning she was new to town. That's when he had told her about the job opening at his office. She had interviewed the next day and got the job.

Then she had lied in wake until she was able to become Mrs. David Gallagher.

That had been nearly sixteen years ago.

Now, the bags under his eyes were dark and his hair was unkempt. He was still wearing a button down shirt and tie, always dressed to the nines. He looked as dashing as ever, even if he looked a bit worn out.

"Darling, you look exhausted. Are you getting any sleep?"

He sat down across from her, and the guard left the room. It had been part of her plea deal. She would tell David everything, but only David. They could record their conversation, but he was the only person she wanted to see.

"No, but let's not waste time talking about me, Sweets. Tell me what they want to know."

She tilted her head. "Aren't you going to ask me how I'm doing? I'm locked up in chains after just having been shot. Look at this place!" She looked around the room, her lips turned down. "It's disgusting. And you should see the cells."

Lauren shivered. They were all repugnant lowlifes. She didn't deserve to be here. She was too good to be in prison.

"How are you?" he asked softly.

"Well, if you must know, I'm doing awful." She leaned closer to him and whispered, "Get me out of here. *Now*."

He shook his head. "You know I can't do that. I've tried. So, tell me what you did so you have a chance at getting out. If you hold up your end of the bargain, the lawyers can work out the rest."

She huffed and pouted at him. That look had always gotten her what she wanted but she had an inkling that it wouldn't work here.

She groaned and tossed her head back. "Fine. I'll tell you."

"Start from the beginning, before you came to Auburndale."

Lauren waved him off. She hated talking about her parents; she was glad they were dead. They had been her first kill, at the mere age of sixteen.

"I'll give you the CliffsNotes version. I was sleeping with a teacher for a better grade. That's how it started, anyway. But, like all good love stories, it developed into something more and we wanted to spend the rest of our lives together." She sighed. "My parents found out and forbade me from seeing him. They said they were calling the police and having him arrested."

She conjured up his face. Young and handsome. He had a five o'clock shadow that she loved to stroke. He was a man, and she had been tired of all the little boys who were pining for her. Even at sixteen she had been far too beautiful and sophisticated for the boys her age. None of them were good enough for her. But he was. And she wasn't going to let anyone keep them apart.

"I walked into the kitchen, grabbed a butcher knife and slaughtered them right in my living room. The mess was far more than I had anticipated." She giggled. "I put on my cute little pink dish gloves and tried to scrub everything with bleach, but that only made it worse."

David shifted in his seat. "What happened next?"

"I knew I wasn't going to get the blood out and I had no idea how to dispose of their bodies, so I called *him* for help...except he didn't help me."

Her eyes glazed over as she allowed herself to get lost in the memory she had pushed out of her mind for so long. The moment that made her into the monster she is, the moment that released The Beast from his slumber.

Her cries for help had alarmed him when she had called. He had rushed over, thinking she was hurt. When he had seen what she'd done, he had been mortified.

She still got enraged every time she remembered his face in that moment.

"Allison, what did you do?!"

"I did this for us! They wouldn't let us be together and they were going to call the police. I saved you."

"You're crazy! We were never going to be together; it was just sex! You're a damn sixteen-year-old. You're one of my students."

He had left then, vomiting outside the house as he did.

She continued, "I knew he was calling the cops to arrest me, so I got all the money out of my parents' safe and left. I quickly learned how to find people with connections in order to become someone else and disappear. It's thrilling what a little manipulation and a small favor will get you in the criminal underworld."

"What happened to the teacher?"

Lauren lifted a brow and smiled. "An anonymous tip came in about his...extracurriculars with his students. Last I heard he survived a prison jump...much to my dismay."

"Is that when you came to Auburndale?"

Lauren nodded. "It was nearly four years later, but I needed a small town to blend into."

An alarm screamed and she slammed her fist onto the table, anger burning inside of her.

She hated it here.

David leaned closer to her. "Was I just a pawn to you? Did you use me for some sick game?"

She scrunched her brows together and gasped. "Darling, I've loved you from the moment we met. You were never a game to me."

She wanted to reach out and touch his hand, but her chains restricted her. She wanted to scream with rage at the shackles she wore and the cell she was now confined to. She wanted revenge for Hailey and Sara destroying what she and David had built.

But more than that, she wanted Trinity dead for taking away her freedom. If she hadn't been shot, she could have gotten away.

She inhaled deeply, calming herself. *Everything will be fine.*

Nothing could ever come between her and David. Their love was far stronger than any prison cell or the shackles that bound her hands and feet.

"Then why were you with Ryan?" he asked.

"I figured out that he was your son. I thought he may be my best chance at winning you over. Until I realized his paternity was a secret. I thought: if I couldn't have you, then I could have something that is a part of you. But it was never enough."

"Is that why you killed Morgan?"

She smiled. "Darling, I killed her to free you. I knew you would never leave her, and you would be miserable unless she was gone. Honestly, I hadn't planned to kill her that night, but I saw everything through the window. You left the front door unlocked so I let myself in to see if she was really dead."

She had stood over Morgan for ten minutes before doing anything. She wanted to savor this woman's death, to have it engrained in her memory. But then Morgan started to make soft noises.

Lauren had felt for a pulse and found that the woman's heart was still beating. She couldn't let her live. So, she wrapped her hands around Morgan's throat and squeezed the life from her.

Lauren could still feel Morgan's body going limp as her life left her.

Lauren shivered, delighting in the memory. Morgan had been so confused to see that *she* had been the one to take her life from her.

"And everything was fine until Hailey started poking around. But you already know about all that," she said with a wink.

David didn't react and that angered her. He always loved when she winked at him; he found it sexy and seducing.

Why was he upset with her? This had all been for him, for them.

She tilted her head. "Darling, I did all of this to protect you. You're the one who came to me when Hailey started snooping and I was the one who convinced you to get Ryan to do your dirty work, to silence anyone who knew about your secrets. I even gave you an alibi for that night."

"He was only supposed to scare them," he growled. "Now you've made more of a mess for *me* to clean up. And having Ryan kill Eli was flat out stupid, Lauren. He was in so deep with me he never would have ratted me out."

She shook her head and smiled. "I killed them, not Ryan. I knew you'd never agree to it, so I did what was necessary to protect us, to protect what we've built and the secrets that needed to be kept hidden. Ryan merely helped me clean up the mess and I knew he'd make the perfect fall-guy, better than Sara." She cursed. "I just wasn't expecting him to go rogue, and by the time he did, I couldn't get him to stop. His hatred for you was more than I accounted for. And Eli..." She waved her hand. "He was on death's door anyway. He was a liability, whether you want to see that or not."

"Why didn't you have Ryan kill them if you wanted him to take the fall?"

"I learned early on that if you want something done right you need to do it yourself. Plus," she beamed, "I *wanted* to do it. There's something so thrilling about taking someone's life, playing God. Didn't you feel that way when you thought you'd killed Morgan?"

He didn't answer, but he couldn't mask the hint of joy that flashed through his eyes.

She giggled. "I knew we were soulmates. Our souls bonded over her death. There's a darkness in us, David. It's unique and very few people understand it, but it bonds *us* together.

He simply nodded and said, "What about Hannah?"

Lauren was getting bored with all these questions. *Who cares about Hannah?*

She rolled her eyes. "She was snooping, too. She saw me talking to Nicole a few days before I killed her and started following me. She confronted me when Nicole 'disappeared,' so I went to her house, claiming that I would tell her everything. Little did she know she'd turn up dead too.

"Thankfully, I was able to strangle her and didn't have a mess on my hands. Then, I created that shrine in the back of her closet. It was easy to find photos between our house and Genevieve's old scrapbooks. I even paid a stranger to take photos of us through the window. Plus, I had my own stash from before

I killed Morgan. From there, it was easy to have Ryan hide Nicole's body at Hannah's house and pin everything on her and Ryan."

A vein in his temple throbbed. "Why did you kill Nicole?"

She stiffened at the jezebel's name. Filth. Whore. Lauren hated Nicole more than anything, even Morgan.

"Don't you ever say her name to me," she hissed. "She was coming between us."

"What are you talking about?"

Lauren tried to go to him, her hands still chained to the table. She screamed and pulled at the restraints, her eyes bulging from her face as she tried to break free so she could go to him.

Realizing she'd lost control, she stopped and closed her eyes, inhaling deeply to steady The Beast that raged inside her.

After a moment, she said, "I never planned for any of this to happen. I only wanted to kill Nicole. She was vile, a seductress. Even Ryan wanted her dead." She laughed. "Can you believe that? Even her own son wanted her dead. And she would have been the only one, if Hailey hadn't started snooping around. Then more people had to die."

David yelled, "Why did you kill her?!"

"Because you were sleeping with her again!" Lauren screamed back. "Even after all I did for you, you still couldn't break away from her spell and I wasn't going to become like Morgan."

David leaned in. "I wasn't seeing Nicole."

"Don't lie to me! You were leaving on trips and working late hours. You were doing the same thing you did with Nicole when Morgan was alive. I was there, remember. I was in charge of your books, so I knew when you were having an affair and when you weren't."

He froze and his blue eyes darkened. "You told Morgan on purpose, didn't you? The night she died, she told me you were the one who mentioned I was seeing Nicole. I thought you had no idea the history we had. But you did, didn't you?"

Lauren smirked. "You were never going to leave her, so I helped speed the process along. I freed you from the marriage you hated, Darling. She was suffocating you and I saved you."

David shook his head.

"Not like any of it mattered, you still went back to *Nicole*. But she was never good enough for you. She didn't love you like I do. I killed for you. Would your *whore* do that?"

David slammed his hand on the table and Lauren jumped. "Don't you ever call her that or I'll kill you with my bare hands. She was everything to me and you took her from me."

Lauren saw red. Hot rage burned through every inch of her. No one would threaten her.

She narrowed her eyes at him and grinned. "That's what I did to your precious Nicole. She didn't even see it coming."

David started; breath caught in his lungs.

Good, she had his attention.

"She invited me in, you know. She wanted to see what the new Mrs. Gallagher had to say to her. She just didn't expect me to end her life."

She inhaled, remembering the smell of iron and the warmth of the blood that soaked her clothes. Lauren traced her hands with her fingers, feeling the blood of her enemy as if it were still on her skin.

David shifted and she continued, "At first, I wanted to strangle her like I strangled Morgan." She giggled. "A little poetic flair. But she somehow overpowered me. So, I got a knife from her kitchen and stabbed her until my hand cramped." Lauren lifted a brow. "She called out for you, you know. But it only came out as a gurgling sound as blood filled her lungs. She wept a single tear and then her chest stopped falling as her heart gave out."

She grinned, proud of her dirty deed.

The Beast had been pleased that day.

Her husband was grasping at control, but he wasn't strong enough. She could see his rage, feel the fire inside of him. He wanted to kill her. Part of her wanted him to try so she could prove who was the superior monster.

He narrowed his eyes and stood up, towering over her. "I wasn't seeing Nicole again. I have cancer. All of those meetings and late nights were because I was at the doctor getting pain therapy and taking care of my estate so that *you* would inherit it all."

Lauren stilled; her lungs gasped for air. "Cancer? What do you mean?"

In that moment, nothing else mattered to her. Not his betrayals, not his hurtful words, not his anger toward her. Not even Nicole or Morgan mattered.

He couldn't be dying. They had a life together. They were supposed to be together forever. Didn't he know monsters don't die?

She had beat death, he would too.

David walked to the door and tapped on it. "Goodbye, Lauren. You won't ever see me again."

Panic filled her body as she clawed at the chains, "David, no. You have to come back. You can't leave me here! We're soulmates, Darling."

The officer opened the door for David to leave but he turned around and said, "Lauren?"

She stopped. Had he seen her desperation, realized their love was too strong for him to leave, that they were destined to be together?

Lauren said, "Yes, my love?"

"I loved Nicole more than I could ever love you."

He walked out the door and she tried to follow but her chains kept her in place. She frantically began fighting against them, blood dripping from her wrists, as she screamed, "David, please! You don't mean that. We can make this work."

She began to hyperventilate. He couldn't be dying. They had so much to live for. They had hopes and dreams.

"David!" she shrieked one last time before crumbling onto the floor in tears, her wrists still chained to the table.

Epilogue

One year later

Sara zipped up Hailey's dress and handed her the bouquet. Hailey turned around. "How do I look?"

Angie beamed. "Like the most beautiful bride I ever did see. Well, aside from me, anyway." Angie winked.

Hailey smiled and shook her head.

The day still felt surreal to Hailey. She was about to be Mrs. Trey Harbor, and she was counting down the seconds. She had almost opted for a courthouse wedding, but Trinity convinced her to have the wedding of her dreams. Trinity had been right. Hailey and Trey deserved a beautiful ceremony surrounded by their friends and family as they vowed to love each other forever.

"You're supposed to have something old, something new, something borrowed, something blue." Trinity said as she handed Hailey her gold locket. "The locket is something old, but Dad took it to the jeweler to have the stones switched to a blue topaz. It's a stone from one of your mother's rings that Genevieve still had- which is something blue." Then, Trinity handed Hailey a gold bracelet. "And this is new and matches the locket."

Hailey teared up. "These are beautiful, I love them."

Trinity rolled her eyes. "You don't need to cry, Mom."

Hailey chuckled. "Okay, I'll stop. Is that why you two were gone so long a few weeks ago?"

Trinity smiled and shook her head. "Yes and no. We dropped it off at the jewelers but…" She handed Hailey a piece of paper. "I'm officially Trinity Harbor."

Trinity had asked to change her last name months ago and Hailey had happily agreed. It had just taken her longer than she anticipated with wedding plans.

"I love you." Hailey beamed. Trinity fought and nearly failed to hide her smile.

"That's sweet," Sara said dryly. She handed Hailey a bobby pin. "Here. This can be your 'something borrowed.'"

Hailey lifted a brow. "How sentimental."

"It's the one I use to pick locks with so don't lose it. I want it back."

Hailey laughed and hugged Sara. Sara hugged her back and said, "This is the one time I'll let you hug me and it's only because it's your wedding day."

Hailey shook her head and pulled away. "You're so dramatic."

Angie brought over a makeup bag. "Sara, sit. We need to do your makeup."

Sara made a face as Angie began laying out foundation, brushes, and eyeshadows. "Do I have to?"

Angie stuck her hip out. "Don't be a brat. My house was almost destroyed while I was gone so you owe me."

Sara smiled. "I see you're not going to let that go."

"Not a chance," Angie chuckled.

Hailey walked to the window and stared down at the guests who were trickling in below.

Today had been a whirlwind of emotions, much like the last year had been. Her father had passed away eight months ago and, though it angered many people, Hailey refused to give David a funeral. She and Sara were the only people to stand over his casket as they lowered it into the ground. They wanted to make sure he was buried six feet under.

Lauren had been put on suicide watch when the FBI delivered the news about David's death. The day David left her in prison, Lauren had screamed bloody murder, begging David to come back. They ended up having to sedate and restrain her. Her reaction to his death had been far worse. She tried to kill a guard, two inmates, and herself.

Since then, she hadn't spoken to anyone, so they revoked her plea deal, and she was now looking at life in prison.

After Lauren had divulged her crimes to David, the FBI found letters she'd written to him from prison that he never opened. Of course, that knowledge had sent her into hysterics. She tore her cell apart and beat her cellmate so badly the woman had to be life-flighted to a specialty hospital.

And she likely would have gotten away with everything if it wasn't for the hair she had left at the crime scene and Ryan going rogue on her. The hair they found in Nicole's car was linked to the death of Lauren's parents and, from what Hailey could gather, the facts of the case were still hazy and being investigated.

After finding Cecilia's phone in Ryan's car, the FBI surmised that Ryan had been stalking the girls in an attempt to kidnap Trinity. They assumed he overheard their conversation about sneaking out and when the opportunity presented itself, stole Cecilia's phone and texted Trinity to lure her out of the house.

Unfortunately, Trinity still had nightmares, but they were happening less frequently now. Therapy was helping and she enjoyed talking to Agent Garcia. He seemed to calm her nerves quite a bit. Hailey even found her daughter spending more and more time with Sara, though Sara still wasn't sure what to do with the teenager.

Sara was also working with a lawyer on a lawsuit against the state. From what the lawyer said, it was very promising. For now, Sara spent her days running down leads for Jasmine Johnson. Hailey was shocked to find the woman actually paid her twin very well.

That turned out to be a blessing because many of David's assets had been frozen so there was no money left for the twins to inherit, though the house had been given to them upon David's death. But after some thought, neither Sara nor Hailey wanted to keep it. They decided to give it to Genevieve who had the idea to turn it into a wedding venue, stating that good memories needed to be made at the estate.

And after fourteen long years, their mother could finally rest in peace.

A knock at the door drug Hailey from her thoughts. Gavin poked his head in. "Are you ladies ready? It's almost time."

Hailey took in a deep breath as butterflies filled her stomach. She couldn't believe this was happening. "We're ready," she said with a smile.

Angie handed everyone their bouquets and the four of them lined up. Gavin looked at Sara up and down. "You single, miss?"

Sara rolled her eyes. "Unfortunately, no."

He laughed. "Well, that was rude."

She laughed back. "Go. You shouldn't keep Trey waiting."

He came in and stole a kiss from her. "Promise to catch the bouquet at the reception, okay?"

Sara blushed as he walked out.

"Oooh, I like him a lot," Angie said.

Hailey laughed. "I think Sara does, too."

Assessing her reflection one last time, Hailey smiled and stood behind Sara. Angie opened the doors and led them out of the room and into the foyer of the church where they waited for the chapel doors to open.

Angie walked out first, followed by Sara, and then Trinity. Without skipping a beat, Trinity walked over to Trey and gave him a fist bump, sending a wave of laughter through the crowd.

Cecilia agreed to be a flower girl and Angie's nephew, Jax, agreed to be the ringbearer, despite both of them being Trinity's age. The two made their way down the aisle as Hailey waited for her bridal music to start.

The doors opened one last time, and she looked directly at Trey. He was smiling from ear to ear, and she found herself needing to pace herself. She wanted to run down the aisle, fling her arms around him, and skip everything but the vows.

She couldn't wait to become his wife.

The music played and everyone in the audience stood as she made her way toward the altar where she and Trey promised to love each other forever. A promise they both intended to keep.

<hr>

Six years later

Lauren sat in her jail cell waiting for her next visitation. She was excited to see him again. She had been surprised when he had started visiting her. She had been even more surprised that he knew about her.

She smiled inwardly. He would help her, and nothing would stand in their way.

She thought about Trinity, loathing her. Rage burned within Lauren at the thought of her. That little bitch tried to kill her. What she wouldn't give to unleash The Beast, to tear Trinity to shreds for taking away everything she loved.

She may have been a kid when she shot Lauren, but she wasn't anymore.

And now Lauren was plotting her revenge.

And he was helping her.

Trinity thought she was safe. She thought these walls and bars and chains would hold Lauren in.

But soon, Lauren would be free. The Beast would need to be satisfied.

And Trinity would need to run for her life.

From the Author

Sixteen years ago, I sat in my high school cafeteria as Hailey Gallagher's story came to life. Over the years, her story has changed many times. Characters have come and gone, villains have changed, and even complete plotlines have been scrapped. But, even after all that time, I could never get Hailey's story out of my head. I spent the better part of those sixteen years writing and rewriting, plotting and replotting, until I finally found a story that I loved. And now, I'm sharing that story with all of you.

I would give anything to go back to that moment in the cafeteria and tell my fifteen-year-old self that one day, her 'silly little story' would be published and her dream of becoming an author would be reality. She'd probably tell me to shut the...well, fifteen-year-old Lindsey is a lot like Sara Gallagher, so, you know exactly what she'd say- ha!

Kept in the Dark truly holds a special place in my heart. It's not only my debut novel into a genre that I love, but it's also the story that sparked my desire to write and share my stories with the world. I hope you all loved Hailey and Sara Gallagher's story as much as I do!

So, here's to Kept in the Dark: may it be the first of many wonderful stories that you all love.

Dear Reader,

I'm so glad you decided to pick up a copy of *Kept in the Dark*. I hope you loved getting to see the cute little town of Auburndale, Florida and all it has to offer. It's truly such a special place!

Of course, Hailey and Sara's story leaves off on a bit of a cliff hanger and I hope to give this story (or, rather, Allison Duval's story) the ending you all deserve; and the ending Allison Duval deserves. But don't worry, we'll briefly meet Trinity again in my next thriller *Forget Me Not*. Except this time, she's all grown up, but still full of sass, sarcasm, and the straightforwardness we all love.

Now twenty-six, Trinity has her own badge and gun, working in the Violent Crimes Division of the FBI. She sees the worst of the worst but is determined to leave her mark on the world by putting away as many offenders as she can.

So, when her childhood friend, Sergeant Jax Moretti, calls her to help with a case involving a sick and twisted serial killer, she quickly finds herself back home in Auburndale, Florida. But nothing is what it seems and the monster they're hunting is escalating.

Forget Me Not follows the story of Sergeant Jax Moretti and his partner Detective Jules Reid as they hunt down a serial killer and rapist who has been stalking the streets of the Polk County area for years. With little to no evidence, Moretti and Reid are desperate to find this killer. And Jax soon finds himself falling for Ali Knox, the woman who may hold the answers they've been searching for.

But nothing can prepare him for what he will find. Sometimes, the truth is better left forgotten. And sometimes, you'll do anything to forget it.

Lindsey loves connecting with readers! Please visit her website to find her social media platforms, to access character photos/profiles for all of your favorite *Kept in the Dark* characters, and for more information regarding event booking, book club appearances, etc.

If you enjoyed this story, I would love for you to leave *Kept in the Dark* a review. Reviews help so much in pushing out the book to other readers who would enjoy this book like you did! As always, thank you so much for your support!

www.lindseyacosta.com

www.ingramcontent.com/pod-product-compliance
Lightning Source LLC
Chambersburg PA
CBHW030105310726
48970CB00004B/1150